a boy like you.

by
GINGER SCOTT

ISBN: 0-9968734-6-5
ISBN-13: 978-0-9968734-6-8

For daddy.

"Show me a hero and I'll write you a tragedy."
F. Scott Fitzgerald

PROLOGUE

I'm not sure which one of us invented the races—Taryn or me. But we run them together. They are *ours*. When the bell sounds at 3:20 every afternoon, there's a sprint to the wooden gate in the alley leading to my back yard.

My house is the perfect place for them. I live on the last street, in the last neighborhood, before the rows of corn and cotton begin. My yard is at least twice the size of most of the others in south Bakersfield. It also slopes up maybe eight feet at the end. Daddy says they built the berm to keep the dirt from the farms out of our neighborhood.

I think they built it for racing.

It's hot outside, but I know that won't slow anyone down. I bet we'll have more kids at my house today than we've had all year; maybe even the entire third grade will come. It's the final week of school—only two days left. Everyone in Bakersfield is ready for summer. The pools don't open until next week, though, which is why our races have become so popular.

"Are you going to run home? Or did you bring your bike today?" Taryn whispers behind me. Her desk touches the back of my chair.

"Brought my bike. I'll beat everyone there and get the coffee can and tickets ready," I whisper over my shoulder, ignoring the suspicious glare from Mrs. Grandel. I raise my book on my desk, propping it on its spine so I can watch our teacher *and* look like I'm reading. "Do you have the trophies ready for tomorrow?"

"Yeah. They're drying in the garage," Taryn says, a little too loudly.

"Ladies? Something wrong? Or do you think you can manage to give me five minutes of learning before you completely shut those brains off?" Mrs. Grandel doesn't have to stand; her voice is loud enough from her chair to make her point, even when her back is to us.

"Yes, ma'am," Taryn answers for us. I cough out a short laugh at my best friend's formal response. *Ma'am—ha!*

"Josselyn Winters, you could stand to learn a thing or two about respect from Taryn. I wouldn't think her proper answer is as funny as you seem to," she says, bothering to put her own reading down on her desk and turn her body to point her eyes right at me. I don't like being embarrassed in class. Everyone is looking at me, including Christopher, the weird kid. My cheeks feel hot as I cross my legs and slide them underneath my seat, shrinking a little. I lean my head to the side, just enough to catch Christopher peeking at me over his book. I scrunch my lips up at him, squinting my eyes, and he looks away quickly.

Good.

Luckily, the bell sounds just as my eyes fall to my desk, and I jerk back to life, springing to my feet, shoving my book in the small cubby under my desktop. Backpack slung over one shoulder, I sprint through the classroom door, down the hall and around the gated fence where the bikes are stored. I didn't even bother to lock mine this morning, instead just twisting the chain around my wheel to make it look like I had. I wanted to make sure I had time before the others showed up, and my padlock is old—the combination part is really rusty, and it usually takes me four or five tries to pull it loose.

With two hands, I push my bike forward, kicking with one foot as I do, the other planted on the outside pedal. I scooter my way through the main entrance of the school, and as soon as my tire hits the road, I sling my other leg over and begin to pedal fast, not sitting once. I cut through the alley, slowing slightly to make sure I can twist and turn my tires through the bits of glass people throw out here. I flick open the clasp on the gate, pushing my bike through with me, then dumping it on its side in the corner of my yard.

I rush through the sliding door, yelling a quick "Hello" to my mom as I run through the kitchen to my room. I exchange my school bag for the can and tickets then sprint again to the backyard, this time smiling at my mom and stopping for a quick hug and a kiss. She laughs at me and tells me to have fun, shutting the sliding glass door behind me.

I pull the small plastic bag from the can, opening one end a little to let the powdered chalk I'd spent the night grinding up from my box spill out in an even line. Then I walk slowly around my yard, beginning at the gate, curving up along the hill, then back down the other side until I connect the oval. There's enough left for me to be able to touch up the track tomorrow.

When I step through the gate, I see Taryn rounding the alleyway, her dark hair pulled tightly under a jeweled band and her feather earrings blowing along her skin with her fast walk. She doesn't look like she should be fast, but she is. She fools everyone at the races, especially the boys. A line of kids trails her, some cutting others off. Our regulars all hold their arms out stiffly, not letting anyone pass. They know better.

Everyone stops at the gate, and I hand the roll of tickets to Taryn, pulling the lid off the coffee can and hugging it in front of my body.

"Okay, racers. We've decided to hold a tournament. Everyone who gets a ticket will be in the race today. Tomorrow will be the championship…for trophies! If you don't get a ticket, then you can sit at the top of the berm and watch. Stand still, and I'll walk down the line."

Taryn rips a ticket off for her and me first, and I stuff mine in my back pocket so I don't lose it, following behind her as she hands out tickets. The kids in the front are the same ones who have been with us since the beginning, since we started the races last summer: the Marley twins—who usually win—Taryn's cousin Emily, and Noah Santos, the boy who kissed me in kindergarten and then got me sent home for the day for punching a boy in the face.

The weird kid is here too. Christopher has gone to my school since the middle of last year. He's a foster kid, and he's living with the Woodmansees. They have a lot of kids—twelve, counting Christopher— and half of them are foster. That's not what makes him weird, though.

He wears the same brown, corduroy pants every day, and by Fridays, you can tell they haven't been washed. His hair is a dull brown, and it's a little longer than most of the boys in our class, and it curls up on the ends, resting on his neck. It's always sweaty. He also hums while he eats, and he sits alone at a table near the trashcan and exit for the cafeteria. When kids walk up to throw away their things, he hums louder, but never looks up. I tried sitting with him a few times last year, because Taryn dared me. The first time I sat at the table with him, he stopped humming completely. He also stopped breathing. When he passed out, I screamed for the teacher on duty. When the paramedics came to check him out, Mrs. Woodmansee showed up too. She just took him home. He was out of school for the rest of the month.

Today is the first time he's shown up for our races, and it surprises me. I can tell Taryn's noticed him, because she glances at the small roll of tickets in her hand and then back up at the line—there's enough for him to make it into the race. *Our* race. She stops a few kids short of where he is and turns to face me, her expression giving me all I need to know.

"Just let him have one," I shrug and whisper, leaning into her enough that the other kids can't hear.

She takes a deep breath, then looks down at the five tickets left in her hand, her fingers slowly clasping around them, folding them into her palm.

"He'll ruin it," she sighs.

Her head moves up, her eyes trained on my hands, and then there's a flash of an idea that crosses her face, her eyebrows raising. "Give me the can," she says, reaching for it and tugging it quickly.

My brow pinches, but I give into her easily. While I've always been the fearless one with the muscle, Taryn has always been the one with the ideas. I let her lead often, and I let her lead now.

With the can in her hands, she spins around, tearing apart the last five tickets and putting them inside before holding the can above her head and backing away from the line a few steps.

"We have five tickets left. Five *golden* tickets," she says.

"They don't look gold," Conner Marley, one of the twins, says from behind her. She glares at him and growls through her teeth.

"Shut up, Conner! I *know* they're not *really* gold. I meant it like as in special, okay?" she scolds him, her long, dark ponytail slapping against her shoulders as she turns to face the rest of the line. Conner mimics her behind her back. It makes me laugh.

"These are the last tickets into the tournament. To get one, all you have to do is answer a trivia question correctly. Are you ready?" she shouts.

A few of the kids yell *yes*, but most of them just blink and stare at her, waiting with nerves in their bellies, their hands twisting in front of them, not sure if they should just shout answers out or raise their hands. Taryn steps on top of a jagged wooden crate that has lived in my alley for almost a year, and everyone quiets down when she does. Somehow, the extra foot of height has given her authority.

"Question one: What is my favorite color?"

The second the question leaves her lips, four girls from the end of the line shout out "Purple!" Taryn picks her favorite of the bunch, a quiet girl named Megan, who skips forward to claim her ticket.

"Second question: Who won the race yesterday?"

There's a longer pause this time, mostly because everyone who was at the race yesterday is already standing behind us with tickets in their hands. Conner and Kyle Marley begin coughing, and eventually a few of the boys clustered near Taryn pick up on their hint. The first one guesses Conner, but he's wrong. The next boy guesses Kyle and is awarded the ticket.

"Question number three...whose house is this?" I smirk at her question, but keep my face low so I don't give anything away. It's funny how many of the kids have no idea where they're at. They just know they *had* to be here.

This answer takes longer, and Taryn starts to make a ticking sound, as if time is running out. Finally, a shy girl in a dress raises her hand, and Taryn nods at her to speak. "Is it…your house?" she asks. Taryn tilts her head to the side and bunches her face before looking at me. I raise my hand in the air as if I'm stretching, then point a finger to myself, over my head. "Oh, I mean…it's…it's *hers*. It's her house!" the girl quickly corrects. She doesn't even know my name, which irritates me a little, but it doesn't seem to bother Taryn. She pulls one of the tickets from the can and hands it over. I guess I don't know that girl's name either, so at least it's even.

"Two left. Who's going to win this one? Hmmmmm, let's see," she says, hopping down from the crate and taking a few steps along the line. Everyone is incredibly quiet, waiting for her next question.

"I know! Question number four," she smirks, glancing at me, then facing the line again. "Who was Joss's first boyfriend?"

"Taryn!" I shout, my eyes wide and my mouth a hard line. That same burn from before—when everyone was staring at me in class—is back on my cheeks. I hear a few giggles, and I turn quickly to try to find where they're coming from. I'm mad that I'm not wearing my hair up today, instead the dirty-blond strings stick to my bare arms and neck. It was hot out, and I wore my favorite yellow tank top, but I was running late for school this morning, so I forget to pull my hair back. I look tougher with my hair that way, and right now—I want to look tough.

The giggling continues, but eventually one of the boys from the end of the line shouts out Kyle's name, and Taryn hands him a ticket. Kyle chuckles, muttering something about how it was only a dare at his birthday party a few months ago, and how I kiss like a duck. I kissed him on the cheek because Taryn pushed me into it, and I hated every second of that day where everyone called me his girlfriend. I never want to be anyone's girlfriend again—especially Kyle Marley's. I turn around and kick him in the shin.

"Owwwww!" he whines. He quits talking about me, and my duck lips, though. I secretly hope his shin is bleeding under his jeans.

Oblivious to the drama she fueled, Taryn continues with the giveaway, holding the final ticket above her head. My stomach feels sick from the embarrassment moments before, and I take the can away from her so I have something to hold in my hands. I lean against the brick wall of my yard and pull some of the ends of my hair in front of my face to look at the split ends.

"Last chance. All you need to tell me is Joss's middle name," Taryn says to an oddly quiet alleyway full of kids. I don't like that she's using me, but I know she wants to make this question hard. I'm not sure anyone will know it, besides Taryn, so my guess is that the last ticket will just go unused.

I push off from the wall and slide my feet slowly in her direction, drawing a line in the dirt along the way as I drag the heel of my shoe forward. I turn to Taryn and meet her gaze, her left cheek pulled high into a smirk.

"Five seconds left," she says, ticking again…like a bomb.

I reach out to take the ticket from her, and the second it meets my fingers, one syllable destroys what we thought was the perfect plan.

"Grace," Christopher says, reaching his hand up and pulling the ticket promptly from my hold. He never looks up, and he pokes the small paper into his front pocket along with his hand as he moves to the opposite side of the wall to stand next to the other racers.

My eyes flash wide to Taryn's, and her mouth forms an O. "Say that's not your name!" she whispers, but loudly enough that the few kids near us hear. They all snicker because nobody really wants Christopher here.

"But it *is* my name. Taryn! Why'd you have to ask that?" I say, stepping in closer to her. My heart is thumping as I look at the faces of the kids around us, a few of them turning to leave now that *he's* in the race.

"How was I supposed to know he'd know that? How *does* he know that?" she says, her eyebrows raised.

"I don't know! I never even talk to him!" I'm being loud now, and the voices behind me have all quieted. I turn around with my lips pushed together tightly to see Christopher standing against the wall, the final ticket held in front of him. He's turning it over in both of his hands.

"Let's get started," Taryn says, walking past me, through the gate into my yard. The kids with tickets begin to follow her, and the ones who have stayed to watch begin to climb up the top of the berm, sitting along the block wall that lines the alley.

"Here," Christopher says behind me. We're alone in the alley, and I know the other kids are going to make a joke about it. I turn halfway, not wanting to completely look at him, and shrug for him to come on in.

"No, really. Here," he says again, his hand touching my shoulder. I twitch from the feel and spin to face him, his hand holding the ticket up for me to take. "I...I don't really want to race," he says, his eyes focused on the ticket pressed between his thumb and index finger. His lashes are long, and it keeps his eyes from my view, but I can tell from the soft slope downward on his mouth that he's sad, and my stomach drops seeing it.

His hands are dirty. His thumb has already left a smudge on the top of the ticket. My eyes move down to his pants, and I notice he's wearing new shoes—bright white Nikes that practically glow against the dingy brown of the material on his legs.

"Are those new?" I ask. His eyes come up to mine slowly, and I notice that they're glossy, kind of like mine are when I hear Mom and Dad arguing at night and I try to drown out their voices with my blanket. He's trying not to cry.

"Yeah, I got them yesterday," he says. His eyes are blue, like mine, but lighter.

I can hear Taryn calling racers to the line on the other side of the wall, and I can feel my heartbeat in my stomach. I should take the ticket and just let him go. He's still holding it out for me, his elbow propped against his stomach as he holds his arm between us. But his eyes are sad, and he got new shoes. He wore them today—here, to my house, for my race, where he knew everyone would make fun of him. Where he knew nobody really wanted him.

Nobody wants him.

"Keep your ticket," I say. His eyes widen. He's looking at me, but not directly. It's like he can't. "I like your shoes," I say, wanting to say something nice. He seems scared, and I don't feel very good about myself because of it.

I can't face him anymore, so I pull the coffee can against my side and sweep my hair over my other shoulder, hating the way it sticks to my neck. When I look back at him before I turn to walk through my gate, I catch his eyes on me, and I notice the small smile on his mouth, and it makes me feel better. Suddenly, I feel faster—like I might win today.

"I'll see you in there. You'll be up soon," I say over my shoulder, staring ahead again quickly, knowing that Christopher is watching me walk away. I kind of like the way knowing that feels.

I will not tell Taryn any of this.

The rules for the races are simple. You have to gallop or skip. No running allowed, and if you're caught, you can't argue about being disqualified. Taryn and I are the judges, and we're honest. I've disqualified her before, and she's called me out twice. The only person who ever argues is Kyle. Sometimes, Taryn lets him through. Today, though, he plays by the rules.

I win my race, beating out five new girls who have never been to our races before. Taryn loses to Kyle's brother Conner, and he teases her about it through the next six races, until he finally loses—to Christopher.

I had no idea he was this fast. He hasn't been cheating. I know he hasn't, because Taryn and I have watched him closely. After every race he wins, Christopher walks away from the now-scattered chalk finish line at the edge of my yard to the plastic box propped against my house under the patio. He stomps his shoes a few times to shake away the dirt, and then spends the rest of the time between races leaning forward, trying to clean away the marks with his fingers.

"Why are you watching him?" Taryn says, scaring me out of my daydream. I was watching Christopher care for his shoes and thinking how he probably doesn't get new things often. I don't like that Taryn caught me.

"Oh, I wasn't even looking at him. I was daydreaming, about how I'm going to beat Kyle," I say, turning my body completely away from Christopher. I want to look over my shoulder, to see if he heard me, to see if he got the dirt off his shoes, but I don't want Taryn to see, so instead I walk away with her at my side.

"Yeah, you better beat him tomorrow. I don't want him to win the trophy I made," she huffs.

Taryn climbs to the top of the dirt berm, and the twenty or so kids left in my yard all peer up at her, squinting at the sun setting behind her.

"Okay, be here right after school for the finals tomorrow. I'll have the trophy here for the winner," she says.

"My trophy," Kyle yells, high-fiving his brother.

"Or Joss's," Taryn yells back, lowering her brow and sneering at the cocky twins dressed in their favorite football jerseys.

"Yeah, right," one of them laughs.

"Don't worry," I say quietly as I stand next to her. "I can take him."

I'm faster than Kyle Marley. I have been since kindergarten. But he's not the one I'm afraid of losing to.

Christopher is the last one to leave, and I watch him balance along the thin brick border that leads to my gate, teetering as he walks with one foot in front of the other, trying not to step in the loose dirt. Once his feet hit the gravel of the alleyway, he turns toward me, and our eyes meet. I don't smile, and I pretend I don't notice, looking off to the side after a blink. He doesn't smile either, but I know being here, and winning today, meant a lot to him.

I kind of want him to beat me tomorrow. But I won't make it easy. He'll have to earn it.

I had planned on speeding home again before everyone got there, but that was before my bike tire was flat this morning, and before I found out we get out of school at noon today.

My parents must have forgotten too, because my mom sent me off with my lunch. It hasn't gone to waste entirely—I snuck most of the pretzels as a snack during reading time, and sold my cookies to Conner during our end-of-the-year desk clean up.

As busy as we've all been with the last day of school activities, the race is all everyone is talking about. It's down to four of us—Kyle, me, a fast kid named Miguel, and Christopher. Even though the race is small, I have a feeling the crowd coming to watch will be even bigger than yesterday's. That's why I want to beat everyone to my gate. I want the track to look nice, and I thought about putting out a few towels and blankets on the hill, so the other kids have somewhere nice to sit.

My knee has been bouncing at the same pace for the last four minutes. I've watched the minute hand creep closer to the top of the clock hung above Mrs. Grandel's head, and at one point, I swear it went backward. It's teetering now, and I've managed to pull my backpack over my arms and turn my body to the side without her noticing.

As if I'm backed into starting blocks, I position my feet against the metal legs of my chair, and the instant the bell sounds, I'm off and out the door. I'm the first one through the gate, and when I glance back over my shoulder as I round the block that leads to my street, I slow down, satisfied that I don't see anyone behind me.

I push through the gate quickly, dropping my backpack, which is stuffed so full with my graded worksheets and art projects that the zipper may soon explode where the bag rests on the patio. I jerk on the sliding door, but it doesn't budge. I pound my hand against the glass and press my face to the window, but I don't see any lights on or a sign that anyone is home at all.

Letting out a small growl in frustration, I slap at the window one more time before running to the front of the house. I slide to a stop quickly when I notice the garage door is raised, my dad's station wagon parked inside.

My dad works at the high school. He's a PE teacher, and a baseball coach. He must be home early too. I'm not sure why he didn't hear me at the window. I step through the door into the house and call out for my dad. When he doesn't answer, I yell for my mom.

My heart is pounding, and as much as I want to grab the chalk and run to my backyard and draw fresh lines before my friends show up, I also don't want to make a sound.

Something is off.

I peer my head around the corner of the hallway that leads to my parents' bedroom. Their door is closed, but the light is on. Just knowing the light is on, that they're probably in there, that I'm not alone—it all makes me feel safer.

I step closer to my room, and when I reach the frame of my doorway, I finally hear my dad's voice. What he says feels like a nightmare.

"Is Joss even *my* daughter, Claire? How do I know you haven't been lying about that too? How do I know she's not his?"

Not...his?

I swallow and hug my doorframe, half of my body in my room, the other half out here in the hallway waiting for my mom's answer. It doesn't come. Instead, my doorbell rings, and my dad flings their bedroom door open. His eyes land right on me, and I grip the wall tightly at the sight of his face. This isn't the happy man who throws a ball with me in the driveway. This man looks scary—his eyebrows raised, his face red and his mouth turned down, denting in the corners as he clenches his teeth.

He looks away from me quickly as he storms down the hallway to the main door, throwing it open with enough force that it dents the wall on the other side. I hear him yelling at whoever came to visit, and I run to the doorway behind him to make sure it isn't one of my friends. When I get there, I see another man holding his hands up, shaking his head, and repeating that he's sorry. He's wearing a Cal State sweatshirt and jeans; the kind of clothes my mom wears.

"Get the fuck out of my house!" My dad smacks his hand hard against the door when he yells, and I jump, stumbling back a few steps, my heart now a rapid drum inside my chest.

When I turn around, I see my mom standing in the hallway, her eyes red and puffy. She's been crying, and when she looks at me, she shakes her head, her lips mouth, "I'm sorry." Her eyes close slowly as she holds up a hand and stumbles to the bedroom, closing the door behind her to the sound of her wailing.

I move into the kitchen, and I notice a few of the kids now lining up along the wall of my backyard. My dad is still yelling on the other side of the wall, and my mother is crying and gasping for breath down the hallway. I am trapped.

When I hear the front door slam, I halt, waiting to hear my father's steps coming down the hallway. Instead, I hear nothing. They must have both left, or gone to the front yard. Maybe I can get to Taryn, tell her we need to move the race. Or maybe no one will notice what's happening inside.

Forgetting about the chalk in my room, I unlatch the glass door leading to my backyard and pull the curtain to a close behind me as I shut it, wanting to hide the things happening inside. I see Taryn at the gate's entrance, balancing on the small crate and directing kids to the berm so they can watch. She's brought the trophies for first and second place, and she's holding one in each hand. Yesterday, winning the tall one was all I could think about. Today, I just want to erase the look on my mom's face that's now burnt into my mind—to rid my head of the echoes of my father yelling at some strange man at our door.

Maybe nobody will notice what's happening here. Maybe this will be fine. When the race is done, I'll go back inside and everything will be…normal.

I blink a few times before walking over to my friend. No matter how hard I try to pretend, though, my ears are constantly listening for clues to what's happening on the other side of my house.

Kyle shows up next, and his brother is standing behind him, hands on his shoulders, squeezing them as if he's sending Kyle in for a fight. Within seconds, Miguel and Christopher step through the gate, and Taryn is ordering us to the starting line.

I zone out as my friend goes over the rules. I know the rules; I made up the rules—two complete laps, no running, no cheating, and no touching another player on the course. That last rule is new; I added it when Kyle Marley tripped me at the finish line a few months ago.

My legs feel like jelly. I bend down to retie my shoes, thinking that maybe I've pulled the laces too tight. But that isn't it. I know it isn't.

The yelling is still there. Nobody else seems to notice, but every now and then I hear hints of my dad's voice. It's how he sounds when he's out on the field, when I'm watching his practices and he's upset after a loss. It's almost like he's barking. I'm focusing on it so much that when Taryn calls for the race to begin, I don't take off right away. I cover my misstep with a twist of my ankle, pretending I fell instead of admitting that I'm not paying attention. My mind, my heart—all of me—is somewhere else.

I make up ground quickly, skipping with long strides to the back of the yard, banking off the berm and gaining speed. And then I hear the long squeal of tires and the crunch of metal striking into metal hard and fast.

The sound stops everyone and everything.

My breath stops too.

Taryn looks at me, and I'm sure my face shows nothing but emptiness and fear. I walk down the hill, off the course, and begin to jog through the middle of my yard, picking up speed the closer I get to the side door that leads into our garage. My heart is beating wildly, and my ears hear nothing—no clues, no questions from my friends, no more yelling, or cries from my parents. All I hear is the *whoosh* of air and blood inside my head and over my ears. Everything else is quiet, and the quiet scares me.

I push through the side door and step into the garage, the man who was arguing with my father is standing in the driveway, his hands on his head while he paces like a lion circling prey around his car parked in our driveway. The scratch in his sports car is long and deep, and my mom is pressed to the screen of our front door, watching him cry over his car while she cries over him.

My eyes are wide, and I can't decide where to look. The kids from the race are slowly streaming through the door, and everybody is seeing this— everyone is seeing something awful happen to my family. I'm just not sure what it is, and what this man with the blue car has to do with it, and why Mom cares about his car so much.

Why does she care about him? And where did my daddy go?

My head is dizzy as I spin, looking from one thing to the next, my feet full with the urge to run away, but my strength unable to take me anywhere. The thunderous rumble of the engine comes first, followed quickly by the shrill scream of rubber digging into road, of brakes pressing on the wheels. Smoke pours from the sides of my dad's car. His wheels spin wildly, and then there's a loud pop as the front tires of his station wagon lift over the small hump in the driveway, catching at least a foot of air before crashing down.

The headlights zero in on me.

My father's eyes hit mine.

He looks terrified.

I open my mouth to scream, but no sound leaves my lips. My father is clinging to the steering wheel, madly jerking it with his hands, and I shut my eyes, bracing myself for the inevitable.

I am going to die.

My body is thrust so hard I'm sure this is it—it's over—when I open my eyelids again, I will be in heaven. But something keeps pushing me and pulling me all at once. All breath escapes my lungs, and I fight to find air, my back flat in the dead grass several feet away from the driveway where my father's car now rests, steaming, the front end enveloped by the sports car my dad drove into—*through*.

I was going to die. But someone saved me.

I gasp and I howl, a panicked search for feeling in my body. My skin is numb and I can't breathe. Air. Air! All I want is air, and I reach and claw at the body next to me, trying to sit up, to swallow, to make a sound—any sound! My fingers grip at a gray T-shirt, and the arms wearing it cling to me. Thin arms, like mine. I don't think they've ever let go. My dad runs to me. My mom bursts through the screen door. The mystery man is covering his mouth, still looking at his now smashed-to-bits car behind us all.

And Christopher is holding me.

My lungs stutter, and I start to cough hard, the sensation of wind passing through my throat almost too much to take after living without it. I choke, leaning forward, my parents both pulling at me, each wanting an arm, each wanting to take me and save me.

But Christopher is still holding me. He won't let go, even when they tell him to. He fights away people tugging against us—blood dripping over one of his eyes. I don't want him to let go. I want them to leave. I want him to take me away.

I begin to cry, and my body shakes, but I suck in a hard breath because the kids are still watching. Everybody is watching. Everybody is going to know that something bad happened here today. Christopher squeezes me tighter, and I wrap my hands around his forearms, holding them to me.

He holds me until all of the other kids go home.

He holds me until the police arrive.

He holds me until I tell him it's okay to let go.

And then he disappears.

For good.

CHAPTER 1

Eight years later

I'm ditching softball practice. It's not required, not that *required* would make me go either. They need me to win, and as long as they need me, I'll show up when I want to. When they don't need me anymore, I'll quit.

Wouldn't my father love that?

He probably wouldn't even notice, truthfully. My dad hasn't watched me throw a ball since I was nine. My life was moving in one direction—the perfect postcard family, smiles always on our faces, food on our table, holidays, vacations and all that happy-home shit. Then my mom left in the middle of the night after my dad crashed his car into the one owned by the guy she was having an affair with. Seems Dad wasn't supposed to be home that early and catch her packing her things to escape with some dude named Kevin who was eight years younger than she. My dad was gone when she finally left, drowning all his problems in a bottle of Jack at some seedy, hole-in-the-wall bar in Southside.

I didn't really know what was happening then. I just knew that I had to spend the summer with my grandparents in Fresno while my parents "worked things out." Turns out, working things out meant my mom disappeared completely. I'm not sure what hurt more—the fact that she didn't say goodbye to me, or that she didn't want to take me with her…wherever it is she went.

I hate her for leaving. But I hate my dad even more for not being there to stop her. He's never been the same—*checked out,* except for the three months of baseball he coaches every spring. He treats the guys on his team like sons. Me? I'm the roommate that sometimes he bothers to lecture when he's pissed off about life and needs someone to pass it off on. I get the man who stumbles in late at night after the bar, sloppy and blubbering about how sorry he is.

He's only sorry when he's drunk. He only makes promises about being a better dad when he's wasted. His promises are made in slurs. Other times, he's just mean—the angry drunk, who says truths that I know live somewhere deep inside. In the morning, I go right back into that box he keeps me in—the one that's labeled: DO NOT TOUCH. More like, DO NOT LOVE.

When I turn eighteen, he won't have that luxury anymore. He'll have to start taking his problems out on someone else. Maybe he can turn on himself. Though, I guess he does that already too.

Whatever.

It's the last day of winter break, and I'm waiting for Taryn at the junior high baseball fields. She's skipping softball practice too. This week was just tryouts for the newbies. Coach knows what I can do. And Taryn doesn't get to play much anyway.

It's our last day of freedom before we go back into the chaos of South High. I can't miss any more days of school this year. Dad got a letter. *I* got a lecture. I rolled my eyes at first, but then he said he'd transfer me to Carden if he had to. That's where they send the fuck-ups. And as *fucked up* as I am, I don't belong at Carden.

A white truck pulls up on the opposite end of the field, kicking up dust from the dirt road. It's hard to tell from here, but it looks like three guys my age are getting out. I don't recognize them, and I wonder if they're here to do a deal. That happens here sometimes; dealers figure the junior high is the last place cops will look. The fields are hard to get to, so a patrol car would be totally obvious.

Maybe that's why I wanted to come here.

My phone buzzes in my pocket, so I slide it into my hands so I can keep an eye on the boys in the truck while I answer Taryn's text.

TARYN: Almost there. My lighter's jacked. I had to buy a new one.

ME: K. Three dudes just pulled up in a truck. Maybe they have some stuff.

I don't hit the hard stuff. But sometimes I like to smoke a joint or take pills, like vikes or OC. I tried spice at the last party Taryn and I went to, but it made me super paranoid. I don't need to add to my anxiety; I need to escape it. I don't think I'll be getting anything from these dudes, though. They're pulling bats out of the back of the truck and a bucket of balls, which means they're probably coming over here.

Shit.

My phone vibrates again against my leg with another text.

TARYN: I don't want any shit today. But are they cute?

I laugh softly, pressing the edge of my phone to my lips as I glance up at the three figures walking toward me. The one in the middle is the tallest, and he's wearing a dark blue sweatshirt and black shorts. It's hard to tell from here, but his hair looks like it's light brown, maybe a little long. It sticks out from the sides of his hat. The other two are wearing gray sweatpants and black T-shirts, and the one on the right is African American. They don't look familiar, and I wonder if they go to North.

ME: Can't tell yet, but looks promising.

She sends me back the thumbs-up emoticon and says she's two minutes away. I push my phone into my back pocket and twist the cap from my water bottle to take a drink, giving me a good cover to stare at my approaching company a little longer. The wind is picking up, so I take the hair tie from my wrist and pull my hair back in a ponytail then pull the sleeves of my flannel shirt into my palms to keep my hands warm. It doesn't really get cold in Bakersfield, but in January, with the wind, the sixty degrees feels colder than normal.

I can tell the guys are talking about me as they cross into the infield area and step up on the mound, setting the bucket down and dropping their bats in the grass. The tall one pulls his hat from his head and smooths his hair back before sliding his hat on backward. He looks right at me when he does, and I dare myself not to look away or change my expression for his benefit at all, even though his blue eyes are freaking unbelievable.

He's unbelievable. He pushes up his sleeves and stretches one arm over his chest as he talks to his two friends, but he keeps glancing at me between his words. I don't give in, and I watch him the entire time. I won't smile. He doesn't. We're both being stubborn. It's like I'm invisible, and he doesn't even acknowledge the fact that he's looking at me. His expression is blank.

"What'd I miss?" Taryn asks, sliding in next to me on the bleachers. She hands me her lighter, and I grab it without looking away.

"Nothing," I say. "They just got here. They parked over there."

I nod across the field to their truck, my eyes still on him as he bends down for a ball, swinging his arm around a few times in the throwing motion to warm up—still looking at me.

"Huh," Taryn responds. "Well, at least they're cute."

Yeah. They're cute. The shortest one seems to have the biggest arms, his biceps completely filling the sleeves of his shirt. He's blond…I think. I don't look at him long, because I don't want to lose this staring contest with Mr. Backward Hat. I was right about the other guy being African American, and Taryn claims him as hers the second he pushes up the legs of his sweat pants, revealing the dark, strong muscles of his calves while he takes a bat in his hands and sways it side to side.

"Damn, girl. I hope he's new. I'm totally gettin' on that welcoming committee," she says, her eyes locked on his broad-shouldered figure, the bat now stretched across his back.

I don't speak, instead bringing my fist up to my mouth, my elbow rested on my knee while I chew at my knuckle and concentrate on the boy on the mound. He quit looking at me when his friend crouched behind the plate, pounding his glove for a few warm-up throws. Now that he's not watching me, I can study him more closely.

21

He tosses the ball up a few times in his bare hand, then readies himself along the rubber on the mound, kicking his foot in a few times to loosen up the hard dirt. The junior high field is old and small, so they've used one of the bucket lids as home plate, moving it back a good fifteen feet from where the younger kids' one is. Finally satisfied with the ground under him, the pitcher stands perfectly still for a few seconds before stepping into his windup motion, his arm taking a long path from far behind his head and around his body, the ball hitting the glove with a crisp snap.

"Shooooooooot," Taryn hums next to me. "That was fast."

"Yeah," I say, my lips still pressed along my knuckles. I'm grinning against my hand, but I don't want anyone to see that I'm impressed—not Taryn, and not the guy throwing the ball.

He repeats his motion six or seven times before his friend finally steps up to the plate. There's no way in hell he's hitting him.

I lean back, letting my legs drape forward along the bleachers, the shoestrings from my Vans dangling along the sides, my skinny jeans hugging my ankles over my socks. I click the lighter a few times in my palm next to me, holding the flame on until I feel the heat as I watch Hat Boy pull up his knee and stretch the length of the mound, firing off a pitch a good ten miles per hour faster than his warm-up throws. His friend swings and misses.

"Jeeee-zussss," Taryn says, leaning back next to me. She hands me a cigarette, but I shake my head. I don't feel like smoking. I hand her the lighter and she puts hers to her lips, burning the tip and puffing once while we watch the catcher throw the ball back to Hat Boy, who shakes out his arm and lines himself up on the rubber again.

"So that's how it's gonna be, huh?" the batter says, shrugging his shoulders a few times and tapping his bat on the edge of the plate.

The catcher chuckles, mumbling something that makes them all laugh, and I wish I could hear whatever it was he said because Hat Boy is leaning forward now, looking in for a sign with one side of his lip raised in the cockiest fucking smile I've ever seen.

I was smitten with his eyes. They're pretty to look at, a unique blue, bright enough that I can tell their color from fifty feet away. His smile, though—well…as Taryn said—*jeeee-zussss.*

He pulls his arms together and presents for his next pitch, and I sit forward again, watching the details of his movement. He turns the ball in his glove, the lines of muscles along his forearms ticking with each twist until his fingers are gripping the ball just right.

He's going to throw a curve.

As the ball releases, I stand and jump down over the two rows of bleachers to the ground, walking closer to the backstop while his friend swings and misses again, the curve sailing low and away. He never had a chance.

"That fucking dickhead," his friend who's batting mutters through a laugh to the catcher. The blond guy scoops the ball low, throws it back to Hat Boy then pounds his fist in his glove to knock away the dirt.

"It was a good pitch, man. Good swing, he just got ya—that's all," he says, tapping his glove on his friend's leg.

"You call that pitch?" the batter asks.

"Nah, man…you know better than that. He never throws what I call. That was all him," he says, pounding his glove one more time and adjusting his body on his heels. "Come on, dub. Give him something to hit!"

The pitcher adjusts his hat again; pulling it forward now, low on his brow—the brim casts a dark shadow that obliterates the blue in his eyes. I hate that I can't see his eyes—it makes me feel uneasy. He runs the side of his arm along his brow before twisting his neck, the same smirk from before the curveball sliding across his lips. I watch him pull his hands together and work the ball in his glove, his lip ticking just a hint higher when he settles on his grip.

"Watch the changeup," I say, my fingers now curled through the chain link and my forehead resting against the backstop.

The batter glances at me quickly, his brow low. He makes the typical *who the fuck are you?* face, then turns back toward Hat Boy, digging his feet into the batter's box a little harder and *tsking* at my suggestion as he rolls his shoulders. His leg is twitching to step already, and his bat is wiggling up and down his shoulder.

He's going to miss.

Hat Boy winds up the same way he did the first two times. His body is impressive—not just in a hot guy sort of way, but like an athlete. My father would love him. His control is ridiculous. And he wears the game face my dad's always telling his guys to have. Intimidation, he says, is fifty percent of the game. For me, it's always been ninety percent.

If I were to overlap video of all three pitches, his release point would be exactly the same. His gift, though, is his ability to make the ball move anywhere he wants it to—at any speed. The batter anticipates, just like I knew he would, and his swing is done by the time the ball sails by, landing softly in the catcher's mitt.

"That's at least fifteen slower," I whisper to myself.

The batter hears me, though, and looks up with one eyebrow cocked.

"Dude, Wes, that was killer. Throw that again, man. Lovin' it…lovin' it!" the catcher says, pulling his mask off and tossing it on the ground. He throws the ball back to the pitcher.

His name is Wes.

"Hold up," the batter says, flashing a hand to Wes and the catcher. He walks over to me, and I feel my stomach clench. I used to think I hated confrontation. I don't. I love it. And I'm good at it.

I wear my game face.

"You were late," I shrug, one lip pulling up to the side as I kick the toe of my shoe into the bottom of the backstop. I feel Taryn walk up next to me. She drops her cigarette in the dirt, stepping on it to put it out before grabbing hold of the fence too.

"You called a changeup," the guy says, his mouth a hard line and his eyes looking at me with suspicion. He thinks I made a lucky guess, and he's a little pissed I made fun of him. I probably shouldn't have, but there's something about these three that makes me want to bring out my snarky side.

"Yep," I say, leaning away from the fence while holding on, stretching my arms. I glance at Wes over his shoulder, his hat still low over his eyes. He's looking at me—his weight leaning on one leg, his glove propped against the hip of the other. "Want me to show you how to hit it?"

The catcher starts to laugh behind him, his hand balled in a fist over his mouth. "Day-umm. She just called you out, TK!" he says.

TK swings his bat around his body, sliding it through his hand and holding the grip side out, his lips pursed and his eyebrows raised in expectation. I chuckle to myself, and look down, shaking my head.

"Oh, you don't *really* want to show me? Is that it?" he taunts, holding his other hand out to the side as he takes slow strides backward toward the makeshift home plate.

"Don't be an asshole, TK. She was just being nice," the catcher says. I like that he's sticking up for me, but he's wrong—I wasn't being nice. I was calling TK out on his weaknesses.

I glance to Taryn, who knows I'm not leaving here without sending the ball back at the pitcher's knees. She laughs quietly then moves to the front level of the bleachers a few feet behind us as I step around the backstop, my hand dragging along the fence until I reach the end. I stop before the dirt, bending down to tie my shoes, then pull my flannel shirt from my arms, tying it around my waist. I wore my black tank top with the thin rose painted down the middle, and my arms chill from the wind. I can't swing in anything clingy, though, so I rub both of my arms a few times before reaching out for his bat.

"TK," I say his name, taking the heavy bat from his hands. I flip it around to read the numbers; it's a few ounces heavier than I'm used to. I tap the barrel against the bottom of my shoe a few times, then close one eye as I look back up to my sparring partner. "So does that stand for Technical Knockout?"

He laughs once through his closed mouth, the sound rumbling from his chest. I smile at the sound because he reminds me of Conner, except Conner's laughter bellows, because he's about two hundred pounds of his mom's pies and cookies. TK is two hundred pounds of Mack Truck.

"Uhm, that would be TKO, Cherry. And no, it stands for Thomas Kennedy," he nods.

"Cherry?" I scowl, slapping the bat in my hand like I'm tougher than I actually am.

"Yeah, your cheeks are all red and round. They look like cherries." The same laugh mixes with his words. I join in, looking over at my friend, now sitting in the center on the bleachers, her legs folded up underneath her. She shakes her head, because she knows me—I don't do nicknames, especially not ones like *cherry*.

"Ahhhh, I see," I say, stepping up to the plate. Wes shuffles his feet around the rubber on the mound. Up this close, I can see his eyes under the shadow of his hat, and I catch him rolling them, his mouth a hard line. He's not amused, and he thinks this is a waste of time.

"I thought cherry was a commentary on my virginity," I say, steadying my feet into place as I swing the bat around twice before resting it on my shoulder. I feel them all freeze at my mention of the word *virginity*. "If that were the case... TK... I ain't no cherry."

The blond guy starts coughing to cover his shocked laugh. TK and Wes remain silent, TK running his hand over his mouth while Wes's jaw flexes and his tight mouth bends into disapproval. Fuck him—now I really *am* going to take out his kneecaps.

"You gonna pitch? Or you wanna stand there a little while longer and judge me?"

Taryn whistles softly behind me, and TK chuckles while he takes a few steps back.

"A'right, Wes. Let's see what she's got," the catcher says, crouching down and patting his glove a few times.

Wes turns his head, tucking his chin into his shoulder, working the ball in his fingers against his thigh. His lips part, and he says something to himself. I can't hear him, but I'm pretty sure he didn't say anything nice.

I dig my foot in while he shifts his body, readying for the throw.

"Show him how it's done, Cherry!" Taryn chants from behind the backstop. I pull my hand from the bat and flip her off. It only makes her laugh again. I'm sure she's giving me the finger back, but I don't bother to look.

Wes shakes his hand by his side, then brings the ball into his glove, his eyes lazily looking at the plate as he cocks back and tosses the ball with an arc to the catcher. I drop the bat and snag it before it hits his glove.

"Don't," I say, shaking my head at him. I fire the ball back, hoping the sting of it punctuates my point. He lets the ball sit in his glove in front of him, his eyes squinting at mine, his jaw working while he chews at the inside of his mouth. "Don't treat me like I'm not just as good as you."

My cheeks burn a little. I'm letting him piss me off, and that pisses me off. I swing the bat around again and rest it on my shoulder, twisting my back foot into the dirt. He tosses the ball in his hand a few times then steps back to the mound, repeating the same presentation as before, never once adjusting his grip or moving the ball in his hand. He's going to throw me the heat.

Good.

His wind up is the same; his motion—the same, and I arm my muscles early, knowing I'll have to swing fast. My bat is at the plate the second the ball is, and I foul it off behind me over the fence, into the dirt lot overrun with weeds.

"You're finding that," TK says.

"Whatever," I answer, nodding for Wes to pitch me another.

He bends down and grabs another ball from the bucket behind him, rubbing it on his shorts a few times, his thumb twisting it in his hand until his fingers have all found a seam. He doesn't adjust again, and I know he's going to try to catch me off balance.

Wes winds up, and everything in my world slows down—I hear my own breath stop, I see the way his sweatshirt rides up around his waist, I notice how low his shorts rest on his hips and how absolutely touchable his stomach is. His mouth gets tight, his face showing the restraint he's putting into every frame of his movement, and his eyes look driven. When the ball releases, I watch the rotation, sitting back just long enough to step with the pitch and send the ball to the fence down the third base line.

I didn't hit it at him like I wanted to. But I hit it hard. I made my point. And the fact that he's resting his glove and throwing hand on his head, watching my ball bounce to a stop about three hundred feet out leaves me more satisfied than any high.

"I'm Levi Stokes, and I think I want to marry you," the catcher says, taking the bat from my hand.

I laugh lightly, unable to stop my smile at his over-the-top line. It's sweet. And while most girls would probably swoon over a guy that looks like him—blond hair, green eyes, muscular build—Levi Stokes is not my type. I don't want a type, really. But I also know I have one, and Wes—he's pretty much the paint-by-numbers version of my greatest crush weaknesses.

"Thanks, Levi," I say, glancing to the mound where Wes is now pacing, tossing a ball, bored with me already. His indifference stings, and I hate that I care. "But I don't want to have to take care of a man all my life." I add this just to get a reaction. It catches Wes's attention, and he takes a few steps closer. "Marriage is shit—*no offense*. You can give me and my girl here a ride home, though."

"Deal," Levi says, reaching out his hand for me to shake. I take it, and his grip is hard—masculine.

"Damn, Cherry. That shit was tight," TK says, holding out knuckles for me. I smirk at his hand and pound my fist lightly into his.

"Thanks, Knock Out," I wink. "And you can call me Joss."

"I don't know, you're pretty sweet—like a cherry," he laughs.

"If you call me *cherry* again, I'll punch you," I say quickly. He shakes his head with a chuckle, holding up a hand to point at me.

"Okay, Joss. Joss the boss," he winks.

I roll my eyes, but when I turn around, I smile because boss is a whole lot better than cherry.

"We're just going to hit a few more. You girls okay sticking around?" Levi asks.

"Fine by us," I say, rounding the fence and sitting on the bottom bleacher next to my friend. "We'll just wait here so we can, you know, give you more pointers?"

"Ha...teach me anything you want, Boss," TK says, stepping back into the box.

I stand to untie my flannel from around my waste, sliding my arms through again. I let the sleeves drape on me, though, letting one fall off my shoulder enough that it exposes my bare skin and the black strap of my tank top. Levi looks at it, and licks his lips before sliding his mask over his face and kneeling down next to TK. He's so easy. He's also not the reason I did it.

Wes is wearing his hat low again, and he reaches up to adjust it before digging his foot into the mound. He's counting on the shadow of his brim to mask him, but it's not dark enough. I can still see his eyes—and they're on me. I let my lip curl on one side as I tug my hair loose from the ponytail before I sit down to watch, my blond strands twisting and knotting in the breeze. I sweep my hair over my other shoulder, happy that Wes is watching every movement. And between each pitch, those eyes...they always come back to me.

The boys hit for about half an hour while Taryn and I both smoke a cigarette. I'm stomping mine out when TK hops back over the fence from grabbing the ball I fouled off into the field. He steps up next to me, nudging me with the bucket of balls.

"That's bad for you, ya know. You should quit," he says, nodding toward the butt on the ground.

"Yeah, well...I've got a long list of shit I should quit, TK. Trust me when I say smoking every now and then is the least of my problems." I smile at him after I talk. I think I'm clever, but he doesn't look amused. It makes me a little uncomfortable; I look away quickly, bending down to pick up the smooshed cigarette end. I may have a laundry list of bad habits, but littering isn't one of them. I carry it in my palm to the trash at the end of the dugout then fall into step alongside TK, Taryn on my other side. Levi and Wes walk several steps in front of us. Levi looks over his shoulder a few times; Wes only picks up his pace, like he can't drop Taryn and me off fast enough.

"So, Boss," TK says. I sigh, but I give in to the smile. I hate to admit it, but I kind of like this new nickname. I think I also like that he's moved on from my smoking and other flaws. "That's some swing," he says, gesturing toward the field behind us with his neck. "You play, right?"

Before I can answer, Taryn snickers. I roll my eyes and push her off balance, making her stumble a few steps.

"Joss Winters is the best shortstop in California," she blurts out, sticking her tongue out at me as she takes a step to the side so I can't hit her again.

"Ah, I don't know about that," TK says. "I'm pretty sure *I'm* the best shortstop in California."

I look down at my feet and let my smile crease my cheeks before I pull my phone from my pocket and pretend I'm getting a call.

"What? Who are you looking for? TK?" I say to my fake caller. I hold the device in my hand to face him, and he pinches his brow. "It's the President. He wants you to know that you're actually number two now."

It takes a few seconds for TK to let his laughter break through, but when it does, it's easy and comforting. I like that I can tease him.

"You all go to North?" Taryn asks. I can tell TK's answer is the one she really cares about. She's never been good at hiding her emotions, and she bites at her bottom lip now like a child asking Santa for the latest hot toy.

"We start at South on Monday. Just moved here," TK answers. Taryn nods, her eyes flashing a *hell yeah* to mine in a split second. I think about his words for a few seconds, glancing up at the rest of the *we* walking in front of us.

"You *all* just moved here?" I let my question spill out slowly, noticing Wes doesn't pause or even seem to acknowledge my question at all. I'm starting to get the sense that he's not real thrilled about giving us a ride home.

"Yep," Levi says, spinning around and walking backward for a few steps. "We're brothers."

I nod, sucking my lip tightly while I do my best to attempt to understand how they all fit together without asking.

"You're…seniors?" I settle on nailing down their ages first.

"Close, Cher—" TK starts, stopping his slip up mid-word, shaking his head, and chuckling to himself. "Damn, that became habit fast. I meant *Boss*. And no…we're juniors. You?"

"Me and Taryn are too," I say, tugging my shirt snug to my body as the sun starts to set. The wind is picking up some.

We're getting closer to the truck, and Wes hasn't said a word. I'm not even sure he actually speaks. He reaches the locked gate first, stepping up easily and placing one foot on the chain while he swings his body over to the other side. He turns his hat backward before reaching to the top of the fence to take the bucket of balls from Levi, but just before the exchange, his eyes move to mine. It's such a small glance, and I'm right in front of him; there really wasn't anywhere else for his gaze to land. But somehow it also feels choreographed, as if he'd been working this trip out several steps ahead of the rest of us just so he'd have this chance to silently confront me, study me, and look at me like this through a thin layer of chain link, close enough to touch if it weren't for the metal barrier between us. My stomach knots, and I feel uneasy under his scrutiny—it feels like a warning.

This is unfair coming from eyes like that.

"Hey, wait…" Levi says after passing the bucket over. Wes turns away the second Levi speaks, so I give him all of my attention, my eyes wide, and my lips sealed. "You're not related to Eric Winters, are you?"

I squeeze at my sleeve, which is now bunched in my palm, and rap my knuckles against my thigh as my teeth clench and my lips force out a smile. It's not Levi's fault he's so enthusiastic about my connection to Coach Winters. He plays baseball, and my father will love him. He'll love all three of them, actually. And Eric Winters is a big deal when it comes to California baseball. Seven state titles, forty-plus college players, and a dozen drafted into the majors. Unfortunately, his statistics in the *father* department suck ass.

31

"That's why you're so good!" he says, taking a step back, as if he's surprised. I try to remind myself that his reaction isn't his fault. It's normal, the same assumption everyone makes. It still irks me, and my mind still runs through the same sarcastic response I usually give. Yes—this is the secret to my success, Levi. You've pieced it together. I have spectacular genes when it comes to running bases and throwing a ball. No effort of my own went into my talent on my part whatsoever.

"Or maybe she just practices harder than you do," Wes's voice breaks through my inner dialogue. He rolls his eyes at Levi, taking the bats through the fence as he defends me without my asking, without knowing he should. His eyes graze over mine again as he turns, pausing for a beat—long enough that I feel it and blink.

He was giving his brother shit, mostly. But he was also saying what I wouldn't. *Thanks.* The word passes through my head, through my chest, but then the second he turns and steps to the truck it's gone.

"Right, no…I didn't mean that. I only meant that's cool and all—your dad," Levi stutters, glancing to me before climbing over the fence, focusing on his hands and feet. I see him shake his head to admonish himself; he's embarrassed.

"I know what you meant. Yeah, it's…cool…I guess," I say, looking to Taryn before fitting my shoes into the fence holes so I can climb. She holds her mouth in a tight line in response, because she's been with me through it all, and she knows my father's failures all too well. No sense in tearing him down in front of these three, though.

We all clear the fence, and Wes secures the equipment against the cab in the back of the truck. Levi and TK jump in the back, insisting Taryn and I sit up front. I climb in reluctantly, not really wanting to sit so close to Wes, but Taryn doesn't follow. I should have known she'd want to ride in the back near TK. I'm going to be in here with him—Mr. Talkative—completely alone. I guess I can fill most of the time with directions to my house.

I scoot closer to the door and pull it shut before reaching for the seatbelt. I hear Wes's door close, but I don't look at him. On instinct, I start to hold my breath, like I'm in the middle of some dare, being trapped in a box—a box with a boy that I can't deny is hot, if not for his personality shortcomings.

The seatbelt won't click, and I feel my lungs starting to ache from the lack of breath, and the more I fumble with the metal clip and the buckle, the more panic seeps through my veins and starts to take over my muscle control.

Wes clears his throat before sliding his hand along the seat toward my failed attempts, and my eyes widen at the sight of his fingertips moving closer to mine. I let go of the belt completely, but before it has a chance to retract and slide back over my body, Wes catches it. My eyes dart to his, and he holds onto our stare while he easily clicks my buckle in place.

"You were putting it in the wrong side," he says, the edge of his mouth lifting, briefly. It makes a temporary dimple on his cheek, and my eyes zero in on that while it's there.

"Oh, thanks," I say. My hands tingle with the shot of adrenaline I feel from talking with him, this close, alone. I curl my hands tightly and bring them in my lap to rid myself of the sensation. I don't like it—it's out of my control.

He pulls his own belt over his chest then turns the key, the truck shaking a little with its effort to start. That one small fraction of a smile and those few words are all I'm going to get—he's focused completely on his mirrors and the dirt road ahead now.

I pull my sleeves over my hands again, looking at my short, ripped fingernails. I spare a glance to my left and notice Wes's eyes on my hands, so I pull my sleeve ends completely over them before tucking my hands under my thighs. His eyes move back to the road when I do.

"So, you, TK and Levi…you're…brothers?" My heart pounds a little harder in my chest. I'm not good with new people. I usually either avoid them or dominate them from the beginning, figuring they'll either bow to my aggressive style or steer clear of me. But Wes intimidates me more than most. I don't like that.

Wes doesn't respond verbally, instead looking at me to make sure my eyes are on him when he nods.

"Cool," I say, immediately feeling stupid for having asked the question. The quiet takes over quickly on our side of the glass, while the two boys in the back with Taryn are laughing loudly, talking happily—smiling. Nothing but serious tolerance going on in here.

"Which one of you…" I start, but stop, my mouth not sure of the right way to form the words dashing around my head. I don't know why I'm compelled to talk to him—I don't know why I really even care, other than the fact that I now know I'm going to see him at school, probably more, given his skill and my father's love of pitchers just like him.

He'll be my dad's new favorite.

I pull the lighter from my shirt pocket and run my finger over the switch a few times, a nervous habit I've picked up. Sometimes I crave having something to hold and touch more than the actual drag of a cigarette. "Who's adopted? Just TK? Or…you?" The three of them look nothing alike—TK's skin a deep brown, Levi's pale and freckled and Wes's somewhere in between.

The truck stops slowly at the edge of the dirt road, and Wes leans forward, looking both ways and squinting into the setting sun. The light plays off the ends of the hair sticking out of the back and sides of his hat, turning the strands gold.

"We all are," he says, his answer short. A semi passes in front of us and Wes turns left onto the highway. I open my mouth to start giving him directions, but he interrupts me, glancing down to my lap where my finger is still nervously clicking the lighter. "You smoke?" he asks.

He knows I do. This feels like a trick.

"Sometimes," I answer, not wanting to give him any more or any less, but inside, my voice keeps going. *Sometimes I do a lot of things, and nobody has given a shit for years, so don't pretend you do.*

Part of me is tempted to light a cigarette now, just to see how he'd react. I don't, though. Instead, I slide the lighter back into my front pocket and push my hands back under my thighs, turning my attention to the rows of houses streaming by outside my window.

"I lived with a foster family when I was young—the mom smoked a lot. She died of a heart attack at, like...forty," he says, his lips parting to say more. A breath escapes, the kind that someone takes before they speak—a courage kind of breath. But his lips close just as quickly, and he glances over his opposite shoulder, switching lanes.

"Yeah, well...like I said. I only smoke *sometimes*," I say. He didn't tell me to stop. He didn't say it was bad for me. He just smacked me with a small dose of guilt.

Asshole.

We reach the light for our neighborhood street, and I sit up, readying myself to tell him where to turn, but he pushes the blinker and moves into the left lane on his own, so I stop myself. How the hell does he know where I live?

The laughter in the back of the truck kicks in again, and I let the sound fill the small void as he turns at the arrow and maneuvers through the narrow street and cars all parked along the curbs.

"So you're all...Stokes?" I ask, my eyes keeping a suspicious hold on him as he glances up in the rearview mirror. The small dimple comes again before he speaks, and the sight of it makes my heart beat harder for that second.

"Yeah. Three mix-and-match triplets," he says, making the slight turn toward my house.

I lower my eyes and twist my head forward to peer out the front window before looking back to him. Taryn's voice is faint through the glass behind me, and I hear the two guys laugh along with her again. Maybe she gave him our address while I was busy untangling my hands from the seatbelt.

"I'm the third one on the left," I say, my eyes not leaving his face. His jaw twitches, but he nods slowly at my direction.

Shit. Maybe he's a creeper. He's a *hot* creeper, but totally a creeper.

I move my hand to my seat buckle, and the second he pulls up to my house, I unfasten my belt, and flip open my door. Wes doesn't leave the driver's seat. Taryn and I say goodbye to Levi and TK and wait at the edge of my dirt front yard while they climb into the cab with Wes.

"Did you give him directions too?" I ask Taryn, for some reason not wanting to admit I didn't tell him where to go. I don't want my best friend freaking out over this. It's probably nothing. But then, it also feels like something—at least something I should pay attention to.

"No, you know I suck at that. I figured you had it handled. Why, did he get lost?" she asks, glancing at me, but only for a second before smiling and waving to TK.

"A little," I lie, pinning my lower lip in my teeth and holding my breath. My thoughts race in search of any reason Wes Stokes should know where I live, and just before he pulls away, he looks at me through his window, his blue eyes locking on mine, and there's a flash of a much younger face behind them for the briefest moment when he blinks.

The familiar feeling is gone quickly, but it leaves a trace of something behind. A memory. Wes Stokes has been here before. My chest constricts as I glance to the place in my front lawn a few yards behind me, the place where a boy once saved my life, and I live in that memory for a few long seconds before shelving it again—burying it back under everything I've promised myself to forget.

CHAPTER 2

Christopher.

It's funny how that name has become such a part of my life. His face. His eyes. The way his rapid breath was synchronizing with my heartbeat pounding in my ear the day I should have died. Sometimes, I wake up from nightmares hearing that sound. Not that it's a bad sound. It's the opposite, really. The hum of his chest as he's breathing hard, fighting to protect me, is the sound that wakes me—saves me from whatever bad thing is about to happen in my head.

When I was younger, I would fall asleep imagining him holding me, tugging my blanket tightly around my body to feel safe—the way I felt in his arms, in the only real hug I'd ever had. I haven't done that in years…until last night. The blanket didn't have the same effect as it did when I was a child. I know better now—I understand pretend and fantasy.

As much as I know I can't conjure up that feeling from that moment in time, I still indulge in imagining his face. *That* is something I've done nightly since the day he disappeared. Sometimes the boy I'm looking at in my head is the one from that day—like I'm trying to hold on to his memory, not forget his details. Other times, though, I lie awake and imagine what he looks like now. The one happy constant in my crap life is my thoughts of him.

It's a secret I keep for so many reasons. I asked about him before I was shipped off to Fresno for the summer. I had heard he got hurt saving me, that my dad's car hit him just as he grabbed me. The neighborhood kids were talking about it. There was blood, but when people tried to help him, he just waved them away, instead tightening his hold on me. They all called him a freak. But he didn't seem so freaky to me anymore. That happens when someone saves you, I suppose.

After my mom left us, my dad wrecked his car a few more times—driving drunk, and by the time I got back from Fresno, *that's* all the neighborhood kids were talking about—my fucked up family and how my dad was going to lose custody of me if he kept acting like this. That wasn't the threat that got him to stop drinking, though. It was baseball—the risk of losing his position. When that hung in the balance, my dad learned to keep his drinking to the bar down the road, the one within walking distance, and he saved his drunken rants and outbursts for our home.

For me.

In the midst of it all, Christopher became an afterthought, and when I brought him up, I got the "Oh, him…yeah…" response with foggy looks and disinterested shrugs. Subjects changed quickly, and his name was lost to everyone but me. He had disappeared. The rumor that he was in the hospital for injuries proved to be a lie, and when I made Taryn ride her bike all the way to the Woodmansees' house four miles away, all Mrs. Woodmansee could tell us was that Christopher went back into the system, that he wasn't working out at their house. That's also the day Taryn told me it seemed like I had a *thing* for Christopher Woodmansee. I told her she was being stupid, and I never brought him up to her again.

Taryn didn't understand. Nobody would. It wasn't a crush or some obsession or whatever. It was a boy who saved my life, and I felt like I needed to at least tell him thank you. I needed to know he was okay, even if everything else was not.

I've held on to this stupid thank you card I made for him when I was nine, stuffed it in the box with my class pictures and the few birthday cards I've gotten over the years from my grandparents. No cards from my mom in the box. No calls from her. No letters. I guess no broken promises either, that way. Though, I feel like when you have a child, you sort of make a quiet promise to always be there for them. So that one's broken for sure.

My mom, Kristina Winters, was living a double life. There was the woman who smiled at me, hugged me in the way I *thought* was a way a mom hugged her daughter, and coddled me when I came home from school every day—and then there was the one I never knew very well at all, other than the fact that she lies, and she never really cared much for her life here with me in Bakersfield. That Kristina was a stay-at-home mom who filled her day from the time I left to the time I got home with motel rooms and parked cars on the outskirts of town with the man she really wanted to be with. I was collateral waste. Just like my dad.

I'm glad I don't have any cards from her in the box. They don't belong in here with Christopher's card.

It has to be him. I spent the night wishing I'd taken one picture of Wes Stokes, just his eyes. In my mind, they're exactly the same. But now I worry that I'm imagining—pieces of my dreams finding their way into my waking moments.

I pull the card from the box, replacing the lid and sliding it back along the floor under my dresser. The paper has yellowed and the edges are soft and slightly bent, but I can still see the vase and flowers I drew in pastels. I thought I was an artist then. The picture is so elementary now, but it felt important when I drew it. I flip the paper open and read my childish message: *Thank you for saving me from the car. I'm glad you were in the race. I was hoping you would win. I hope you didn't get hurt. Your friend, Joss.*

I smile as I read it back. I haven't looked at the card since the day I came home from the Woodmansees with Taryn. I hid it from her after she teased me, and I slide it in my algebra binder now, my cheeks still burning with embarrassment. Years later, and I still don't want people to think I have a crush on the weird kid.

Taryn honks twice outside, so I zip up my backpack and grab a pack of cherry Pop-Tarts from the pantry on my way through the kitchen. My dad leaves for school early—he opens the gym for morning workouts for

39

his players. I know sometimes nobody shows up, but he opens the doors every day anyhow—even some weekends. I think he just prefers to be in the car alone. The few times he's driven me to school, all we've done is fight. He tells me how I'm throwing away my gift by not trying hard enough and by ditching practices, and I tell him I'll listen the day he starts treating me like his daughter instead of one of the guys on his roster. Somehow, eventually, it always ends up with one of us bringing up Mom. She's like our trump card; we throw her out when we want to really hurt each other. I say she left because of him, and he laughs, saying it's the other way around. The real story is she didn't want *either* of us; so, we both lose in the end.

"TK would have a field day with your breakfast choice, Joss," Taryn says, motioning to my cherry pastries. I smirk and roll my eyes, my stomach growling as I tear the package completely open and take a large bite out of one of the tarts.

"I notice you're a good twenty minutes early this morning. Someone you want to see on campus, Taryn?" I tease her.

She texted me last night that he had called her. She didn't give me details because he was on the phone when she sent the message. I'm assuming that's what has her so amped for school this morning.

"He's actually waiting for me," she says, her red lips curved into a smug smile under her sunglasses. "We talked on the phone all night. I am going to crash hard at practice."

"Look at you," I say through my full mouth. I grin at her and nod my head in support. "So where's he meeting you this morning? Hot date under the bleachers?"

"No!" She scrunches her face, looking at me briefly before returning her eyes to the road. "He's going to your dad's workouts, actually. I said I'd meet him by the gym."

"Ugggghhh," I grumble, small crumbs falling from my lips. I catch them in my lap and wrap up the second pastry in the napkin, tucking it in the front pocket of my backpack for later.

"You don't have to come inside. Besides, your dad's always busy talking to people. He won't even notice us," she says.

I purse my lips because I know better. My dad will notice. He'll wonder why I'm here early and not working out myself. Then he'll ignore me, in front of everyone, which actually feels worse than having him ride my ass about being lazy.

"Fine, I'll drop you off at the front of the school so you don't have to come with me. You can hang out in the library," she shrugs. It's a pissed off tit-for-tat kind of gesture, because she knows I hate the library. Nothing against books or reading—it's just the place they send me for detention, and I get those…a lot.

I don't have my own car, so I always ride with Taryn. Her grandma wasn't able to drive anymore, so she gave her car to Taryn. It's a giant, white, Crown Victoria that looks like an undercover cop car until you get really close. I'd make fun of it, but I won't have a car until I can find a way to afford one. No grandmas hanging up the keys and giving away cars in my family anytime soon.

We drive up to the front, and Taryn slows at the curb. She doesn't even feel guilty about any of this, flipping her visor down to check her blood-red lips in the mirror. She's going to wear off all of that crap on her face; I'm not sure why she's bothering to touch it up.

"I guess I'll see you in history," I say, not bothering to look her direction as I kick open the door and push it closed behind me with my ass. She doesn't linger, and I hear her cop-motor rumble through the lot to the other end of campus behind me.

It's early enough that the hallways are empty, which somehow makes everything feel darker. They pulled all of the lockers from the walls last year. Our principal said it was for safety reasons—one less place for kids to hide weapons. I kind of think they were hoping it would be one less place for kids to hide drugs, though. Finding what you want—pills and other shit—is pretty easy around here. I doubt stripping away our lockers is going to do much to stop the drug trafficking that happens in the school parking lot.

They haven't painted yet, so the walls are still full of holes and bare spots where metal doors once lined up. It looks like a warzone, which I guess is also appropriate.

The library is at the very end of the main hall, five hallways jutting off it to other parts of campus. I notice a few students sitting at tables when I open one side of the double doors. They never look up at me, so I slide past them to the back. It's the first day of school after break. Who the hell is studying now?

I dump my heavy bag on a table in the far corner, then kick my feet up next to it with a weighty *clunk*. Mrs. Tierney, our librarian, clears her throat and wiggles her finger at me in a circle before pointing down. I bunch my brow and she raises hers, repeating the gesture. She wants me to put my feet on the floor. I got it the first time. I just don't like being pointed at with her spindly finger.

I pull my feet down, but the second she looks away, I compromise and wedge my toes in the metal ledge right under the table top and lean my chair back on two legs. With my phone in my hand, I type Taryn a message: *You're a real bitch for making me hang out here.*

She writes back, sending me a picture of her lips. I roll my eyes and flip through my apps, finally settling on a game where I have to shoot paper airplanes into a trashcan. My dad won't buy me a car, but a phone he'll pay for. Thank god I have this paper airplane game.

After about ten minutes, I've managed to beat my all-time high score, when I notice the main library door swing open again. Wes is holding a sheet of paper in one hand, his backpack slumping over his opposite shoulder. He's wearing a different hat today—this one's a brown mesh Padres hat, trucker-style. It's fucking cute, and he's lost, which makes him super compelling. I chew at the inside of my cheek, fighting the urge to bound to my feet and help him before some other girl does. Which is a stupid challenge, because I'm in here with two girls who are way more focused on studying for SATs than the soap opera that is Wes Stokes and how he fits into my twisted world.

He finally looks up at me, and my feet slip from their grip, my chair clunking forward and my butt sliding slightly off the chair. I have to lean over and grab the table to keep myself from hitting the floor.

Shit. That was embarrassing.

"Hey," he says, unfazed by my chair aerobics. He slides a crinkled paper in front of me that looks like he's just pulled it from his back pocket. My hair is flung in front of my face from all of my…flailing…so I push it back with both hands in order to see what he's showing me. It's his schedule, just as I figured.

I slide it forward and spin it around with one finger. He's in my first period. Of course he is. Before speaking, I scan the rest of his classes and feel both sad and relieved that we only have one other class that's the same—photography. I had to pick an elective, and taking pictures sounded easier than drawing them. I bet Wes actually has some skill, though. He coughs lightly, and I slide his paper back to him, realizing that I have yet to say a word.

"Lost?" I arch a brow as I look up. His blue eyes hit me the second I give in, and my fingers grip the sides of my chair as my mind zeroes in on the almost decade-old homemade card tucked in my backpack. I swear it belongs to him—this is Christopher.

"I planned on being early so I could find my way around, but we had weights in the gym." His words trail off and he picks the paper up, squinting at me with one eye as he rubs his neck with his other hand. As adorable as the stupid trucker hat is, his squinting and neck-rubbing thing is better—or worse, depending on how I look at it. It's definitely irresistible, which is messing with my whole resisting-him plan. Maybe I just don't resist him.

"My dad's a big believer in building muscle…like…in every spare moment," I say through light laughter. Somewhere deep down, I feel the pang of loss of the relationship I *used* to have with my dad, when I was little watching him lift weights and he told me how muscle would make me dominant in the batter's box. Wes's lip twitches on one side into a faint smile, and a small chuckle leaves his mouth. It's also adorable, and it erases that pang the second I see it.

"Yeah, I got the lecture at tryouts yesterday. That's why we were hitting at the field," he says.

Wes holds his breath, staring at me quietly, his lips forming a tight, nervous smile. I feel like a little of the power has shifted back into my reigns, and I don't really care if it's just because I know where I'm going and he doesn't. I need whatever power I can get.

"You're in my first period. I'll show you where to go."

I zip my bag up and manage to untangle myself from the table and chair without making a scene. I lead Wes through the doors and down the long language arts corridor. His steps are a few behind me, and I'm tempted to turn around to see if he's looking at me or is just distracted by new classrooms and other students passing by. I never look, though, because I'm pretty sure it's the latter, and I'm not up for feeling disappointed this early. I'll stick with my fantasy where I'm the shit and he wants me but can't have me—at least until I confirm this hunch I have about his past.

"This is it," I say, turning quickly and pressing my back along the door, my hand pushing down on the handle. Wes is staring at his phone—totally not staring at me—and I feel just like I thought I would. Disappointed.

"Thanks," he says through the side of his mouth, his eyes never registering the fact that we're having a conversation, his attention on the text he's drafting.

"Sure," I say, my response short, my eyebrows raised and my lips pursed as I take in a slow breath and back through the door, spinning around so I don't have to watch him ignore me. He said thanks. I guess that's enough. It still felt...I don't know...rude?

I move to the last row along the wall of windows and drop my bag at the feet of the middle desk. A few seconds later, Wes shuffles in and nods in my direction, taking the seat directly in front of me.

My brow lowers as he slides in and shifts to get comfortable. I glance to the rows of empty seats next to me. Why here?

I can't help but focus on his details from this view—the ones...*behind.* His shoulders are wide, and his hair seems freshly trimmed. No split ends in sight. It's still long enough though that the back dusts his collar, curling at the ends from the shape of his ball cap, which I look down and notice is tucked in the top of his backpack. I smirk, because Wes is a rule follower. Dress code doesn't allow for hats inside. It's a stupid rule, because it's not like we're wearing top hats or some distracting thing on our heads, and some people would frankly be *less* distracting if they covered that shit up with a hat.

There's still a good five minutes before the starting bell, so I lean forward, tapping my pencil on the tag sticking out from his T-shirt. "Your washing instructions are showing," I say.

"Thanks," he throws over his shoulder, reaching his hand to his neck and tucking the tag in, ending that conversation just as quickly as it started.

"Okay," I mouth to myself, tilting back in my chair. I pull a pencil from the front pocket of my bag and twist my hair over my head, pushing the pencil into the knot through the side to hold it in place. It's winter, and it's seventy-four degrees. I'm hot.

A few more students trickle in, and I glance at the door, noticing them notice Wes. He's hard to miss. And not just because he's somehow a little better looking than every other guy at South, but because he's also noticeably bigger. His legs are straddling the chair in front of him, and his body has to sit back at a slant just to fit in the seat. I laugh silently when I realize how much he looks like a giant at a tea party, but the longer I let my eyes zone out at his form, the more my mind drifts to curiosity.

"Hey, so…" I say, scooting forward again. He still doesn't turn to face me, merely tilting his head to the side, his phone still in his hands. I chicken out on asking him if he by chance used to be called *Christopher* and instead ask about the code-red texting he's rapt up in. "Is there a crisis or something? You're kinda lighting up that keyboard with your thumbs."

He sighs and leans his head forward, swiping his phone off and twisting to one side to push it in his back pocket. He shifts in his seat completely to look at me, and I find home in his eyes the second he does.

Christopher.

"TK's ditching first period," he shrugs.

I laugh out a short breath and offer a closed mouth smile, silently studying his face while we talk.

"I guess that means Taryn will be missing first period too," I say, knowing that if they're ditching first period, I probably won't see them until lunch.

"TK makes stupid decisions sometimes," he sighs, and the hairs on my neck stand ready in defense of my friend.

"Meaning?" I lower my brow.

"Nothing," he says with a slight shake of his head as he spins back around in his seat, bending down along the way to pull out a notebook and pencil. I don't like how he ends conversations. He always has the last word, and it leaves my stomach feeling gross.

"He's a big boy," I say. He responds with a short breath, and I know he's rolling his eyes. I notice that his tag has curled back out from his collar, and my lip ticks up in a smirk. I'll keep it to myself this time. *Tiny win, yeah!*

"So…" I start again, glancing to the last few students as they straggle in through the door. Mr. Coughlin isn't here yet; I still have time. And now that I'm a little pissed at Wes the Rule Follower, I feel brave enough to test my theory. "You all just moved here, but did you ever live here before?"

I watch his back for any reaction. After a second or two, he takes a deep breath. "We lived in Nevada," he says, his pencil balanced between two fingers, bobbing up and down against his notepad.

"I meant, maybe…I don't know, before you were adopted?" I ask.

"Still Nevada," he says, his voice sounding bored. I nod behind him, my head accepting Nevada, but my gut rejecting it all.

"Oh, okay. You just…" I halt, biting my tongue and giving myself a short breath to make sure I say this exactly the right way. "You remind me of someone…" I settle on that, and I watch his shoulders, hoping for a memory to be triggered—for *something*. All he does is shrug, though.

"Hey, how'd you know how to get to my house?" I ask, fitting in one more question as Mr. Coughlin steps through the door and claps once, a leftover habit he's had since teaching first grade years before. It's funny how it makes seventeen-year-olds jump the same as seven-year-olds.

"We knew where coach lived," he says over his shoulder. I squint my eyes, not sure if I should believe him. "He said we could stop by whenever we needed anything, gave us directions at the end of tryouts yesterday. Your dad seems like a good guy, said his players are like family. Must be weird for you, players dropping in for dinner or whatever."

He sort of chuckles out that last part, amused as he imagines an open and welcoming house. I hold my mouth firm and keep the painful laugh I want to respond with inside this time. "Yeah, he's a good coach like that," I say in an even tone.

Truth is, other than Kyle, one of my dad's players has never just *dropped by for dinner.* If someone did, though, I have no doubt they'd be treated like royalty, and nothing like family at all. If his players were like family, they'd feel like ghosts that drift around our house, only acknowledged when they *really* screw up. I wish he treated his family like his players.

Slumping back in my seat, I resign myself to having concocted an amazingly lavish fantasy, and I go back to just thinking Wes Stokes is a hot new guy at school with an abrasive personality. And I'm almost convinced of it, until Mr. Coughlin reads through roll call for the day.

"And what do you prefer to go by, Mr. Stokes? Wes or…"

"Wes," He interjects quickly, his shoulders suddenly stiff. "I go by Wes…"

"Got it, so the other name…" he says, clicking through the list of students on his computer and eyeballing the rest of us.

"Just Wes," he repeats, his voice a little firmer, shoulders stiffer.

"What about the other name?" I say quietly, barely under my breath, a whisper escaping. Wes turns his head a fraction to the side, and I know he heard me, but he leans forward instead, increasing the distance between my body and his. I bet he's regretting his seating choice now.

Taryn and TK both showed up at lunch, as I predicted. I caught him nibbling at her neck just outside the cafeteria as I was walking up. He headed out to the parking lot before I approached them, and I saw him jump into the back of the truck with his brothers.

I picked at my fries throughout lunch while Taryn caught me up on all things TK—he likes football better than baseball, he's a good kisser, and he's taking her out this weekend. Those were the highlights. We usually hang out at Conner and Kyle's on Saturday nights, so it's looking like I'll be walking there. They only live a few blocks away, and the slightly risky walk at night is still better than hanging out at my house and waiting for my dad to stumble in, or better yet, to call me and beg me for a ride. It's cruel every time it happens—the only time I can drive his damn car is when I'm picking him up from puking on himself.

I'm trying not to be snarky with Taryn over TK. She does this with guys, though—gets a crush, and it accelerates at a hundred miles per hour until she's suddenly neck deep in a suffocating relationship with the guy in a matter of days. Guys just fall for her—*hard*. Taryn Rodriguez is beautiful. Her body curves, and her boobs are enormous. It's one thing she's always had that I envied. I'm jealous of her home life too—two older sisters in college and married parents who think she walks on water, even when we land our asses in trouble. Yeah, I'd trade my best features for her bra size and dinner at their family table any day.

Taryn is still crushing on TK while we load the balls back in the bucket from hitting practice. She's starting to repeat things, and normally I call her on it, but the boy standing next to my father three hundred yards away distracts me.

Of course, my dad likes him. And he doesn't just like him. He's living vicariously through him, practically foaming at the mouth over the fact that Wes Stokes is his to coach and train. My dad was a pitcher in college until he hurt his arm. He and my mom had been dating for three years, and she married him right before they graduated. I think she had high hopes that he'd make a comeback and get drafted by a team. Instead, she wound up married to a high school PE teacher and coach who preferred to live in rural California and hated L.A.

My mom loved the city. The compromise was Bakersfield, which is *very much not* a big city. My dad became a legend of a coach here, and he'll die here. I know this much. My mom must have too.

I'm careful how I watch Wes. Taryn's already asked me if I have a thing for him, and I told her he was hot, but seemed like an asshole. A fair summation, I believe, even if I left out a few details, like my twisted theory that he's literally my childhood hero.

He's working on grip technique with my dad now. I can tell by the way they're trading the ball, practicing stances while Wes moves the ball in his hand behind his back. I smirk, because I'm so much like my father. Wes doesn't hide his grip very well; it's how I knew exactly what he was going to throw. My dad picked up on that right away and aims to fix it. I'm glad. I'm also sick because I'm like him.

Maybe I'll die in Bakersfield too.

"Trying to get over the fact that he's an asshole are you?" Taryn teases, throwing a ball toward me and bouncing it off my thigh. Shit. Caught.

"No," I sigh, glancing back at them a few times. "Just watching him with my dad. He really likes him."

My mouth falls into a tight line, and I busy myself with the balls and the tee, balancing one for my next hit. I check my feet and ready my swing, but before my bat moves, Taryn grabs the ball into her hands.

"Taryn, don't," I protest. She's reading into this the wrong way now.

"You should talk to your dad, Joss. Tell him you miss how close you were. You know he misses you too. He'd love to get back to that time when you stood there with him like that," she says, nodding toward Wes and my father.

"We've had those conversations, Tar. They don't work. You know they don't work, because I come live with you for a week after every time," I say, holding my hand out for the ball. She huffs and puts it on the tee for me, and I pull back and unleash a hard swing. I bend down and replace the ball with a new one, ready to swing again. "And I'm not jealous of my dad's latest pet project. I'm just pissed that he's telling him how to hide his pitches better. Now I won't be able to read them so well."

I take another hack and load another ball, but Taryn pulls it away again.

"I swear to god, Taryn, just stop…" I say, wiping the beads of sweat from my brow and letting my bat slump over my shoulder.

My friend rolls the ball in her hands a few times, her lips parted and ready, but after a few seconds she closes her mouth and puts the ball back in place, then takes a few steps back so I can swing.

"Fine, I'm wrong…I guess," she says. I cut through the ball, sending it ricocheting off one of the poles holding the hitting net. "But…" Taryn starts again. I breathe harder, the heat and the hundreds of swings I've already taken starting to catch up to me. I'm too tired to argue with her any more. I look at her, my lips pursed and my eyes wide—I'll tolerate one more lecture.

"You lied about one of those things, Joss, and I know it. And it's okay, but you know you did," she says. I shake my head in response, rolling my eyes. "Either you're jealous of Wes Stokes or you're into him. It might even be both, Joss, but it sure as hell ain't neither."

I want to protest, but I also want to drop it, because Taryn's right. She's more right than I thought she would be too, because yeah…it's both. But it also doesn't matter.

Coach Adams blows his whistle when the sun is starting to set, and I linger behind the rest of my team. I've always been a lone wolf out here, Taryn the only real teammate I care to hang out with off the field. The other girls are just different from me. They're focused on the matching hair ribbons and bows for their cleats, while I'm focused on crushing the competition and the celebration after—with shots and maybe a few of those pills that make everything feel fuzzy and far away. They all also get to go home to bright and shiny families. I'm sure some of them have their own problems, but they're nothing like mine—and they're nothing like me.

I pull the gate closed on the batting cage after putting the buckets of balls away. When I'm locking up, I notice Wes is sitting at the end of the bench in the dugout across from me, also alone. I chuckle to myself because as much as he's my dad's pet, he also can't compete with the six o'clock happy hour at Pete's that I have no doubt my father is already halfway on his way to.

Wes is leaning forward on the bench, his hands moving near his feet, doing something to his cleats. I step to the end of the cage where the netting is thinner and I have a better view, but I stop shy of walking all the way into the open. After a closer look, I realize he's wiping away the dust and dirt from his shoes, and the scene makes me suck in a breath and hold it.

He drags the corner of his towel around the toes and sides of his shoes, then stuffs the cloth into his bag, lifting it up and rolling it behind him until he reaches the exit for the dugout.

The infield dirt is loose, just like the farms a mile or two away, and there's really no way to walk through it without making deep prints and leaving puffs of dust clouds in your wake. Wes pauses, lifting his bag by the straps up over his shoulder, then steps slowly along the edge, rounding the dugout to a small strip of concrete that runs to the main sidewalk near the locker rooms. I watch him the entire way; he never sees me.

It's been eight years since I've watched a boy walk along a balance beam in attempt to keep his favorite pair of shoes clean. And I know in my heart I've just seen that same boy do it again.

CHAPTER 3

Taryn and TK have defied the law of averages, and as much as they appear to be into each other, there also doesn't seem to be a sign of them getting sick of one another. A week would actually be a record for a Taryn Rodriguez relationship, and dare I admit, I'm rooting for a new record.

I'm looking forward to getting to know TK more. Taryn talked him into coming to Kyle and Connor's tonight. I think the Marley boys like him too. Conner seems to like all three Stokes brothers, actually. But Kyle hasn't said the nicest things about Wes since I've gotten to his house tonight. I think he's just threatened by him. I only know what I've seen from my side-glances during practice this week, but even from far away I can tell that Wes is ten times the pitcher Kyle is.

"Why do you like coming to my house so early, Joss? Hmmmm?" Kyle says, his mouth right over my shoulder as he passes behind me, two cases of beer in either hand.

"Clearly, it's because I'm secretly hot for you and can't get enough, Kyle," I say in my bored voice. He laughs hard once, then presses his lips down on my bare shoulder in a friendly peck before moving all the way into the kitchen.

Kyle is me. I'm Kyle. As much as Taryn is my best friend, Kyle is the one I turn to when I need to be destructive, when I'm angry and I want to vent, when I need to show my ugly parts and talk *truth*. We grew up together, and we both played tee-ball for my dad as kids. Kyle was always my dad's favorite. Though, my dad goes through his favorites like I do brands of cigarettes. Kyle fell out of favor the first time he got hauled in for drag racing with me in the car. My dad was too drunk to pick me up from the police station, so Mr. Marley took me home.

My dad benched Kyle for two weeks, and as bad as I felt for my friend, it felt nice that my dad was upset over someone putting me at risk. Then I overheard him having a conversation with Kyle outside his coaching office. He told him he didn't think I was a good influence on him and that I would ruin his chances at making it to the next level in baseball. Kyle told him he would never walk away from me, and then he called my father pathetic. He's been last in the rotation ever since. He worked his way up to starting by the end of last season, but only because he throws hard. Wes throws harder; I don't think he'll have that luck again this year.

"So what's up with your girl and TK?" Kyle smirks, wiggling an eyebrow at me while he rips open one of the beer cases and begins loading his kitchen fridge.

Kyle's dad is a wildland firefighter, and his parents are divorced. His dad's schedule leaves an empty house most weekends, so as long as we help him clean up on Sundays, he always hosts.

"I don't know, yo. My girl is pretty smitten with your new shortstop. He seems like a good guy," I say, tapping my pack of cigarettes in my palm and offering one to Kyle. He shrugs it off.

"I'm quitting," he says, and I bunch my brow. Kyle's the reason *I* smoke—*what the hell?* "What? I'm allowed to quit. That shit really is bad for you, and you should quit too."

I flip Kyle off and place my cigarette between my lips, standing up from my seat to feel for the lighter in my back pocket.

"TK, though? Yeah…he's a good guy. He's fitting in with the team," Kyle says, and I know he's leaving something out.

"How about Wes and Levi?" I ask, checking my front pockets as well as the floor beneath me for my lighter.

"Yeah, they're a'right. Wes is a little…I don't know…quiet, I guess," he says, swallowing in the middle of his speech. That's a jealous swallow, but I give him this one, pretending I don't notice.

"Dude, have you seen my lighter?" I ask, both hands deep in my back pockets again as if that four-inch space against my ass cheeks is going to suddenly produce the Zippo it's been hiding all along. The second I turn around, I'm face-to-face with Wes. I smile, cigarette still perched in my lips, and I feel like an asshole.

"You probably forgot it. You're always forgetting it," Kyle says behind me.

"Yeah," I say, pulling the cigarette from my lips and sliding it back in the pack I've left on the counter.

"You should quit anyway," Wes says, moving into the seat next to the one I'd just left.

"Probably," I say, refusing to make eye contact with him again. "I've been hearing that a lot lately."

Kyle chuckles, and I hold up my middle finger against the other side of my face, which only makes him laugh harder.

"Joss! I feel like I haven't seen you since you lit my brother up on the mound," Levi says, reaching around me for a hug. It surprises me; my hands awkwardly pat at his arms. I catch Kyle's face over his back as he's laughing at me so hard he's squinting, and I scowl, which only pushes him into a gut-busting kind of laughter.

"Joss lit you up?" Kyle finally asks, leaning over the other side of the counter, handing a beer to Wes. He takes it in his hand and pulls back the tab, which surprises me. I didn't expect Rule Follower to drink. I also didn't expect Kyle to be so hospitable to him. It's a night full of surprises it seems.

"She did," Wes says, nodding before taking a long chug, which I swear he's doing just to prove to me that he does, in fact, break rules. I watch his lips leave the can and the movement feels like it happens in slow motion. I look down after one side of his mouth lifts into a smile again. He's grinning because he caught me watching him. I wince knowing everyone saw me looking at him, and I bet I looked all doe-eyed.

"It's because you don't know how to hide your grip," I shrug, daring to glance up at him as if looking at him is no big deal to me. His eyes meet mine instantly, and I inelegantly attempt to look away.

"We've been working on that," he says through a soft laugh that comes from his chest. It makes me turn my head to the side and glare at his chest, and the way his dark gray shirt hugs his muscles, and the thin chain that peeks out from under the collar of his T-shirt, and his neck, and the golden color of his skin. I get up and move to the other side of the counter next to Kyle so I stop looking at him, so others don't make assumptions, and to check myself.

"I knew my dad would like you," I say softly, my eyes trained on the beer now cuddled between my hands on the counter. Kyle's foot rests next to mine, and I know he's telling me it's okay, that Wes replaced him too.

"Who wants to play *I Never*, bitches?" Taryn busts into the kitchen with TK's arm around her, more beer in his other arm. He slides it on the counter and slaps hands with Kyle, pulling him in for a hug. He's hugging me seconds later, and I can't help but laugh out loud through the grin pressing into my cheeks. It's as if TK has been in our circle since it was formed.

I let go of him, letting him return his arm to Taryn, who snuggles in quickly. She's fallen hard, but somehow, this time feels different. I notice Wes stand up nearby, crinkling his can and moving around the counter toward Kyle, holding it and asking where to recycle. His can isn't even empty yet. He looks anxious, and I see the subtleties in his eyes. He's looking for some place to go, something to do. He's hiding, even though it's out in the open, and I realize—as much as Levi and TK are at home—Wes is an alien.

I notice Conner, Kyle's brother, in the living room, so I nod over my shoulder for Wes to follow me into the other room. I'm not sure he's come with me until I feel his weight sink in next to me on the worn leather sofa.

Conner is lining cups around the coffee table, and Wes tilts his head with a strange look. I recognize it, so I fill in the blanks for him.

"They're twins," I say.

"Ahhh, yeah. They're like…identical," Wes says, his eyes still stuck on Conner with the same amazement as he would have watching baby chicks hatch.

"Yep, identical. That's a thing," I smile. He shakes his head slightly and looks to me with a lopsided grin. "They must not have any weird oddities like that in Nevada?"

"Ha, yeah…they do. I just…I didn't know there were two of them," he says, gesturing to the kitchen where Kyle is still talking with Wes's brothers.

"We're totally different, though," Conner finally speaks, stepping around the table to shake Wes's hand. He rarely speaks. Not that he can't, he's just not the social butterfly his brother is. Two carbon-copy blond hotties—though only Kyle has the surfer body—and green eyes, the Marley twins are meant to walk two diverging paths in life. Conner will probably be our class valedictorian, whereas Kyle will scrape by with a 2.0. However, Kyle can take a punch and throw an eighty-five-mile-per-hour fastball. Conner couldn't break a window with a rock.

After another minute or two, the others join us in the living room. Kyle brings in a dozen cold beers ready to fill the cups, and I tap the one in front of me. He quirks a lip, and I tell him to shut up and fill it.

"Always so eager to get right to the buzz, Joss. I don't think you even taste half the shit you drink," Kyle says, filling my plastic cup to the top, knowing I'll drink most of it down before we even begin to play.

Wes is looking at me; I can feel it, but he's not saying anything.

"Yeah, well, I'm a hot drunk and you know it," I say with a wink, emptying my cup in seconds.

"Woooooooo, she's not messing around tonight. Taryn, I hope you're ready to take your girl home later," Kyle teases, filling my cup again. I feel Wes shift next to me, moving forward, his arms on his knees, his hands clasped in front of his body.

I feel his disgust.

I start to tip my second cup back, but Taryn reaches across the table, pulling my arm down lightly with a few of her fingers, her eyes catching mine, her warning loud and clear.

"What?" I mouth over the cup's edge, my tongue taking a small taste of the liquid beaded around the edge. I hate the way beer tastes, but I love how it makes me feel—drink enough, and everything sharp gets softer.

"Stop it," she whispers back, the worry line deep between her eyes.

My lips purse as I pause and decide if I'm going to engage, like I normally do, or listen to my friend and not fall into my usual pattern, which I know would ruin her night with TK. Kyle is me, and I am him, and nobody tests the nerve that runs through me like he does. He likes to push me into things. I like to let him. I hate that he's quitting smoking, because he's the reason I started, and part of me wants to get shitfaced in minutes just to spite him. But Taryn's right. Besides, that's what he wants. He wants the push—and I think part of him is showing off our connection in front of Wes just to prove to the new guy that he doesn't get to be *everyone's* favorite.

I put my cup down and sink back into the couch, ready to play the game. My buzz will come soon enough, and I'm willing to wait the hour it might take before the reality of what I'll have to deal with at home sinks into me.

Taryn starts things off easy, with statements like "never have I ever kissed more than one person in the same night" and "never have I ever slept in the nude." I drink for both because I've done both, and I feel Wes's eyes on me for my confessions.

The admissions get heavier as the hour wears on, and I've only sat out a few of them. I haven't been arrested—officially—so I don't drink for that, and I've never kissed a girl. Kyle asks this question every time we play, and I know it's because he wants to see me finally check that box and kiss Taryn in front of him. That check doesn't happen tonight though.

I notice Wes has hardly drunk any, and I wonder why he even bothered to come. Conner's girlfriend, Layla, showed up late along with Taryn's cousin, Emily, our friend Noah, and a couple of other girls I sort of know.

They've all had more to drink than Wes. The new girls are also quite taken with him. The way he sits, holding his half cup of beer in one hand, arm slung over the back of the sofa, his shirt tight around his biceps, hair falling in his face—it's almost laughable how good looking he is. He doesn't belong here in this dark room on the poor side of Bakersfield in a house with olive-colored carpet and wood-paneled walls. And god, the way he smells. I'm feeling my beer pretty good at this point, and the only thing keeping my wits with me is Wes's cologne. I keep trying to follow the scent into a dream, but whenever I do, I end up staring at him.

"I have to pee," I announce, standing clumsily and knocking over a few half-filled cups teetering on the edge of the coffee table.

"Shit, Joss. You're making a goddamned mess," Kyle says, laughing halfway through his lecture. He's as drunk as I am, and at least that feels right.

I stumble down the hallway to the bathroom and spend several minutes looking at myself in the mirror after I've taken care of business. My eyes are heavy, and my hair is down. It's tangled around my shoulders. I pull the band from my wrist and twist my hair up, fastening it in place before running a finger under each of my eyes, smearing away some of the excess eyeliner. My head falls forward and I let out a faint laugh when I realize how silly I'm being. I'm trying to look good for Wes, but I also want to call him on his bullshit and make him admit he's Christopher— and beyond that, I want him to quit looking at me like I'm doing something wrong. He has no idea what it's like to live in my house. Saturday nights are my one escape, at least until my phone rings and reality comes calling.

My phone hasn't rung yet, though. Maybe tonight I'll get a break. I wash my hands and flip off the light before entering the hall, running right into Wes's chest when I do. My palm finds the center of it, and his hand finds my wrist, steadying me when I startle and scream.

"Sorry, I didn't know you were coming out. I was waiting for my turn," he says, same stupid crooked smirk.

"It's okay," I say, and I smile back at him. Doe-eyes are back, and I feel them, so I straighten my posture and pull my lips tight, taking my arm from his grasp. "We'll wait for you before we start again, Christopher."

I just let it slip out. My heartbeat drums quickly in my chest, and the last vestige of sober me fights to act nonchalant while I watch Wes's face for a reaction. His eyes never flinch, though, and his reaction is nothing but natural. One eyebrow quirks up, and he points to himself. "It's Wes, and I think maybe you've had enough," he says.

"It's not Wes; it's Christopher," I say, squinting at him and pointing my finger in his chest. He glances down at it, his face still resolved, which pisses me off even more. "And I'm not even *close* to drunk yet."

I leave him there in the hall, but before I turn the corner to the living room, I run into Kyle. He grabs my elbows when I stumble, and glances behind me before looking in my eyes. I see him look back at Wes again before he disappears behind the bathroom door, and then he turns to me with a question.

"He was waiting to use the bathroom, and he scared the shit out of me in the dark," I say.

It's the truth, but somehow it reads like a lie, and I can now feel my heart beating in my stomach. I shirk off Kyle's hold on my arms and step over Taryn and TK, who are practically spooning on the floor. I get back to my spot on the couch and fill my cup with one of the beers—drinking it down almost completely before Kyle and Wes get back to the game.

McKenna, one of the girls who showed up late, has somehow wormed her way to Wes's other side. There really isn't a seat there, so her leg is pressed into his as she attempts to split the couch cushion with him. She's not even subtle about the way she's maneuvering her body so that her skirt rides up just enough to catch his eye. It works. Hell, every human that's not spooning on the goddamned floor has ogled her leg by now—me included. But I still feel the tingle of jealousy in my veins, amplified by alcohol.

"Let's play more," Kyle says, interrupting my jaunt down envy lane. "I…" he says, standing in the center of our circle, his finger out as he spins slowly, pointing to each of us as if he's the prize wheel and we're the prizes. He stops at me, and the right side of his lip rises.

Shit.

"I…have never, not ever made out with Josselyn Winters." His declaration comes out smug, and he brings his cup to his smiling lips quickly, drinking his entire cup empty and setting it down with a smack on the table right in front of Wes. He just made me a challenge, like I'm some trophy he won. Most of the room rolls their eyes—aware of the few hook ups Kyle and I have had over the last couple years—none of them caring. But his turn wasn't for them—it was for Wes, for Kyle to prove he's already had me, in some small way, and that he had me first. Wes is holding his cup in both hands between his knees, spinning it slowly, his lips pursed, and his jaw twitching. It would be sweet if it were because he's jealous, but it's not—it's because he doesn't like people paying attention to him. Just like Christopher.

Reaching forward, I smack my hand flat on the table to get everyone's attention, and when they all look at me, I sit up tall, pulling my cup into my hand.

"I have one! I have never ever pretended to be someone I'm not," I say, my words coming out ugly, but clear enough that everyone hears. I hold my breath and scan the room slowly, stopping when my eyes reach Wes's. I wait for him to drink, but he just stares at me, his brow slightly lowered, his face full of concern, maybe even disappointment. I look back at him, my breath slow and even, when something else comes over me. Maybe he's pretending to be someone else, but so is everyone here. Kyle, Taryn…all of my friends—me! We're pretending to be okay with the fact that we live where we live, that not one of us can afford college and that the kids who live on the north side all have nice cars and two parents who have jobs with suits and business meetings and fancy parties. We pretend to be tough, to be grown up and ready—but we're not. We're so far away from any of that.

"You're all fuckin' liars," I say, holding my cup against my lips, my breath held. I don't flinch, my eyes playing defense against Wes's stare as I tip my cup back and swallow the remains of my last beer. I feel the vibration of my phone in my pocket, so I pull it out to confirm my father's cell phone number before putting it away and turning to face Wes one last time. "I know who you are. Why are you ashamed to admit it? Is it because I wasn't worth saving? Is that why?"

His brow is furrowed as he keeps his eyes on mine, his head shaking slightly side-to-side like he's trying to understand my language. To the rest of the room, this sounds like my usual drunken rant—nonsensical, meaningless conversation that will be forgotten in the morning. But my wits are there by a thread, and I'll remember this.

So will he.

"I'm out, Kyle. As always, thanks for taking me away from the shit for a while," I say, stumbling over the legs of the girls I don't really know and wrapping my arms around Kyle.

"You want me to come with?" he asks, and I squeeze his shoulder before bringing my face to his.

"Nah, I got it this time. I'm good," I shrug.

I kick at Taryn's feet, and she tilts her head to one side. She feels guilty because she's usually my ride home, but I know she's staying here with TK. And Taryn's seen my nightmare enough. She deserves a night off.

"I'm good. I promise," I say, tripping over her feet a little. It makes me laugh, but I catch myself quickly, holding up a hand and crossing my heart with the other.

"Okay, call me if you need me?" she says from her position wrapped deep in TK's arms. I hold my phone up and waggle it at her. I won't call, and she wouldn't answer—not tonight. And that's okay.

"It's been real, TK…Levi," I say, pounding both of their knuckles on my way through the living room. Conner and his girlfriend left the party a long time ago, so I don't bother with anyone else, instead giving over my attention to the *buzz* of a message on my phone.

I wait until I'm completely out of the house and walking down the driveway before I dial in and listen. It's the same message it always is, my dad's voice coming and going as he holds the phone at various distances from his face.

"Fucking assholes say you need to come get me," he puffs out, his face muffling his words as the rough stubble of his cheek presses into the phone. "I'll be out front. You can take the car…"

"Shit," I mutter to myself, looking at the time stamp from the message, feeling the vibration of my father's next call. It's only been two minutes. This is how it goes, though. He calls until I answer, or until I show up. I quit answering months ago, because it doesn't get me to him any faster, and not answering means I can enjoy these few minutes before I *have* to talk to him in person.

"You need a ride?" His voice comes out of the complete calm of the night behind me. My legs buckle from the adrenaline coursing through me as a result.

"Shshshshit!" I say, pressing the buzzing phone against my chest.

"Sorry," Wes says; I think maybe wincing a little.

"I'm fine. Go back to the party," I say, shaking my head and sighing with relief that the ringing has stopped. I push my phone back into my pocket and turn to head to the end of the block. Wes stays with me, though.

"You're lit," he says. "I don't feel comfortable with you walking home in the dark."

I laugh loudly, and turn to face him, continuing to shuffle backward. "Welcome to my every Saturday night, Christopher," I say with my hands out on either side.

"Right, uhm…I'm Wes," he nods, which only makes me laugh harder. I hold my hands to my stomach to exaggerate it, but he talks right through me. "You're not in a position to be walking along the road in the dark. Come on, I'll take you home."

"Ah, yeah, right…cuz you know where I live!" I say, holding a finger up. "Give it up. I just wanted to say thanks for what you did, but if you want to pretend that you're not him, whatever."

I'm slurring more, and my feet feel heavier. I can tell I passed the line, and I know I'm probably going to get sick any minute, but I have to make it to Jim's first. Wes walks away, and I turn around to go forward because this backward shit is making me dizzy. My phone buzzes in my pocket, and this time I pull it out and silence it.

I do my best to pick up my stride, and I'm close to the end of the block when I hear the familiar idle of Wes's truck pull alongside me. I chuckle to myself, and stop, turning to face him with my thumbs hanging from the pockets of my jeans.

"You left your jacket, Joss. I have it in the truck. Just…just get in," he says, and as if Mother Nature is in his corner, the breeze picks up, sending a chill over my bare shoulders, blowing the fabric of my tank top tight against my stomach.

"Fine," I say, feeling the buzz in my pocket begin again. I let it go this time, and when I slam the cab door shut in his truck, I can hear the phone's sound vibrate against his seat.

"You need to get that?" Wes asks.

I remind myself that he hasn't done this dance before, so I'm polite—or as polite as I can be with a burning esophagus, fading consciousness, and rancid taste of bile in my mouth.

"It's fine. He'll call back," I say, fumbling with the buckle. This truck doesn't even work right. Wes tugs the belt away from me and snaps it into place, pausing with his hands on the wheel before shifting into drive.

"Who'll call back, Joss?"

"My dad. It's…it's always my dad. It's fine; just…take me to Jim's. It's like, super close. You probably know where it is, though, because you, like, know everything," I say, and it comes out both sing-songy and bitchy. I don't mean it to, so I try to correct it. "It's okay that you know everything. I mean…whatever, right?"

He sighs heavily, laying his forehead against the steering wheel while he pushes the gear into place. I curl my legs up sideways and rest my head on his window, willing myself not to be sick.

"I don't know what Jim's is," he bites, and I roll my head to the side against the glass to meet his stare. His head is lying on his hands, against the wheel, and he looks as frustrated as I feel every time my phone vibrates against me. Maybe he doesn't know Jim's. Maybe he doesn't know anything at all. Maybe I've hit rock bottom, and I'm making things up in my head because I want to feel like I did when Christopher's arms held me away from the harms of the world. That was the last time I ever felt safe, and it was the day I almost died. I've been chasing that feeling for years, and maybe I just want to find it so badly that I'm seeing things.

"Fifth and Washburn," I answer in a whisper, mostly because I'm pretty sure if I speak any more loudly, I will lose everything in my stomach. "Just go three blocks to the right, and then turn left at Fifth. You'll see it."

His only response is a heavy exhale as he drives forward. His truck rides rough; every turn makes my stomach clench, and by the time we reach Jim's, I kick open his door just in time to puke all over the gravel parking lot beneath my feet. I hate the way it tastes. I hate everything about this part. But not enough that I won't do it again next weekend. I'd do it every day if I could, but my dad is home too often during the week. Not that he'd care, but it's just too much when it's both of us living in the fog. I can always count on Saturdays, though. I probably won't be able to afford college, but Jim—if there even is a Jim that this bar is named after—is probably driving a Mercedes by now, thanks to my dad's patronage.

"You okay?" Wes says, his hand tentative against my back. I shudder from his faint touch, and he pulls his hand away. I regret it instantly.

"I'm fine," I say, running the sleeve of my zip jacket along my jaw and stepping wide around my mess. My stomach feels better, but I know I'll do that again. I just hope I can wait until I get home. I don't want to throw up inside Wes's truck.

Per the norm, my dad is sitting on the bench outside of Jim's, his phone in his hands while he repeats hitting the dial button over and over.

"Quit calling me; I'm here," I say, grabbing his arm and slinging it over my shoulder. Wes steps to the other side, pulling most of my father's dead weight against him. I'm embarrassed, but too grateful that I don't have to fall and drag him like I normally do to feel the sting of it right now.

"Awwww, Josselyn. Goddamnit! Don't bring him into our mess," my dad says, his eyes watery from his usual self-pity cry.

"This isn't our mess, Dad. It's yours. It's always yours," I say through gritted teeth. Maybe it is ours. But at least when it comes to *my* half, I never need any help getting home in the end. I'm like the family cat nobody wants; I could be dropped at the ends of the earth and somehow still find my way home on my feet.

"It's okay, Mr. Winters. I'm here to help," Wes says, and I wave my other hand to get his attention.

"Don't bother. He won't remember any of this," I say.

"I remember everything!" my dad interjects. I shake my head *no*, because he's just mirroring our conversation. He never remembers this. He only remembers the things *I* do wrong.

I climb into the truck first, and Wes helps my dad onto the seat, buckling his safety belt for him and shutting the door carefully around his feet. I shake my head to myself as Wes rounds the cab and climbs in next to me, his body pressed against mine. I wish I could enjoy this instead of survive it.

Jim's isn't far from our house. It's why he goes there. He walks—every Saturday, practically jogging on his way there in the late afternoon and filling his body with whiskey until he can no longer see. Sometimes he can get back home on his own. But that's happening less and less.

I keep my eyes focused out the windshield as we pull along the curb of my house. I'm done being sick, but my head is starting to pound now. And I'm not drunk enough to forget any of this, which makes it all hurt more.

"I'll go get the door," Wes says through a slow, steady breath. I feel his chest lift next to me, and I wish we were attached so he could breathe for me too. He closes the door behind him, and in the time he walks around the front of the cab to my father's door, my dad lets the word *bitch* fall slowly from his lips. I'm glad Wes didn't hear it, because he wouldn't understand. I know my father doesn't mean it—he doesn't mean any of this. He's drunk, and when he's sober, he's strictly indifferent toward me, but never hateful. The hate only comes out when it tangles with him missing my mom and blaming me.

"Come on, Coach," Wes says, pulling my dad's arm over his body and lifting him from the truck. My dad fights the help when his feet hit the sidewalk, and he swings his arms wildly. I climb out and move to him, and he shoves me away too.

"You're not even mine!" my dad seethes, his eyes having a hard time focusing on my form as he wobbles backward on his unsteady legs, tripping in our dead lawn. I know it's a lie, because as soon as my mother left, my dad followed through with a blood test. It still hurts. It hurts every time he says it.

Wes steps closer to me, and I pull my arms around myself, holding one hand up to the side, urging him to just let this all be.

"It's fine," I say.

I always say it's fine. My mantra—*fine.*

I'm a liar.

"We're home now, Dad. Time for bed," I say, treating him like a toddler. I reach for him again, and he shrugs me off, standing sloppily on his knees and eventually pulling himself back up to his feet. As much as I want to hate him, I can't. I miss him. And I don't like Wes seeing him like this.

"You waste your time," my dad says, holding his unsteady finger at me. For a brief second, his eyes fade into reflections of the man lost inside, and they tear. I think for a moment he's going to cup my face and reach for me, but just as quickly, that warm feeling is gone, and he bends forward, vomiting on himself as he collapses into sleep on the ground.

"Fuck!" I yell so loudly that my voice reverberates off everything around me. I grip at my hair and close my eyes, but all they do is twitch, fighting to stay open. I couldn't escape my nightmare if I tried.

Wes has my dad in his arms in seconds, and I part my lips to protest because I'm ashamed, but give up quickly and let him carry my father inside. I drag my feet behind them both, unlocking the door and nodding toward the long hallway in the back.

"Last room at the end. Just lay him on the bed," I say. Wes marches down the hall, setting my father on top of the quilt my grandmother gave them when they first married. It was always my mom's favorite, and the fact that it's all he'll put on that bed is so telling of the many, many things wrong in this house.

Wes starts to pull my dad's shoes off, but I touch his arm lightly. He freezes at the feel of my fingertips on his skin.

"Really, just leave him. He'll erase all of this in the morning," I say.

Wes's jaw is working with his thoughts, but eventually he nods slowly as he swallows and faces me, his eyes holding mine. They're full of pity.

"Don't look at me like that," I say, turning and walking back to the front door to guide him out.

He's slow to follow me, and when he reaches the door, he pauses again, his lips opening with the intent to speak, but no words coming. His eyes stay on me for a few more seconds, and I dive into them, finding the familiar. I don't even care if it's make believe at this point. I'm dizzy, and I'm my own mess, and something about Wes makes me feel better.

I give in, and I step into him, letting my forehead press deep into the center of his chest as I bring my limp arms around him, my fingers gripping the fabric of his shirt on the back. His chin slowly falls to the top of my head and his own arms circle me tentatively at first, until finally they lock around me, his palms sliding in slow tender circles along my skin. I'm overcome with his strength and the feel of his embrace, and I do something that I regret the moment it starts.

I cry.

CHAPTER 4

Sunday was for hiding. Taryn called to check on me. She knows the Saturday routine. I told her I was fine, but not feeling well. I wasn't feeling well. As much as Saturday nights numb things for a few hours, they also suck to remember the next day. The bad parts greatly outweigh the good.

The one solace was Wes. By the end of Saturday night, when he finally stepped away from holding me and typed in my phone number, texting me, begging me to call if I needed anything, I was satisfied with him simply being him, not some ghost from my past. I didn't call him. I wouldn't. I don't want to need him. I *don't* need him. But I think of him. I think about him a lot.

When Monday came, everything in my life reset, just like it always did. My dad left for school early, opened the gym, and Taryn picked me up so she could meet TK after he was done lifting. The routine carried through the week, and my father and I were cordial, at best, when we passed each other coming and going from our house. Saturday's scene a blur to him, and just one more in a long line to me.

It was...fine.

I'm also starting to get comfortable with life in the library early in the mornings. It's peaceful in there. I suppose an empty room can be that way, but being in there without being forced to go there feels nice. I've even started reading again—something I loved to do when I was young, and quit when stories weren't offering enough of an escape from my reality. A few teachers who have seen me in the library have even commented on how proud they were to see me working hard. I let them believe whatever they want, because it feels good, even if I'm just here because I have nowhere else to go.

Last semester, I would kill time smoking while sitting on the abandoned brick and wood scraps in the alley behind the school. Sometimes, I'd miss most of my morning classes smoking and drawing with a marker on the brick wall. The tardiness always landed me in detention, which brought me to the library anyhow. I'm just skipping steps now. I also haven't smoked in days.

I guess I'm quitting too.

The week has been on a pleasant mode of autopilot. I'm actually excited about softball, and I'm almost enjoying my teammates. Almost. They're still young and bubbly and insistent that I let them braid my hair before games. With ribbons—ginormous ribbons. I doubt I'll ever understand the ribbons. But for the first time...well...ever, I considered saying *yes*.

I spend practices working hard, and watching Wes with my dad in the small breaks in between activities. He's like a compass for my eyes, drawing my gaze to the point where I seem to know where he is and what he's doing at all times. Wes and I have only talked a few times, in our first period English class and in photography, which so far has been nothing but lecture. I have yet to take a picture. Wes never brought up what he saw, and when I thanked him, he shook his head and gave me a look that said I needed to forget about it too. What I didn't tell him is I'm normally good at forgetting those moments with my father, but I can't seem to shake this last one—and it's because of him.

My father loves Wes. It's different than when he works with Kyle, and I think Kyle sees that too. I can tell it's hurting him. A year or so ago, Kyle was the golden *it* boy. He hasn't been that boy in months, and he was starting to get used to it. Seeing my father fawn over Wes has brought things back to the surface. I haven't said this to my friend yet, but I think my father would have favored Wes no matter what Kyle had said or done. It's about what they're both capable of. My father looks at Wes like he's his own—he sees himself, only better. He's even skipped the bar every night this week, instead watching slow-motion video he's taken of Wes and going over new workout techniques online.

"We've been replaced," Kyle says, pushing my feet off balance. They fall to the ground from the wall I've propped myself up on. He straddles the wall next to me, lying back and tossing a ball above his face into his glove.

"It's a wonder you have teeth," I tease.

"Ha ha," he says, not missing a beat and continuing to toss the ball while kicking me gently with his right foot.

I'm waiting on Taryn to get out of the locker room so she can give me a ride home, and I'm also watching my dad and Wes out on the field.

"*You've* been replaced. I'm still just the girl who plays this silly little sport they have for girls, in between partying and throwing her life down the drain." My voice is monotone, my attention devoted to watching Wes stand tall on the mound and go through his motions slowly, my father tweaking and adjusting inches along the way.

"You're better than all of us," Kyle says, sitting up and leaning into me. The funny thing is, I know he means it. He would never say it in front of others, but with me—alone—he's always been my biggest fan.

I let my head fall to the side to look at him and give him a lopsided, closed smile. "Thanks," I say, glancing down at my nails, the dirt wedged underneath, scratches on my hands from sliding practice today. "You know, he's never seen a single one of my high school games."

"Who, your pops?" Kyle asks, leaning back on his hands, spitting sunflower seed shells off to the sidewalk.

"Not a single one," I answer. It's quiet between us for a few minutes, and we both watch my dad shake Wes's hand and pat him on the back. My dad makes the slow climb up the hill to where we are, but Wes stays out there, working alone, the sun barely up and dark clouds closing in on what little light is left.

My father gets closer, and our posture shifts into that of two grade school kids sent to sit along the wall after getting in trouble on the playground. In an act of defiance, Kyle spits one more shell out toward my father's feet as he nears us. It makes me chuckle.

"Wes is starting Monday," my dad says. I look down, wishing I could disappear and give Kyle privacy. I can feel disappointment radiate from him without looking. He knew he wouldn't start, but my dad is rubbing it in by saying it in front of me.

"Okay," Kyle says, his voice even, despite the rage I know is brewing underneath.

"Joss," my dad says, not moving, waiting for me to look up. I take my time, because the only thing I can do to show Kyle support is make my father wait. After a few seconds, I flutter my eyes open on his and sigh. "You had a pack of cigarettes in your jeans. I found them in the laundry. You said you were quitting."

"I did quit," I say. I glance to Kyle, who smirks at me because I gave him shit for quitting a week ago. I shrug then look back to my dad.

"I'll believe that when I see it. You have a pattern of not following through with things," he says, pulling his phone from his pocket and checking a message, no longer looking at me while insulting me. He walks away without another word, but before he rounds the corner, I fire off something brave.

"I'll quit when you quit," I say, just loud enough that he pauses at the edge of the building, rolling his shoulders and pulling one hand from his pocket to make a fist. I hold my breath and wait for him to turn around, but he doesn't. I hit him with his own flaws, and there's no comeback for that.

"You didn't have to do that," Kyle says, leaning forward with his hands on the handles of his gym bag. "I knew Wes was going to start and not me. Really, I'm fine with it."

"He was still being an ass," I say, rolling my head to face him. He gives me a quick grin and leans his head in my direction. "And no offense, but that was more for me than you. Last weekend...got ugly."

71

Kyle nods slowly, standing and walking over to me, resting one hand on my knee while leaning forward slowly to kiss my head. "I'm sorry, Joss," he says, letting his forehead fall to the top of mine. He means it. When nobody is watching, Kyle is incredibly sweet.

"Thanks," I sniff out. "Wes…he was there. He…helped."

Kyle steps away, and I know it's because I mentioned Wes's name. I didn't want him to find out from anyone other than me. If Wes were the one to tell him first, he would think I was hiding it from him for other reasons. I haven't mentioned it, because I've wanted to forget. But my dad just brought the memory roaring back to the forefront of everything.

"Glad you weren't alone," he says, his back to me as he picks up his bag, tucking his towel inside before zipping it closed. "Hey, I'll see you tomorrow, yeah? We're still on for Slasher Saturday?"

Kyle, Conner, Taryn, and I have gone to the Bakersfield Nine Drive-Ins for slasher films every February first since we were old enough to pedal our bikes that far. When we were younger, we had to sneak in under the fencing near the projector building and pretend we were with our parents when ushers would ask, pointing at random cars and lying, saying that was our family. Last year, Kyle drove us there, and I fell asleep next to him to the sounds of chainsaws and screaming. He woke me when we got to my house, and he looked at me like he wanted to kiss me—*really* kiss me, the kind of kiss that meant something, different from the other times we'd hooked up just for fun. I haven't kissed him again since.

"Wouldn't miss it," I say. I feel a strange sense of guilt from the way he turns his body, careful not to look at me while he walks away. His words are guarded, and he's hiding how he feels, but I still see it. I leaned on Wes instead of him. He holds up a few fingers and walks a little faster to the back parking lot, his gaze never lifting to me until his engine roars and he's ready to pull away. He holds up a hand one more time to wave goodbye, but he doesn't smile.

When his car pulls out of sight, I let my eyes drift back to the field, where Wes is throwing balls to nobody, letting them hit the backstop. I push from the wall and throw my bag over my back, my cleats untied and

72

loose around my feet as I trudge through the outfield toward him.

"I can catch for you…if you want," I say. He turns quickly at the sound of my voice, startled.

"Oh…uh, thanks, but it's okay, I was almost done " he says, jiggling his arm against his side as if it's sore and tired. He hasn't thrown many pitches at all today, though. I know, because I've been watching.

"You know, eventually you're going to have to give in to the fact that I can handle you," I say, my eyes leveling him with a challenge. He laughs lightly to himself, his lip held between his teeth as he tugs down on the bill of his hat, shadowing his face, until he finally nods at me.

"A'right," he relents, shrugging to home plate.

I step over to the backstop and throw the dozen or so balls he pitched on his own back to him, and he drops them in his bag near his feet one at a time. I brush the dirt from home plate with my glove, then crouch down. I hold the pose for a few seconds while Wes stares at me, and eventually he shakes his head with a quiet laugh.

"What?" I yell, dropping my arms to my knees. I hate catching; it's miserable. I only did it because it was him—he needed help. No…I *wanted* to help. And now he's laughing at me?

He jogs toward me in long, slow strides, and I stand, leaning with my glove against my hip. He's wearing dark blue shorts over black compression pants, and unlike the other boys on my dad's team, he actually looks good in them—like a *real* ballplayer. I look away and take a step or two back when he gets closer, but he reaches for my arm, catching my elbow with his fingers. My eyes go right to his hold and then to his face where he's waiting for me with the same expression I have.

"Sorry," he says, letting go of me quickly. I feel the loss of his touch.

Kneeling down, he urges me to do the same next to him, shirking his glove from his hand and holding his palms on the insides of his thighs. "You are sitting like this. It's unsteady, and you're going to get tired…fast," he says, his eyes gliding over to my legs. He licks his lips, and sucks in a slow but heavy breath, before putting one knee down and bringing his hand to my leg, glancing at me quickly for permission before resting his fingertips on my kneecap. His touch is cautious and purposeful. It's also powerful, and I feel it.

"If you just turn…like this, and then shift your weight," he says, tugging my knee out gently before clearing his throat slightly as his eyes run up my thigh. He stands abruptly, and I let down one knee to rest my legs. "Anyhow, I just figured maybe you never caught before, and I could show you something. You probably already knew that though, so—"

"Thanks," I interrupt him before he steps away. I'm not warm and fuzzy. I make him nervous. And I regret that. "Really," I add, as he tilts his head sideways over his shoulder, glancing back at me. "My dad use to show me stuff like that, but…it's been a while."

His lip pulls up with sympathy, and he looks down before glancing back at me with a sideways tilt of the head, raising the ball in his hand. "Let's try a few," he says, walking back to the mound.

I kneel just as he taught me, and my legs shake a little at first, so I adjust my knees more, giving myself a base. "I'm good," I say, pounding the center of my glove and holding it out for his target.

Wes nods, then winds up for a pitch. He throws a changeup, and I know he did it because he doesn't want me to get hurt catching anything faster. The fighter in me wants to spit and tell him to give me the real stuff, but the girl I am—the one that likes the way he looks at me—is okay with the fact that he wants to protect me.

"That looked good," I say, throwing the ball back to him. His lips twist into a crooked grin, and he tugs his hat low again before winding up for another pitch. I praised him, and he liked it.

I liked that.

He throws twenty more, and somewhere in the middle of it all, Taryn walks down to the dugout to watch us. I saw her coming, but Wes doesn't notice her until he finishes his last pitch. He seems to retreat into his shell when she claps at his final throw.

"Thanks for helping me out, Joss. Sorry, I didn't mean to keep her," he says, pulling the hat from his head with one hand and running his other arm over his forehead and hair, wiping away the sweat. I get a little lost in watching it and don't notice Taryn step next to my side.

"So you're a catcher now, huh?" There's a gleam in her eye and an inflection in her voice that's teasing me.

"He was working on some stuff. I saw my dad helping him," I say, shrugging. I don't lie to Taryn well, so I swallow slowly and busy myself with my own bag, zipping my glove away and looping it over my shoulder.

"You know, I could maybe have some place I need to go. In fact, I think maybe I do. Ugh, that's right. I just remembered…I can't give you a ride home," she says as my back is to her. I twist up to look her in the eye, ready to argue with her for ditching me or being impatient because I wasn't ready and waiting for her outside the locker room. When my eyes hit hers, though, I catch the soft hint of a smile on her tight lips just as she winks.

"It's not like that," I sigh, standing and urging her to walk away with me.

"Sure it's not," she says. "Hey, Wes? I have somewhere I need to go, and I'm late. Think you can take Joss home?"

My eyes are wide on her as my back is to him. I mouth the word "bitch" and she winks at me again.

"Yeah, that's fine," he says. My eyes flutter closed because his response couldn't possibly have sounded less excited.

"Thanks," Taryn says, holding her phone out toward me and whispering for me to text her later. I flip her off, and Wes catches me, which makes my body rush with a mortifying heat.

I watch Taryn walk away, and Wes gets a few steps ahead of me before pausing and looking back. "You ready? I have to take my brothers, but I'll make them ride in the back," he says. He's talking logistics. Taryn was playing matchmaker.

"You know what, it's okay. My house is close. I'll just walk," I say. His brow pulls in as his head jerks back a little in response. A second later, he steps back the few paces to me and tugs my bag from my shoulder. I hold the straps tightly in protest, but he jerks them free, throwing my bag on top of his as he walks toward his truck, leaving me behind.

"Quit being stubborn," he says. "Just come on."

I let him get a few more steps ahead before I follow. His back muscles could not be more perfect—the way they curve and dip and flex with every motion he makes. His arm is bent through the straps of both of our bags, and his hand is gripping them at his shoulder. He's godlike. And I'm in a pair of cutoff sweatpants, the legs different lengths, and my shirt is two sizes two big. The longer I walk behind him, the more ridiculous I feel being paired with him, and the less I think he could possibly be the scrawny kid from my youth.

As we step into the parking lot, his brothers are already waiting in the cab of the truck. Seeing me, they both climb out, but I hold up my hands and yell before they step into the bed.

"Seriously, I can ride in the back. It's fine," I say. I don't give them a choice, instead just lifting my leg over one side and sliding my back against the glass, getting comfortable.

Wes pauses at the back of the truck, sighing with a slight shake of his head. He lifts our bags over the tailgate and pushes them to one corner before walking to the driver's side. I cross my legs and fold the bottom of my T-shirt around my cold hands, readying myself as the truck rumbles to a start. I hear both doors close, and I start to shut my eyes, embarrassed and angry at Taryn for putting me in this spot. Before I shut down completely, though, I see Wes step from the other side of the bed, climbing in to the space next to me. He turns to face the glass behind us and knocks twice, letting his brothers know he's in. As he twists back around, he stops to look me in the eye, his eyebrows high on his forehead.

"Stub-born," he says, punctuating both parts of the word. I shrug, and wrap my hands tighter in my shirt.

Before we get to the main road away from campus, Wes leans forward and tugs the thin long-sleeved shirt from over his head, turns to the side, not giving me much choice as he pushes the fabric over my head. He rests back against the window, crossing his arms at his chest after tugging his hat low on his head.

I sit there looking ridiculous for a few seconds with a scarf made of his shirt looped around my throat. I give in quickly though as the wind picks up, pushing my arms through. There are holes at the ends of both sleeves, and I slide my thumbs through, making fists of what's left of the material. As thin as it is, it's surprisingly warm. And it smells exactly like him.

"Thank you," I squeak out, inhaling slowly so he doesn't catch me. I pull my knees in and rest my head on them along with my folded arms. Wes doesn't look at me, but he smirks and leans into my side.

"You're welcome," he says.

We ride in silence most of the way, and with every shift and adjustment Wes makes of his body, he moves fractions of inches closer to me. At one point, both of our hands are flat along the bed of the truck, bracing our bodies for the impact of a bumpy road, and the jostling forces his pinky finger to loop over mine. We both look down at the feel of our touch and pull our hands away when we realize we're both aware.

There's a block left to go before we turn down my street, so I reach up and tug the band from my hair, letting it come down in waves and blow in the wind as we ride. I usually hate the way riding in a truck makes my hair knotted and dry, but the urge to let it down in front of Wes was stronger. I want to look soft for him—not the abrasive...*stubborn* girl he's only gotten so far. It's a desperate move, though, and the second I feel my hair fly loose in the breeze, I regret it, and pull it into my hand, holding it at the base of my neck. I'm not the pretty girl. I'm not ribbons and bows. I'm being stupid.

"I've been meaning to ask you," he says, pulling me out of my own head. "Would it be okay if maybe I called you sometime?"

My gut reaction is to tell him to grow a pair, to ask him why he'd want to do that? My instincts are to shut down and ward him off because I'm messy, and I have miles of issues, and I don't want to let myself like him like that. But I'm holding my arms near my face, and his shirt is warm and soft, and it smells nice, and as much as I shouldn't fall for fleeting things like that, I can't help myself.

"I would probably answer," I say.

Fuck, it sounds flirty. I sound flirty, and I'm smiling and trying to hide it behind my arms. I'm actually hiding my face. We're at my house, and I know I should just give him his shirt back, but I don't want to do that either. I want to keep it. I want to keep it forever, so I step out of the truck quickly, grabbing my own bag and waving to his brothers, careful not to look him in the eye. I walk fast, opening and shutting my front door behind me, and then I let myself breathe.

"Was that Wes?" my father says, stepping out of the darkened kitchen area, a cup in his hand that I've long learned is not coffee.

I nod, but look away, instead carrying my things past him toward my room. He stops me before I can get far, though, lightly pressing his hand on my shoulder and leaving it there until I meet his eyes.

"Leave that boy alone," he says before bringing his cup to his lips for a taste. I watch him swallow, and I wait for his eyes to relax and soften, but they never do. He lets me by and moves into the living room, to the chair he likes to sit in at night to watch TV until he passes out. He's not watching pitching videos tonight, it seems.

I stand still, and bring my wrist to my nose slowly, breathing in Wes's scent. I think about Taryn's father, and how he warns her away from boys constantly, because he never thinks any guy is good enough. That's not what my dad was doing though. He was looking out for Wes—because I am nothing but trouble. He's probably right, but he made me this way. And I don't think I can stay away from Wes Stokes even if I tried.

CHAPTER 5

I wore Wes's shirt to bed last night. When I woke up this morning, I took it off quickly, folded it, and tucked it underneath my blanket, pillow, and piles of clothes on my bed. I'm not sure if I was hiding it to keep it or just felt foolish that I wanted to keep it so badly.

What *really* felt humiliating was the way I kept checking my phone for a text message from him all night and again this morning. I'm one step away from putting bows and glitter in my hair.

Instead of waiting for nothing to happen, I put on my running pants and push my earbuds in, letting my latest playlist fuel me for a run. I used to run every morning my freshman year. That was when I was still under the illusion that if I tried hard enough, I'd impress my father. He never noticed, though. He called me lazy no matter how hard I worked, how early I rose, or how many miles I trod. So I quit.

I'm not sure what's pushing me to go this morning, but when my eyes opened and saw the sun barely up, something felt different. My dad's door is open as I pass it, his bed made. I shake my head because he probably left after I walked away from him last night and just never made it home from wherever he went. If he ran into...*trouble*...he didn't call, so that's on him—not me.

I lock our door and shove the house key into the small pocket on the side of my pants along with my iPod, then stretch for a few minutes before testing out my legs in a jog. The burn comes faster than I remember. This is what happens when I haven't run like this in months.

My pace is slow, but I refuse to stop, and I make it six or seven blocks before I turn back into the neighborhood. I'm winding through streets aimlessly, but I'm on a constant watch for Wes's truck, wondering which house is his. My curiosity keeps driving me forward, pushing me for one more block, one more quarter mile, until before too long, I find myself at my high school's football field. The track is empty and the center covered with weeds—because our football team is an afterthought. We're a baseball school. My breathing is so heavy I feel like I can't catch up, so I slow to a fast walk and eventually come to rest in front of the bleachers with my hands clasped over my head.

This used to be so easy. All of it—easy. It seems impossible now. My lungs feel as if they've been punctured by millions of staples, and my sides ache with cramps. I look up at the stands and see flashes of my youth. My dad liked to run. He said just because he was too old to play ball didn't mean he couldn't run faster than other men, so when he'd run on weekends, I'd join him here. My legs were always too small to tackle the steps of the bleachers, but I'd still try. My hand instinctively goes to the tiny line that measures about an inch at the bottom of my chin, a decade-old scar from a missed step that brought my face down hard into the metal. My dad carried me home, his shirt pressed on my chin to stop the bleeding, then he drove me to the ER for stitches. My first of many.

My chest still working in and out, my shoulders tight and my legs pleading for me to quit, I reach into my pocket for my iPod, crank the volume up, and begin to climb. It takes me a dozen or so steps before I find an easy rhythm, but I run up and touch the bar at the top, turning around and letting my weight carry me back down the sixty steps to the bottom. I do it again, only this time faster, and I slow when I take the steps down so I can feel the sting of my muscles working hard. I repeat the pattern six more times, until my final sprint up the stairs ends in a trip on the last step. I lunge forward and catch my body on the top seat, my iPod slipping from my pocket and sliding along the metal and over the edge. I grab the cord with my fingers, but not before the weight of my device breaks it loose, and I hear it career off the metal support beams until it busts to pieces forty feet below.

Fuck.

I let my head fall to the cold step beneath me and roll onto my back, pulling my legs into my chest with one arm and tugging my useless headphones from my ears with my other hand. Balling the cord up in my palm, I let my fist come down next to me a few times, vibrating the metal. I hate running without music. I have no idea how I'll be able to do this again tomorrow.

Maybe I'll just quit.

"That's it! Yes, do that again. Just like that."

My dad's voice echoes off the gym wall, and I stand quickly to see where it's coming from. I lean over the back of the bleachers and scan the parking lot and tennis courts behind me, but the grounds are just as empty as they were when I ran through them. I step up on one of the bars, locking my knees in place for balance and scan the rest of the area, looking out at the ball field on the other side of campus, and just as I see him, I hear his voice again.

"Yes!"

His words are faint, and I only hear them because he's yelling and it echoes. He's catching for Wes. It's maybe seven thirty in the morning, on a Saturday, and my father is crouched down in the dirt just like he use to do with me. The vision hits my already-exhausted chest hard, and I kneel down, letting my face rest against the metal handrail while I watch something amazing happen—without me.

My father praises him after every single throw. It's as if I'm watching a stranger the way he's excited, positive, and full of vigor. He throws his glove down and jogs over to Wes several times, both of them facing each other, the intricacies of what they're working on with grip and fingers too fine for me to see from here. The longer I watch, the more it hurts.

I don't lie to myself. I'm jealous. This is envy, and I let the tear fall down my face while I hide up here like a frightened stray cat. My fucking

81

iPod is broken beyond repair on the pavement below me, and I'm not even sure I'll pick it up when I leave. I should care about that more, but I'm consumed with what's happening hundreds of yards away.

When I can't take it anymore, I fill my lungs with a cleansing breath and resolve not to look at them again. But I won't leave. I won't quit what I started. I put in ten more passes up and down the bleachers until my legs are jelly and I can barely feel my toes. My body is beating with heat, and I'm winded, but I did it. The only person I wanted to prove something to was *me*.

Before leaving, I pick up my cracked and jagged music player and hope by some miracle it still works after a little love and attention. I jog home, slower than I came here, and I shower and leave my house to spend the day at Kyle's. No note left for my dad. No checking for messages from Wes. Nobody cares where I am, so whatever.

On a last-minute whim, I grab Wes's shirt, mostly to torture myself later with thoughts of him, and stuff it in my backpack, under what's left of the Jim Beam I take from my dad's cabinet. He keeps it locked, but he also hangs the key about a foot away from the cabinet—apathy at its best.

Kyle is already in full slasher-mode by the time I get to his house. I arrive just in time for the classic *Halloween* showing, and in the middle of the movie, Conner sneaks in and jumps over the sofa, wedging himself between us, his arms slung over our shoulders. We both punch at him, and the scene turns into a wrestling brawl as Kyle lifts me over his back and starts to spin, trying to fling my wild legs at his brother.

"I am not your weapon! Put me down!" I scream. Kyle slaps my ass hard, and I hit him in the gut, sending him to his knees on the sofa. We're laughing and rolling with each other when Taryn walks through the front door with TK, Levi, and Wes beside her.

"Always with you two," she says.

"I didn't know you were bringing anyone," Kyle says, letting his hand roll down my arm and onto my leg slowly—affectionately. I look at it curiously then glance to Wes, who is also watching Kyle paint me with his touch. Irritated, I fling his hand from me and move from his lap, flipping him off as I storm out of the room.

"What?" His question comes out so innocent, which only pisses me off more.

"You don't fucking own me," I say, turning and squinting my eyes so there's no mistaking how I feel about what he just did. I glance to Wes again, who is pretending not to hear any of this, then I look to Taryn, who smirks. I flip her off too.

I escape to the kitchen, but Taryn follows. I ignore her at first, pulling the bottle from my backpack, and not bothering with a glass. I take a long drink, and the familiar warmth fills my chest and numbs my urge to care. I hold the bottle out for my friend, but she just twists her mouth in a half frown before backing up and pulling herself to sit up on the counter across from me.

"Suit yourself," I shrug, taking one more, smaller drink before putting my bottle away.

"You're going to have to tell one of those boys the truth tonight, you know?" I don't respond, but only stare at her as if I have no clue what she means. "You like Wes, and you don't feel that way about Kyle."

"I've been through this with Kyle. He knows we're just friends," I say.

"Doesn't mean he's not going to put up a fight," she says back quickly. Her words stress me out. I don't want to deal with them. "And Wes…"

Before she gets a chance to finish, the door opens and everyone spills into the kitchen. Taryn keeps her eyes on me for a few seconds, leaning her head toward Wes as he walks by, letting her eyes follow him before coming back to me.

He could not possibly look any more perfect. Dark, loose jeans, a white T-shirt and a gray Y&R hat, always low on his brow. Every detail about him is simple, but in the perfect place: his hair poking from the back of his hat, the brown leather band of his watch on his bronzed arm, his Vans shoes, and damn, whatever the hell it is he wears for a cologne. I'm sporting my two-year-old state championship sweatshirt with torn cuffs and the smell of Jim Beam. My hair is pulled back tight, but when I run my fingers through the ends, they're knotted from not drying my hair after my shower.

He and I—we don't match.

"So, you threw with my dad this morning," I say, sliding into the stool at the end of the counter. Wes looks up at me surprised, and I notice my words get Kyle's attention too. I know this will make him jealous, that my father's giving Wes extra time. I guess I want Kyle to be just a jealous as I am.

"Yeah, uh…he offered after practice. Said he'd be there, if I wanted to show," Wes says, taking short looks to Kyle. This isn't fair; I'm putting him in an awkward spot. "Did he say something about it?"

His eyes catch mine under the shadow of the brim of his hat, and they practically glow, they're so crystal clear. I get lost in them for a second, but shake the trance off quickly, breathing out a short laugh through my nose and shaking my head, giving my attention to Kyle. This makes Kyle's day.

I feel Wes watching me though. And I feel bad. It's not his fault he's gifted. It's not his fault that he was able to get my dad to do something I haven't been able to for years. None of this is his fault—but damn if I don't blame him anyway.

The theater grounds don't open for a few more hours; to kill time, Kyle spreads out a few of his movies for us to pick from. Taryn is always the most vocal, so we end up going with *Jaws*, which isn't really a slasher movie, but we all love it anyhow. We spend the next two hours mocking the naïve swimmers on the beach, and Taryn and I overdo our screams in reaction to the shark. TK finds her girly scream adorable, and before the end of the movie, she's nestled between his legs, her back against his chest and his arms wrapped around her body while his mouth plays along her neck.

I envy Taryn now too. Not that she's with TK, but that she's with someone, gets to feel something like that. I've never had that. I've never really wanted it. But lately…

I've found my way to the middle cushion of the sofa, right between Kyle and Wes, and the three of us don't move an inch for the last thirty minutes of the movie. The tension is suffocating, and the second the credits roll, I step over the coffee table in front of me in lieu of choosing a side to walk in front of, leaving the two of them alone as I retreat to the kitchen to sneak another shot of my whiskey.

"Kinda early for that, isn't it?" Wes startles me, and I hold his stare, the lip of the bottle resting against my mouth. He leans against the wall opposite me, and loops his thumbs in his pockets, waiting me out. My lip curls up on one side, and I tip the bottle back, letting it coat my throat and chest again. I keep looking at him, and make slow deliberate steps in his direction until I'm close enough to touch him if I wanted to. I hold the bottle up and raise an eyebrow. He only pushes my hand away and steps to the side.

"I'm good. Not big on whiskey, especially at four thirty, before a drive-in movie," he says, every word rife with disdain.

"You're not my parent," I say, running my arm along my nose. I choose those words purposely, keeping them trite and clipped. I point at him with one finger, the rest still wrapped around the bottle, and I hold the hard line on my mouth. I think about taking one more drink right now just to spite him. I don't, and that's because his reprimand worked on me. A little. A lot.

"Besides, it makes the movie *way* better," I say instead of drinking, closing the cap while I drown in my own cocktail of liquor and shame.

I put the bottle away again, turning my back to him, hoping he'll leave—*hoping he'll come closer*. He doesn't move at all, but I hear his breath shift, ready to speak. I no longer intimidate him, which is exactly what I wanted, but it also makes me vulnerable.

"You saw us," he says. My mouth grows tight and my jaw clenches in an automatic reaction, but I don't turn to face him. Instead, I shift my things in my backpack, feeling for his shirt, and I clutch it in my hand. "I can tell by the way you reacted when I asked if your dad told you. He didn't tell you, and that's why you're mad. You should have come, if you saw us. I bet your dad would have liked that."

Ha! That statement gets me. Not wanting to play psychoanalysis with him anymore, I pull his shirt from my bag, spin on my heels and grab his hand in mine, stuffing his shirt in his palm, closing his fingers around it. The feel of him is instant, and my knuckles become stiff and rigid, fighting against letting go of my hold. It's the whiskey making me feel that, which means I've had enough—for now. I take a big step back to force distance between us, but I keep my eyes trained on his, and I keep my voice calm.

"I'm not mad that he didn't tell me, Wes. I'm mad that he picked you instead of me. And no...he wouldn't have liked it if I joined you two. That's the real problem. My father...he doesn't really like me much at all," I confess, my throat finding it hard to swallow as I breathe. Wes's eyes flash with the slightest realization and quickly wash over with sympathy, which is too close to pity, and I don't want that.

"Thanks for the shirt," I say, grabbing my bag from the counter and reaching in for one last thing. "And you owe me a new iPod. I broke mine, trying to keep up with how great you are, so...here."

I lay my busted device in his other palm, the cracked screen facing him, and then I walk back into the living room and convince the rest of our group to leave for the movie festival a little early so we can get a good spot.

Taryn rides with the Stokes boys, and I hop into Kyle's backseat, which throws off Conner's plan to sit next to his girlfriend. I'm sort of done with boys for the night, though, so when I refuse to make eye contact with him, Conner finally relents and takes the front seat so I can pout in the back next to Layla.

I like Layla. She's quiet and shy. She likes to be in the room with us, but never really participates. And she never asks questions. I'm done with questions. In fact, I'm pretty done with talking for the rest of the night if I can manage.

The gates are open when we arrive at the drive-in, and because we're so early, we get a prime spot. I ditch everyone and hit the snack bar, wasting time walking from screen to screen, munching on full bites of buttery popcorn until my stomach hurts. No matter how far I roam, though, my eyes are always quick to find Wes sitting on the top of his truck, his legs hanging against the back window.

The sun is finally starting to set, and it paints the sky with strokes of purple and orange. The colors make me sleepy, and they also give me peace. Not quite ready to return to chaos, I pull myself up on top of a wooden fence that divides the car spaces from rows of plastic chairs. Two little girls are playing in the sandpit in front of me. What starts as a castle they work on together—quickly turns into a war over who gets to decide how their kingdom is built. They remind me of Taryn and me, though I never argued. I just let her have her way, and when I really wasn't up for it, I went and played by myself. That doesn't seem to be the pattern for these two, though, as within seconds sand is flying in the air as they kick towers of dirt at one another and start a screaming match.

"Hey, girls," I say, not even garnering as much as a head turn. I'm hit with some of the sand from their fight, so I pull my fingers to my mouth and blow a loud whistle that gets them both to stop. The one on the right lets the grains of sand trickle through her fingers, and I grin at the thought of her dropping her weapon.

"Come here," I say, urging them closer. They're timid at first, but when one starts to come closer, the other one shoves her in the arm, and they both suddenly sprint until they're touching the fence post next to me. "You two are friends, yeah?"

They both glance at each other and crinkle their noses, wobbling their heads because they're still mad and they don't want to admit that they're friends. That means they're probably best friends.

"How about you forget about the castle and the sand and all of that crap…" I say, chuckling to myself when their eyes widen at the word *crap,* "and you take the rest of my popcorn to share during the first movie?"

The one with dark hair, clearly the *Taryn* of the pair, grabs my bag without question, while the other one stands behind her, her mouth slowly stretching into a smile.

"We should wash our hands," she says to her friend, her words lisping through her missing front teeth.

"Nah," I say, kicking off from the fence and wiping my buttered fingertips along my jeans. "It's just dirt. Germs are bullshit."

I wink at them both and walk away to the sweet sound of their giggling. I feel proud. As stupid as that was, I accomplished something huge back there. I might have saved a friendship.

My phone buzzes in my pocket, which halts me instantly, and the good feelings from before drain fast. It's Saturday. It's still early, but…it's happened early before. I gaze around the various lots to get a feel for how crowded things are, to see if Kyle would be able to get back in if he had to take me somewhere. The drive-in is far, but I could still walk. And my dad could wait. I prefer to make him wait.

I unload a heavy breath and pull my phone out, ready to feel the sick feeling that comes over me every single time I go through this. But it's not my dad. It's Wes.

Nice work in the sandlot. The movie starts soon. TK snuck in Cokes. I saved you one.

I read his short text over a few times, and I keep my head low so he can't see my smile. But I am smiling. The grin on my face is unmistakable, and the fluttering in my chest feels better than the whiskey did earlier. I write him back:

Thanks. Be there in a sec.

After I hit send, I glance up and notice Emily's car now pulled next to Kyle's, and I also see a girl sitting next to Wes on top of his truck. It's McKenna, and she's wearing a dress out here…on one of the coolest nights we've had. The skirt is blowing up her legs in the breeze, and she's holding her arms around her body, rubbing her hands on her bare arms. I sense it coming before I get there, so by the time I step up to the bed of the truck and see McKenna wrapped in the shirt I slept in last night, I can do nothing but laugh.

I feel like a fool.

"Cokes?" I say, quirking an eyebrow up at Wes, pretending to be unfazed by the fact that Malibu Barbie is tittering inches away from him.

"I set yours up here," he says, turning to reach for it behind McKenna, only to see her clasping it in her hands, taking a long sip.

"Right, you know what? I'm good," I say, pointing to Kyle's car, where I left my bag and where I plan on hiding for the next several hours.

"Joss, wait," he says, sliding down from the roof, his feet heavy when he lands on the ground. McKenna leans over and watches his every move, and when her eyes make it to me briefly, I blow her a kiss, which makes her smile fall flat.

"You're a bitch, Joss," she fires at me.

"You, too, Kenna. You too," I say, shaking my head and refusing to give her any more of my time.

"What the hell, Joss?" I'm so shocked by him saying anything remotely assertive to me that I freeze and stare at him, blinking. "Why do you have to make everything so damn hard?"

Still blinking. After a few seconds, I shift and look back up to McKenna, her fingers tapping on the side of the can while she pretends not to watch our conversation. She's hanging on every word. God, for a second there, when he texted me, I thought he was into me, and I actually felt a rush. It's amazing how in two seconds my brain can whiz through scenarios where—he's kissing me, I'm holding his hand, I'm lying on his lap watching these stupid movies. When I replay it now, he just said the movie was starting and he saved me a drink.

"I'm not making anything hard, Wes," I say, glancing behind him toward the roof of his truck. "Oh, she looks cold. I should let you go."

He opens his mouth to speak and moves like he may take a step toward me, but I ignore it, turning and walking over to Kyle's car, shutting the door behind me as I crawl into the backseat and pull out what's left of my bottle. Yeah, I am making this hard. But I also know how this ends. Wes gets to be my dad's darling, and I'm the girl who isn't good enough. I'm just the worthless mistake that ended my parents' marriage—at least, that's how my dad sees it. Wes can have him.

"What are we drinking?" Kyle asks, opening the other door and sliding in next to me.

We both press our feet against the backs of the front seats and lower ourselves from view. As pissed as I was over Kyle's acting like there was more to us earlier, I hope Wes is watching us now. We're just below the window view when I pass the bottle into his lap.

"I shouldn't…I'm driving," he says, holding the edge of the bottle against his lip.

"Yeah, like that shit's stopped you before," I say, tipping the bottom up so the liquid hits him. He jerks back, and a small bit spills down the front of his chest.

"Fuckin' Joss, now I'm going to smell drunk no matter what," he says, sitting up and leaning forward, blotting at his shirt. He turns his head sideways, and at first he looks genuinely mad. The left side of his mouth gives way to a grin though. "I might as well drink now, then, I guess."

"Hell yeah, Marley," I say, knocking my knee into his while he takes a long drink, letting out a slow breath after it slides down his throat.

Kyle and I stay huddled in the back for the next five hours. I only break out once when I have to pee, and while I don't look fully, my eyes catch enough to see Wes sitting on top of the truck and McKenna sitting next to him. I force myself to ignore it on my way back, quickly climbing into the car and sinking into the dark cave of Kyle's backseat.

The bottle was half empty when I took it, but there was still enough for Kyle and me to string along a pretty damn awesome buzz throughout most of the movies. The last show starts at eleven, and I can tell Kyle's getting restless. He pushes open his door and walks to the rear of his car, not bothering to go all the way to the restrooms to pee, and I hear Taryn chastise him for it. It makes me laugh, so I get out and threaten to do the same thing.

"You two always get our asses kicked out of this thing," Taryn says, picking up a handful of gravel from the ground and tossing it at us.

"That's the best part and you know it!" I yell, turning in a full circle with my arms stretched out. I'm spinning slowly, but the way the stars swirl above me makes me dizzy enough to stumble on my feet. My back finds warm hands before I run into anything, and when I gaze up, I see Wes's eyes peering down on me.

"We should get you home," he says, his mouth a firm line. I spend a few seconds weighing my options and enjoying the feel of him against me as I tip my head back even more. He's tall enough that he's a full head above me, and with my forehead pressed into his chest as I lean back, I can see his eyes clearly, and that same familiar feeling from the first time I met him floods me again.

"Oh, Christopher," I say, reaching my arm up and around his neck. "Didn't you hear me before? You…are not…my parent."

I feel him sigh against my back, and I start to laugh, happy I'm frustrating him. Seconds later, my legs are swept out from under me, and I'm being rushed to Kyle's car, carried in Kyle's arms.

"Hey," I giggle. I'm a little drunk. I'm more than a little drunk. I should put up a fight, but I'm too happy being carried around. I like that Kyle's greedy for me, even if he isn't the one I want.

"You and me need to race, Stokes. Come on; let's get out of here. We'll hit the old highway," Kyle says, jingling his keys by his face. A few people parked nearby start to yell at him to be quiet, and he tells them all, "Watch the fuckin' movie!"

"Kyle, stop. I'm not racing you, man. Just calm down," Wes says, holding one hand up and shaking his head in apology to the still-angry people around us. Kyle holds his hand up, waving it haphazardly, mocking Wes.

"Dude, Wes…it's like Joss said…you ain't my fuckin' parent," Kyle says, his laughter stopping abruptly before he leans forward and spits on the ground. "Now get your ass out on Fairfax Road, pussy."

Kyle climbs in and closes the heavy door of his piece-of-shit car, firing it up and revving the engine. I stand at the passenger side, the open door in my hand, one foot inside, resting by the seat.

"Don't do this, Joss," Taryn says, walking up to me, bending forward, and looking inside the car to survey Kyle. I hold her stare for a few seconds, while Kyle yells for me to get in. I'm about to give up on everyone, to slam his door shut and to begin my long walk home, when Wes steps up behind her.

"Don't get in that car, Joss," Wes says, tipping my danger scales instantly.

Lowering my brow, I do my best to scare him, smiling just enough that I feel like the devil himself has taken over my body. "Stop me," I say, climbing in quickly and slamming the door shut, my fists slamming down on Kyle's dash.

"Go, go, go!" I scream.

Kyle doesn't hesitate, spinning his tires and kicking up dust and rock that has the already-angry crowd now getting out of their cars ready to attack him. They're too slow though, and he's peeling down the dirt drive and through the exit in seconds. I crawl up on my knees and hug the back of my seat, looking through the window and counting until I see Wes's truck pull out behind us.

"He's coming. You've got at least seven seconds on him," I say, turning back to face the empty roadway ahead while Kyle speeds toward Fairfax.

Farmland hugs us on both sides of the road, and the rumble of Kyle's motor echoes loudly, filling our car.

"We need fast music," I yell, flipping through stations on his radio until something good finally comes in, Foo Fighters blasting through his speakers. I pull my sweatshirt over my head so I'm only wearing my thin tank top, and I push my body out my window, sitting on the frame of the door and holding my sweatshirt by the hood like a flag.

"Woooooo!" I scream, pieces of my hair flying loose from my hair band and slapping at my face. "They're getting closer, Kyle. You better press that shit to the floor!"

Kyle looks up at me as I lean into the window, and laughs. "Joss, this is as fast as this car has ever gone!"

The car swerves as he looks back to the road, and my body shakes with the jerk of the tires along the shoulder of the road. The thrill of almost flying free fills my body with adrenaline, and I go from terrified to high in one heartbeat.

The lights of Wes's truck behind us are all I see. He's flashing them and honking, and Kyle and I are laughing harder. I push myself to sit on the door frame again and hold my sweatshirt high, finally letting the hood slip from my fingers and watching as my shirt sails through the air, smacking against one of Wes's headlights on its rapid decent to the roadway.

"Oops!" I say, covering my mouth and laughing.

"We're not going back to get that," Kyle says, each time he takes his eyes from the road, swerving more, sending more of that wonderful drug through me.

"Joss!"

I lean back, my fingers gripping the roof of Kyle's car while I look to see who's yelling my name. Wes's head is out his driver's side window, and it looks like Levi's holding his wheel and pressing the gas.

"That's not very safe, Wes!" I shout, unable to be serious for more than a second, laughter taking over my chest quickly.

"Joss, make Kyle stop the car!"

"He wants you to stop the car," I say, leaning down so Kyle can hear me.

"Tell him to fuck off," Kyle says, leaning forward against the wheel, trying to find one more level, to push his Impala just a little faster.

"Kyle says to fuck off!" I howl.

Wes purses his lips and slams his palm against the outside of his door, leaning into his cab again, defeated.

That's right, Wesley *Christopher* whoever the fuck you are. You are not our parent, and you can fuck off!

The lights from town are but a bright haze off in the distance behind us, which makes the stars above even more powerful. With my arms stretched out, I lean back and look at the harsh line where the clouds end and the swirls of stars begin. It's beautiful, and I want to live in this feeling forever, never to come home. I'll disappear in that sky.

I let my eyes start to close under the lull of the wind beating against my face from our sprint along the highway when the car swerves once more, and I feel my legs slide too far.

The rush hits my veins instantly. It's good. It's amazing. It's chilling.

It's death.

It all happens so slowly, the stars above me sliding into beams of light as the car beneath me fights to grip the road and my body gives itself over to chance. Somewhere in the middle—I decide I don't want to lose. My fingers are frantic, my arms frenzied as I hunt for something to hold onto, for my balance, and any way out of this that doesn't end with my body on the road.

And then Kyle's car begins to pull to the left, the rough dirt of the shoulder taking it, pulling it into its control while Kyle struggles with the wheel. The car is losing. Kyle is losing. I am losing. I am going to flip from the vehicle; I can feel my legs losing their grip and my body sliding more off balance. I open my mouth to scream in terror just as Wes's arms wrap around me. He's holding onto his open door, his brother now in the driver's seat, taking over control of his truck while he reaches for me. He kicks off from his truck, pulling my body against his tightly as we both roll along the sharp gravel of the road and into the tall grass and irrigation canal of the adjacent farm.

Everything mutes, but the sound of Wes breathing. My fingers are deep in his back and sides, my face flat against his chest, my elbows bleeding and my legs skinned and bruised. His chest rises and falls in fast pants, and his hands keep a firm hold on me.

It feels like we lie here forever, like hours have passed before my senses return. I hear my name, Taryn's voice, and the sound of steam pouring from Kyle's car. TK's the first to find us.

"Is she okay?" he asks.

"I think so," Wes's voice vibrates against my ear, his chest still keeping its rhythm. Are we dead? Did we die? I cling to him harder, pressing my ear against him, searching for the beat of his heart, but I can't hear anything over my own. I feel his hands run slowly up and down me, though, and I know he's okay.

"You're bleeding, Wes. Fuck, man…we need to get you to the ER," TK says.

"That's her blood. I'm…I'm okay. But she's hurt. It's her arms. Can you see? I can't let go," Wes says, and everything inside of me clings to those last words.

I can't let go.

"Yeah, man. Hang on. I think she's okay," TK says, kneeling down until his gaze meets mine. "Hey, Joss. You're okay. I'm just going to look at your arms, yeah?"

I shiver at his touch and grip Wes harder, suddenly living eight years in the past—my dad's car wrecked, my family ruined, my friends horrified, everyone looking at me. Wes's hold is tight, and his chin comes to rest over my head as I lay on him, his body the only thing between the ground and me.

"It's okay, Joss. Let him look. I'll stay. I'm right here," he whispers against my face.

It's okay. I'll stay.

I loosen my grip, letting TK roll my arms side-to-side one at a time, taking his own shirt and wrapping it around one of my elbows to stop the bleeding.

"She's going to need to clean that up, so it doesn't get infected, but it doesn't look broken or anything. Maybe she hit her head though? Wes…we should take her in," he says.

"I know," Wes whispers against me, and I grow rigid and clutch him again.

"Oh shit! Joss! Joss!" Kyle's voice is frantic and his run turns into a stumble at my side as he falls to his knees and pulls me from Wes's grasp. "Joss, oh fuck, Christ! I'm so sorry. Are you okay? Please say you're okay," Kyle cries, holding me to him.

"What were you thinking?" Taryn yells, not hesitating to shove Kyle, even though I'm in his hold. I take the distraction as an opportunity to retreat back to Wes, who is now sitting with his knees bent, picking debris from his clothes and skin. When he sees me scurry toward him, he pulls me in.

"I don't know. I…fuck, Taryn. I could have killed her," Kyle says, fighting against himself to find his balance. He stands in the center of us all, his body swaying in circles, his hands folded on his forehead as he looks at his car. "Shit! There's no way I'm getting that home."

"There is *no way* you are driving *anything* home," Wes growls, holding me and lifting my body to a stand with him.

"I know, I know. You're right, man. I'm so sorry. Joss! Joss…" Kyle breathes, stepping into me, reaching for my face. Before he can get close enough, though, Wes turns me, putting his body between Kyle's and mine.

"Do not touch her!" Wes shouts, his finger pointing from Kyle to his truck. "Get your ass in the back of the truck. We'll figure out how to get your car tomorrow."

"Don't keep her from me, asshole. I need to see her and know she's okay," Kyle says grabbing Wes's arm, only to be shaken off onto the ground.

"You can see her tomorrow. You're done tonight," he says, anger radiating from every move he makes.

"I did this," I say, my voice almost croaking out quietly behind him, surprising him—surprising everyone. "Don't be angry at him. I did this. I'm the one who always does it. I didn't have to get in the car. I didn't have to sit on the window. Be angry at me."

"Oh…believe me. I'm plenty angry at you!" Wes yells, his eyes leveling me with disappointment. I stand there under the scrutiny of his stare for a few seconds, my breathing still strong from the terror moments ago, my nostrils flared.

I challenge him long enough that he finally shakes his head and swears under his breath, and I step toward Kyle and offer him a hand to stand up from the ground. I weave my fingers through his and walk with him to the truck, climbing in the back to sit with him. I'm about to lower my body to the truck bed when I hear the heavy thump of Wes's feet step onto the tailgate and move toward me.

"You can call me whatever you want. You can be pissed and tell me I baby you. Whatever, Joss. I don't fucking care, but you're not riding back here. Not after we both just rolled down the highway. Not while my brother's shirt is the only thing keeping blood from dripping down your arm. And certainly not while I drive this fucking cocksucker home. Now get in the cab!"

Wes's hat is off, thrown onto the ground on his way into the truck, and every movement of his muscles is forceful and strong. He's actually showing an emotion, and it's inciting the fight in me.

"No!" I yell, kicking my sore leg at him, barely grazing him with my foot.

He doesn't warn me again, instead, bending over and lifting me over his shoulder, leaping from the back of the truck and pushing me into the cab despite the battle my loose arms and legs put up. When the door closes behind me, I grip the handle and work to push it open, but TK is holding it, his body leaning against it and his face full of pity. I fucking hate pity.

I crawl to the driver's side, hurrying when I see Wes bend down to pick up his hat, but everything hurts, and I wince with a pain on my side just as Wes climbs through the driver's side door.

"What? Your side? Is it your rib?" he says, reaching for the bottom of my T-shirt. I slap at his hand.

"I don't think so, asshole," I yell.

"Goddamnit, I just want to know you're not hurt any worse, that you're not bleeding internally or some shit. That's it; we're going to the hospital," he says, pulling his seatbelt over his body and starting the engine, glancing over his shoulder to make sure all of our passengers are in the back.

"No, I'm fine. No hospital," I say, reaching over and grabbing his arm. Both of our eyes fall to where my hand touches him, and I let go quickly, scooting back to my seat. "Really...I hate hospitals. Please. I'm fine."

"You probably broke a rib," he sighs, his head fallen to the side. I hold my breath and make a silent wish to go back to that brief second where I was under the stars and life felt free. I want to pair those few seconds with the feeling of his arms around me. Those few simple things are my happiness, as pathetic as they seem. His hold and the stars; it's enough.

I tug my shirt up my stomach to the edge of my ribs, and I push in with my hand a few times, pressing against the bones. The skin is tender, and there's a deep bruise already forming, but I don't think anything's broken.

"I'm okay," I say, my voice coming out in a gravely whisper.

Wes's eyes scan down my body to the bare skin on my side then back to my eyes. He nods once and turns to face the steering wheel, closing his eyes and breathing deep before shifting his truck into drive.

We get about a mile away from the crash when I remember my backpack and the empty bottle inside it. I don't want that coming back to haunt Kyle.

"My bag!" I sit up, turning to look out the rear window. Wes moves a hand to the top of my knee, recoiling as soon as I flash to him.

"Levi got it. It's in the back," he says, swallowing hard as he stares into the rearview mirror.

"Thanks," I whisper, falling back into my seat.

Unlike the last time I was in his cab with Wes, this time the passengers in the back are quiet. Nobody is having a good time with any of this. I meant what I said to him before—I did this. I *always* do this.

We pull up to Kyle's house first, and TK, Taryn, and Kyle all climb out.

"Taryn will drop me off later," TK says, reaching through the window to pound his knuckles against Wes's.

"Thanks, Wes. That was solid," Kyle says, his eyes now showing their redness. He was too drunk to drive. And I'm too drunk to make smart choices.

I did this.

Kyle holds his fist through the window just like TK did, and Wes looks at it for a second before sighing and pounding his fist forcefully and speeding away.

"I just have to drop Levi off, then I'll take you home," he says, his eyes looking everywhere but at me.

"That's fine," I say.

I take these few minutes to study him, to watch how he moves, to survey how badly he's hurt, when I realize…Wes isn't hurt at all. His jeans are ripped, and his shirt is soiled with mud and grass stains and small tears from the road. He has scrapes and some blood where his clothing was torn, but that's it. He wrapped himself around me and took the force of everything when I fell, and it barely left a mark.

Within minutes, we pull up to a small white house with a single porch light on and nothing else. There's an old station wagon in the carport and a plump orange cat waiting to be let in at the front door.

Levi pounds on the side of the truck when he gets out and holds up a hand. Wes circles around and rolls down his window, leaning out to talk to his brother. "I won't be long. I just want to make sure she gets home. Tell them not to worry if they're even up."

"Yeah, yeah. Hey…" Levi answers, leaning up and in the window to gaze at me. "I'm glad you're okay, Joss."

I want to thank him, but I know the only reason I'm able to speak at all is sitting right next to me. So instead, I smile tightly and hold up one hand to say goodbye.

"A'right. See you later," he says, patting the outside of Wes's door as Wes rolls the window to a close and pulls away again.

We're only a few blocks from my house, so as much as I want to sit here in silence and escape any more judgment, I don't want to waste the time.

"You're not hurt," I say, pulling one leg up to the side so I can see how Wes reacts.

"Uh," he says, checking mirrors and then rotating his own arms and feeling along his chest and sides. "Yeah, no. I think I'm okay. Some cuts is all."

I wasn't really asking, more just stating the fact. Wes isn't hurt. I was sheltered in his arms and my body looks like it's been fed through a shredder. He's dirty. That's it.

We turn down my street, and I chew at the inside of my cheek, trying to decide what any of this means—he looks like Christopher, which means if it is him, that's twice now that he's saved my life. And he isn't hurt. He isn't hurt at all. The inside of the truck is spinning a little; my mouth feels cottony and dry, and I definitely didn't eat enough popcorn to soak up what I drank. But I'm aware enough to know that I'm not imagining these facts, and that they're adding up. I just don't know what the equation equals.

Any chance that I'll question it tonight evaporates the second we pull up alongside my house, and my favorite day of the week rears its ugly head. My dad is on the front lawn on his hands and knees, heaving into the dead grass like a rabid dehydrated dog.

"He said he wasn't going to do that," Wes sighs, shoving the car into park forcefully and leaping out before I can catch him.

He said?

I get out after him, and the soreness from the evening overwhelms me, my legs weak under my body. I clutch the side of the truck and watch helpless while Wes bends down and pulls my father to a stand, walking him inside quickly, neither of them looking at me.

I reach into the back for my bag while he's inside, and by the time I'm done looping my arms through the straps he's walking back through the front door toward me as he talks to himself. I shut my eyes tightly—praying I can hold my weight up when I let go of his truck—and open them on my first step. Everything hurts, but I'm able to move. It doesn't stop Wes from weaving his arm under mine and behind my back. He sweeps my legs up over his other arm and lifts me easily, kicking the screen door open with his toe and pushing the main door closed behind us with his elbow.

"You can't live like this, Joss. You guys…you're killing yourselves," he says. His words don't feel like they're for me, necessarily, though. He isn't talking *to* me; he's just talking. He's narrating my pathetic existence.

"Bathroom?"

"That way. By my dad's room," I say, my eyes laser focused on his. He looks tired, and he looks sad.

I did that.

He sets me on the edge of the tub in the bathroom and slowly unwraps his brother's shirt from my arm, the cotton now soaked through completely with my blood. The sight of it makes my stomach turn a little, and I bring my other arm over my mouth, pressing the inside of my elbow to my lips.

"You okay? You need to be sick?" he asks quickly, his hands under my arms, ready to move me. I shake my head and point to the shirt.

"That's a lot of blood," I grunt out.

He refolds the shirt inside itself, masking the stain some, then sighs. "Yeah. You're gonna have a scar from this. That...what you did..." he says, his eyes flipping from my arm that he's now holding under the faucet of the tub to my eyes, "that was stupid, Joss. I'm sorry, but that was just..."

"I know," I say, looking down. The water stings, and I don't let myself look away from the blood washing down the drain. Wes has to brush my cuts with a wet towel a few times, cleaning out the dirt, tar, and rock from the road. Every time he pulls a pebble from me, more blood rushes into the water. I watch it all.

After a few minutes, he shuts the water off and moves to our cabinet, pulling out the alcohol and boxes of ankle tape and bandages. We're prepared for sprains, but not intoxicated leaps-of-faith it seems.

"I'm going to have to use this; it's all you've got," he says. I lift my shoulders and move my arm to the sink where he wraps it in ankle bandages and tape, loosely enough that it can breathe.

When he's done, he pushes the empty boxes to the trash and moves the alcohol back into the cabinet, closing the mirrored door, but stopping when something catches his eye. My heart stops, knowing what he sees, and when his giant hand wraps around the three nearly-empty bottles of pills, I decide it's better not to wait for his question.

"When I was little, my dad caught my mom having an affair. He went bat-shit crazy and tried to hit the guy with his car. This kid I knew..." I flit my eyes to his, which are focused on the small bottles of Oxy and painkillers in his hand. "Christopher," I pause again, studying him. His eyebrows lift with a twitch, and his eyes move to mine. "He pulled me out of the way. Kinda…just…in…time. I should have died. It sort of left me…I don't know…broken? Definitely fucked up. I'm definitely fucked up. And sometimes, it all just gets to be too much."

I tap my finger on my head a few times, then ball my hand into a fist, and move it to my chest, pounding there softly. All of my pain—locked away in my head and my heart.

"These aren't in your name," Wes says, turning one of the bottles to the side, rolling it in between two fingers.

I lean my head sideways and look at the tiny print, trying to remember how that particular pill made me feel. Funny, I can't even remember. But when I took them over the summer, I couldn't get enough.

"Nope," I answer, letting my gaze slide to his eyes. He pulls away from the bottles briefly, looking into me, and his hard swallow lets me know he understands.

"I haven't bought in months," I say, letting things fall out of focus, not wanting to look at my life so closely.

"Your dad doesn't see them in here? Right…like…in the open?" Wes asks.

"He would have to care," I say, reaching up and taking one of the bottles from his fingers. He grips for a second, but I shake my head, encouraging him to let go. I open the bottle and spill the four pills left into my palm, looking at them. So tiny. So potent. I tilt my hand and let them roll free into the toilet, and then I do the same with the other two bottles in his hand, flushing away my darkest days.

Those days weren't so long ago. They were before Wes. And these pills—they aren't the only ones hiding.

He leans back against the frame of the door, pushing his palm into his brow as if he has no idea what to do with me. I'll make this easy.

"I'm good. You can head home. I'm going to crash soon or get sick, and no offense, but I don't really want you here for either," I say through quiet, humble, nervous laughter. I sit back down on the edge of the tub and survey my wounds, then look up to give Wes a tight smile. His mouth hasn't ventured from the despondent line it came to rest in when he finally got me alone in the cab of his truck. "Really, I'm okay."

He doesn't look away. He stands there with his arms crossed as he inhales and exhales slowly through his nose. He doesn't want to leave me, and that thought feels so good. If only he wanted to stay because it's me. But that's not it. I could be anyone. He just feels…liable.

"You're not my parent, and…" I hold up my hand before he jumps to the wrong conclusion, "what I mean is, don't feel that you have to be responsible for me…for…any of *this*."

He looks down at his feet, which are crossed at the ankles, and slowly starts to nod in acceptance. I so very badly want him to stay, but just as much I want him to go. I want him to go because I feel foolish. Because I was stupid. And because he isn't hurt at all, and his face…god that face. It's familiar. But my head is spinning, and I'm not sure what's real and what isn't.

I know what happened tonight though—that tumble from the moving truck—Kyle wouldn't have come through unscathed. Nobody would have.

He did.

"Okay," he says, bringing me out of my thoughts. My eyes meet his quickly, and I feel our brief connection in my chest, the rush of it sweeter than the whiskey and the thrill of hanging from the car. The way his gaze feels scares me. It feels…addictive.

"I'll walk you out," I say, standing up and faltering on my unsteady legs. Wes steps forward to catch me by the arm, and I suck in a hard breath, shutting my eyes because his touch brings the same flood of emotions.

"I know my way," he says. My eyes are still closed but I can feel that his face is close to mine. I feel the slight breath from his words, his heat— the way the air changes just from him breathing it. I keep my eyes closed and suck in my lip, nodding slightly in concession.

"Come on. Where's your room?" he asks, picking me back up in his arms without even asking me. I've been here so much tonight I feel used

to it. It doesn't make me feel weak at all, either. It makes me feel *special.*
And that scares me too.

"Across the hall. It's…it's messy," I say, cracking open one eye and
cringing.

Wes chuckles, and the vibration hits my jaw where it rests on his chest.
"My brothers and I share a room. *We* are messy. I swear…I won't judge
you," he says, the left side of his mouth raised. There's a short pause while
he holds me here in my dim hallway, a stupid smirk on his face and our
noses close enough to touch. The feeling, whatever it is, doesn't last long,
but I know we both noticed it. I did not imagine that. That was real.

Wes reaches with one hand to open my door, and steps inside without
turning on my light. I'm relieved because I wasn't kidding about the mess.
I leave food in here because I don't like leaving my room. I'm embarrassed
enough as it is that he has to kick clothes and equipment out of the way
to make a path to my bed, and when he sets me down on it, I have to
push the pile of dirty clothes to the floor just to find my blanket. I push
my hand under my pillow the second I feel the coolness of the sheets on
my skin, and my fingers search for the feel of his shirt, only it's not
there…because I gave it back to him, and he gave it to McKenna. That
thought kicks me in the gut.

"You're sure you'll be all right?"

"I'm sure," I say through a heavy sigh.

"Okay, I'll lock your door from the inside when I go," he says.

"'Kay," I breathe out, my body already succumbing to the pull of
exhaustion. My world is spinning a little, so I let the sleep drag me in, not
wanting to feel anything bad until the morning. I hear my door begin to
close, though, and I manage to wake myself enough to see Wes before he
leaves. "Hey, Wes?"

"Yeah?" He rests his head against the side of my door, and I'm grateful
this is the last thing I'm going to see tonight. The look on his face right
now is sweet, and it's only mine.

"Thank you," I say, my eyes as wide as I can hold them. It's too dark
to see the blue in his, but I know it's there.

All he does is smile, but it's enough. He gently shuts my door, and seconds later I hear the sound of the front one close followed by the start of his engine. My phone buzzes in my pocket shortly after, and I fumble awkwardly, trying to make my hands work well enough to find it. My father's home, so I know it isn't him, but Taryn's probably worried.

I finally pull it from my pocket and bring it in front of my face just as I hear Wes pull away. The text is from him.

You really scared me tonight. And not because I was afraid someone was going to get hurt. I was afraid YOU were going to get hurt.

His words are powerful and sad, and I cry almost immediately. My heart also soars. Maybe it shouldn't, and it's probably selfish that it does, but it does. I clutch my phone in my hand and think of what to type back, but the pull of sleep is strong, so before I succumb, I simply write *I'm sorry.* I won't promise that I won't scare him again, but I do vow to myself that I will try. I will try because I don't care about much anymore, but I care about Wes. And I don't want him to be afraid.

CHAPTER 6

My body is going to be a painful reminder of stupid decisions for a few weeks. The gash on my elbow is deep; the blood soaked through the bandages overnight, leaving me with a dried and hardened cast of my own making around my arm. I showered with the bandages on, letting the water melt them away rather than peeling them off and risking opening up wounds. Things are going to be raw no matter how I look at it though, and I am going to need something better than ankle wrap to heal.

I put on a loose sweatshirt and my running pants and pull my wet hair through my favorite Giants ball cap so I can walk to the drug store a mile or two away. Normally, I'd call Kyle or Taryn to take me, but I wasn't ready to face either of them, for different reasons. I'm pretty sure they're okay having a little space from me too.

I'm too sore to run. My overzealous workout from the day before has left my legs feeling weak, and my two-man tumble from the moving car took care of anything that didn't hurt. So I walk. I walk slowly. In an hour, I get to the store and spend the last twenty that my grandmother sent me for my birthday over the summer on real gauze, ointment for my cuts, a king-sized Reese's pack, and a *thank you* card. I borrow the pen at the counter to write a short note to Wes, then lick the envelope closed while I walk back into our neighborhood, this time counting until I see Sycamore Street—Wes's street.

I did my best to commit it to memory last night. Somehow just knowing where he lives feels better. It makes him less of a mystery, but it makes me more, curious all the same. I woke up thinking about what he did, the text he sent and the fact that he walked away unscathed. I'm not stupid enough to think that superheroes are anything real, but Wes…he makes a mighty good argument.

The closer I get to his house, the more I start to think that coming here in the first place is a tremendously bad idea. I'm a driveway-length away, and I have time to bail, but before my brain sends the *run* signal to my feet, TK stands up from the bed of the truck, a bucket in one hand and a washrag in the other, soap dripping over the side.

"Hey! Look who's up and walking today. I do believe it's the dead!" His laugh is raspy as he sets his cleaning supplies on the tailgate of the truck and hops down next to me, shaking the water and suds from his arms before pulling me into a tight hug I don't see coming. I stand there awkwardly and let him hold me for a few seconds, my hands clutching my pathetic *thank you* card and quickly-melting chocolate and peanut-butter candy.

"Hey…uh…yeah," I say, looking at my feet as we pull apart. "So…I'm sorry for what you guys had to deal with…yesterday—"

"Stop," he interrupts me, swinging his hand toward me and brushing my arm. I look up at him, squinting from the glare of the high-noon sun. He's smiling softly, and it's almost making me feel worse. I think I'd prefer if he were just pissed at me. He's not though. "We're just glad you're okay. You talk to Taryn yet today?"

I shake my head *no* and let my eyes fall back down to the comfort of my running shoes with a hole in the toe.

"You should call her. She was pretty upset last night. Not…not at you. More, *for* you, if that makes sense?" He's looking right at me when I tilt my head up, and I offer a barely-there smile and nod.

"I'll call her tonight. If you talk to her, just tell her I'm okay," I say.

TK nods in return, then gives his attention back to the bucket of water on the truck, pulling it to the ground now and kneeling to wash the tire rims. There's mud crusted everywhere.

"That from last night?" I ask.

TK tilts his head up with a slight laugh before answering. "Yeah, that was as close to off-roading as this truck's ever been. It's sixteen years old. I'm kind of shocked it held up."

"Sorry," I say. He just waves a hand at me and goes back to work on the wheel. I watch for a few minutes, glancing toward his house every so often, nervous to ask if Wes is home. I feel like practicing talking with TK is good for me, so I set my things down in the plastic bag from the store and reach into the bucket for another rag, moving to the front wheel to begin scrubbing.

"You don't need to do that," he chuckles.

"I want to," I say, my sore arm no match for the clod of caked-on mud deep inside the rim grooves. I do a decent job, but save the tough cleaning for TK. "You three share this thing?"

"Yeah, it usually works out because we're going to the same place. We try to respect one another and not take it out for long if we know one of the other guys has plans or needs to go somewhere. And we can take our mom or dad's cars if we really need to. They work so much, though, that their cars aren't always home."

"That's cool. It must be nice to have two brothers, to grow up like that. Have you all always been close?" I'm fishing now because I'm so hungry to know more about Wes—and TK and Levi seem to be deeply woven into his life.

"Yeah, we've always been tight. We were adopted around the same time, when we were like nine or so," he says.

I pause and think about his answer. *Nine.* That would be about the age Christopher would have turned.

"You guys ever fight?" I ask. I wait a few seconds for an answer, and I start to think he didn't hear me, so I begin to ask again. My words are stopped cold by the blast of water that hits me from behind, soaking through my pants and shirt in an instant.

"We like water fights, Joss. And you have just been christened," Levi is yelling, poised with the hose behind me, the end capped in a sprayer that gives him precision accuracy and makes the water sting when it hits me.

"You shit!" I yell, dunking my rag in the soapy water and throwing it at him. It hits him with a *thud* in the chest, but he laughs it off, spraying at my legs as I scurry to the other side of the truck.

"Come on out, Joss. Nowhere for you to run," TK says. I'm tucked behind one front tire to hide my legs, and I can hear them behind the other, the pressure of the water building up and making the hose buzz. I left my bucket on the other side of the truck, so I'm completely unarmed. But I am fast, even though my legs are on fire with every step. Still, I might be able to make it. I think about making a break for it when I feel a hand flatten on my soaking, wet back. I startle and turn to look Wes in the eyes, holding my tongue when he has a finger pressed to his lips. I'm sure he can feel my heartbeat against his hand through my spine.

"I'll come out when you put down your weapon," I say, holding my gaze on Wes and buying us time. His lip curls into a slight smirk on one side, and I suddenly want to kiss it.

"Yeah, that ain't happenin' sister. Might as well give up now," Levi yells.

Wes's hand finds mine without looking, and my breath catches at the feel of his fingers sliding through mine. He holds his finger against his lips again, and for a brief second, his eyes slip to my mouth then back up again.

Breathing is becoming harder.

Wes leads me several feet from the truck until we have a chance to make a break for it to the side of the house. He tugs my hand, encouraging me to run with him until we find the safety of the brick wall, our backs flat against it. His hand lets go, and I miss it. We both hear TK taunting me, under the assumption that I'm still where I was, and it makes both of our mouths pull into tight smiles, holding in laughter.

"There's a hose on the other side. We have to go fast. Come on," he whispers into my ear. I'm suddenly grateful that my arms are beaded with goosebumps from being wet and cold, because the shivers from his voice against my neck and ear would have the same effect, and I don't want him seeing that.

Now in his backyard, we both run around to the other side of the house, unlooping the heavy hose from the hook anchored to the wall. Wes bends it, cutting off the water supply, and nods to me to turn the water on high. I do it and then step up next to him, our bodies touching on the sides. He's wearing a torn tank top and sweatpants, and I can see his stomach and ribs through the large holes on the sides. I'm distracted by the thought of running my hand inside his shirt and feeling his tight body as we creep slowly behind his brothers, but I shake myself out of my fantasy quickly when Wes looks down at me and nods again.

"You better run, suckers!" I yell, just as Wes cuts the hose loose and lets the spray drench Levi and TK, who both run, leaving the second hose behind. I grab it quickly, and Wes and I each take on a brother, soaking them until they climb up into the back of the truck and grab the last bucket of soapy water and fling it at both of us.

Wes shakes his head fast, the wet ends spraying in all directions. Jesus holy hell does that boy look good all wet.

TK manages to pull the other end of my hose away from me, and I reach for it, but too late—he tugs it to his body quickly, pointing the spray right at me, soaking anything that was remotely close to dry. Wes comes to my rescue quickly, spraying his brother in the face until he has to turn and let go of the hose.

For the next ten minutes, we run around the driveway, using their truck for protection, and take turns spraying and laughing. This is what it must be like to grow up in a house full of brothers. The joy in my chest is intense, and my cheeks hurt from smiling.

The water war finally breaks up when an older sedan pulls up next to the truck, and a heavyset man with a full mustache and beard steps out. He's carrying a box under one arm as he moves around the front of his car and eyes the boys' truck.

"You know, the cleaning thing only works if you actually get the water on the *truck* right?" he says, teasingly, quirking one eyebrow at Wes.

I'm standing behind the truck with my arms folded over the bed when he notices me. The man's lips grin, and he glances over at Wes's brothers.

"Well she's too pretty for you hooligans. Anyone want to fill me in on our guest?" He hands the box to Wes, then dusts his hands against his belly, wiping away dust and dirt from whatever he was carrying.

"This is Joss. She's coach's daughter," Levi answers. Wes busies himself with the box, letting his brother's answer stand on its own. I don't know why, but I want him to say more, to make me...*more*. I'm not coach's daughter—I'm something to Wes. I have to be.

"Nice to meet you, Joss. You stayin' for lunch?" he asks, pulling his glasses to the tip of his nose and looking at me over the rims.

"Oh, no…it's okay. I was just stopping by," I say, remembering my lame card and chocolate, which is probably both drenched and melted in the driveway.

"You should stay," Wes says, not looking away from the box. His shoulders are stiff, and the fact that he's refusing to look at me almost means more than if he did. My lip pulls up into a smile against my will, and my tummy goes all butterfly gooey. I hate it. I love it.

"Okay. Uhm…yeah, sure. Thanks," I say, smiling and nodding to the man. I still don't know his name, but I'm too awkward to ask, and I'm pretty sure my bra is outlined through the shirt I'm wearing.

TK and Levi throw a few more wet sponges at each other, but pick up the buckets and walk over to Wes, looking in the box with him.

"Sweet. Dad got the part," Levi says, pulling out some shiny chrome something that I'm guessing is for the truck.

"I'll work on it next weekend," Wes says, dropping the part back in the box and carrying it into the garage.

"See ya inside, Joss," TK says, smacking Levi on the back of the head as he takes off toward the house, Levi running after him.

Wes walks back out toward me when the garage door shuts behind him, his brothers leaving us alone. My body shivers once from the breeze blowing against my wet skin.

"Your dad seems nice," I say.

Wes smiles with a short nod, his hand rubbing the back of his neck as he steps to the front of the truck, leaning against it. He dips his head forward and runs his hand through his hair, pushing the wild strands back from his eyes.

"He is. I'll introduce you the right way when we go inside," he says, his eyes not quite making it to mine, glancing away from my body and darting around the truck and front yard. The outdoors suddenly feels suffocating, and I can't think of the next thing to say. Wes fills the gap for me.

"Don't forget whatever you have in the bag, over there?" He points to the end of the driveway, and my stomach grows tight remembering my original plan. It feels even sillier now.

"Oh, yeah. That's…I sort of…I brought something for you," I say, holding up a finger and jogging to the back and bringing it to the front of the truck. I stop closer to Wes and set the bag on the hood. He watches my hands, but still seems to be avoiding my eyes. He takes a deep breath and covers his mouth with his palm.

"Here," I say, handing him the card and a very heavy package of Reese's. "It's a thank you card. It's…it's dumb. I didn't really know what else to do though, so…"

"It's nice. Thanks," he says, taking the card and dragging the melted candy bar closer to him along the hood.

"I didn't really think through the chocolate," I say with a light laugh. Wes chuckles too, picking the bar up and holding it on top of the envelope.

"I'll put it in the freezer," he says, his eyes finally sliding over to meet mine. They halt there, and I don't move or breathe under their scrutiny. I keep my embarrassed half smile in place as my fingers work against my palms in awkward fists at my sides, my heartbeat speeding up the longer Wes's eyes hold me hostage. They are blue and perfect and exactly as I imagine them when I close my own.

Slowly, his gaze falls to my mouth and chin and then to my chest and shirt, and I notice his lip twitch as he stares at the rest of me for longer than I think he wants to, eventually bringing his hand back over his mouth as his eyes flit to meet mine.

"I have some dry clothes you can wear," he says, and my eyes shoot wide in realization. I glance down and see my breasts on full display, every curve of my body obvious as my wet clothes cling to my skin. The cold air has made my nipples hard, and I am overcome with the fact that Wes was staring at them.

"Oh my god," I say, folding my arms and leaning against the warm truck. I lay my head forward and rest it against the hood, rolling it away from him, wanting to die.

Oh my freaking God!

"Come on," he chuckles, reaching for my hand and forcing it into his. He turns his back to me, but tugs me along behind him. "Just stay close to me."

I step closer, until my front touches his back, and Wes pauses when our bodies meet. He sighs, and I lean my head against him, feeling both mortified and turned on from this touch.

"I'm so sorry," I squeak out, feeling his body rise and fall with his long breath.

"You're a beautiful girl. Don't be sorry," he says, his head tilted to the side enough that I am given the gift of looking at the line of his jaw and chin. His eyes glance over his shoulder and meet mine briefly before he inhales once more and leads me through the door while I replay what he said over and over.

Beautiful girl.

"Sandwiches okay with you, Wes?" his father hollers from the other end of the house. I can hear pans and cabinets moving and opening.

"That works," Wes yells back, looking side to side, I'm assuming for his brothers, as we step into what is clearly their room.

"Your friend okay with that?" his dad yells, a hint of teasing to his tone.

Wes winces as he shuts his eyes tight, leaning his head out the door, but looking back at me quickly first. "You okay with that? It's probably ham or turkey. It's always ham or turkey," he whispers.

I nod and laugh to myself silently.

"Yeah, Joss likes sandwiches. Thanks. We'll be in to help in a sec. Just drying off!" He closes the door carefully, resting his head against the wood. I'm standing behind him with my arms still folded, and I swear I can feel the pull of something bigger trying to push us together. Wes presses the lock in before turning away from me and moving to a set of drawers, pulling out a dry pair of sweatpants. He takes a few steps backward and bends down to pick up a black hoodie and two shirts that he holds to his nose.

"You weren't kidding about your room," I say through my grin he can't see.

"Yeah, we're fuckin' pigs. Sorry about this," he says, throwing his first selection of shirts into a pile in the corner and picking two more up from the floor.

He's finally satisfied with a gray one and he turns to the side, handing everything to me.

"These are clean…ish," he says, shaking his head with a short laugh, still careful not to look my way.

"Thanks," I say. "You know, I'm still clothed. You can look at me now."

Wes chuckles again and steps to his door, opening it and resting his forehead against the edge, peeking at me briefly.

"I better not, Joss," he says, tapping his knuckles a few times against the wood grain and laughing as he turns away. "I better not. I'll wait for you out here."

The door closes behind him, and my smile comes hard and fast. I really like this boy. I bring his clothes to my face and inhale, happy that his things smell like him. I slip my wet clothes from my body, including my soaking bra and panties, and step into Wes's sweatpants and shirt, letting the soft material hug my body.

Before I pull his sweatshirt over my head, I pull out a few new bandages from my drug store bag and replace the wet ones on my arm, throwing the old one in my bag and tying it shut. I gather my pile of wet things in my arms, stepping through his door to find him leaning against the opposite wall and waiting for me in a dry shirt of his own. He smiles the kind of smile that meets his eyes and leans his head to the side as he looks at me.

"Thanks for letting me borrow this stuff. Do you have a plastic bag or something? I'll just put my shoes in your yard or something to dry," I say, trying to hold my wet belongings away from my now-dry self.

"Here, I'll throw everything in the dryer," he says, reaching for my things.

Without thinking, I give him everything and follow him to a small closet-sized room right off of the garage. He opens the dryer and lets my clothes roll from his hands into the machine, but my bra slides out from the fold of my shirt along with my panties.

"You…uh…you changed everything, huh?" Wes says, swallowing hard.

"Had to," I say, my voice cracking as I clear my throat.

"Right. No…of course," he says, punching buttons and starting the dryer before turning around to face me. I'm fully covered, but for some reason, when Wes turns to look at me again, his eyes lingering just a hint below my eyes, I feel barer than before.

"Lunch is served," his dad says, his voice echoing down the hall, snapping us both out of a trance.

Wes finally looks up into my eyes and nods toward the door for us to leave, but not before swallowing hard one more time. I walk ahead of him toward the kitchen, and I put more effort into every step than I ever have before. I'm purposely working my hips, and when I realize that I'm trying to draw attention to my ass, I feel ridiculous. I really am close to bows and glitter in my hair now.

Fuck.

"Joss, really glad to finally meet you," his dad says as I step up to the counter and grab one of six plates with a sandwich and chips on it. "The boys have told me all about the girl that hits Wes's curveball."

His dad laughs through the end of his words, laughing even harder when Wes rolls his eyes and sighs.

"It wasn't a curveball. It was his changeup," I say, sitting down at the table next to Levi on a long picnic bench. I put a whole chip in my mouth and glance to Wes, offering a smug smile.

"It was a slider," he says, raising his eyebrows at me in a challenge as he lifts his plate and carries it to the seat opposite of me.

I hold his stare for a few seconds and wait as he takes a bite of his sandwich, proud of his pitch. I lean back and pull one leg up next to my body and chuckle before popping a whole chip in my mouth and crunching it.

"Like hell it was," I say.

Wes quirks an eyebrow and pauses mid chew, and I lean forward on my elbows and stare into his hypnotic blue eyes. I'm lost to them, but I'm not losing me and going all gushy just because he's the cutest boy I've ever seen.

"Change. Up." I bite down after the last syllable and give him a matter-of-fact, tight-lipped smile. TK busts through the quiet quickly, laughing so hard, he actually chokes on his sandwich.

"I like her," his dad says, stepping into the bench seat next to Wes and leaning into him. Wes is still frozen in his reaction to me, but I can see the amusement in his eyes, and when his mouth slowly starts to chew and grin at the same time, everything inside me goes warm.

"Joss, you can call me Bruce, by the way," his dad says, wiping his hand on a paper towel and reaching it over the table to shake mine. I grasp it firmly, to show I'm not weak, and I can tell his dad notices that as well. "How's your sandwich?"

"Good sir...I mean Bruce. Thank you," I say, never fully taking my attention away from the boy across from me.

One thing about a table of athletes is they never eat for long. We're all done with our plates in a matter of minutes, and I help Levi clear the table and rinse dishes off, dry them, and put them away. There's a Warriors game on the television in the living room, and I follow Levi in, stopping behind the couch when we reach the rest of his family in the room. He hops over the back and sinks into the well-worn blue sofa, patting the cushion next to him.

"Oh, no…it's okay. I should go," I say, glancing at Wes, whose eyes are bouncing from the TV to me. If he wanted me to stay, I'd think he'd ask, or at least be more interested.

"Ah, come on, Joss. You can't leave the middle of a Warriors game. It's bad luck," Bruce says, holding up his bottle of water to toast me. I'm struck by the irony that in my house, that hand would be wrapped around a beer. And my dad wouldn't be toasting me, either.

Reluctantly, I round the couch and slip into the corner of the sofa, giving most of my attention over to the TV. TK and Levi seem to be more into basketball than Wes or Bruce, and eventually, the room is divided into two conversations, one over who the Warriors *should* have picked in the draft, and one about whatever truck part was in the box Bruce brought home.

While Wes is involved in his conversation with his father, his eyes keep glancing to the side, checking on me, and it feels nice. I catch him more than once, and I smile and even give a thumbs-up once or twice to let him know I'm okay. After a few minutes, he gets up and says he'll be right back. I stand to follow him, but he holds up a hand.

"Just checking something on that box Dad brought home," he says, urging me to stay where I am. I like that he doesn't want me to leave his home, so I step back toward the couch, this time sitting on the other end, closer to his father.

TK and Levi are engrossed in the game. The Warriors are playing the Lakers, so I get it.

"You guys have a favorite baseball team?" I ask, immediately getting three different answers. TK says the Dodgers, Levi the Padres, and Bruce is a Texas fan. I laugh at how different they all are.

"Maggie, that's my wife, she likes the Yankees," he says, and I wince, because I'm more of a Red Sox kinda girl. Bruce laughs at my reaction. "I know, and to think," he says, leaning forward and whispering, "I married her anyway."

He leans back again with heavier laughter, the full-belly kind that shakes his shoulders. I've only met him today and yet feel like he's some uncle I've had for years. I like Bruce. I like his entire family, and I bet I'd like his wife too.

"Thanks for having me over," I say, pulling my legs up and tucking them underneath me so I can sit sideways and talk to him more. This is how Sundays should be. I have vague memories of mine being this way. I was young, too young for the memories to really stick—but before my mom left, I know we used to do things like this. I watched games with my dad on the TV, and Mom would make us snacks. Everything was perfect. Fake...but perfect.

"Wes...he likes you, you know?" Bruce says, surprising me. My stomach drops with rollercoaster strength, and I work to keep my reaction away from my eyes.

"He's really nice," I say, my cheeks warming with my blush. Bruce's cheeks dimple with his smile as he looks at me sideways and takes a drink from his bottle. He sees right through me, and he knows I like Wes too.

"Yes he is," he nods with a soft laugh. "You know, Mags and I always talk about the things we love most about our boys. What makes us proud of each one? Levi is loyal."

"Like a dog," Levi answers over his shoulder, barking twice. TK hits him on the shoulder, but Levi shrugs it off, going right back to the game.

"TK is our funnyman. He brought joy to this house the moment he jumped up for a piggyback ride and let me carry him through the door," Bruce says. TK threatens to stand up and jump on him for a ride now, and Bruce holds a hand to his back. "That only worked then. You're twice my size now."

"Maybe this way," TK says, patting his head.

"Ha ha, very funny," Bruce grunts out, folding his hands over his belly. He gives in with a real laugh soon, and TK moves into the kitchen to grab another drink.

"What about Wes?" I ask, wanting nothing more than to sit here for hours and hear stories about the boy hiding out in the garage.

"Well you had it right. Wes is kind. I'd like to say we raised him that way, but he just came that way. We adopted him at nine, after a few months of living with us as a foster kid," he says, staring down at his hands and smiling at the memory. "We threw a birthday party for him before the official adoption. Mags had just lost her job at the bank, but we didn't talk about that stuff in front of the kids. Somehow, though, Wes...he must have heard us. He crawled up next to her on the couch the night before his party and said he didn't want any presents. When Maggie asked him why, he just shook his head and said there was nothing he needed. But she knew...and so did I. He didn't want us spending money on him when we didn't have much to spend."

"That's sweet," I say, my chest squeezing, trying to picture the little boy who did that. My head pictures Christopher instantly. I'm about to ask for a picture, when the front door opens and Wes steps inside, and all of my inner thoughts fizzle at the sight of him. Seeing him—looking at him—it takes over everything.

"It's the wrong size. Thanks for trying though, Dad," he says, wiping his hand with a rag from the garage. "I saw the receipt. I'll take it back today; get the right one. No big deal."

"Ah damn. I'm sorry. I was guessing," Bruce says.

Wes is standing by the front door with the truck keys in his hands, so I stand and move toward him, my eyes meeting his.

"I should go too," I say, offering a hand to Bruce. "Thanks again for the sandwich. And company."

"Anytime," he says, patting the top of my hand before letting it go and sinking deeper into his seat.

I turn to Wes, who is still at the door with the keys in his hands. "Mind if I grab my things?" I ask, tugging on the shirt that isn't mine and looking down at the rest of my borrowed wardrobe.

"Yeah, here. I'll give you a ride," he says, shutting the door, jogging past me and dashing into the laundry room. I hear him inside, pulling things from the dryer as I step to the doorway. He walks out just as I'm about to enter, and we press into each other, the hot clothes in his arms between us.

"Sorry," I mumble.

"It's…it's okay," he says, not moving. His fingers are grasping my clothes, and I blush at seeing my bra in his hands, my mind immediately imagining him touching me. "Your shoes aren't very dry. More…hot really. Sorry."

"It's okay," I say, sucking my top lip in, not falling fully into his eyes. I move my hands slowly around my things, and we brush over each other on the exchange.

"I'll get you a bag," Wes says, stepping into the garage. I follow him out the door, and he quickly shakes out a plastic grocery bag, holding it open for me to drop my things inside. I do it quickly, tucking my bra and panties in the bottom. I tie the handles in a knot, then hold my warm, damp things to my chest.

"I read the card," Wes says, looking down at my feet, the right side of his mouth tugging upward before he peers at me, one eyebrow raised. My mental state is instantly shot to the level of humiliated. I was feeling sappy and spontaneous when I bought the card. I wrote that I thought he was my hero, and that I'm not sure how he was able to save me, but that I'm glad he did, and I'm glad it was him. I gushed, and went on and on to the point that I even had to write the rest of my note about how amazing I think he is on the back, drawing an arrow for him to flip the card over as if he would think that I actually stopped mid-sentence.

Stupid girl. *Gah!*

"I'm not that special, Joss," he says, his head to the side. I can't bring myself to look up into his eyes for long, so I just give him short glances while I shrug my shoulders to my ears.

"You kinda are," I say. His dad was right about what he said inside—Wes is kind. But he's more, and I just wish I could see his full story. To do that, though, I'd have to ask things of him. I'd have to share pieces of me.

I feel him step closer to me, and my heart picks up its pace until it's almost doing nothing but squeezing inside my chest. His fingers touch my chin, and he tilts it higher, forcing me to look at him, and despite how tiny my movement right now, it's the scariest, most honest gesture of my life when my eyes finally hit his.

"I love the way you see me. I do," he says, his breath held until the last second when he painfully exhales, and his shoulders fall along with his hand from my face. His expression is soft, but serious. "You make me want to live up to your expectations. I'm afraid I'll disappoint them, though."

"I don't have any expectations, Wes. I learned about disappointment a long time ago. I just wanted you to know I appreciate what you did. That's all," I say, lying. It's a lie, because I used to not expect anything. I didn't have hope or wishes or dreams or plans—none of it. I had the next day. And then the next. And I filled the in-between with whatever distraction I could find in the moment to get me through.

And then Wes Stokes showed up and changed everything.

If I could, I would fold into myself. I don't like this feeling—the one I get talking about feelings. Not that we're *talking* about feelings, but we're dancing around talking about feelings. I'd rather go back to making fun of his pitching, or to water fights and trash talk over the basketball game. This…this is uncomfortable.

"I should get home. I can walk…really," I say, my hands working to untie the bag and fish out my wet shoes. I don't get far in my quest as Wes's hand moves over mine.

"Your shoes are so wet you'll get blisters. Get in the truck, stubborn girl," he says, winking and not waiting for my answer as he walks to the driver's side and gets in, starting the engine.

I move to the passenger door and climb inside, instantly feeling the pressure of less space around us. I tuck my wet bag between my feet and wait, until after a few seconds I look up at him and shrug.

"Why aren't you going?"

He laughs and turns to face the front window for a second, shaking his head before twisting his body to the side to look at me, his arm resting over the steering wheel. "I have a rule with you. It's a new rule, and it's sorta your fault," he says.

"Okay…" I swallow, not really sure where this is going.

"Whenever I'm responsible for you, like, say…when I'm driving you home in my truck, you will follow every single safety precaution ever suggested. That means buckle up, and lock your door, because I don't want that thing mysteriously *flying* open in the middle of a tight turn," he says, pausing as if he's waiting for me to agree with him. I hold his gaze for a second and think about arguing for the sake of feeling more comfortable in my combative skin, but there's something about the way he tells me to be safe, and the way he's looking at me right now, that makes me just smile, pull my belt on, and click the door locked.

"Was agreeing with me so bad?" he laughs out his question, shifting the truck and pulling out of the driveway.

"You have no idea," I sigh, earning a short laugh from him. He bites his lip when he shakes his head. It's the slightest thing, but it's sweet and vulnerable too.

Wes flips the button on the stereo, bouncing between a few stations and settling on classic rock. It makes me smile when I notice his lips moving along with the Journey song. I love Journey. My dad used to play it in the garage when he'd throw me whiffle balls and let me hit them into the net. It's a good memory, and somehow I've kept it pure. Steve Perry's voice still makes me smile, and I lean back comfortably into my seat and add the memory of Wes lip syncing to the list of happy thoughts associated with this sound.

Whatever part he's returning is in the box between us. I pull it closer to me with two fingers and look inside, not really sure what it is, until Wes explains.

"It's a main drive gear and a pilot bearing…it's…just parts for a transmission," he says, glancing at me quickly, then moving his eyes back to the road. I notice his hands are quite literally at ten and two. He's being serious about by-the-book safety. I smile at that too.

"Is yours broken?" I ask. I know nothing about cars. I haven't bothered to learn, because I have yet to drive anywhere. I got my license, but my father allowed that only so I could drive my grandmother around when she came to visit. He knew he wouldn't be able to most of the time. I'm covered under the minimum of family insurance plans, so unless I get a job, I'll be hitching rides and running most places I go.

"It's just acting funny," he says, glancing at me again with a tight smile.

I look down at the part, not really sure how it works. The truck seems to have been fine the last time I rode in it, though I can hear the engine more today—like everything under the hood is working just a little harder. I listen to the hum of his motor, to the way everything sounds like its playing catch up when he accelerates after pulling to the stop sign near my street. I look over to Wes and watch him, and even though I know he can sense my eyes on him, he keeps his forward, his lips pursed—he's holding the truth in.

"It was from last night, wasn't it? When you had to drive so fast to catch Kyle?"

He doesn't answer, but after several long seconds, he pulls up to my house and exhales a heavy breath before looking at me. He doesn't *have* to answer. With that one look, I know.

"I'm sorry," I say.

"Don't be sorry. It's an old truck, and it was going to need some work soon anyway," he says.

The good feeling I had listening to Journey is gone. Now I just feel guilty. I step from the car and pull my bag of bandages and damp clothes out with me, rounding the truck and pepping myself up to turn and wave thanks. I'm not expecting Wes to be waiting outside his door when I get to him—but he is.

The motor is still running, the grind coming in waves. I understand why he's going to exchange the part today. The transmission isn't going to last much longer, and I know enough to understand that part is probably fairly important in the truck going anywhere at all.

"I'm really sorry, Wes," I say, not able to look up at him. His hand finds my chin quickly, righting my gaze back to his. His smile is warm and genuine, and it breaks me a little more.

"Joss, please…do not be sorry. It's an old truck. I swear," he says, his eyes willing me to accept what he says. He's lying. But he's lying for me. It makes me feel both worse and amazing all at once.

"Wes, what are you doing here?" My father's voice breaks through everything, and on instinct, I step away, like a child caught touching something expensive and breakable. At the last second, though, Wes reaches for my hand, clasping it and not letting go. My father's eyes see it.

"Hi, Coach. We had Joss over for lunch. I'm just bringing her home," he says, as if this is normal—as if me going to his house is a thing I do often, a thing my dad accepts. It isn't any of those things, and that's painfully clear in the expression on my father's face.

"That's thoughtful of you, Wes. Joss, I'm sure you have homework or something you're probably ignoring inside. Why don't you head in. I'm going to chat about our opening week of games with Wes for a few minutes," my dad says over his shoulder, his focus not really on me, more *at* me. His jaw is rigid, and his neck muscles are flexing.

"I don't have any homework," I sigh.

"And maybe that's part of your problem. She's got straight *Cs*," my dad answers quickly, almost proud to point out my faults and failures in front of Wes. I feel my gut clench, and I suppress my desire to argue with him.

"Sure it is," I say, biting my tongue on the rest.

I hold up a few fingers and mouth *thank you* to Wes as I shuffle my bare feet toward the house. I stop at the edge of the garage and open my bag to pull my damp shoes out to let them finish drying. I take the opportunity to study Wes and my dad, looking for clues on their conversation. It looks like they're only talking baseball, even though my instincts tell me they're probably talking about me.

Wes clutches his keys a few times and nods at my father, glancing at me when he can, his expression remaining the same. When my father places one hand on Wes's shoulder, patting him twice, I know their conversation is done, and I fumble with the knot in the plastic bag, trying to get my shoes out faster.

"What are you wasting your time with now?" my dad says, pulling the bag from my hands and making short work of the knot. He holds one of my wet shoes up and tilts his head.

"We had a water fight," I say, regretting sharing anything about my day with him the second the words leave my lips.

He sneers, letting a short puff of air escape his nostrils as he pulls out my second shoe, tossing both of them in the full sun of the driveway before handing the bag of clothes back to me.

"You should get a job, quit wasting your time on things that won't get you anywhere. Maybe it will make you focus on studying more too," he says, moving into the garage, toward the door to the house. He pauses to kick my softball bag further into the corner, out of his way. It feels like he's kicking me. "I'll pay your phone bill this month. Next month, it's on you. And Joss…"

I don't even bother to look up as my father turns. My name sounds like disappointment coming from his lips as he stands there, one foot already inside the house. I keep my eyes on my three-year-old bag of equipment that's falling apart, the handles taped together, one sewn to the bag with fishing line I got from Taryn's dad.

"Don't bring Wes down with your…drama. That boy's talented."

He doesn't expect me to answer. He expects me to obey. The door closes behind him, and I think about how I probably should follow his orders. But then I think about how I'm talented too, and the man who's supposed to believe in me couldn't give a damn about that.

Somewhere along the way…he forgot.

CHAPTER 7

"It won't be so bad, Joss. We'll get to work together sometimes too."

All morning, Taryn's been talking up the job she got me at Spider's Jungle Gym. She works there on Sundays, so when I called her yesterday afternoon, after the ultimatum from my dad, she put in a word with her manager before she left. All I have to do is fill out the application and drop it off this week and voila—the job is mine.

I guess I should be glad the process was easy. And the gig isn't anything hard. I have to run the party room, and then clean up the gym when they close three or four nights a week. As a bonus, my father won't be able to count on me on Saturdays anymore, because that's the biggest reason I got hired—they lost their Saturday person, and Taryn said I could fill the slot. I'm sure my dad will call anyway, but he'll have to wait. And maybe…just maybe…eventually he'll quit calling period.

"I know. Thanks for getting me the job, T. I was kinda thinking of getting one anyway. I guess I just hate that my dad put his foot down like that," I say, knowing it sounds whiney. It's not that I don't want to work, it's just that I don't understand the things my dad decides to care about when it comes to me.

"Girl, you know my dad made me get this job. I turned sixteen, and he was like, *hello* sweet sixteen and *goodbye* allowance," she laughs.

I smirk and lean into her while we carry our bags from the locker room toward the bus idling by the main field, our cleats scratching and clapping against the pavement. We have an away game with North today—not a far drive. Taryn's family is coming to watch. I like it when they come, because they usually cheer for me too. Without them, I'd have nobody in the stands.

The boys have a game at home, and as I step up onto the bus, I see Wes throwing his warm-up pitches in the bullpen, my father right behind him, measuring his speed with the gun.

I see Kyle run from the locker room to the field, and I'm relieved. He wasn't at school for most of the day, and he ignored the text I made Taryn send him. I'm still too uncomfortable to text him on my own; I don't know what to say. I'm glad he's here though. I didn't want him to miss his game. Even if he isn't pitching, I'm sure my dad will play him. Kyle's too good to leave on the bench.

Taryn and I shuttle our bags to the back and each take a seat in the rear of the bus. There are no senior girls on our varsity squad, so we're the oldest. We're also the toughest. I'm not sure how I became a leader, other than the rest of the girls were just natural followers. They still try to put braids in my hair, though, so I must not intimidate them too much. I succumbed to one ribbon today—our catcher, Shelby, insisted. I pulled the bow part out when she wasn't looking, so I'm only sporting two long strands of red ribbon now. I saw her notice, and I could tell she was itching to fix it. I don't know what I'll do if she touches my head again.

"Looks like Wes has a fan club today," Taryn says, nodding over my shoulder. I sit upright and turn to see McKenna and a few other girls walking out to the baseball field wearing shorty shorts, high socks, and red baseball jerseys.

"Whatever," I say, turning back and pulling my headphones from my bag, pushing them in my ears and cranking LCD Soundsystem up as loud as it will go. Taryn keeps her eyes on me, her lip twisted in a smirk. She knows I care more than I'm letting on, but I'm still not taking these earbuds out of my ears, and I'm not acknowledging Wes's entourage of hooker wannabes either.

I might be a little jealous.

My phone only has thirty percent left, so after a few songs, I turn the streaming music off, but I leave my headphones on for the rest of the trip so I don't have to answer any questions about Wes or McKenna…or my lunch at the Stokes house. That's the problem with Taryn dating TK—he told her I was there Sunday, and when I didn't mention it to her, she called me on it, eyebrow raised, arms crossed, and suspicion and teasing twinkling in her eyes. I'll have to answer her questions eventually, but not before our game—and not on a bus full of over-excited freshmen and sophomores who would absolutely *die* knowing Joss Winters has fucking fluttering going on in her tummy over a boy.

I put my phone and earbuds away when we get to North's campus, and Taryn and I are the last two off the bus. The North girls are supposed to be pretty good this year, and our team's young. I'm anticipating getting our asses kicked, but I plan on standing out.

Coach has me at shortstop, and after we unpack, stretch, and warm up, we take infield. For the first time all day, I feel all stress and anger leave my body. It's a team sport, but when I'm out here, I'm on my own. Nobody tells me what to do—they just let me *be*. I field cleanly, turn my double plays, and even make a diving grab that gets the attention of the other bench. I can see them whispering about me, and that makes me excited. I get off on their fear—I live to intimidate.

I am home.

It's an honor to bat fourth. That's what my dad used to say. When the first three girls strike out, though—and we can't seem to get an out to save our lives so I can get back up to bat—being fourth in the lineup kinda feels more like a curse. Our only outs are the two balls hit to me, until finally someone reaches for a slow pitch and pops it up to Shelby. I'm almost willing to let her retie the bow in my hair I'm so happy she caught the damn thing.

North has one of the best pitchers in the state, and she's throwing hard. I notice a few men in college jackets sitting on the front row of the bleachers right behind the backstop, all of them with speed guns in their hands and cell phones in the other. I hope their cameras are rolling when I'm up to bat, because I plan on disrupting her seventy-mile-per-hour strike fest.

I step into the box and take two balls before she throws a strike, and I purposely let that one go by. I didn't like it.

Don't swing at just any strike, pumpkin; swing at the right one.

As broken as we are, my father's words run through my head every time I touch the ball and my feet hit the dirt. I will never get away from him completely; he and I are woven together in this game I love. It's the hours together in the back yard of me throwing the ball incorrectly, and him training my arm to do it the right way. It's the moment I swung the bat and finally made contact. It's the first home run I had in T-ball when he carried me from the field on his shoulders. Like listening to Journey, playing this game reminds me of when everything was good. And as bad as he turned out to be as a father, he was always one hell of a coach.

The right pitch comes along next, and I see it before it leaves her fingertips. I shift my weight and cock my arms, loading my swing so by the time the ball reaches the plate, I hit it so far I don't even have to look to know it's gone.

Home run.

I hear the ump say the word, but in my head, it's my father's voice. I round the bases and let my teammates hug and jump on me once I step on home plate. I celebrate with them, and I talk shit with Taryn about how I plan on doing that again.

I only get to bat two more times, thanks to the falling sun and the absolutely pitiful fielding by my teammates, who seem hell bent on letting the other team run up the score. But I get on base both times—two doubles, right up the center, and just low enough that the pitcher gets scared. I blow a kiss to Taryn after my third hit, and the ump gives me a warning. I'm used to warnings, though, so when he turns his back, I blow one to him.

We end up losing twelve to two, but I hold my head high knowing those two—they're *me.* The ride home feels lighter, and I don't feel the need to hide behind my music and headphones. I even give in and let Shelby loop the bow correctly in my hair. It seems to make her happy, and when Taryn makes fun of me, I tell her not to shit on my girl Shelby's bow-tying skills. Shelby smiles and lights up at the fact that I call her my girl. I love that I seem to matter to these girls—to all of them. They should hate me, but they don't.

"Looks like the guys are still going," Taryn says, and at first, I'm not sure what she means. A few girls in front of us push down their windows and whistle out toward the field, and I turn to look out mine, seeing Kyle now on the mound.

"He must be closing," I say to Taryn, gesturing to our friend.

"TK is so fucking hot in those pants," she responds, not even hearing me. I laugh because…yeah, of course, that's what she notices.

We climb from the bus, and Taryn, Shelby, and I walk toward the bleachers for the baseball field, dumping our stuff on the ground and climbing up to the seats in the back. We had maybe a dozen fans watching our game, but the baseball team attracts at least a hundred every game. I get it; I'd be here too, if I didn't have a game of my own to play.

Kyle is throwing hard, and the score is four to three—us. My dad is in his lucky spot, crouched down in the catcher's position at the front of the dugout, hands moving quickly from his ear to his nose to his knee. He's giving the catcher signs. If I wanted to ruin his day, I could walk over to the other dugout bleachers and call them all out. They'd know every pitch Kyle was about to throw.

But I wouldn't do that to Kyle. And this is Levi's first game catching, so I wouldn't want to screw him over either. If I'm being honest, there's also still a small part of the little girl I used to be deep down inside of me—and she likes to see her daddy win…even if I won't be acknowledged in the celebration.

It's the first batter of the last inning; Kyle lets one slide into the zone, and the batter rips a line drive to TK. He handles it easily though for the out, and Taryn squeals like a Pee Wee football cheerleader.

"Wow, if you're gonna do that, I'm watching from over here," I say, pointing to the other end of the dugout where the bleachers end. She rolls her eyes at me and continues to jump up and down.

I leave her with Shelby, but not because I'm embarrassed. I recognized Wes's form almost immediately, his body leaning in the corner against the fencing of the dugout wall. I'm dying to know how he did. I'm also dying to put myself between the view of him and the front row of the bleachers taken up by his giggling fan club. I walk in front of them on purpose, and I take special care to give McKenna a tight smile as I pass by.

"Still hoping Daddy will let you play with the boys, Josselyn?" She immediately breaks out into laughter with her friends.

My blood pressure rises from her taunt, but I check it quickly, spinning on my heels to walk backward and look at her. "I can play with *these* boys anytime I want, McKenna," I say, and I move to turn back, feeling satisfied.

"Not *every* boy, you can't. Why don't you ask Wes about the beach this weekend?" she says.

The whispers and snickering pick up quickly, but I don't let myself turn around again. If I weren't already almost to the corner of the dugout wall, I'd go back to my original seat. But I don't want McKenna to have any power, to know that her words matter to me. They shouldn't, but they do.

"Hey," Wes's voice comes out raspy. "I was hoping you guys would get back in time. I made it six innings. I gave up a home run, though. Seems they can still see my changeup."

"Ah, so now we're admitting it's a changeup and not a slider, are we?" I say, linking my fingers through the small bit of chain-link fencing between us. I can still feel McKenna's eyes on me, and I hate that I'm letting her get to me.

"I admit nothing," Wes says, wincing when he shifts his weight and moves the ice pack around his arm. "I threw you a slider. You just hit that too."

His lip curves on one side as his head tilts up just enough that I can see his eyes under his hat. Even the red-and-white South High Toro uniform looks perfect on this boy.

"Looks like Kyle's taking care of business, though," I say, resting my head against the fence. We both look out to the mound to see Kyle strike out the second batter. They're one out away from a win—Wes's first win.

"Honestly, I think he's better than me. He should have started," Wes says, not looking back at me for a reaction. He didn't say that just to be nice. He said that because he meant it.

"He's not," I say, waiting Wes out until he finally meets my eyes. He stares at me with a serious look, not believing me. "Really, my dad wouldn't do you any favors just to make you feel welcome because you're new or whatever. My dad plays to win—no matter what."

After a few seconds, Wes nods in agreement and slowly takes the ice pack from his arm, hissing as if it's painful.

"You get hurt?" I ask.

"Nah. I could probably throw tomorrow. Honestly? I always hate the icing down shit we have to do. Cold hurts way worse," he says through a light laugh, standing and tossing his ice pack in the cooler. He pulls on his sweatshirt, and I let myself admire the way he runs his fingers through his messy hair before putting his hat back on.

"You ever really throw out your shoulder or elbow—and I bet you won't think the ice is so bad," I say, thinking how I should probably heed my own advice. I never ice my muscles, for the same reason Wes hates doing it. Cold sucks.

"Yeah, you're probably right," he says, stepping up on the bench and sitting on the seat back, bringing himself closer to me.

I glance back at his fan row on the bleachers, and only McKenna is watching. She's pretending not to. I recognize it, because that's how I look at Wes—while pretending not to.

"So…your *fan* over there mentioned something about taking you to the beach?" My stomach hurts the second I let the poor excuse for fishing for information leave my mouth. Since the moment she mentioned it, my mind worked for a natural way to ask Wes about it, to find out if it's a date with her or anything remotely like she wants me to believe it is. I feel stupid asking, and I'm scared to find out his response.

"Oh, yeah..." he says, standing and not finishing his answer. I'm hanging on his words, but he's on his feet against the other side of the dugout, watching, because the other team's big hitter just hit a fly ball deep to right field. Our fielder is tracking it, all the way to the fence, and at the last minute, he lifts himself up, reaching over the top and snagging the ball out of the air.

"Hell yeah!" Wes shouts, pumping his fist in the air and running from the dugout, piling with the rest of his team and lifting Kyle up in a bear hug. It's the most animated I've ever seen Wes Stokes. He's also celebrating Kyle, giving him full credit. I have a feeling though, he had more to do with that win. Six innings is a lot.

The team moves back toward the dugout, and I stand in my place feeling more awkward and out-of-place by the second. I'd join Shelby and Taryn, but they're already walking down the bleachers toward me—along with McKenna and her friends.

In all of the chaos of social circles colliding, I've somehow missed my father stepping into the dugout, and when I turn back expecting to see Wes, I'm a little surprised to see his tired face staring back at me. He has a toothpick in his mouth, a thing he does at school because he can't chew tobacco here. The king of all hypocrites, he chastises me for picking up smoking yet spends a minor fortune on Skoal.

"You win?" he asks.

"No. Regina Foles pitched. Most of the team couldn't hit her," I say, my eyes staring at the worn toothpick, splinters actually coming apart where the wood meets my father's teeth. He must have been stressed.

"You hit her?" he asks, pulling the pick from his mouth and tossing it on the ground. I'm a little surprised by his interest in my game, so it takes me a second or two to answer.

"Yeah," I say, and when I meet his eyes, for a brief second there, I see pride.

"Good, you shouldn't let speed scare you at the plate," he says, giving his attention over to TK and Levi when they come in and threaten to dump the cooler of ice water over his head. "Now I know you're not gonna dump that on me after only one game, right? You make it to the end, win us a pennant, then you can start lifting coolers. Any sooner, and you'll be spending some serious time out here running bases."

TK flashes a look at me quickly, and I nod once with a tight-lipped smile to confirm my father isn't kidding. He's never kidding when it comes to winning.

"Sorry sir," TK says, setting the cooler down and turning his focus to picking up his gear and cleaning out the dugout.

"Punk little shits win one game and they think they've got something to celebrate," my father says at me, his eyes out at the parking lot beyond my shoulder. I don't respond. He's not asking for one. His opinion and method for winning is something he's *always* right about.

"I went three for three," I say instead, not sure why I felt the need to prove myself to him, but for the first time in a long time, I wanted to tell him about my game. His eyes snap to mine quickly, but his expression remains flat.

"You should. You hit any over?" he asks.

"One," I say, my hands flexing at the memory of the crack of the ball against my bat before it sailed over the fence. I start to smile, when my dad cuts our conversation short.

"You can do better," he says, patting his hand against the brick of the dugout. With that, he grabs his clipboard from the nail on the wall and walks out across the field back to his office.

"He just meant you're our best player, that's all," Taryn says, immediately going into *make-Joss-feel-better mode*.

"No he didn't," I sigh. "He meant I'm not good enough. It's fine. Whatever."

Before I get too deep in my pity party, Kyle comes around the wall, wrapping one arm around my stomach and swinging me up over his shoulder, spinning me a few times.

"I'm gonna throw up, dude. Don't!" I yell through my laughter. Kyle and I haven't talked for a couple days, and when he sets me down, the tension I feel when I look at him is heavy. Before it's too strong to handle though, I register the dark bruising around his eye, and suddenly all of my anxiety is replaced with worry for my friend.

"Kyle, oh my god!" I say, reaching a hand up to his face. He catches it in his own and shakes his head.

"I'm fine, I'm fine," he says, pulling his cap from his head and running his arm across his forehead. He drops my hand and puts his hat back on with both hands before bringing his face square with mine again. The bruise looks fresh, and I wonder if it happened during the game.

"Did you take a line drive or something? I thought you only pitched the last inning?" I'm trying to reach for him, and he's still backing away, when all three Stokes brothers walk up to join us.

"Wes hit him in the locker room, right before the game," Levi says, a giant grin on his face at getting to be the one to tattle on his brother.

Boys.

"He...*hit you?*" I ask, my gaze bouncing between Wes and Kyle. They both look sheepish—lips pursed, and shoulders raised.

"He sure did. Kyle was late to the field because of it, and coach made him run down to the canal and back before the game," TK says.

"Yeah, sorry about that man. I didn't mean for you to be late," Wes says, his gear at his feet and his glove still on one hand.

Wes pulls his hand free and drops his mitt on the ground, stepping in front of us all and holding a hand out to Kyle. "I'm sorry. That was a cheap shot. We all good now?" he says.

Kyle studies his hand for a few seconds, and I notice his jaw flex in a way that probably *only* I would recognize. He's nervous. I'm not sure if he's afraid Wes is going to hit him again, or if it's something else entirely, but he's uneasy about accepting this truce. He does, though, shaking Wes's hand, his grip tight. Before they part, Kyle grabs Wes's forearm with his other hand, stopping their shake until Wes looks him in the eye.

"Just so we're clear here, I know I deserved that. I hear you. Won't happen again," Kyle says, this time causing Wes to flinch, his eyes twitching the slightest bit as his tongue pushes at the inside of his cheek.

Finally, he blinks and nods at Kyle before glancing to me as he picks up his gear and walks to the locker room.

McKenna and the few other girls who have stayed with her rush to catch up to him, and my eyes go right to her, counting every time she brushes his arm, flips her hair, laughs, and does all of those stereotypical perfect-girl-things that are stereotypical for a reason. I wish I knew what Wes thought of it…of *her*.

"You gonna tell me what that was all about?" I say to Kyle, my eyes still on my crush a hundred yards in front of us.

Crush. I have a crush.

"He told me if I ever put you in harm's way again, he'll kill me. And I agreed to let him," Kyle says, bringing my eyes to him instantly. Kyle doesn't add anything more, instead, just looking at me for long seconds while I stare back at him wide-eyed and afraid. Finally, he laughs out a breath to himself, then bends down to pick up his things, grabbing mine too.

"What's funny?" I ask, folding my arms over my chest while we walk— until I realize exactly how it looks when I'm pouting. I release my hold and instead move my thumbs to my back pockets, splitting my attention between Wes in front of me and Kyle beside me.

"Nothing's funny, Joss. This isn't funny at all," he says, his eyes straight ahead. "I just realized that I'm never going to get you to look at me like you look at him. What's worse is I'm totally okay with it. Wes…he's the kind of guy you deserve. And maybe I just love you enough to want you to have it all. Fuckin' hurts though; not gonna lie about that."

I slow my pace at his words until eventually I stop. Kyle makes it a dozen or so feet ahead of me before stopping and exhaling, the weight of both of our bags sagging his shoulders. He never turns toward me, but tilts his face to the sky so I can hear his words.

"Don't feel bad. I'll get over it," he says, glancing just enough to the side that I can see the ache in his eyes. "Now come on, let me take your ass home."

I catch up to my friend and help him load our things in his father's truck. I wave to Taryn in the distance, letting her know I have a ride and that she can take TK in her car. Levi and Wes are just pulling away from the lot, McKenna between them in the cab of their truck, and the other girls cackling in the bed. I don't really know any of those girls, but I hate them.

"Your dad let you use his truck, huh?" I say, wanting to just pretend things are normal, that they *could* be normal, after the words Kyle just said.

"Yeah…sorta," Kyle sighs, starting the engine and finally twisting to look at me. He's forcing a smile, but his eyes tell the true story. They look heartbroken. "He's buying a new one, but I have to work off the debt on this. Looks like you and I will *both* be taking on shifts at Jungle Gym."

I smile at the thought of working there with Kyle, even though it feels different now than how it would have before. "Really? You call in a favor with Taryn too?" I ask.

"Yep," he says, eyebrows raised as he turns his attention back to the front, putting the truck in reverse and pulling out of our spot. "We might have a few shifts together. But I'm the lucky early-morning snack-bar guy. I get to make all those awesome boiled hotdogs and fill those cups of processed cheese at five every morning before I haul my ass to school."

"I might be a little jealous," I laugh, clicking my belt and putting my feet up on his dashboard so I can untie my cleats.

"I thought you might be. I know how you like shitty-ass nacho cheese," he says, feigning serious. Neither of us ever breaks into a laugh, but we both know we're kidding. It's almost normal between us, even though deep down, it will probably never quite be normal again.

CHAPTER 8

I stuck to riding with Taryn for the rest of the week. I also stayed on my own ball field, avoiding venturing over to the baseball side during practice and after games. It kept me away from Wes, and it kept me away from the uncomfortable feeling that now accompanies being near Kyle. Most importantly, I avoided the entire nightmare that is standing between Wes *and* Kyle while McKenna looks on.

I smoked a cigarette this morning with Taryn on our way to school. I blame all of this girl drama. I'm back to zero days of no smoking in a row. I might just chalk today up to a total loss and smoke one on the way home too. I'm walking, because riding with Kyle just stresses me out too much now, and Taryn took off to her empty house with TK.

My father passes me in his car, never once slowing down as he pulls out of the faculty lot in front of me. There's no way he doesn't see me. I'm the reason the crosswalk is blinking. Of course, he ignores the YIELD and blows through the stop anyhow.

It was Friday, light practice, and we were done by four, which apparently is why the beach plan was hatched. I heard about it, but I haven't been formally invited. All of my friends are either going or have plans on their own, so it looks like I could have started my job at the Jungle Gym tonight—like Mike, the boss, originally asked.

There's forty bucks missed out on.

Wes and Levi drove out before my father left. They turned right out of the lot, toward the main highway, which means they're going to Pismo along with everyone else. I will be walking home to the left, to the home I used to sprint to as a kid—the place I couldn't wait to be. Now it's just the place my dad stores his liquor and I go to sleep when I don't have anywhere else to go.

"Are you seriously moping?" Kyle's voice breaks into my pity party, and I cringe because I'm going to have to talk to him—and yes, I was in fact moping.

"I'm just tired," I say, shrugging.

"You're a shitty liar. Get your ass in my truck. I'll go pick up Conner and Layla, and I'll drop you off at your house so you can change," he says, reaching across the long seat to push the passenger door open. I just look inside without moving.

"Change for what?" I ask, knowing what, but putting off excuses as long as possible because…well…I need to think of one.

"Don't play that with me. You can bullshit other people all you want, Joss, but you and I both know you're pissed about McKenna, and the beach, and you want to be there. This act is just your front because you're pissed Wes didn't ask you. But you know what? It wasn't Wes's thing. This whole bonfire idea was McKenna's…and she doesn't *want* you there, which is exactly why you should go. So can we cut through ten minutes of you lying to me and pretending like you're not going to end up there tonight anyway and just get moving?"

I do my best to look tough, but my exterior cracks quickly, and my tight lips stretch into a smile with a breath of a laugh.

"You're a fucking dick, Kyle. You know that?" I say, throwing my gear and backpack in the truck bed and climbing into the seat next to him.

"Yeah, you've called me that before too. Whatevs. I'm right, and you know it," he says.

The sense of awkwardness kicks in after a minute, and the reason I avoided Kyle comes screaming back. I glance at him as he drives to my house, but he works hard never to turn his face enough that his eyes catch sight of me. His discomfort is all over his face, and I feel guilty. I'm kind of mad at him that I feel guilty, which I know isn't really fair. You can't help feelings, but Kyle is me—I need my other half. And when he opened his mouth, I feel like he took that half away, because I didn't feel the same way he did.

"You can quit looking at me with pity too," he finally says. I crack a smile.

"I wouldn't dream of pitying you," I say. I mean it. *No, I don't.*

"Look, you and I—we've been friends for a long time. And I'm not stupid…ah…don't you contradict that," he says, holding up a hand. I laugh, because he caught me—I was about to give him shit. "I'm not throwing away my best friend just because she doesn't love me *that way*. I meant what I said before—I'll figure this out, get over it, or whatever. But you can't ignore me and avoid me on top of it. That shit just hurts, and it's mean. Like, meaner than your normal mean to me."

We both sit in silence as I stare at him and watch his eyes dart around traffic, his jaw twitching as he chews at the side of his mouth. Finally, I breathe, and while the awkwardness is still there, it does somehow feel a little less.

"You called me mean, dude. That hurts…right here," I say, pounding my fist on my chest.

"Yeah, well, you can be a real bitch too. How's that for ya?" he says, his familiar teasing tone back.

I punch him in the leg and he swerves a little because of it.

"Oww! Fuck, Joss!" he chuckles, but he grows serious quickly, righting his hands on the wheel and sitting up straighter. "Don't do that shit when I drive. I meant what I said to Wes too. I'm not going to do risky shit like that with you anymore. It scared me too much."

This time, the weight I feel is different, the guilt different. The accident wasn't Kyle's fault entirely. I didn't have to climb out his window.

"Why are you taking me to the beach?" I whisper my question.

Kyle glances at me a few times before looking forward again, his brow furrowed as he turns down my street.

"Why, Kyle? You know I only want to go because of Wes. You even said so. Why are you helping? Is it because you feel guilty about the accident and you want him to not hate you for it? Or because you feel guilty about me getting hurt?"

I hold my breath and wait for his answer as his truck stops in front of my house. I look over to my driveway long enough to register that my dad's car is gone.

"Maybe a little of everything," Kyle says, his arms gliding down to the bottom of the wheel as he sits back in his seat. He tilts his head to the side to take me in, and after a few seconds, he laughs a breath through his nose and shrugs. "And I also think McKenna's a bitch."

I let my grin slide into place and linger before moving my hand over to take Kyle's. I squeeze it once, memorizing my hand on his, then move my gaze back up to his genuine smile waiting for me.

"I do love you, you know," I say, my chest hurting when he takes a harsh, deep breath that lets me know he knows exactly what I mean— exactly how I love him. It's not the same as his love for me, but it's still real.

"Yeah, yeah," he says, shifting in his seat and pushing the gear into park. "Go get your ass changed. I'll be back in ten minutes."

I nod and climb out the passenger side, reaching over and grabbing my things from his truck, patting the side of the bed when I'm done to let him know he can leave. He doesn't look back when he drives away, but I watch just in case.

Within the few minutes Kyle is gone, I manage to go through seven possible outfits. I'm not good at this kind of stuff, and I wish I had Taryn here to help me with it. I finally settle on my original choice: my rolled-up loose jeans with holes in the knees, my Vans, and my black bikini top. I grab my white sweater to wear when the sun sets and the temperatures fall into the fifties, then sprint out to Kyle's truck with my small backpack to hold my phone, wallet, and knit cap. I haven't earned a dime from my new job, so the only cash I have on hand is in quarters.

"That's what you're wearing? " Kyle says, nodding to my sweater when

I climb into his truck. Layla and Conner snuggle together in the small half-seat in the back.

"What? It gets cold at night," I protest. He doesn't shift gears and keeps his stare on me, his forehead wrinkled as he waits on the brink of laughing at me. "Damn…fine. I'll take it off," I say, stepping out of the truck for a few seconds to pull my sweater away.

I climb back in and shove the sweater into my backpack, then buckle my safety belt before looking back at Kyle, who still hasn't shifted into drive. This time he's staring at me with his eyebrows high, so I hold my palms out in front of me. "Jesus…what?"

"Nothing," he says, spinning to the front, shifting into drive and swallowing hard. We drive for a mile or two before he finishes his thought. "It's just McKenna isn't going to know what to do. No way she looks like *that* in any damn swimsuit she shows up in."

My cheeks burn instantly. I'm not used to boys noticing things like that about me. I get noticed for being tough, for throwing hard, for being Eric Winter's daughter, and walking the line between good and bad, often venturing beyond it. I do not get noticed for being beautiful.

"Thanks," I say, my teeth nibbling at my bottom lip while my fingers play with the zipper at the top of my bag.

When I glance back at Kyle, he holds my gaze for a beat and rubs his hand over his mouth and chin, finally nodding slowly, returning his focus back to the road. He keeps it there for the next hour and a half, and we all let the music and Conner's bad jokes fill in the empty space all the way to Pismo Beach.

We pull up next to Wes's truck, and I can't help but start searching for him the moment my feet hit the sand. I walk with the Marley boys and Layla to the fire pit about a hundred yards away from the waterline. Kyle brought an old blanket, and I help him stretch it out so we have a place to leave all of our things. My attention is constantly elsewhere though. I'm searching.

I don't find Wes, but I do find Taryn and TK, and I can't help but feel the sting of my best girlfriend ditching me to come here. I walk up to her and before TK can warn her, I cover her eyes with my hands.

"Guess who?" I say, doing my best to put on a flowery, girly voice full of pep and cheer.

"Joss, I can read right through whatever accent you think that is. Besides, your fingers always feel different," she says, stepping out of my hold. I pull my hands in front of me and look them over, a little ashamed of the calluses and short nails with dirt underneath.

"So were you going to tell me you went to the bonfire *after* it was all over? Or were you just going to hope it never came up?" I'm standing with my hand on my hip when McKenna walks by, pausing to talk to one of her friends near me, her pose exactly the same. I let my arm fall free and shift my stance accordingly.

"I'm just as pissed that I'm here as you are. Believe me," she says, kicking her feet free of her sneakers and holding them between us to dump out the sand. Her eyes flit to mine as she purses her lips. "My parents cancelled their getaway. They decided they wanted to spend their anniversary at home instead, having movie night with me…and my new *fella.*"

I can't help but laugh, and she rolls her eyes at me when I do, stomping over to the blanket we brought and dropping her shoes on the corner next to mine. "We were about to…*you know*…when my parents came barreling through the door with movies and steaks and plans. I snuck TK out through the garage door and when my parents told me their plan, I apologized and said I'd already told TK I'd come to the beach with him."

"Aw, that's sweet they wanted to spend their special day with you, though," I say, my smile tight and holding back the floodgate of laughter.

"Yeah, great. Now I'm a bad daughter *and* I'm sexually frustrated," she says, folding her arms and huffing. She frowns until TK moves his arms around her and kisses at her neck from behind.

"This beach plan ain't *so* bad," he says, his eyes moving to me with a quick wink.

"Yeah, I guess not," she giggles, turning into him until their lips lock and I'm forgotten.

I excuse myself quickly and walk over to where Kyle and Conner are standing with Levi. My stomach tightens because Wes isn't with his brothers. It means he's somewhere else—with *someone* else. And it doesn't take me long to spot him.

Wes isn't standing next to her, but he's close enough that she occasionally reaches forward while she talks, touching his arm and kicking at his legs as she laughs. He doesn't seem interested, honestly. But he also doesn't seem to move.

One of McKenna's friends drives one of those giant Jeeps, and they've pulled it partially into the sand from the parking lot. I've seen people get busted for doing that before, but I have a feeling, with my luck, nobody will be patrolling by foot here tonight. And even if they were, I bet McKenna would bat her lashes and manage to worm her way out of any ticket or trouble for her friend.

The Jeep has a big speaker in the back, and that's what's sending the music over our growing crowd. The bonfire isn't really lit yet, but the spots near it are already getting taken up by blankets and towels as people claim their space. I hope McKenna's towel catches on fire when they finally light it.

I'm not being bashful about my stare, and when Wes looks my direction, I don't move, instead raising my hand to the side and offering a stiff wave with my eyebrows high. Wes sets his cup down on the back of the Jeep and says something to McKenna, which causes her to turn and glare at me as he walks my direction. My stomach both sinks and beats with my heart's rhythm at the same time.

"Hey," he says, glancing back at McKenna, whose eyes are locked on us like lasers. I lean sideways beyond his profile to make eye contact with her and hold my hand out in an overly-enthusiastic wave. Her brow lowers as she picks up his discarded cup and begins to follow in his footsteps toward us.

"Your date's a little pissed off that you abandoned her," I say. When he bunches his forehead at me, I nod over his shoulder so he can see McKenna's angry stomp in our direction.

"She's not my date," he chuckles.

I start to smile and breathe deep, but it's cut short when McKenna steps up to his side and slides her arm through his, handing him his cup.

"You forgot your drink, babe," she says.

Wes quirks an eyebrow at her, but takes the cup from her hand. "Uh, thanks," he says, glancing up at me. I'm waiting with my smug grin, sorry to be right.

"Hey, Joss!" Levi yells, and I turn to give him my full attention. He's holding a bat in his hand and a giant mushball in the other. "Whataya say? Quick game?"

"Hells yeah!" I say, ditching Wes and the bitch he says isn't his date.

Taryn and I are the only girls who decide to join the game, and I insist we play on the same team. Levi gets mad when Kyle picks me first, so to protest, he convinces Wes to join his team. With teams of six settled, we toss a coin to see who hits first, and Levi wins. I offer to pitch, because it's mushball, and there isn't much to it other than tossing it underhand near the batter. Kyle's fast, and we need him to catch and field the ball—he knows he can throw it to me at home plate.

I aim as Levi steps up next to the folded towel we use for our plate, and he hits the first pitch I throw. The heavy ball doesn't go as far as a normal one, but Kyle still has to dive to make the catch.

"Keep that up, and I'll tell coach you're good at that shit. He'll have your ass in center," Levi taunts. Kyle runs his hand under his chin lightly, giving Levi the finger.

Wes steps up next, and I do my best to ignore the way he's looking at me. I throw three pitches and he lets them all go by, so before I throw the fourth, I walk up to him and hold the ball out for him to examine.

"Those are all hittable. Don't be a prick," I say.

"I'm not being a prick," he says, letting the bat drop to his shoulder as his head tilts down to meet my eyes.

"Then hit the damn ball," I say, challenging him.

"You're standing too close," he says.

"Fuck that. I'm standing just fine. Now swing," I say, spinning around and walking back to the line in the sand.

Wes sighs, then drops the end of his bat against the towel.

"Pitch it with an arc so I can hit it over you," he says.

"Screw you. You don't get to call your own pitch," I say, throwing the ball flat and level. He lets it sail by him, and Taryn catches it then tosses it back to me.

"I don't want to hit you, Joss," he says, the bat once again slumped on his shoulder.

"If you hit me, I'll catch it," I say.

Several long seconds pass as we stare at each other in this standoff of the sexes. I'm making it about that. But I know it's also about *more* than that. Wes legitimately doesn't want to hurt me. I'm getting ready to step into my windup, even though he isn't ready, and I'm going to lob one in with an arc, just like he requested, when McKenna actually cheers for him.

"Come on, Wes baby. You can do this!"

Baby.

I rear back and heave the mushball toward Taryn, another flat pitch. Wes shakes his head as it passes.

"If we had an umpire, you'd have struck out looking," I say, clapping my hands in request of the ball. Taryn tosses it back to me, and I repeat the same pitch.

"Steeee-rike!" I shout. I'm almost pleased when Wes sighs, his chest falling with his disappointment in my behavior.

"Come on, Joss. Do you want me to pitch? Just give him what he wants!" Kyle shouts from several feet behind me.

I refuse though, and I pitch another ball exactly the same way. Wes lets four more pass—but every time, I see his muscles flexing more, his bat lowering, his body weight shifting and getting ready. I'm pissing him off, and I like it.

Finally, I send one to him, throwing it hard and fast, a dream pitch if it weren't a soft mushball, and Wes boils over, swinging his bat through its center, slamming the heavy canvas ball straight at my chest.

My reaction happens in milliseconds—the ball slowing as it spins in

146

the air, the trajectory right at me. I ready my hands and slide a fraction of a step to the right, giving my arms room to cushion the impact of the ball in my fingers, and when I blink, it's in my hands.

"You're out," I say, tossing the ball a few times in the air. Wes steps away from the makeshift home plate and tosses the bat end over end into the sand.

"This is all such bullshit," he mutters to himself. I start to feel guilty for pushing things so far, but then McKenna jogs over to him and places her hands on his shoulders, squeezing and giving him a massage, and my guilt vanishes.

We quickly get one more out and then it's our turn to bat. Levi's team isn't as strong. All six of us get on base safely. We're on our second pass through the lineup and the sun is cresting along the water, threatening to take away the last few rays of light and end our game. Wanting one more chance, I step up to the plate and hit the ball quickly, running to first, where Wes is playing, and sliding into the towel base when Levi misses his throw.

He swings his arm around a few times, making an excuse, like his arm is sore before complaining that he's not used to throwing balls this size.

"You got schooled by a chick," I tease.

"Ah, come on. Are you seriously telling me that a mushball is anything like a baseball? Please," he says. He bends down and picks up a rounded rock from the sand, tossing it a few times before looking back at me. "I bet if I threw this, I could strike out your boy Kyle."

"In your dreams," Kyle laughs, tapping his bat on the towel and gearing up as if he's really going to hit.

"Yeah, okay. But I know I could strike out Conner," Levi says.

"How much?" Conner says, standing from his comfortable spot in the sand. He brushes the grains from his shorts and stretches his arms, taking the bat from his brother.

"Twenty bucks," Levi smirks.

"Guys, this is a bad idea. We can hardly see," Wes says.

"I see just fine," I talk over him, ignoring his presence next to me even though I can hear the way his body shifts and his posture changes in his frustration with me.

"You're on," Levi says, moving to his pitching stance.

Conner steps to the plate, and Kyle picks up one of the folding chairs from nearby, aligning it so Levi has something to aim for. He throws the first one, and it sails by Conner, his swing almost a second late.

"I was getting my timing down," Conner jokes, reaching his arms behind his back and twisting a few times.

"Yeah, sure you were," Levi snorts.

Kyle tosses the rock back to him, and Levi readies himself to pitch again. This time, his delivery is slower. Conner's swing is a little faster. Both of them adapt just enough that the metal clings against the rock, and just like that—nobody knows where it went.

Nobody.

Except Wes.

And me.

His eyes find mine quickly.

My heart is racing.

My eyes are tearing, and every breath is coming out with a hard force through my nose.

"Shit, I don't even see it!" Conner says, running slowly around the bases in celebration.

"How the fuck did you hit that?" Levi says, kicking at the sand, spraying grains in the air around him. "Shit!"

"Twenty bucks, buddy. Twenty bucks!" Conner shouts, his hands held over his head as he rounds the last base, pumping his right fist in the air.

I swallow hard and allow myself to blink once—quickly—for fear I'll miss something, a sleight of hand or illusion. I know what I saw, though. The rock sailed off Conner's bat and was going to hit me between my eyes. There wasn't time to move. No time to react. There was only enough time for my brain to register that pain was coming my way—and it was going to be bad.

"Let me see your hand," I say to Wes, my voice low and even, so the others don't hear.

"No," he says, his jaw growing rigid and his eyes shadowing as they look at me.

"Show me. I know what I saw, Wes. Show me," I say.

Our group is already picking the towels up and moving toward the bonfire. Wes takes his eyes off me long enough to bend down and lift the towel near us, and when he stands, I ask him again.

"What's in your hand, Wes?"

This time he doesn't say a word. He takes a step closer to me, and with his height against mine, he's looking down on me. There's a towel in one hand and a fist hiding a secret on his other side. His lips are in a hard line, and I'm sure the hazed expression in his eyes is meant as a warning.

"Wes…" I begin to challenge. He shakes his head.

"Don't…" he grits his teeth, shutting his eyes slowly, his chest exhaling every bit of air in his lungs.

"How did you do that?" I ask, moving past the proof. I don't need it; I know what I saw.

"I did nothing, Joss," he says, stepping even closer, so close that I'm unable to see anything but him now. My hand moves to his chest, and I press my palm flat against his soft, blue T-shirt just to feel him breathe. I watch my fingers spread as my hand stretches to cover the center of him, struggling to feel the beat of his heart over the pulse of my own blood pumping through my fingertips.

Slowly, deliberately, I move my hand to the right, my fingers running along his hard chest, his shoulder, and down his bicep until I meet the bare skin of his forearm and eventually his wrist.

"Wes," I say quietly. His name comes out as a plea for him to trust me. I have to see it. I need this—the confirmation. I don't know what it means, or why I'm fighting so hard for him to give in, but my heart is telling me one thing, and my head needs to make sense of it.

I look up, and when I do, Wes's eyes are waiting for me. I stare into them, ignoring my name being called a hundred feet away from us. The waves pound, and the air grows chilly as the last piece of the sun falls away. I ignore it all. There's only Wes. And as his eyes fall to the place where my hand touches his wrist, I follow him, whispering a wish.

"Show me," I say.

He turns his hand over within mine, relinquishing his fingers one at time until eventually the smooth orange stone slides from his grasp and falls to our feet. My breath falters, and as much as I want to grab the rock and hide it, I can't move.

"Wes, are you coming?" McKenna's voice breaks into this dream—our own private dream. She's an invader, and I hate her instantly. My eyes flash to Wes's, and his expression is blank.

"Be right there," he responds, never once pulling his eyes away from me.

We're bathed in dusk's cloak of darkness and far enough away that our words are only ours. Now is the time to ask. Now is the time to tell the truth.

"Tell me," I say, my lips trembling with hope.

Wes's name is called behind me, and his eyes move to the sound briefly before coming back to me. He was almost there. I know it. I felt it.

Christopher.

But that small break from my gaze—it was enough.

"There's nothing to tell, Joss," he says, his face back to its rehearsed and empty expression as he steps around me, walking into the light of the embers over the pile of wood in the center of my circle of friends.

He goes right to McKenna, and she doesn't hesitate to tuck herself under his arm—my only relief the fact that he seems so awkward with her, his hand not quite closed around her shoulder, his fingers stiff and straight.

You're still here…with me.

I wait in the darkness until Wes breaks away from her to join his brothers. I see Taryn looking for me, so I jog closer and catch up with my friend, urging her to walk with me toward the truck with the keg in the back. We step up just behind McKenna, and even though Taryn is talking a million words a minute—loud enough to fill an auditorium with her voice—I'm not taking in a single sentence.

We both step up to the tailgate together, and I let Taryn fill her cup first, wanting to linger and listen over McKenna's conversation with a few of her friends. She's talking about Wes, but she also knows I'm here, so she's speaking low. She's probably also lying. I hear her mention that he was at her house, but the details are drowned out when my friend turns to me and tells me she'll meet me by the fire.

There's a line building behind me, so I pull my cup from the stack and begin to fill it, dividing my attention between this task and McKenna. As I stop the flow from the keg, I notice McKenna step away, telling her friends she'll be right back. Her drink is sitting on the end of the truck, inches away from my hand.

My mind races through a litany of possibilities, some more vile than others. I settle on simple, inconvenient, and embarrassing. I tug the stud from the top of my right ear quickly, pushing the sharp post through the side of her cup on the side, just enough for a slow trickle to drip.

I move my hand to my ear to replace my earring when McKenna comes back, her eyes finding me, and her lips sneering instantly.

"Who invited you?" she says, taking her drink in her hand.

Drip. Drip. Drip.

I smile, feeling more satisfied than I have in days, maybe weeks. "Kyle did. Just to piss you off," I answer, knowing Kyle won't mind one bit.

"Yeah, well it worked," she says, shrugging one shoulder and moving her drink to her lips. I smile as the first few drops hit her white shirt, the drip coming out heavier with every tilt.

"Good," I say, turning before she has a chance to even flinch. I walk toward Taryn, but notice she's with all three Stokes boys, and Wes's eyes are on me. He saw. He saw everything. And with one sigh and the tilt of his head, I feel like a petty, ridiculous child.

Shit.

Instead of joining the group, I step by the corner of our blanket and retrieve my sweater, slipping it over my chilled arms and neck, tugging the sleeves down low enough to cover my hands. I cross my arms over my body and begin to walk slowly, not wanting to draw attention.

Not wanting to be followed.

I make it most of the way along the main pier, my body camouflaged in the darkness of the far end where the lights have yet to turn on. "What are you doing, Joss?"

I knew he'd come.

"Just going for a little walk," I say. My words come out in a giggle.

"Alone?" Wes asks. He's closer. I can hear his feet along the wood now. He's wearing shoes. He put them on to come find me. He wasn't wearing them for our game. He wasn't wearing them at the bonfire. But I hear their heaviness now.

"I'm not alone," I say, pulling my arms and body free of my sweater again, holding it outstretched above my head, letting the wind catch it like a flag. "You're here."

I let the sweater drop behind me. Wes's feet stop moving. He's picking it up.

"How about we both go back to the fire, huh? It's cold out here," he says.

He's nervous. *Why are you nervous, Wes? Are you afraid I'm going to ask questions?*

"I like it out here," I say, walking past the small observatory at the end of the pier, out to the very edge. The moon is only half, but it's enough to make the water's ripples light up like crystals.

"Yeah, I'm getting that," Wes chuckles, moving next to me. I don't look at him completely, but I see his body from the periphery. He's staring out at the water too.

We both stand in silence for almost a full minute. The time passes so slowly that it eventually becomes a test for me to see how long I can go, how long I can survive in silence this close to Wes. My body shivers once, betraying my strength, and I feel the fabric of my sweater tickle along my arm. I turn to see Wes offering it back to me. I refuse it.

"I'm fine," I say, my right lip rising in a short smile as I return my focus to the deep black of the ocean.

"Sure you are," he says, punctuating it with a short laugh that causes me to turn and look at him again. "Is that why you poked a hole in McKenna's cup? Because you're fine?"

I hold my tongue against my top lip, fighting off the embarrassment at getting caught, moving past it. My eyes meet his, and after a few seconds, I grin. "No, I did that because McKenna's a bitch," I say, my mouth stopping in a tight smile.

Wes shakes his head, and I turn away, letting him take in my profile. He won't look away, though.

"You know McKenna and me, we're just friends, right?" he says. "Hell, we're not even really friends. We're just…I don't know…*friendly?* I barely know her."

I start to laugh softly, letting it drift off into quiet before I speak again.

"Wes, I don't care what you are to McKenna," I lie.

Really, I do care. I care more than I should, more than I want to. McKenna's lucky I stopped at the hole in the cup. My other visions of revenge were less couth. I take a deep breath before turning, so my back rests against the wood railing at the end of the pier and my eyes catch Wes, ready to dare him.

"I care about the fact that a rock was hurled at my head—at a hundred miles per hour—and you snatched it out of the air. Your hand—it isn't even bruised," I say, knowing he won't show me otherwise as proof against my theory. There's nothing to show. Instead, he slides his hands in his pockets and moves his feet, shifting his weight as he looks down at the planks of wood beneath us.

"What I care about, is the fact that you grabbed me in the air and wrapped me up in your body as we tumbled along a jagged highway. You were unscathed, Wes. Scratches—mere scratches," I say, holding up my arm and twisting it to the side to show the huge gash still healing on me.

His eyes lift to meet mine, but his lips remain closed. Tight. He swallows once, hard.

"What I care about…" I say, my hand reaching for him, but closing in a fist and falling to my side. "All I really care about right now, this minute, is the fact that you saved my life when I was just a child. The most horrible thing to have happened in my life happened right in front of you—and when it almost killed me, you stepped in the way and stopped it all. And you won't admit it. You won't admit to any of it at all, but that...*that*...the fact that you're Christopher, that you're the same boy I knew then—you'll deny that most of all."

"Joss," he sighs, his lips parted and ready to give me more lies.

"No," I say, holding up my palm. "Tell me, Wes. What would you do?"

His brow pinches, and his eyes lower on me, his mouth unhappy, almost angry.

"What would you do, Wes, if I just..." I pause as I feel with my bare feet behind me until one foot finds the first beam of the wooden ledge. I step up on it and quickly lift myself to sit on the top of the railing.

"Joss..." Wes moves toward me, uttering my name nervously. His eyes are wide, but his movement is guarded.

"I don't swim. Did you know that? Not well, at least," I say, moving my feet to the next rail, standing slowly.

"Joss, stop. Stop! Joss...you're scaring me," he says, lunging for me. I slide out of his reach down the railing, the wood only thick enough for my feet.

"Tell me, Wes. I want the truth. Give me the truth," I say, our eyes locked in a game of truth or dare. His eyes are paralyzed—stuck on my movement—and behind them, so much is happening.

"Joss, there's no...*truth*. I don't know what you're saying. The rock was coming for your head, and I just stopped it. I got lucky, Joss. Jesus! Just...fuck, Joss. Get down from there..."

"I don't think so," I say, falling backward in a leap of faith. I have faith...trust in Wes. In Christopher.

I will be okay.

The fall is farther than I realized, and about halfway down, my heart is rushed with adrenaline. I stepped off feet first, and my arms swing wildly. But I don't scream. I'm too much in shock for noise to leave my throat. The impact is harsh, and even though my feet break through the freezing surface first, the movement of the water rushes over all of me, twisting my body and battering my face with salty wave after wave. I ingest breaths of water, and I choke and fight with my arms to right myself.

But I'm never fully afraid. I think I never screamed because I always knew he wouldn't let me drown.

I don't hear him. I feel him. Wes's arm loops around my chest and under my arms and he kicks hard to bring us both to the surface. He battles every wave until we're near the shore, the sand rushing up to meet our feet. I cough as I climb from the water, the waves still wrapping around my legs, my wet jeans clinging to my thighs and my body shivering from the cold air.

"I knew it," I mumble, teeth chattering.

I keep walking until the sand is dry, then I look at the sky, my smile wide on my face, and I begin to laugh.

"Damn it, Joss!" Wes scolds me as he steps behind me. I wrap my arms around myself, and turn to face him, the smile never leaving my lips.

"I knew it!" I say, my voice louder now.

"Knew what? Jesus, Joss…you're talking like a crazy person. You…you could have died doing that! What were you thinking?" Wes's voice is angry, and his face is harsh, a deep line between his eyes, his skin beading with bumps from the freezing water and air as his wet jeans and shirt hug his body.

"I knew you'd save me. I *knew* it! Say it, Wes. Tell me. You're him, aren't you?"

"Goddamn it, Josselyn! Stop this!" Wes shouts, stepping at me with angry movements until his hands wrap around my wrists. He doesn't shake me, but he holds me in place, lowering his head to look me in the eyes. "I am not some super hero! And you—you are not immortal! You have to stop, Joss. You have to stop this crazy idea that seems to have stolen away your ability to logic and reason. I've been lucky."

"No, you haven't. I know it," I begin, but Wes quickly speaks over me.

"Yes, I have, Joss. Jesus, I've been able to protect you with the help of miracles. How you see me? As this…what? Invincible guy from your past?

Joss…I've been lucky. Listen to me…" He holds me close, his grip on my arms almost desperate as his eyes look down on me. "You can't keep testing me. You can't keep acting out with these crazy delusions, Joss. One of these times—I'm going to fail. Do you understand? I will fail, Joss."

"No…you won't," I whisper, my voice cracking. I'm losing him.

He backs away, running both hands through his wet hair, his fingers gripping at the ends and pulling as he looks up to the stars and begins to turn in a slow circle.

"Yes I will, Joss. I will fail. And I won't be able to save you," he says, stopping his solitary slow dance when he's facing me once more. His head falls forward, and his eyes fill with sadness. "I can't save you from you, Joss. Please…give up."

He stares into me a second longer before turning to walk up the rise of the sand toward his truck. I stay in the shallow water, my body already adapting to the coldness—I'm becoming numb. Wes stops to say something to TK and Levi, then walks to his truck. He sits in it for several minutes, the engine idling, the taillights glowing, before finally pulling away.

I leave my sweater on the pier. A sacrifice to the gods—proof that I was in fact here.

I don't mind the cold.

And maybe Wes is right. Maybe I know nothing at all.

Maybe…maybe I *have* been lucky.

CHAPTER 9

I am the fool.

So often, I am the fool.

But I also can't seem to shake the memory of what happened Friday on the beach. Wes denied it, but his expression said otherwise. The rock was inches from my face when he snatched it from the air as if it were a feather. When he looked at me, the flash in his eyes was beyond familiar.

His eyes were warning me, but they were also fearful.

I know I have to let go of these thoughts—Wes and Christopher. Even so, I don't want to. I can't.

When Kyle dropped me off at home after the beach in the early morning hours, my house was quiet. I expected it to be empty, but I paused at my father's open door, his body lying face down on his bed, his shoes at the foot of the bed and the clothes he wore that day still on. He made it home on his own. I was given a rare night off.

Every night has been a different story, though. The drink in my father's hand is a fixture after games or practices—even the late ones. Yesterday, I had to help him to bed. He stopped somewhere between his chair and the hallway, and I couldn't just leave him there. I'm strong, but my father's stronger—and when he's stubborn, it's impossible to maneuver him. He doesn't bend to my will when he's drunk. He fights me. He hurts me. It took an hour to get him from the living room to his bed thirty feet away.

Yet somehow, he gets up every day and returns to his other life. I can see it taking a toll. It's been taking one for years—slowly eating away his personality. He doesn't have any friends. He has a team. And I think that's why he gets up in the morning. He lives for that team. He sure as hell doesn't live for me.

He's had two games this week—games that were far, and took both he and Wes out of school early to travel south. My games were home. I played well. Nobody cares, though. When I came home, I stayed in my room, or went to Taryn's, to avoid him, timing it just right so when I stepped into the living room I could pull the half-filled glass from his loose grip and turn the light off by his chair. As sad as this routine was, it was bearable.

I could live like this.

What I couldn't live with, though, was this new feeling between Wes and me. He was avoiding me. Maybe I was avoiding him a little too. We acted like strangers in the two classes we had together, and when one of us would walk up to join our small circle of friends, the other would leave.

Taryn has noticed. And she's focused on my jealousy as the cause. McKenna has been an easy scapegoat, and perhaps on many levels, she is the reason I'm avoiding Wes. But she's not the only reason.

I am the fool. This is the reason. I believed so hard that he would save me, with all of my heart—but his reaction made me start to think he's right. He's been lucky. I've been lucky.

He might fail.

I might die.

"You're really so inflexible about things that you won't even shop for a dress with me?" Taryn breaks into my thoughts. I shake my head and look up at her. I must have missed part of this conversation.

"Dress shopping?" I ask, pouring a packet of salt into my small mound of ketchup for my fries.

"You aren't even listening to me. Awesome. What was the last thing you heard? Or…actually, you know what? I'll just take McKenna with me to buy a dress," she says, the snarkiness of her tone apparent.

"Don't be a bitch," I say.

"Ohhhhh, I say *McKenna* and I get your attention," she says.

I roll my eyes at her and turn my attention back to my fries, pushing the red around my paper plate in swirls.

"The Valentine's dance, Joss. That thing you always say is stupid, and that I actually always wanted to go to—but never have, because my best friend always talked me into getting drunk with the Marley twins under the bleachers instead," she says.

"I've never kept you from going," I say, my lips pursed.

"Sure," she says back, her expression mirroring mine.

"You're going this year, so whatever," I say. "I told you, I've got too much to do. The new job, and I want to save my money to replace my iPod and get some new cleats. A hundred bucks for a ticket and a dress is not part of my plan."

"Yeah, but just come shopping with me. I want you there to pick out something pretty, something you think TK will like," she says, her lips morphing from a hard straight line to a pout. "Please?"

I sigh, but know I'm going to give in.

"I don't know why you think *I* would be a good judge for what makes a dress pretty or whatever, but fuck—fine. I'll go," I say, stuffing my saturated fry in my mouth and picking up another, pushing the ketchup around again.

"Yay! And I know…yes, I just said *yay*. But I'm so excited you're going with me. And I know you don't hate the idea as much as you say you do," she winks.

I do hate it. Just as much, if not more. But I love Taryn. Love wins.

I eat a few more of my fries and fold what's left of my pizza slice into my napkin, piling my plate on Taryn's tray, smirking when she shoots me an irritated look. She'll throw my trash out for me—it's a small request in exchange for dress shopping.

As she steps away from our table, I move my gaze out the window and catch TK, Levi, and Wes pulling into the student parking lot from lunch, McKenna and two of her friends riding in the back. Her hair is blown wild, and I know it's going to piss her off. This pleases me.

"So, is it another beach Friday today?" I ask when Taryn returns.

"I think some of them are going. TK's coming over for dinner tonight, though. God, I *wish* we were going to the beach instead," she says, her eyes wide.

"Wow, so he's reached meet-the-parents status, huh?" I say, more surprised than I let on. TK is one of only a few boyfriends she's had meet her family. And I'm sure he's the only one who has met them on purpose.

"Yeah. He asked to. He said it was important," she says, her thumbnail lodged in her teeth as the corners of her mouth flex into a shy smile.

"Don't be embarrassed," I say, leaning into her. "It's sweet."

I smile at her genuinely, but my enthusiasm fades when I see Wes walk into the cafeteria alongside TK, McKenna wrapped in his jacket. Taryn follows my gaze, then looks back to me just as I'm stepping from the bench seat of our table.

"You know he's not with her or anything. Shit, Joss, she probably took his jacket out of his truck when he wasn't paying attention," she says, jumping to the usual conclusion. "What's with you two? You've barely talked all week, and you keep running whenever you see him."

"I couldn't care less if he's with her, T. I just have things to do. I'll see you this weekend. I'm the late shift Saturday too, remember?" I say through the fakest of grins. I knock once on the table and disappear just in time to avoid looking Wes in the eyes.

He was looking at me when I left. He looks at me often. I feel him. And even with my close calls, I can't avoid him completely. I'll see him in a few minutes in our photography class. But in there, I can hide.

The photo room is usually a wonderful escape. As much as I took this class just to fill a credit, I've fallen in love with the idea of it. We started actually shooting, finally. Nothing complicated, portraits of each other mostly. I paired myself with this girl, Courtney. She's an overachiever—student council, cheer, and about a dozen other clubs. I think she might be number two in our class, just behind Conner. She's all business, though, so our partner assignments in class have been perfect, and always done before class was over.

Today, we get to check the cameras out for the weekend, and I won't be working with Courtney. Our assignment is to shoot a series of stills of something intimate—an item that tells our story. My story is short, and it's sad, and while Wes looks over at me, I'm filled with the sense that in many ways he's my item. But I can't shoot a photo of him. It would be misconstrued. People would laugh. They would gossip. They wouldn't understand.

He wouldn't understand.

He'd tell me to stop.

When the final bell rings, I linger, letting everyone else check cameras out first. Wes leaves in the middle of the group, and he doesn't look back in my direction. I'm not relieved; I'm disappointed.

My camera in my hands, I tuck it into my heavy school bag and move the straps over my shoulders, pulling my phone from my pocket to let Taryn know I don't need a ride. If I'm also working Saturday and Sunday, I'll need to shoot my assignment today before I go to my first shift.

Don't forget—dress shopping Saturday, she writes.

I tell her it has to be before two, so I can work, and she sends me a photo of her lips kissing at me. I smile to myself as I step outside, happy that at least my friend is happy.

A line of cars streams by me, and I notice McKenna's Jeep pass, Levi hanging out the back. He waves at me, but as McKenna turns the corner quickly, his weight pulls his hand inside. I wait for a few more cars to pass as my finger pushes the crosswalk button, and when the light switches to red, Wes's truck pulls up next to me.

"Are we done?" he says, his window down, his arm hanging out the side, and his eyes forward. I've never wanted a WALK sign to flash more in my life.

"Did we start something?" I respond, eyes forward, my expression aloof.

The crosswalk signal changes, and I step into the street, his motor revving as his truck idles into the intersection beside me. I turn quickly to look behind him, a line of cars waiting, held up by the red light.

"Excuse me, but you need to yield to pedestrians," I say loudly.

"Just making sure you get across safely," he shouts. "I can't count on you making smart decisions, you know."

I stop in the middle of the road and slam my fist on the hood of his truck, and when I look at him through his front windshield, his damn smirk is waiting for me. "Fuck you, Wesley Stokes," I yell back, my eyes low and my temper full-on flaring.

My tantrum only makes his smirk tick up on one side, so I take two steps away, ignoring the flashing signal that will soon send traffic through the intersection. I step to the driver's side door, and without pause, kick it twice with every bit of strength I have, pointing at him when I finish.

"Fuck. You!"

The light turns green, and the car right behind Wes honks. I don't know the driver. Some guy I think might be a senior. I flip him off too, and he calls me a *bitch*.

I kick Wes's door one more time before pulling my bag tight against my shoulders and walking to the other side of the street.

"So are we done now?" he asks, pulling into the bike lane and driving slowly next to me, cars honking at him as they pass. He doesn't even flinch. He's leaning into the middle of the truck seat while he drives so he can shout at me through the passenger window.

"I don't know what it is you have to do, Wes. I'm doing my own thing, so how about you just go join your girlfriend at the beach and let her make you feel like big man on campus," I say, my cheeks burning at the sound of myself. That last part slipped out—the buried shit coming out for him to hear. I'm mortified. But I'm also still pissed.

"Big man on campus," he chuckles, repeating my last words.

"Whatever!" I yell, picking up my pace. I hate this feeling—I hate how I'm acting. I just want him to drive away, yet the moment he does, my heart sinks.

"Whatever," I whisper to myself, shaking my head. My hands feel my back pockets out of habit, looking for the release of a cigarette. But I threw everything away again after last weekend's smokes. I'm on a five-day smoke-free streak. *Yay me.*

I look up and notice Wes's truck is parked a block ahead. Pulled around the corner, the passenger door is open, framing the view of him sitting with his arm slung over the wheel, his hat pulled backward so I get a full look at his cocky smile—which I can't quite make out from this distance, but am sure is there anyway.

I don't slow down, but I don't walk quickly either. I walk like I would have if Wes hadn't interrupted my journey. But my heart races—it speeds like the goddamn Daytona 500. I reach his truck and move beyond the open passenger door to cross in front of him. I think I knew he'd get out. I wanted him to. I'm testing him like a foolish girl with a crush.

I am a foolish girl with a crush.

"Are you stubborn about everything in your life? Or just with me?" he questions as he meets me halfway around his truck, his arms out, as if he's ready to tackle me if I attempt to run by him. The idea of testing him on this amuses me.

"No," I say, my lips in a hard line. "I'm stubborn about going dress shopping with Taryn too. But I already gave into her, so I've spent my weakness for the day if you don't mind. Nothing left for you."

"Where are you going?" he asks, ignoring my response, walking backward in slow steps and moving in front of me every time I try to pass him.

"Well…" I say, sighing hard, and pulling my heavy bag from my shoulders, dropping it to my feet to give my arms a break. I put my hands on my hips and squint as I look at him, the sun hot and bright behind him. "It seems my dad thought it would be a good idea for me to get a job. I do have expenses—you might recall a broken iPod?"

He grimaces.

"And since our photo assignment is due Monday, and I have about three hours of sunlight left, I'm going to do my homework," I say, shaking my arms out at my sides and bending down to pick my bag up again. Wes reaches for it before I do, though, and lifts it easily, stepping around me and setting it in the cab of his truck.

"Josselyn Winters, the girl who doesn't care about school, cares about her grade in some elective," he says, turning and blocking the door so I can't reach in and retrieve my bag. His taunting pisses me off.

"Yeah, well, I give a shit about things I like. And I like taking pictures, so get the hell out of my way, because I don't really give a shit about you," I say. My lips twitch as soon as the words leave my mouth. Wes's twitch too, frowning, and he looks down at his feet, moving his hands to the pockets of his faded blue jeans.

"I see," he says, sucking in his top lip as his eyes remain on the ground between us. "Well then…how about I help you get where you need to go. Something you dislike so much shouldn't stand in the way of something you love."

My chest hurts over the lie I told. But it's better to act this way with him. It keeps me from getting crazy ideas. It keeps me from falling. It keeps me from believing.

"It's fine, Wes. I planned on walking. I have enough time, but I need to get going," I say, reaching forward for my bag. His hand finds my wrist, and his touch is fast, but tender.

"Joss, it's just a ride," he says. I glance at him, his lips lopsided with an innocent expression.

Walking away would be smarter. But I give in to easier. I give in to weaker. I give in to him.

"Fine," I sigh.

He steps out of my way and waits while I buckle, I think a little unsure if I'm really going to stay or bolt the moment he leaves the door. The thought did cross my mind.

Wes climbs into his seat, shutting the door and shifting the truck into drive. He makes a U-turn and stops at the corner, his head falling to the side as he talks. I love when he looks at me like this. Just once, I'd love him to do this and say something sweet—something just for me.

"Where to?" he asks, and I laugh lightly to myself, because his question—it's sweet enough.

"Just pull out on Main. Take it to the flower farms. There's one in particular, but I forget what road it's on. I'll know it when I see it," I say.

Wes nods and makes the turn, driving us through the outskirts of town, past rows of combed dirt ready to grow the next season's crops, until we hit the messier farms, the ones with clusters of green jutting from the ground in haphazard patterns, with splashes of color and splinters.

"It's a few more ahead," I say, leaning forward and propping my elbows on his dashboard. I catch his smile on me as I do.

"You like the flower farms, I take it," he says.

"I love them," I answer without looking at him. My response is instant and from my heart.

When I was a little girl, my dad would come home from road games with a cluster of flowers. He'd always make a bouquet for my mom, but he'd be sure to make a smaller version just for me. One day, he picked me a little cluster of peonies, and those quickly became my favorite. He couldn't find them all the time. Peonies only grow for a short season in California. They're rare here, which somehow I understood. It made them more special. It made the fact that my father would force the team to stop at this rickety stand in the middle of nowhere that much more important.

"Here…stop here," I breathe, tugging my seatbelt loose.

Wes pulls to the side of the road into the dirt, and I open the door before he's fully stopped. His hand reaches for me on instinct, and he grabs my leg firmly. My eyes flash to him.

"Wait…please," he says. His eyes wide, and his swallow hard.

I don't tease him. I don't get angry. I understand. I've scared him enough.

Nodding, I wait for him to shift the truck into park before climbing out and hopping over the narrow canal lining the road. I bend down and press my nose deep into the petals of the pink flower, inhaling the memories that come along with it.

My smile grows automatically.

"What is it?" Wes asks. I was so lost to my moment of bliss that I didn't hear him step up behind me.

"They're peonies," I say, my fingertips brushing over the soft petals of a few fully-bloomed flowers. It tickles.

"I didn't peg you for a pink flower kinda girl," he says. I look up at him, and his smile is just enough. Yet one more sweet thing from his lips. His thumbs are looped in his pockets, and the sun is casting a dust of golden light over his face. He's devastatingly handsome, and suddenly I'm glad he's here to share this with me.

"I need to get my camera before the light goes away," I say.

"Okay, you want me to pick one? This one you were touching?" He bends down and places his thumb and forefinger on the stem.

"No! Leave it. I...I want to shoot it like it is," I say. Wes steps back, his brow a little bunched, but he nods in acceptance.

I rush to grab my things and pull the Canon from my bag, popping the lens cap off and tucking it in my back pocket. I untie the flannel shirt from around my waist and lay it on the ground near the canal, pulling it close to the flower I spotted first, and I kneel on my knees in front of it, lowering myself to my elbows until I'm eventually laying in front of it.

"Here," Wes says, pulling his sweatshirt from over his head and tossing it in front of me. "So your elbows don't get sore," he says, smiling once, quickly, on the side of his mouth.

"Thanks," I say, moving the fabric under my arms. It helps—makes my arms more steady. That's not why I like it though, and it's not why I took it.

It takes me a while to get the focus just right, the pink vibrant and crisp, and everything beyond the petals soft and out of focus. I shoot a dozen shots like this before sitting up and searching for another flower. The ones here look the same, so I loop the camera strap around my neck and pick up the two shirts, shaking them free of dirt and stepping into the rows of bushes.

I glance around the flatland to make sure nobody sees me, but we're out here alone. The workers come in the early mornings. I move six or seven rows in, Wes walking slowly behind me, when I spot my next subject.

I repeat my routine, getting close to the flower, and then I wait, holding the camera still and resting my chin on top for the perfect moment.

"That one looks like it's on its way out," Wes says, kneeling next to me. I'm thankful he's on my right, his shadow not interfering. I don't think I could ask him to move if he were in my way. I like him here too much.

"That's what I love about it. It's already blossomed, but before it goes, it has these last few petals," I sigh as my eyes stare at the soft, wilting, pink pieces clinging to their last moments of beauty in front of me.

"Is that supposed to be you?" Wes asks.

I inhale slowly, filling my lungs with that thought. *Is that me?*

"Sometimes," I answer.

Seconds pass, and I hold my breath, waiting patiently as the golden rays crawl along the dirt and stems of the rows in front of me until finally the color reaches my flower. It's haloed by it—heaven shining down on the end of a life, giving it one last moment of glory.

I capture it all, every last moment, until the shadow of the neighboring flower shades it and the light is gone.

"I think I got it," I say, pushing up to my knees.

I pull the camera in front of me and flip through the dozens of shots— each one minutely different, but the entirety telling a story.

"It's beautiful," Wes says, his breath soft against my neck as he kneels behind me, looking over my shoulder. I close my eyes and keep my face forward.

"Thank you," I say. I mean it for so much more.

He knows. I can tell by the way his breathing shifts; by the way everything seems to slow.

Standing, I pull our shirts up, shaking the dirt from them both and handing his sweatshirt back to him. He waits for me to walk before moving back to the truck, almost as if he's making a concerted effort to be by my side, not to leave me.

The sun is disappearing, and the air is growing colder, so before I climb into his truck, I pull my shirt over my bare arms. I hold the camera in my hands once inside and buckled, and as Wes begins to drive out from the dirt road and turn around, I flip through my shots one more time. Every single photo hits me, and without warning, a tear forms in my right eye. I wipe it away quickly and tuck my camera in my bag.

"Why'd you choose the flower?" Wes asks.

I breathe in deeply, pulling one leg up into my chest and hugging my knee with my arms, laying my head on it and looking at him. His face is different at dusk. It's just as handsome.

"They remind me of my dad. They were kind of our thing—his silent way of telling me he loved me," I say, lowering my leg and moving my gaze to my window. The farms are already giving way to brick walls and business fronts.

"Loves you," Wes says. I look at him with my brow pinched, his eyes waiting for mine. "You said *loved*. But he still loves you."

I hold his gaze until he has to look back to the road, and when he does, I let the soft laugh escape my lips.

"I know it doesn't feel like it. But he does. He talks about you all the time. Compares us to you," Wes says. I turn in my seat, curious.

"You don't have to lie," I say.

He grins and chuckles.

"I'm not lying. He does. At least once a practice," he says. "It's a bet we make every practice—we see who's going to get the Joss comparison this time. Yesterday, it was me."

My smile is subtle, but inside it feels enormous. My chest fills. My heart beats louder. I feel…

"What'd you do? You know, to earn that honor?" I ask, hoping he did something good, that it's not an admonishment to be compared to me.

Wes laughs to himself and squints one eye, chewing at his lip before looking at me. "I hit Kyle in the arm with a pitch for crowding the plate. Your dad said you used to do that when you pitched. You called it *nudging*. He said you did it better."

My smile is full now, the kind of grin that dents my cheeks and aches on my face. "I did do that," I say, remembering pitching in sixth and seventh grade. All that time, I thought my father wasn't paying attention. I thought he was just irritated for having to take time away from his practice to pick me up. He always saw the last inning, and that was all.

"And you did it better," Wes says, pushing me lightly on my leg. He clears his throat when he moves his hand away, but glances at me sideways, nodding. "That's the important part. Your dad said you did it better."

I watch him drive for a minute, thinking about what he said.

"I probably did," I say, pulling a heavy laugh from him. It's the first time I've heard this sound from him, and it fills the space of his cab. It's loud and deep, and I bet when he's together with his brothers and dad, the house is filled with this sound too. It's my new favorite sound.

"You're not humble, Josselyn Winters. I'll give you that. You're stubborn, but shit if you're not miles away from humble."

I shrug, but my smile remains, even as I turn to face my window. We're getting closer to my house, and the good feeling is fleeting.

"Thanks," I say. When Wes tilts his head in my direction, I explain. "For telling me that…about my dad? Thanks. I miss him. How we used to be. And sometimes I feel it more than others."

It grows quiet after that honest moment, and when I look at Wes, his thoughts seem to be lost somewhere. I watch him work through whatever it is, and when he catches my stare, he shakes whatever it is off.

"Why didn't you pick one? Or make yourself a bouquet?" he asks.

I turn back to him, shrugging.

"People pay a fortune other places for those flowers. It's the only farm in Northern California that grows them. Yet, all I need to do is trespass and pick one. I can't seem to do it, though. I've stolen things from the mall. I've walked out with cases of beer from the minimart. I've taken balls and equipment from the school for softball. I can't steal a flower I think is beautiful. I just don't want to rip it from the ground just so it can die in my hands. It needs its roots. It needs its home. I don't know…that probably doesn't make sense."

"It makes perfect sense," he says, returning his gaze to the front as he sucks in his bottom lip. I wait for him to say more, but he doesn't.

Before we pull up in front of my house, I drag my things into my lap, hugging them to my body. My roots were destroyed years ago. My father's car is gone, which means tonight he's returned to old habits. I'll be at work, so I close my eyes and wish for him not to call me while I'm at work. I make a mental note to turn my phone on silent mode.

"He's going to call you, isn't he?" Wes asks, already versed in my routine.

I shrug as I open the door of his truck.

"I never know for sure," I say, looking over my shoulder to the empty driveway and open garage, the only things inside—our lawnmower and my broken bike. "But yeah…" I sigh heavily. "Probably."

When I turn back to him, as my hand holds onto the edge of his passenger door, I notice his eyes on the deep-purple bruise on the inside of my wrist. I twist it, but not quickly enough.

"Is that from the pier?" Wes asks, his eyes unable to leave my arm. I roll the cuff of my sleeve down to cover it more.

"No," I say, knowing he doesn't believe me. I give him more details than I want to just to make sure he knows the truth. I don't want him to think he failed me. He's the only boy who never has. "My dad…he passed out getting out of his chair a couple nights ago, and I didn't get there in time to catch his drink before it fell. It was a mess, and I couldn't leave him there. I had to carry him to his room, but he's heavy, and we fell. So…"

Wes looks to his steering wheel again, nodding once, his lips pursed. He knows the scene. He's watched it, or at least enough of it.

"Call me…if he needs help; if you need help? Call me. I'll come," he says.

I chuckle quietly to myself and look down at my feet as I swing my bag over my shoulder, pulling my hair out from the strap underneath.

"I thought you weren't my hero," I smirk. Wes's face remains serious.

"You shouldn't have to deal with that on your own," he says.

"Yeah, well…you can't save me from everything, Wesley Stokes," I say, my arms stretched out to my sides as I let them fall against my hips. "Besides, he'll find his way home if I don't answer the call. He always does. Hey…thanks for the ride."

"It was my pleasure," he says, a small dimple on his cheek. "I'm gonna have to step up my game after seeing your assignment."

"Who says it's a competition?" I say, my head angled as I look at him.

"Oh Joss," he chuckles, shifting his gear to drive before looking at me. "With you? It's *always* a competition."

I flip his door shut and step back, smiling and blushing a little too. He shakes his head with the laugh I can't hear as he pulls away finally, and I wait at the end of my driveway for a few extra seconds, hopeful that he'll turn around and come back.

Wes stays gone, though, so I move toward my house. Dropping my bag on the floor of my room, I fall onto my bed. I sit up after a few minutes and reach for my bag, slipping my hand inside and pulling the crinkled thank you card I stuffed in there days ago. I smile looking at it, running my fingertips lightly over my childish handwriting. Maybe he's not him, but he's *like* him.

I breathe in deeply and kneel down to slide the small box from under my dresser, tucking the card back inside, then I lift the plastic bag I picked up yesterday from Jungle Gym with my new uniform inside. The pants are black with pockets at the hips and knees. Steven, the manager, told me they make it easy to carry around extra pieces of equipment—scissors, tape rolls, and spray bottles of cleaning solution.

I couldn't possibly look less attractive. To make matters worse, my work shirts all have my name incorrectly spelled over the right pocket—*Jose*. I showed Taryn this morning, and she snapped a photo and posted it on every social media account she owns. Yet one more reason I avoid life online.

Dressed like a metal-band roadie, I pull my hair back with a purple tie and twist it a few extra times into a loop to keep my hair off my neck. It takes me about thirty minutes to walk to Spider's Jungle Gym, so I search on my phone for bus routes on my way. The route is safe, but it still isn't fun at night. Tomorrow, I'll try the bus option.

I still get in a few minutes early. It's almost seven-thirty when I punch in my code on the computer. It takes me a few tries. The screaming coming from the main play area is constant and deafening. At first, I dreaded the idea of working here late at night, of closing up the place and spending hours in the dim lights picking up the remnants of other families' birthday parties. But now that I'm here for the real thing, I think I got the good end of the deal.

How bad is it?

Kyle's text makes me smile. He worked this morning, and he smelled like nacho cheese all day. I gave him a hard time about it, but he told me to wait and see what I smelled like. I think he's right—fresh cheese wins.

I snap a photo of one of the tables, icing caked along the length, and some questionable red liquid dried on a few of the booths. I send it to him and wait for his response.

Is that blood?

I laugh, and type back: *No idea, dude. It sure as hell ain't cheese, though.*

I catch Steven's eyes on me, his finger tapping his watch. I don't know him well, but Taryn told me he's strict about breaks and making sure we're doing what we're supposed to. Another perk to me closing at night. He won't be here to monitor how long it takes me. I know I'm only paid for four hours. But I'll work longer for free, taking my time, just to avoid real life for a while.

I put my phone in my pocket, flipping it to VIBRATE first, then grab the broom and dustpan from the closet, quickly going to work cleaning the main eating-area floor. My task feels futile until the gym closes and children are no longer around to spill Goldfish crackers and rip open candy wrappers, tossing the plastic on the floor.

The night servers all take care of their tables, so I can focus on the gym and main common areas, which are somehow in worse shape. Gum is stuck on the inside of slides, and I've filled a plastic bag with stuffed animals, socks, and shoes that were left behind. I dump the bag once in the lost-and-found bin and move toward the ladder to search for items up high.

"Hey, new girl," one of the guys shouts from the front door. I jog over to where I can see him.

"Yeah?"

"We're locking up. Just wanted to let you know. Go out the back when you're done, and the door shuts behind you, so don't leave unless you're, like, totally done. Steven gets pissed if he has to drive back in to unlock the door," he says.

I salute him and hold up a thumb, then wait as he locks the door with the key. Funny, he didn't give me the option to call him if I get locked out? Seems he gets a little pissy about being called back to work too.

I lower the blinds and return to my bag, climbing up the giant tree-house structure to continue collecting belongings and trash. The music is still on. It's a top-forty station, so it isn't bad. Not my first choice, but it's better than the kiddie songs that they were playing in the dining area when I first got here.

My bag is full of things before I'm halfway through the top part of the gym, so I climb down and return to the lost-and-found, dumping it again. My pocket *buzzes*. I pull my phone out, knowing it's too early for it to be my father.

Need company?

My heart kicks at Wes's text. I look up at the front door, and there's a shadow behind the blinds, the height just about right. I still flip them open and look out before unlocking, and when I open the door to let him in, he commends me for it.

"I was so sure you were going to let in the ax murderer," he chuckles. "I would have bet money on it."

"Yeah, well, this guy I know keeps telling me I need to be safer about things, so…" I say, kicking my foot at him.

"He does," he says, raising one side of his mouth for a short smile.

"How'd you know where this place was?" I ask.

"Kyle told me. He smelled like cheese all day," he laughs. It makes me smile.

I stand with him near the door for a few seconds, wondering why he's here, but too afraid to ask. He might leave. And now that he's here, I want him to stay.

"How do you feel about gum?" I ask, one eye closed, my head tilted in question.

"I…uh…I like it?"

"That sounded like a question. You don't sound very committed," I say, stepping closer to him, my hand holding the putty knife behind my back.

"I love gum. I do. I'm committed. Give me gum or give me death," he jokes.

"Awesome," I say, handing him the blade. "There's a shitload stuck to the side of the top slide, and it's making me gag."

He laughs as he looks at the blade in his hand.

"I asked if you wanted company, Joss. Not if you needed an assistant," he says.

"That's the price you pay to be in the presence of greatness," I yell over my shoulder, my hand holding my bag in the air and my other hand pointing a finger forward, as if I'm leading an army charging into battle.

"A'right. Which one?" he finally gives in, stepping up to the tree-house entrance behind me. I point to the winding blue slide cascading above us. Wes sighs, but passes me, climbing the steps to the very top.

He gives me commentary, telling me about the various pieces of gum, the color, his guess at their flavor. He even jokes about eating some of it just to confirm he's right. But after a few minutes, his banter grows less, and for the last half an hour, we've been working together in silence.

"You know, you don't really have to stay the whole time. I'm almost done in here, and I'm gonna lock up soon, so…" I stop talking when I walk out from the back office area and spot Wes standing in the middle of the main lobby, chewing at his lip and an iPod in his hand. I push the button on the cordless vacuum, ceasing the buzzing in my hand.

"My dad's really good at repairing things, and he's good at finding parts, and well…" he says, unwinding the ear bud cord wrapped around my iPod and unplugging it to hand the device to me.

"Your dad fixed this? For me?" I say, pushing the power button and running my thumb over the smooth screen, then the small dent left behind on the metal casing.

"He couldn't really fix that part, but he got a new screen. I always told him he should open up a side business for this kinda stuff," he says, his fingers nervously twisting the cord of my earphones. I reach for them, and he starts.

"Mind if I test it?" I ask, my eyes barely reaching his. He looks away the moment I meet his gaze. He's being bashful.

"Oh, yeah…yeah. Sorry," he says, handing the cord to me.

I thumb through my playlists and press one of my favorite Foo Fighters songs, smiling when the music drums into my ears. Wes smiles back at me, and I look at him for a second or two with my soundtrack drowning out everything else.

"Thanks," I say. He laughs, and I pull my headphones out of my ears, winding them around the device. "Sorry. Was I loud?"

"You're always loud," he says. I glower at him, and he holds his hands up. "Kidding. You're a delicate, quiet flower."

"Oh, now I know you're full of shit," I say, punching him in his arm. It's a stupid touch, and I choreographed the entire thing just so I could feel him. I take a few steps back, a little embarrassed. I reach for the vacuum again and push the iPod into my pocket opposite my phone. "Seriously, though. Thanks," I smile.

"It was important to you," he shrugs.

You're important to me.

"I'm almost done, really…" I begin my out for him again, giving him permission to leave. He interrupts quickly.

"I'm driving you home. It's late, and I'm driving you home," he says, his serious voice coming out. I hold his eyes with mine for a few seconds, my tongue poking in the side of my cheek as I consider. I finally give up.

"A'right," I nod. "I'll be a few minutes."

I move to the back and finish my passes along the floor until the carpet is completely clean. When I'm done, I tuck the vacuum and other supplies into the metal closet, shut off the lights, and close up the office area. Wes stands from the small bench by the front door, and steps toward me.

"Do you want to just pull around?" I ask. "I can lock it from the inside after you leave."

"Nope. I'll walk with you," he says, mouth in a tight smile.

"Okay," I submit, looking away and leading him through the darkened gym area, shutting every light off along the way. The more darkness there is, the more I feel his presence, until I catch myself holding my breath and draw in a silent gasp of air.

I hold the door for him and test the door behind us. Locked, just as the guy warned. Our arms both swing near one another as we walk slowly around the side of the building to his truck parked near the front under the lone light. My fingers flex, wanting to be reckless, wanting to grasp onto his as they pass, just once…to feel them.

Wes holds the truck door open for me, and I climb inside, letting him shut the door for me. I pull both my phone and iPod out and hold them in my hands, and I stare at them as he starts the engine and pulls out of the lot.

"Thanks," I whisper.

It's quiet for a few seconds, and I look to the side and catch his hand along his chin, his arm resting on the small rest pulled out from the center seat between us.

"You're welcome, Joss," he says, glancing at me with a tight smile, but looking back to the road quickly.

My mind races with all of the things I want to say—with questions, with gratefulness, with hope and stupid flirtatious stuff. I want him to tell me more things my dad says about me. I want him to tell me more things about him. But this is always where things go wrong. So instead, I keep my mouth shut—all the way to my house.

"Shit," I hum finally. My dad's car is in the lawn.

"I got it," he says, stopping abruptly and leaping from the truck ahead of me.

I'm ashamed. This shouldn't be Wes's problem. This shouldn't be my problem. But it is. It's mine.

"Just go," I say, closing my eyes as I step up next to him. He's already reached into the car and unbuckled my father's seatbelt. He stands straight from leaning into the car and meets my eyes. I feel his breath, and I get lost in the blue of his irises. "Just…"

The tears are swift. I cup my mouth and beg my body and nerves to obey—*hold it in, Joss. Hold it in.*

"I got it," he says again, his voice firm. He leans forward just enough, bowing his head to look me in the eyes. He knows how embarrassed I am, so he looks away quickly. He knows.

I don't hate my father.

I hate that I love my father still.

Wes lifts him from the seat enough that my father startles. He mumbles a few things that are incoherent, and for a moment, I think his eyes focus on me. "I'm fine to drive," he spits out. His tone is full of defiance, anger, and all of the self-righteous bullshit that has consumed his soul over the last decade.

"You are *not* fine!" I yell.

That wakes him. It's enough that his gaze flies to me, and all of the resentment behind his eyes comes surging my direction. And just as quickly, his body goes limp against Wes.

"Just…just take him inside. I'll move the car to the driveway so the neighbors don't see it," I say, stepping into my dad's car, the motor still humming. I wonder how long he sat here with it idling. No wonder our grass won't grow.

I back out over our lawn, into the street, and pull forward again into the driveway. I shut the engine off and walk through the lawn, kicking the dirt in various directions to erase the tracks. I don't want anyone to ever know this happened.

It's happened before.

When I walk into the house, I hear Wes down the hallway. I follow the sound to my father's room, and I watch as my father crawls on his knees

177

up into his bed then flattens against the quilt and pillow. Wes pulls his shoes from his feet, laying them on the floor beneath him, and before he turns and steps from the room, he speaks.

"You have to stop this. You promised you would stop," he says.

"What do you mean he promised?" I ask.

Wes freezes, his back to me.

"Wes?"

He turns the small lamp off, then walks from my father's room, closing the door behind him. He doesn't look at me until his toes are nearly touching mine, and the shock of being so close to him chokes me.

"Did you do this for him before? Last week. After the beach. I came home and found him like this. Lying in his bed, his shoes…they were off. You…was that you? Are you helping him…what…behind my back?" My body quakes, and I'm not sure if it's out of humiliation or anger.

"You shouldn't have to do this by yourself," he says. My eyes are locked on his. His body hovers over me, his chin tucked in his chest as he looks down on me. I feel small. I feel weak.

"I think you need to go," I say, my eyes burning.

Turning my head to the side, my focus lands on the family photo that still hangs on our hallway wall in a golden frame—the paint chipping off the edges and showing the cheap wood underneath. I've pulled the picture down a million times. My father always hangs it up again. It doesn't matter where I hide it. He always finds it. I grab it from the wall and carry it with me into the kitchen. I set the frame on the center of the counter and begin pulling open drawers, spilling out bins, tossing papers and old brochures and menus to the floor until I finally find one filled with tools. I pull the hammer out and spin around with one swift movement, my arm raising and falling fast, the metal head crashing through the glass over and over. I pound the photo until the image is unrecognizable, and the glass shards have scattered around me on the floor. I lift to swing again, and Wes grabs my arm.

"Leave me alone, Wes," I say, my breathing hard, my heart pounding.

"Let me clean the glass—"

"I got it," I shout, interrupting him, jerking my arm loose. I drop the hammer on the counter, then turn to the small pantry and pull out the broom and dustpan. With my back still to him, I beg him once more to leave. "This is my problem, Wes. And I don't want you here. I don't...I don't want you seeing this—any of it. Please."

My voice cracks by the end, and my cheeks are stained with tears. I count as I inhale; closing my eyes and begging silently for Wes to be gone by the time I finally turn around. I need him to be gone. I don't know that I can ask him to leave again. And if he stays...if he helps—I will *need* him.

Seven. Eight. Nine. Ten.

The sound of the door closing hits my ears. It isn't loud. It's gentle. It's reluctant. But Wes is gone.

CHAPTER 10

It took me an hour to clean up the mess left behind from my breakdown. I scooped everything into a bucket and took it outside to the trash by the curb. I woke early this morning and heard the garbage truck come and take it all away, and I cried—that picture is *really* gone now.

I let myself feel the weight of that for exactly fifteen minutes. No more. And when time was up, I got out of bed, put on my running pants, a T-shirt and shoes, and grabbed my newly repaired iPod, leaving the house for three hours. I ran for miles. They were slow, and they hurt. But I pushed. I ran up the bleachers. I sprinted around the track. I hopped the fence and ran the bases on the softball field. I pushed myself until I finally collapsed on the outfield grass.

For the next thirty minutes, I looked at the sky, and I thought about my mom. I thought about every single good memory—the chocolate Kisses she slipped into my lunch bag, the way she always made sure to sit up front for school performances, how she kept score for my T-ball games.

The times she kissed my father after a game, when we'd all go out for ice cream.

So much love. Suddenly gone. I would never understand.

I got home in time for Taryn to pick me up for the mall, and for two hours, I smiled and clapped and turned my thumbs up or down for nearly thirty dresses until she found the perfect one. The dress she ended up buying is blue, and it sways right above her knees. It wasn't my favorite. But I could tell it was hers, and that was all that mattered, so I told her to get it.

On our way out, we passed a white dress with a string tie weaving down the back. The sleeves were long and draped, and the dress looked like something a girl would wear to a country-dance. It wasn't frilly or body hugging like the dresses Taryn tried on. It was simple.

It was pretty.

She begged me to try it on, but I refused. I haven't worn a dress in years. I'm not even sure I quite know how. And trying one on today would be like admitting that I have fantasies—the kind where Wes shows up at my front door next Friday and takes me to some stupid school dance.

I have these fantasies, and I do not need to feed them. I need them to go away.

Taryn brought me home in time for me to grab my things and catch a ride with her to Jungle Gym. My father's door was still closed when I went inside to change, and his car was still in the garage where I'd parked. I was relieved, but also a little scared, so before I left, I cracked open his door to make sure I saw his body rise and fall with at least one breath. When I did, I left for work.

The first part of work today was harder—longer. It was also louder. I finally got a set of earplugs from a pizza chef in the back named Marcos. He took me to his locker and showed me a full box, saying I was welcome to them anytime. I plan on taking him up on his offer, because the last few hours have been bearable thanks to the muffling of the screams and crying.

Now that the lights are going off, and the gym is officially closed, I feel the tension leaving my shoulders.

Just like yesterday, the night wait staff cleans their own tables, refilling napkin holders, salt and pepper shakers, and ketchup bottles. Before they all leave, I ask one of the taller guys to help me reach a few of the cleaning supplies up high in the storage room. The schedule says I'm supposed to mop tonight, so I need the bleach.

I follow him back out to the main lobby, wheeling the mop cart in front of me, pausing while they begin to lock up the front door. The same guy from last night reminds me to go out the back, not to call the boss, and the implied *do not call him.* I turn and begin to roll the mop cart to the kitchen, but I'm stopped when he calls my name.

"Hey…Joss?" I spin around, and his brow is pinched, someone standing behind him. "This dude's out here. He says he's your ride?"

My heart thumps. It pounds. I feel it in every inch of my body.

He pushes the door open just enough, and Wes slides to the side, taking one hand from his pocket with a cautious wave. I stare at him without a word, and his eyes apologize even though they don't need to. They shouldn't. He should never be sorry. I should *always* be sorry.

My co-worker clears his throat.

"I'm sorry. Yeah, he's my ride. It's okay. Thanks for checking, though," I say, my eyes darting from him to Wes and back again.

"Sure thing. Always want to make sure you're safe," he says, opening the door a little wider to let Wes step through. He locks it behind Wes, and I keep my eyes on the window instead of the boy who has somehow become more important to me than breathing.

"As long as I don't have to call you," I mutter under my breath, chuckling to myself as my colleague stuffs his set of work keys in his pocket.

Wes's back is to me when I turn, and I allow myself a second or two to take him in. He's wearing gray jeans, a black T-shirt and his usual hat is gone. His hair in soft waves, combed back with his fingers.

My eyes go to my cleaning cart, and I step over to it, grabbing the putty knife. I move around him, not fully looking him in the eyes still, and hold out the knife. "Same slide. Different gum," I say. I move back to my cart and begin to roll it through the lobby. "I'll be in the kitchen."

I move past him, never once glancing his direction. My heart pounds in my chest so hard that it hurts, and when the kitchen door swings closed behind me, I step around the wall out of his sight, and fall against it.

One. Two. Three. Four...

I make it to twenty, then slip the door open to see if Wes is still standing there. Seeing he's gone, I exhale and turn back to my work. Moving to the sink and pulling the hose faucet over the edge, I place the end in the bucket to fill it. I turn the water on high and wait, feeling a buzz in my pocket while I do. I pull the phone out, expecting a text from Taryn or some nacho-cheese joke from Kyle. But it's Wes.

I'm having a hard time deciding what photo to use for my assignment. Can I show them to you?

I chuckle to myself lightly, shaking my head.

Sure. Mine's still going to be better.

I smirk to myself, then reach over to turn the water flow off, drying my hands and picking up my phone again. I wait for almost an entire minute for a response, then figure he must mean he'll show me later. I pull the mop from the holster, dip it in the bleach water, and begin to push it around the floor—weaving in figure eights from one corner to the other for the next ten minutes, moving myself toward the lobby door as I back away.

My phone buzzes just as I'm finishing the kitchen, and I prop the mop up inside the bucket and wipe my hands dry on my unbelievably ugly pants before swiping open a text from Wes. It isn't words...exactly. It's a photo of a letter, the handwriting sloppy, and several things misspelled. It takes me a few minutes to understand what the words say, what it is I'm looking at.

And then my heart breaks.

~~Deer~~ dear Josselyn:

Nobody reely ever talks to me. I hope I did not get you in trubble with your friend for coming to your house. I herd you talking about the races last week and they sounded like so much fun. You are always reely nice to me. You do not have to sit at my lunch table but sometimes you do. I like when you do. It makes me nervuss. That is why I hum. Thank you for liking my new shoes. My casewerker got them for me. The Woodmansees were not happy he did that. It made their reel kids angry. I wanted to tell you that because I like you. I hope it is okay that I like you. You can keep it a seecret. You do not have to like me back. Do you? If you do like me you can tell me. I would be so happy if you like me. If I win the race today I want you to have my trowfy.

Your frend,

Christopher

My body rests against the kitchen door, my back braced by it as I slide to the floor and zoom in again, to every letter of his name. The letters are lopsided and jagged and everything about this letter is imperfect, yet perfect.

"Christopher," I whisper to myself, my finger running over the zoomed-in name. My heart clenches at the memory of his arms around me, at how he felt then, a small boy—so strong and brave.

So much stronger than me then.

So much stronger than me now.

His arms were the same a few weeks ago when he held me in my own house, when I cried into him over my broken life.

I knew. I always knew.

He's telling me.

My phone buzzes in my hand, and I swipe to the next text. The shock from what I see rushes my system—my head feels light, and I fall forward, laying my phone in my lap as my head cradles into my hands.

The image is of two fingers—Wes's fingers—pinching the edge of a small gray ticket: ADMIT ONE TO TARYN AND JOSS'S RACE. The words are worn, the pencil markings smeared. Wes's face is behind the hand, his image blurred, but not so much that I can't see his expression. His mouth is a hard line. His eyes are penetrating me through this captured moment—through a lens.

Clutching my phone in my hand, I pull my legs in and push up to stand. I step through the door, closing it behind me quietly, and I move to the steps of the tree house. The music is low, and I listen for him—hoping he'll call me to him. As one song ends, I hold my breath before a new one starts; all I hear is the rustling of the air-conditioning ducts woven through the ceiling above us.

I step into the tree house, then climb the rope ladder, lifting myself to the wooden attic floor above. My eyes find Wes in the dark. He's sitting against the opposite wall, his phone in his hands just as mine was moments before. He watches me pull myself up into the same space as him, my fingers gripping at the wood floor while I slide to the opposite end. His head falls back against the wall behind him, but his eyes never leave mine. And for minutes, we stare at one another. We rarely blink. We barely breathe.

We remember.

We hurt.

"On the first day of school, Mrs. Grandel read everyone's full names. That's how I knew… *Grace*. I memorized your entire name the moment she said it. I waited for her to say it, for you to raise your hand and claim it as your name. I waited. *Josselyn Grace Winters,*" he says, his eyes on mine, his body still—mine captured with every last word he's said.

I swallow hard and slowly pull my phone out and click to open the photo of the ticket, looking down at it in my hands. My lips part to ask questions, but I don't even know what's left to ask. This unraveling is so deep, so many threads.

"Christopher was my middle name. The Woodmansees already had a Wes, so they used my middle name. I remember pieces. I don't remember everything. My brain was injured, from where the car hit me," he says. My

185

body shudders. His hand moves to the back of his head. "I had a small surgery. But I was okay. I wasn't hurt like I should have been, and I kept it a secret. I told them I hit my head on the driveway when I ran to get out of the way."

"But that…that isn't true," I say. I don't have to ask. I knew then.

He shakes his head.

"Your dad's car hit me when I reached you. I got there just in time," he says, his words stopping as he brings his hand to his mouth. He holds his fist against his lips, and I know he's thinking about what would have happened if he failed.

I would have died.

"My memory was slow to return at first, and it was too much for the Woodmansees to take on. I had some rehab. I had to learn how to do certain things again. I couldn't remember a lot of words. So the state took care of me. I had a caseworker, Shawn Stokes. He always treated me like family. But he wasn't well—a degenerative nerve disorder that eventually took his life. But before he passed away, he convinced his brother to adopt three boys instead of the two my parents were planning on."

"I didn't remember you. Nobody knows about you. I've never talked about you. But then I saw you. The day we were hitting balls at the school. It was like so many missing things fell into place," he says, his eyes leaving mine for the first time, his head falling forward to the phone in his hands, to the same photo I'm looking at. "I kept this ticket. I knew enough to know it meant something…that it was important. And I…" he pauses, chuckling lightly…sadly. "I remembered there were these twins. When I was a kid, they weren't very nice to me."

His mouth twists as he peers up at me, but his lips slowly slide into a soft bend. His gaze lingers and long seconds pass as we stare into one another.

"I didn't remember you being so beautiful," he whispers.

His eyes fall to his hands again, and I move my palms to my face to dry the tears forming in the corners of my eyes. I shift my weight, bringing my legs up in front of me, and fold my arms around my knees. Wes tilts his head to the side, not fully looking at me. He watches just enough to catch my movement. His muscles are rigid, and his jaw is flexing as he lays his phone in his lap and lets his hands squeeze into fists at his sides before relaxing.

"Why didn't you tell me?" I ask, my voice low, my courage lower. His movement stops, and his eyes find me again.

My heart breaks once more.

"The case, with your dad…it's still open."

I breathe in deep and pull my legs in tighter.

"The state has a lot of questions, but I've never been able to remember things. The story was always that he lost control of the car, that it was a terrible accident. But there are a few things that don't add up. There wasn't a sobriety test done. But a few of the kids said they thought maybe—"

"My dad was drinking," I whisper, my gaze falling away from him. I tuck my chin into my body and bring my hands to my mouth, my thumb between my teeth.

"I get questioned every few years about the accident, and I never remember. Nobody really cares anymore. The case, it's just on a list—and it's probably just considered dead. But it's on some numerical radar in some filing system, and they have to check. They're going to call my parents again one day. They're going to want to talk to me. And they're going to know I'm back here—near you. Playing for him. And I will lie. You can't let them know I remember anything."

"Why would it matter? Maybe it would be good for him, Wes. Maybe that's what needs to happen—something that sobers him up," I say, my voice coming out angrier—stronger.

"And what would happen to you?"

Me. This isn't about my father at all. This is about me.

"You're not eighteen. Yeah, maybe they would let you stay with a family friend. Or maybe they'd send you to live with a relative. Or maybe they'd place you with a family you don't know. I've lived with a lot of families, Joss. I've had good families, but I've had bad families too."

"I want your dad to clean up. I want that for you more than anything on this earth. I've been working on it. And I know…" he turns his head to the side, his lips tight, his smile sweet, but short. "I know you don't want me to help. But I refuse not to. I won't stand by and watch you go through this alone. I didn't want your father to get taken away then, and I don't now. As bad as he is, Joss, you still don't need to become a ward of the state. He's not as bad as playing parent lottery—I can promise you that."

I stare into his eyes for several minutes, and he lets me. My stomach aches over the reality of what he just said, but even so, my emotions swing on this pendulum from fear to freedom.

"Christopher," I whisper, resting my cheek on my hands over my knees as I look at him. My eyes have adjusted, and I can now see him clearly in the dark.

"It's Wes, Joss. Just Wes," he sighs.

I move slowly, pulling my legs under me, crawling on my knees closer to him as I shake my head. "No, it's not," I say. I stop at his side, and my breath halts along with his. I place one hand on his shoulder and move my leg over his lap, so I'm straddling his thighs, and I sit my weight on him. My other hand finds his cheek, and I press my palm against his familiar, matured face. "It's not just Wes. It's both. It's…it's you," I say, my chest heaving as I start to cry.

Both of my hands move to his face, holding it and looking him in the eyes, my thumbs stroking slowly along his cheeks.

"My god how I've needed you," I swallow, sucking my bottom lip in and smiling for him.

His hands are slow as they move from the floor to my thighs, and with a cautious drag, he brings them up my body, along my sides and to my arms, until he's cupping my face too. His head falls forward, and he rests it on mine, his lips parting with a breath.

"I love how you look at me. I love how you see me, Joss. I love that you think I'm invincible. You've always looked at me like…like I was something better than the way everyone else saw me, but…" He stops, his thumbs moving to my chin, and he tilts my head up enough so I'm meeting his eyes. His eyes move from one of mine to the other, and he breathes in slowly, his chest filling under me, his touch on me the only thing that's felt right in years.

"I'm not invincible, Joss. I'm just not," he shakes his head. "I will always fight for you. I can't say *no* when it comes to you. I can't *not* fight for you. I can't *not* do everything in my power to keep you safe. But I could fail. And if I ever lost you, if I was too late just once, not strong enough, not capable—"

"I won't test you, Wes," I say, my hand running along his face again, under his jaw. He leans into my touch, his eyes closed, and his lips brush against my palm.

"Thank you," he breathes, his lips kissing against my hand again. "Jesus, thank you. I can't fail you, Joss. I can't—"

"I know," I nod, bringing his eyes back to mine. I nod again for him to see me. "I know."

His hands move into my hair, one reaching the tie twisted in the strands, and he pulls it loose and runs his fingers deep into it, combing along my scalp as his eyes fall over me in the most adoring way. I've dreamt of him looking at me like this. There were times I even thought for brief seconds he, in fact, did. But now that I'm here, in his arms, I know that *this*...this is real. And it is a first for us. Every fantasy I've had could never measure up.

I pull myself forward, into him, my hands running in his hair, and our heads rest on one another again, until his dips lower, his nose grazing along the curve of my neck, his lips whispering kisses along my skin, up my jaw, until his mouth pauses over mine and I feel it slide into a smile.

"I'm about to kiss Josselyn Winters," he says, a light laugh escaping him. "Holy shit."

I give in and smile against him too.

"It's Jose," I laugh, loving the feel of him laughing with me, his body shaking with happiness, the sound thundering quietly in his chest. "And you better make it a good kiss," I add, my bottom lip catching his top lip.

I hold onto it, I taste it and wait for him to make the next move.

He spends time dusting his lips over mine, his tongue finding my bottom lip, taking small passes. Every movement is slow and savored. This is our time—here alone in a pretend tree house shrouded in darkness. We're two kids who found each other when each needed someone to believe in them the most. Our bodies have grown. Our hearts are still the same. And they knew…

Mine knew all along, and his remembered.

"You have always made me feel like I belong," Wes says, brushing another soft kiss over my lips and resting his head on mine, his eyes closed.

"You have always made me feel like I matter," I say back, my head shaking at the memory of his embraces during my darkest times.

He pulls away from me, his eyes searching mine again, as if he doesn't understand how anyone could think otherwise. He's home. He's come back to me. And I fall into him, his hands gripping my hair and caressing my face while his mouth covers mine with a possessive kiss. His tongue moves along my own as his lips tug on my lips, his teeth grazing along my tender skin with each parting pass until he comes back hungrier for more.

We kiss until our bodies are tired and our mouths have memorized every breath and move the other half has made. And then Wes helps me finish my duties, making an hour's worth of work take less than half the time it should. When we leave, he grabs my hand firmly in his own, threading our fingers together as he walks me from the backdoor to the front of the building and his truck. He doesn't let go until I'm home and he's seen me to my front door, satisfied that my father stayed home tonight—even if he's asleep in the chair with a drink in his hand.

I kiss Wes goodnight, then lock up and shut the lights off in the house. I tug the quilt from my father's bed and lay it over him in his chair, kissing his head once while he sleeps, and I pull his drink away.

"I hope your dreams are good, Daddy. And I hope you come back from them soon," I say, for the first time in years, believing he might.

CHAPTER 11

Wes showed up Sunday, just the same, telling my coworker—who I know now is named Jamie—that he was my ride. I didn't even have to ask him to scrape the gum away. He simply grabbed the putty knife from my hand and went to work.

We didn't leave immediately. We spent an hour after my work was done sitting in the tree house talking. I told him everything I knew—reliving what happened the day of the last race, when my father confronted my mom and how he left in a rage. I also told him how my mom left without ever saying goodbye. As crappy as my father is, at least he stayed.

When Wes brought me home, I was in such a state of peace that, for the first time in months, I didn't feel my chest seize up with worry over what state I would find my father in. I didn't search for his car the moment I turned down my street; I didn't scan the lawn for his body, and I didn't dread unlocking the door. All of which made the surprise of opening the door and finding him sitting in his chair—alert and awake, a soda in his hand and the evening news on—that much more startling.

I said goodnight to Wes and acted as if he weren't there at all. We didn't speak, but we also didn't argue or tussle while I tried to wake him and carry him to bed. It was quiet and fast, and the weight of it hit my chest the moment I shut my bedroom door. The heaviness was still there this morning, and I feel it now as I pull up to the front of the school with Taryn, her car slowing at the top of the hill where I usually exit and head straight for the library.

"I think maybe I'll come with you today. To the gym?" I glance at her from my periphery and look away quickly when I catch enough of the shocked expression on her face. I bend forward and zip the side pocket of my bag open. I have no reason to. I have nothing I need, nothing to search for. I just don't want to look at her.

"Ooooookayyyy," she finally says, moving her gear to drive and continuing down the hill.

We park near the back of the gym and walk to the side door where the weight room is. I can hear the *clanking* from the other side of the door before we even open it, and my insides are swarming with a sense of familiar. My hands quake, and I look at them to make sure they're still my own—still the same hands I have now. They are, but everything about me feels like the little girl who used to stop by in the morning with her mom to bring her daddy coffee.

Taryn pulls the door open then glares at me, watching as I stand frozen and look inside. She shakes her head with a sigh, stepping into the room. I grab the door just before it closes and follow her.

"I usually just hang out over here until he's done," she says, moving to the padded training tables near the wall. I set my bag next to her as she pulls herself up and sits with her back against the wall. But rather than joining her, I turn around and let my legs amble on rote memories to the other end of the gym where the jump ropes hang.

"Hey," I hear Wes's voice over my shoulder.

"Hey," I hum, not turning around. My fingers run down the plastic beads of the blue-and-white rope. A few seconds later, Wes's fingers come into view, grabbing the blue-and-red one next to it—his knuckles grazing my own in a purposeful touch that wakes me from my trance.

"Wanna jump?" he says, his right cheek dimpled with a smile. I take it in for a breath, then glance beyond him to my father's desk. He's watching me, and though I expect him to be scowling, he isn't. He's looking at me with no expression at all.

"Yeah," I say, my eyes moving to Wes's. "I do," I grin.

I pull the rope into my hands and move a few steps away to give us both room, then begin to swing. The silent competition sparks quickly, and I do my best to keep up with him, but after a full minute of skipping, my feet finally run out of speed, and the beads tangle with my shoes.

"Yeah, I'm still working on my cardio," I huff, wrapping the rope around my hand.

"That was pretty good," he says. I roll my eyes at him. "No, seriously. I've been doing this every day for weeks, so it was good. You did good."

"Whatever," I say, smiling to myself when I turn away to hang my rope on the hook. When I turn back, I glance at where my father was sitting to find him no longer there. I sigh, my mind instantly replaying his voice, his warning to leave Wes alone. *I'm a distraction.*

I leave Wes on his own, and head to the free weights, loading some weights and working out on my own. He never lets me wander far, but he gives me my independence. After twenty minutes, though, my muscles fatigue, and I slide my feet over to Taryn, collapsing on the bench next to her.

"I'm proud of you," she says through the side of her mouth, not pulling her eyes away from some video she's watching on her phone. "I know how hard it was for you to come in here."

I exhale and lean into the wall behind us, rolling my head to the side. "Thanks," I sigh, landing my fist softly on her shoulder.

After a few minutes, the bell sounds, giving us ten minutes to get to our first period. I pull myself up and lean forward to grab my heavy backpack, but my father's feet are on either side. I look up at him, squinting, my eyes still sleepy. He's holding a folded piece of paper, which I stare at for a few seconds before his hand shakes it once, encouraging me to take it.

"What's this?" I say, my brow pulled in as I stand and shift my bag over my shoulder and unfold the page with one hand.

"Your workout," my dad says as he walks away. I watch him, my lips parted, caught in their usual pose—the one that's ready to defend myself and argue with my father. Only…that's not what this morning was about.

"You ready?" Taryn says next to me. I begin to walk alongside her and read through the routine my father clearly just jotted down in pen—a mix of upper body, legs, and core with specific goals set for two weeks, four, and then six. He made plans. He has expectations. And not just gruff, unattainable ones I'll never meet. These were made with thought.

"Told you," Wes says, suddenly by my side. I startle, and begin folding the paper quickly, stuffing it in the back pocket of my jeans.

"Told me what?" I ask, suddenly aware that he's next to me, near Taryn and TK, and Kyle and Levi are behind us.

"That your dad loves you," he leans in. I stop for a second and consider his words, what just happened.

"This is about me beating the competition. That's all," I say, shaking my head and looking at my feet.

"No," Wes says, his thumb under my chin, pulling my eyes to his. "It's about him *believing* in you and knowing you're better than the competition."

I lean my head to the side and purse my lips, still not ready to give into his argument, when without warning, he leans in close and brushes his mouth on mine, running his thumb along my bottom lip and holding the side of my face while he looks at me.

"It's also about you being too stubborn to consider I might just be right," he says, his mouth raised on one side. I let out a breathy laugh, and immediately blush at the sound of Levi *Ooooooooing* behind us.

My face falls lower, and I start to tuck my chin into my chest, but Wes quickly trails his hand down my arm to my hand, his fingers linking with mine before he tugs gently on my arm to walk with him.

"This might seriously be the first time I've seen a guy hold Joss's hand and not get punched in the face," Kyle says behind me.

"That's because you're usually the one trying to hold her hand, Kyle. And no girl wants that—we'd *all* punch you in the face," Taryn says loudly.

"Ha ha ha," Kyle says back. He's acting like it's no big deal, but I can tell his feelings are hurt. I look over my shoulder to check on him. He smiles with tight lips and winks at me. I mentally do my best to send him an apology. I'm caught between wanting to hide holding Wes's hand in front of him and wanting to showcase it to the world.

He doesn't give me a choice, not letting go until we have to part ways and move to our separate seats in our English class. I catch a few stares on our locked fingers before he lets go, and I know it's only a matter of seconds before McKenna knows. I watch a friend scurry over to her seat, in the front corner—a few rows away from Wes and me. She glances at each of us while her friend talks, but quickly pretends not to care. Inside, I gloat.

The rest of the day, the feeling of having someone like Wes claim me as his publicly, lingers—and I find myself walking the halls a little taller, feeling less of a need to put off a vibe that warns people to stay away. It's a different kind of confidence. I feel...beautiful.

At lunch, rather than leave campus with his brothers, he tosses the keys to TK and stays behind, sitting with Taryn and me. The way Taryn looks at both of us makes me blush, and eventually Wes leans forward, pressing his lips on my cheek in front of her, almost as if he's trying to break the ice and let the awkward out of the bag.

"So you two are really actually...together?" Taryn says. I glance to Wes, not sure how to answer.

"Until she tells me otherwise," he says, grabbing a fry from my plate and popping it in his mouth. I grimace at him.

"If you steal my food, that might happen sooner rather than later," I threaten, teasingly. He reaches for another fry and holds it at his lips, and I lower my brow. "You sure about that?"

He pauses with it there for a few seconds and opens his mouth, about to bite into it, but closes quickly and places the fry back on my plate, brushing his fingertips together to get rid of the left-behind salt kernels.

"Nope," he chuckles. "Pretty much not sure of anything at all."

Wes pulls his own plate closer, folding his slice of pizza in half and

195

eating nearly a third of it with the first bite. I watch as he chews, his long body stretched under and above the table, his legs jutting out into the aisle. He's outgrown this place already, and he's only seventeen.

"So does this mean…you'll be going to the dance on Friday?" My stomach drops the moment my friend puts that out there. I could kill her. Literally, my mind is racing through the millions of ways I want to punch her or push her into traffic, and my face is red and beating.

"You know I hate dances," I blurt out, realizing too late that I cut Wes off, his lips held open, about to speak. He was going to ask? He wants to go to the stupid dance with *me*? I will never know now, because I'm a stubborn cuss who sucks at this whole boy thing.

"Oh, believe me, Joss…I know," Taryn says, finishing her last bite and standing from the lunch table. Her eyes glide from me to Wes and back again, her eyebrow raising a tick just to let me know I fucked up with that one. I raise both of mine and push my lips together tight to signal to her that I know.

Taryn leaves us alone, and the tension makes me slink down a little in my seat. I can tell Wes isn't looking at me. He's feeling the tension too, and it's sucky, and I hate that it's over a stupid dance.

"I just don't really do the whole dress-up thing," I blurt out.

That made it worse.

I spare a glance at Wes. He smiles tightly and nods, but I can tell from the deep inhale that slowly fills his chest that he's still uncomfortable, maybe disappointed? I turn my attention to my things, pretending to straighten notebooks and papers in my backpack as I unzip and zip again. Wes steps away from the table with our trash, and I exhale the second he's gone. When he comes back, he looks around at the tables nearby, his eyes not quite making it to me.

"So you have a game today, yeah?" he asks, still not fully engaged.

"Yeah. You guys are off, right?" I respond, pulling my bag over my shoulder. He reaches for my hand as we begin to walk and a heavy breath falls from my chest in relief that he's still proud to be with me, even if I throw baby fits over school dances. His hand squeezes mine tightly, as if he senses the inner turmoil I'm feeling. Everything about the last two minutes feels so utterly teenager, so unlike me. I need to get back to me—to feel home.

"I bet you ten bucks I can hit the ball over the fence today?" I throw a challenge out there. It's meaningless, but the goal somehow gives me something else to think about—something other than dances and my dream boy and...*dreams.*

I look up at Wes as we pass through the cafeteria doors and into the hall, his lip pinned in his teeth and his brow bunched.

"So, all I get is ten dollars if you don't pull this off?" he chuckles. "I mean it's not like *I'm* pitching to you. It doesn't feel fair."

"Silly Wes," I say through a breathy laugh, shaking my head as we step into the photo lab. "If you were pitching, I guarantee I would hit one. *That* wouldn't be fair. That would be like taking on a T-ball team."

I spin around at my desk, dropping my bag in my seat and folding my arms, standing toe-to-toe with him. My lips are tingling, and I comfort the itch by letting a smirk slide into place. This feels more natural. This is how we are. This is how Wes and I need to be. We're races and tickets and dares. And maybe some kissing too.

Wes steps close enough that his head is nearly resting on mine, and I have to look up at him. I love looking up at him. The right side of his mouth curves into a grin, and he shrugs one shoulder, adjusting the weight of his bag slung over his arm. The noise of more students bursting through the door causes him to turn and look at them, but he comes back to me quickly, his smile reaching both sides of his mouth now.

"All right, Joss," he says, taking two steps back and leaning against the tabletop of the desk across from me. He folds his arms and lowers his eyes, and his smile switches into something almost devious. "I'll take that bet...with a twist. You hit one over the fence today. And if you don't, you are going with me to that dance on Friday."

Well, shit.

I pull my top lip into my mouth and suck. Half of my body is jumping up and down, dying to go to this stupid dance. The other half is pissed, and wants to hit the ball over the fence and prove that I don't need dances and dresses and hearts and boys showing up at my door with flowers.

But I want that too. I want it so badly.

"Deal," I say, reaching out my hand for his. He chuckles and shakes his head, pushing off from the desk and taking my hand in his. He shakes it, but steps closer to me, towing my hand up to his mouth, turning it over to press his lips on my wrist. I swear when he turns away, I'll be able to see a brand from it, I still feel it so strongly. I actually look when he leaves, but it's only my skin—no visual memory of his touch. But my heart remembers. My stupid heart, and the thump in my chest and the numb feeling I have in my toes and fingertips.

I swallow, move into my seat, and pull out my notes on lighting. We spend the rest of the afternoon learning new ways to use shadows to tell a story, but all I think about is how I want to crawl into one. I think about how even if I blow this and weasel my way into a school dance date with Wesley Stokes, I don't have anything to wear, and I wouldn't know what to do when we got there.

I resolve myself to swinging at the very first pitch I get and putting it over the fence to end the misery of living with expectations. And then I regret knowing I will. I simmer in regret until the bell sounds and Wes and I link fingers at the door and walk down the hallway and outside to the gym to change. When his hand leaves mine, I feel lucky and terrified all at once.

Taryn comes in last—she's always late to practice, late to the games, late to coach's meeting. She says that's why she's stuck in right field. But really—she's just not the strongest player. I come in late. And before I met Wes, I used to skip practice all together. But I still played short and batted fourth. Sometimes, skills get you a pass in life. I rode mine for a long time.

Lately, though, I've been trying harder. I've wanted more—more from myself, more out of life, more…

More expectations.

I don't know if it's because of Wes, or if the timing was just fate that I decided to make a change in my life. I would like to think I'm strong enough to fight for things on my own. But I also know that I didn't really care about much, until the boy who saved me once, showed up to do it again.

I take my time lacing my cleats, pulling my socks up high around my knees. My pants are snug against my thighs; my sliding shorts padding me underneath. Taryn is still getting dressed, so while I wait for her—while the rest of the girls have gone and I have this small window in front of the bathroom mirrors alone—I stand still and look at myself.

My chest is flattened under the thick stretch of Lycra. My hair is pulled back tight, the few loose strands around my hairline glued down with water I splashed on them with my hands. As I turn to the side, I take in my figure. I curve, but more in the way that screams of speed and muscle. My arms are still blue with bruises in spots; more green, really. And where they're not, I'm scratched up like a tomboy who spent the day wrestling fish barehanded from the rocky river-bottom.

I turn back to the mirror and step forward, resting my hands on either side of the sink, letting my face get close. My freckles are faint, and my green eyes are muddied, but when I stare closely, holding my breath, I can still see her—I can still see the girl Wes…Christopher…saved years ago.

"She's in there," I whisper, my eyes held open until they start to tear.

I back up and shake my head, clearing myself of that sad feeling that was starting to crawl inside. I breathe in slowly and turn to my right. I don't look like a girl who goes to a dance. And this is the first time I've ever really cared about the outside—what people see and how I fit into their mold.

"You ready?" Taryn yells from the locker room end.

"Coming!" I shout back, lingering on my reflection for one more second—just long enough to clear my head and get on my game face.

I snag my equipment bag on my way to the front door and meet Taryn there to walk along the dirt path that divides the baseball side of our school fields from the softball side. I catch a vision of Wes on the mound, my father standing next to him with a clipboard and the speed gun. It's too far to see their eyes, but their hats are both tilted toward me. Wes reaches up and adjusts his, and I let myself smile because I know it was for me—a sign saying *hello*. And then I think about our deal, and the girl I saw in the mirror, and I look away.

"I guess Trinity really sucks," Taryn says. I glance out to the right side of the field where the other team is throwing, girls dressed in bright green with bows and matching shoelaces. They all have matching jackets, and when I look over at their dugout, their equipment bags all have their numbers stitched on them.

Private schools.

"They look like they have money," I say, dropping my bag on the dugout bench and looking at my own cleats—my laces worn and knotted. I wouldn't trade my shoes for theirs for anything in the world.

"Whatever. Remember last year when we snuck a smoke behind their school before the game?" Taryn says, grabbing a ball from the bucket and leading me out to the field to throw.

I laugh under my breath at the memory, nodding to her when I'm ready for her to throw.

Last year's matchup with Trinity was when my bottom began. I took myself out of the game, pouting from a bad call, and that night was the furthest I went in a make-out session with Kyle. I kissed him and let him get my shirt off in his back bedroom while our friends all got drunk in his living room. I felt ashamed during, and the shame only amplified when I pushed him away after an hour of him hoping things would go somewhere. I don't know how he doesn't hate me, but I'm glad he doesn't.

That's when I started skipping practices and sleeping in, blowing off class. I skirted by with mostly *C*s, and one *D* last year. My grade point average is shit. But I wasn't going anywhere. I didn't want to go anywhere, other than some place that wasn't in my father's home.

I didn't think about limitations. I only thought of not giving a damn about much. But I kind of want to go somewhere now. I kind of give a damn. My stomach twists knowing that my spiral could have cost me the opportunity to go anywhere at all—to go anywhere Wes might go.

"They're ending early," Taryn says, nodding over my shoulder and flipping the ball to me underhand. I catch it and rest it in my glove on my hip, squinting into the sun as I look out at the baseball team huddled around home plate.

"He never ends early. He's probably just lecturing them more," I say, still captivated by the scene on the other field.

Our coach calls us to the dugout, so I join the rest of the team, but I watch as the boys grunt out a chant and begin to move from the field, grabbing their bags and unlacing their shoes. A few of them begin to walk across the field, but it doesn't hit me until I see Wes walking alongside my father—heading this way.

"Holy fuck," I say under my breath.

"What?" Taryn says, flipping her hair up as she kneels on the bench beside me, looking through the back holes of our dugout. She locks onto what I see a second later. There are maybe twenty guys on my father's varsity team, and they are all headed this way.

Every single one of them.

Taryn's laughter starts to brew in her chest, and soon the raspy rhythm of it is filling my left ear, her hand slapping my arm.

"Holy shit, they're coming to watch us!" She leaps from the bench and rushes to the other end of the backstop so she can talk to TK as he walks up to our small set of bleachers. I stay where I am, on the opposite end, working the rough edges of my glove around my hand.

Wes stands behind the bleachers, resting his hands on the top of the back seat. My father is next to him, but only Wes looks my way. He lifts his hand and smooths his hair under his hat, sliding it back in place before giving me a slight nod.

I feel sick.

Thank god we're in the field first.

Our coach gathers us for some warm-ups, and I only half listen to his assessment of the other team. It doesn't matter what his assessment is. I only know one way to play—*my* way. The Eric Winters way. It's just that it's been a while since I've played in front of my father.

I catch my father's eyes over my coach's shoulder. He's watching intently, even though he can't hear anything. As we take warm-ups, I notice him lean over and give commentary to Wes.

It doesn't take long for muscle memory to kick in, and I glide side-to-side, my feet find their natural rhythm for every fielding attempt, for every throw. My head kicks in with my father's voice.

You are better than that. Throw it harder. Don't leave room for errors. Nothing gets by you. Come on!

I toss my final warm-up throw to our catcher, Shelby, and the ball snaps in her glove. She flicks her mask off and glares at me, but I look away. I took that out on her. I'm not proud. But I'm also not apologizing.

We take the field, and Trinity only gets a hold of one pitch, sending a line drive at my knees that I snag easily and flip up to the pitcher on my way in. I notice my father lean to Wes, and I sit alone at the end of the bench in our dugout to think about what he could have possibly said.

Don't flip the ball like that. Nobody needs showboating. Just do your job.

Our first two batters get on easily with walks, and I pull my helmet from the ground and put it on, spitting out the sunflower seeds I stuffed into my mouth seconds before.

"I don't know how you eat those things. They're gross. It's like chewing on pencils," Taryn says, kicking dirt over my pile of wet seed shells. I glare at her. "Don't take your shakes out on me. You're pissy because you quit smoking."

I scowl at her.

"No, I'm not," I say, pulling the small bag of seeds from my back pocket and pouring five or six more into my mouth. "And fuck off."

Truth is, I don't really miss cigarettes at all. I didn't like the way they made me feel. I liked the distraction of them, the fact that they made people think twice about me and leave me alone. I liked that they were one more thing that pissed my dad off.

The girl at bat before me is named Bria. Her ribbon is enormous. I'd make fun of it, but she's actually a decent hitter. And now that I'm the only player not wearing a ribbon, I don't really have much to stand on. Bria gets ahold of a pitch and sends a ball into deep center field, and the Trinity player somehow puts a glove on it. I swear her eyes were closed for the catch. I walk toward the plate feeling the swagger of knowing anything I put out there won't be touched. Bria hit the ball well, but she doesn't hit as hard as I do. I won't give anyone time to react. My ball will be gone before they know what to do with it. My father won't have anything to say. And I won't be wearing a dress Friday for some stupid dance.

Even though that's all I want in the world.

I spit my last round of seeds out in the grass before I get to the batter's box. The umpire glares at me, and I stare back at him, feeling around my mouth for the one shell left inside. I spit that out too, this time on the dirt, and I cover it with a small kick of my cleat.

"Bacon-flavored," I say, raising my eyebrows in a flash. He grumbles and points a finger at the Trinity pitcher, done with me.

I load my weight and let the bat rest on my shoulder until I know she's ready to throw. She winds and grunts, and the ball flies by me, a little above my waist. I let it go.

"Strike!"

I hear everyone cheering in the background. Some of the guys are chanting my name, and my teammates are yelling a string of "Come on, Joss, let's go, Joss, you got this, Joss. Let's go, number thirty-four!"

It's all noise. All of it. None of it matters. I don't let it in my head. That pitch didn't matter. It wasn't my pitch. I tune it all out. I don't hear a thing. Only the sound of my pulse and my breath as it comes in and leaves through my nose.

And then I hear his voice.

"Thata girl. You don't hit those. You hit winners."

My father doesn't yell like everyone else. He speaks. His voice cuts through the bullshit and moves right for my ears. It's all I hear, and suddenly my legs shift, my hands adjust and my muscles flex.

I'm a fighter waiting to strike, and when the pitcher delivers her next try, I hit the ball so hard it not only clears the outfield fence, it bounces into the parking lot.

My feet carry me at an easy pace around the bases, my eyes watching the dirt clouds that puff beneath the heels of every step of the girl running in front of me. As I round third, my team is walking from the dugout to greet me at home plate. I don't look at them. I look right through the backstop, to the back row of bleachers, to the older man standing behind them—smiling.

I'm hugged and high-fived the second I pass the plate, but my eyes never leave my father's. His smile is brief, and if I hadn't looked right away, I probably would have missed it. But I did look. It was there.

It was real.

The rest of the game passes with much of the same. We end up scoring fifteen runs to their two—and the game is called after the bottom of the fourth for time. Our field isn't lighted, and the sun is on its last few minutes of gold.

Taryn packs up quickly and yells that she'll call me later, passing her things to TK, who carries them on one side of his body while he holds her close on the other side. I watch them walk away while I tug my batting gloves from my hand and take my time packing up. I'm the last one in the dugout when Wes steps in behind me.

"So, I guess I owe you this," he says, holding out a ten-dollar bill. I smirk at it and shrug. I don't want it anymore.

"Bet's a bet, right?" I say, taking the ten from him and pushing it into my back pocket. I bend down and pull my cleats from my feet, then zip them into the bottom pouch of my bag, my back to him. I drop my flip-flops on the ground and stuff my feet in, scrunching the socks between my toes.

"Yeah…bet's a bet," Wes says behind me. I sigh and turn to look at him, instantly guilty because I can't seem to just give in and tell him *yes, I want to go to the dance.* He's already left the dugout.

I look out to the home plate area and notice my father talking with our coach. He isn't yelling. In fact, at the moment, they're both laughing, my father with his hand placed on my coach's back, leaning forward and smiling. They both turn to look at me, and the laughing stops, so I step from the dugout and follow Wes's steps toward the bleachers.

"Nice hitting today, Winters. Your dad was just telling me we should get you some work on the left side of the plate. I didn't know you switched," coach says.

"I don't," I answer quickly. I notice my father's response—he leans back with a silent chuckle and folds his arms over his chest.

"She does. She's just rusty. It's been a while," he says, his eyes dancing over me with a familiar fire.

Pride.

I pause my steps and look at them both. I'm expressionless because this feels like a trick. I'm waiting for things to turn.

"We'll work on it," my father says.

My eyes go right to his, expecting something different. I expect a dig or criticism. But instead, I think he might just be making plans.

"Sounds good to me," coach says, patting my father on the back once and moving toward the dugout to grab his things. He spins on his heels and walks backward, looking at us both. "Oh, and you might want to have that ready to go next week. Chico State has a guy coming out to our road game to take a look at you."

"She'll be ready," my father says. He's holding a glove in his hand, and he slaps it once in his other palm before letting it drop to his side. It's something he's always done—he's always thrown with the boys, always done every drill he expects them to do.

It's something he used to do with me.

I feel Wes step closer behind me, but he stops as my father approaches. I'm caught in the middle, like a cat lost in the rain, and every muscle in my body wants to run. My heart wants to stay right here though.

"Whaddaya say you get up early with Wes and me, come out here to the field, and we work on some things this weekend? I mean, you've been getting up early and running on your own anyhow," my father says with a light laugh that turns into a cough. He's nervous. "You're not as quiet and sneaky as you think you are. I hear you in the morning."

"I didn't think you were aware of *anything* in the morning," I say. I hear Wes's breath change behind me, like he wants to interject. I'm attacking, and I know Wes doesn't want me to blow this moment, but I've waited so long to say some of these things with my father in a state-of-mind that was willing to hear them. I have to get them off my chest.

"You're right. And that's fair." My father's words shock me.

I wait for him to give me the *but* portion of the statement; instead, he brings his arms up, his trusty glove still in one hand, and shrugs, admitting his guilt.

"I have work," I say, my chin raised as I deliver my next excuse—the next hurdle to overcome in this *Hallmark* moment.

"We'll work around your schedule, so you don't have to get up too early after coming in late," he says.

"Ohhh, yeah. For *me,* right? Not you and your coming in late. This is about me," I say, turning back to gather my things. I run into Wes, who has moved closer and is already holding them.

"Joss, just give him this. Just listen," he says.

I pause and study Wes's expression. His eyes are begging me to take this leap, to trust that my father is doing something kind right now. This olive branch is real, and Wes wants me to take it.

I spin back to face my father, but his eyes are on Wes's. He's biting his bottom lip, and he stands there motionless, in thought, for several seconds before speaking.

"She has a lot of reasons not to listen, Wes. I know. I have not been…present. I haven't been *there*," my father says.

"You haven't been anything but a drunk, abusive ass!" I interrupt, my voice caught between laugh and cry.

My father swallows hard, his eyes shifting to me as he passes the glove between his hands. He slowly begins to nod, then leans his head slightly to one side, his eyes frosting over with something I don't recognize. It's not quite regret, but it's close.

"I'll be here Saturday, at nine in the morning. And I'll be here for you.

Hope you can make it," he says, walking past me and stopping at Wes to shake his hand before he leaves us both on the field alone.

It's quiet and uncomfortable for the full minute it takes for my father to walk the length of the field to the parking lot where his car sits.

"Joss, I—" Wes starts, and I turn and point at him.

"No! You nothing. What was this? Did you put him up to this? Was this like an intervention or some lame attempt to try to fix our fucked up relationship? You can't fix us, Wes. You can't! We're too broken."

I rip the straps of my bag from his hand, but his grip is hard and fast. We both tug, but I'm no match for his strength, so I halt as he lowers his head and holds my eyes captive.

"Goddamnit, Josselyn! Your dad did this on his own. He planned this days ago, when he saw your schedule was different from ours. He shortened our practice, and told the team if any of us wanted to keep our starting position he'd better see our asses on the bleachers cheering for the girls. *He* said all of that, Joss. Your dad! Not me…*him!*"

Wes lets go of his hold on my things, and the loss of his grip sends me back a step or two. I hold his gaze, and all I feel is foolish. I'm embarrassed because my life is so fucked up. All this boy has ever really known of me is how much my father has broken my heart. He's seen it—from the very beginning. The fact that he's here, witnessing this attempt at making things right—which will no doubt fail—makes me feel more ashamed.

"He's going to disappoint me," I say, the cry sneaking up on me. I suck it in and roll my shoulders, rebuilding my resolve.

"Maybe he won't," Wes says, stepping into me more.

I take one step back and shake my head, looking at my feet and dropping my things.

"He always disappoints me. He's going to do it again," I whisper. I don't say it loud, because I'm regretful to admit I don't believe in my dad. I'm even more ashamed to admit I want to.

"What if he doesn't? What if he wants this more than you?" Wes closes the distance once more.

I swallow and nod to myself, lifting my eyes to meet his, my arms wrapped tightly around my body.

"Are you going to pick me up when I fall? Are you going to be there for me when he fails?" I bite my lip hard, doubt pushing on one side and the little girl who wants this wish to come true pounding on the other.

Wes rests his head on mine and pushes the stray hairs from my face, running his thumbs along either cheek.

"He's not going to fail, Joss. He's not. I looked in his eyes today, and I believe. But I will be there for you, for every bump and setback that might happen. It won't be perfect, and he'll make mistakes, but he's not going to quit. He's not going to fail." Wes's voice is soft, and he tilts my chin with his thumb, urging me to look up at him.

I whimper once and let out a hard breath, looking to the side while I run my wrist over my eyes.

"It's okay to cry, Joss. It doesn't mean you're weak," he says.

"Yeah, it does. And I hate it," I say, refusing to meet his gaze.

"It's okay to cry," he repeats, and his words ignite another sob escaping me.

"Whatever," I breathe, running my hand over my eyes again, finally giving in and facing him. His smile is soft and his head leans to the side while he takes over the work on clearing my face of pain.

"Whatever, as in…you'll try? You'll come out here with us on Saturday morning?" he says, his lips in a faint, tight smirk.

"Whatever," I shake my head. "Yeah, fine. I'll come out here."

His grin stays in place, and his eyes remain on mine, studying me, as if he's drilling down to uncover the secrets underneath them. But I have no secrets. Not from him. He *was* my secret—*is* my secret.

"What?" I finally shrug after long seconds pass under his scrutiny. I feel hot from blushing.

"Are you going to let me take you to this *stupid* dance?"

It isn't chocolate or flowers, and to anyone else—Taryn especially—it isn't romantic in the least. But to me, that one frustrated sentence is the world. It's everything. And it's exactly how I wanted to be asked.

My lip tugs up on one corner, and I nod slowly, still holding his stare. "Yeah, I am."

CHAPTER 12

"If you would hold still, it wouldn't hurt when I pulled on it."

I think Taryn likes feeling like she's the boss of me. It's typically the other way around. She hasn't really been the one in control of things in our friendship since we were kids. When my life turned upside down, she ceded dominance to me. The older I got, the more I realized she gave it to me because she knew I needed it—I needed to be in charge of *something*. So, she let me call the shots when it came to the trouble we got into.

But now—now that she has a handful of my hair in her grip, pins poking every which way into my scalp, hot irons poised to scald my skin— Taryn is once again in charge.

"This is torture for me. You know this is torture, right?" I blow up at my forehead, a few stray curls she's left there to cool sliding across my skin.

"This coming from the girl I watched purposely throw herself from a moving vehicle at fifty miles per hour. Yeah, I'm really sure *this* is going to be the thing that kills you," Taryn says.

"It might," I say, my eyes looking up from the corners, my head held firmly in place with her hand while she pushes one more piece of metal into a thick chunk of my hair. "And I'm pretty sure we were only going thirty at the time. Maybe thirty-five."

"You know, I would *kill* to have thick hair that curled like yours. It's so unfair," she sighs.

"Well, I'd give it to you if I could. You have no idea how many times I've thought of shaving my head," I say.

Taryn's fingers pause and she twists my head so my eyes are looking at her, her hands sliding to my cheeks where she pushes my mouth inward from the sides.

"Please say you're kidding about that. Do not—I repeat—do not, not *ever*, shave your head."

"I'm…kidding?" I say through smooshed lips.

Taryn stares at me for an extra second, then rolls her eyes and jerks my pony tail once more. I'm pretty sure she didn't really need to do that. I zone out on the thought of me shaving my head for a few minutes while Taryn finishes working my hair into something presentable. I really did have the clippers to my head once last year. I even went ahead and took off a chunk in the very back. It was just enough that when I pulled it up in a tie, I could feel the short hairs along my neck. I liked to touch them and think of how easy it would be to shave it all—to be that free.

"Okay," Taryn says, pushing hard on my right shoulder and spinning me around on the kitchen stool we'd pulled into her bathroom. "Time to take it all in."

I don't recognize myself at first, and all I can seem to do is stare at the girl looking back at me in the mirror. Her face is still mine. I refused the extra makeup. I have eyeliner on—heavy—and that's enough. I insisted that my hair be pulled up, because I feel more in control that way. I always have. But Taryn insisted I let her make it look *hot*. It isn't anything big, and the changes she made were subtle, but the girl in the mirror is older, happier, and maybe ready to be kissed on a dance floor in front of everyone who thinks she doesn't deserve it.

"Well? You like it?" Taryn's biting her thumbnail and looking at me in the reflection. Slowly, my lip rises on one side and my eyes slide over to meet hers.

"Yeah," I say. "I do."

"Thank God!" she says, slouching back, resting her weight on the bathtub edge behind her. She looks me up and down, her eyes scanning me almost the way Kyle's do. "You look good like this. I know you say it isn't you, but…it's you. This is you tonight, Joss. And every guy—mine included—is going to notice."

My chest starts to pound and my head feels light. I don't need everyone noticing me; I only need one boy noticing me. All I want is to look good enough for Wes not to regret picking me.

"Okay, do you want to just take the dress home so you can finish getting ready there? Or do you want me to help you with that too?" Taryn says, drifting across her hallway into her room. I follow her, my fingers instinctively feeling the slickness of my hair pulled up on all sides. Whatever she did, my hair isn't moving for the rest of the night.

"Uh, I guess I'll take it home. Wes wants to pick me up there. My dad…he…he said he wanted to see what I looked like," I say, my hand moving to my eye, rubbing the lid because it's starting to twitch. This entire night is surreal. It was never supposed to happen—on so many levels.

"It's good that he does. Maybe…maybe he's checking back in," she says, handing me a plastic-covered dress on a hanger.

"Maybe," I shrug, knowing how quickly he can tune out again.

I fold the garment over my arm and lean into my friend. I'm not a hugger, but I feel like I need to give her some gesture to show her how much this afternoon meant to me. She spent a good hour making me look like a princess—at least the blond parts. The rest is up to me.

"Text me when you guys are leaving to go there. We'll get there around the same time," she says, hanging on her door as I leave through the hallway. I promise her I will, and make my way through her front door, letting the screen slam closed behind me.

"You look beautiful, Joss," Taryn's father says as I pass him at the end of his driveway. He's standing from the kneeling position, holding a car part in an oily towel that he's working with his hands. Her father takes on a lot of spare repair jobs at their home, separate from his work at the garage. It helps pay for her sisters' college tuitions, and it will probably help pay for Taryn's too. "You want a ride home? So you don't have to get your hair all messy?"

The breeze has picked up, and it actually feels nice against my bare neck. I smile at him and shake my head no.

"It actually feels kind of nice," I smile. "I think I'll walk."

"Okay, JJ. You be good tonight, you hear?" He leans forward and presses a small kiss on my cheek. Taryn's father has always treated me like one of his own. He's been calling me JJ since Taryn and I were kids, and I know he said it just now to remind me of the fact that I'm still his little girl. It warms my belly to feel that kind of love.

It only takes me a few minutes to get to my house from Taryn's, and I head right to my room, turning my iPod on and plugging it into my clock speaker. Wes downloaded a bunch of top-forty music to it yesterday, and he insisted I listen to it to get myself ready for the dance. It's all pop, and I know most of the songs—they just aren't what I usually listen to. Nothing hard, and every song has a happy ending. By the fifth tune, I'm almost giggling at the difference between this playlist and my usual soundtrack.

My phone buzzes with a text from Wes, telling me he's on his way, so I pull the silky black dress from the bag and hanger Taryn leant me. It was the dress she wore for her quinceañera two years ago. It's simple and nice, and it will do the job. I slip it on easily, reaching the zipper on my own and working the length down my hips until the hem rests at my knees. I stand on the end of my mattress and press my hands on the ceiling above me to hold my balance so I can see the full form. I'm turning to the side when I hear the soft knock on my door.

"One second," I say, glancing down at my bare legs. It feels too fast for Wes to be here, and I'm not completely ready yet.

"It's just me. He's not here yet," my father says. I slow as I step down from the bed and approach the door. My hand stops on the knob, and for a moment, I consider telling him I'm still getting ready. I don't, opening the door instead.

My father's eyes move right to mine, then fall along my cheek, hairline, and shoulder, taking in my appearance as his head falls to the side. His lips are in a flat line—emotionless.

"Well?" I lift my hands to either side and spin slowly for him. "It's T's dress. I don't really have anything, and…I'm so uncomfortable."

My father only nods slowly, his eyes caught somewhere around my waist while he chews at the inside of his cheek. My hands move around my body, and I mentally begin to file through other dresses I like in Taryn's closet—or sweaters or something that isn't what I have on right now. Then my father lifts the plastic bag from his side and hands it to me.

"That one isn't you. But this…maybe?" His hand trembles with the weight of the bag. It's not that it's heavy. It's that he got something—for me. And I think maybe he just trembles more now too.

My brow pulled in tight, I take it from him and move back to the edge of my bed, sitting while I pull the bag open and reach inside. The white crisscross of the back of the dress is the first thing I see, and I let the weight of the dress and bag fall into my lap under my hands, my eyes jetting to my father's.

"How'd you know?" This is the dress I touched when I was with Taryn. It's the only thing I saw in the entire store that I thought I would actually buy for myself if I had the means to do so. It wasn't incredibly expensive, but it was more than I had to give for a dress. It's not a lot of money for my father, but it's more than he's ever spent on something that wasn't a bat or a glove.

My father shrugs.

"It was Taryn's idea, really. She said you didn't have anything to wear, said I should do something about that. I gave her the money at school, but she dropped the bag here yesterday, said it would be…more *meaningful* if I gave it to you," he says, every word sounding uncomfortable and embarrassed. His eyes dart to mine, but drop quickly to his feet.

"Dress shopping isn't our thing," I say, giving him an excuse. I don't know why I do, but I can see the struggle in his body language. He feels guilty that Taryn had to prod him to do something nice. But still…he wanted to do it. I wouldn't be holding this dress if he hadn't. That's the part that matters…I think.

"I hope she got the size right," he says with a quick smirk.

"It's…it's right," I say, pulling the dress completely from the bag now. My fingers work at the tag, my thumb running over the eighty-dollar price marking. "You…you didn't have to…"

"Yeah…I did," my father interrupts. He leans his head against the frame of the door, and his eyes finally make it to mine. "This is one of those things a father should do for his daughter."

I hold his gaze and let his words burrow into me. After several seconds, I look back down at the dress in my lap and let my hands smooth it out as I nod.

"Okay," I whisper. "Thank you."

"You're welcome," my father says, swallowing as he reaches into his hair, his fingers scratching at his scalp. "I'll let you finish. If Wes comes, I'll keep him busy so you can get ready."

"Okay," I say, my eyes still locked on his as he slowly pulls the door to a close between us.

For a full minute, I remain frozen, my perfect dress in my hands. It takes me that long to feel like I deserve the dress I'm holding. When I slip it over my head, it looks exactly as I imagined it would. I put Taryn's dress back into the bag and set it along with the black shoes I borrowed from her on the chair in the corner of my room, then go into my closet and find the dark-brown cowboy boots I haven't touched in almost a year. They were my mother's, and wearing them feels like a betrayal. But I won't ever get rid of them. I love them as much as I hate them.

Minutes later, I hear the doorbell ring, and even though I'm ready, I wait by my door, listening as my father opens the door and makes small talk with Wes. I put my phone and the twenty I kept out from my first paycheck in the satchel purse that I used to use to smuggle cigarettes and beer into the movies. I cross the strap over my body and pause again with my hand on my doorknob. Wes and my father are chuckling over something, but I can tell they're both really just waiting for me.

My eyes closed, I whisper a prayer. I ask for tonight to be perfect, to be heartbreak free. And then I push through the door. When my eyes open again, I'm given my first indication that my wish was heard. They aren't pandering. They aren't gawking. Their smiles are subtle, and my father's eyes are glassy. Neither of them says a word, until my father holds the door open for us both and reminds Wes to drive carefully.

I feel the tickle of Wes's fingers along my back as he guides me toward the curb, to his truck. I reach to grab the door handle, but he stops me, his hand covering mine.

"No, let me. Just tonight," he says.

I laugh lightly. "All right, just tonight," I say, my palms moving to the skirt of my dress, bunching the folds of fabric together, and getting ready to lift myself into the truck seat. Wes opens the door, and reaches for my free hand, taking it as I step up into the cab. He stops before closing the door, his eyes on mine, his face void of the usual stray pieces of hair that fly loose when he pulls away a hat. With both hands hanging on the top of the open door frame, his head falls forward as his chest lets out a heavy breath.

"I promised Taryn I wouldn't make you uncomfortable with attention and talk about how pretty you are. She said that might scare you. But holy fucking damn, Joss. Just…holy fucking damn," he says, raising his head again, his lip in his teeth and a smile on his face.

He doesn't say anything more, closing the door and walking around the front of the truck. But he pats his hand on the hood twice as he rounds the front to his door, and he bites his lip once more before shaking his head and firing the engine.

I'll take *holy fucking damn.*

"We have to pick up Levi, back at my house. He's bringing some girl on your team. Bria, I think?" he says, driving slowly, his eyes keep glancing over at me, and I cross my legs to try and get the tingling sensation to stop.

"Your legs look really good in boots," he says, his grip now on his neck as he looks at my bare knee where the dress has slid up just enough. I tuck it tightly under me and cross my legs tighter, my body warm with his attention.

"You look nice too," I say lightly. He only smiles in response, giving his attention back to the road.

He's wearing a gray button-down shirt, black pants, and a thin black tie. I notice his shoes—the way they look barely worn, and I smile to myself. I don't ask him if they're new, but I'm pretty sure they are. And it makes me think back to when he was a boy.

We pull up in front of his house, and Wes's family is waiting in the driveway for us. Bria's parents dropped her off, and she's standing with her hands wrapped around Levi's arm. Levi is dressed just like his brother, and the thought that TK probably looks exactly the same warms my heart too. My suspicion is confirmed when Taryn pulls up behind us, and Wes's brother steps from her car.

"Gah! I don't think my boys have ever looked so handsome," a short, red-headed woman says, pushing her way from behind Bruce, her phone poised in her hands ready to take a picture.

"That's my mom," Wes whispers in my ear.

"Boys, come on. Just one more photo," his mother says, urging her boys to stand next to the truck with their arms around each other's shoulders. "TK, knock it off. No flipping the bird secretly. I see it every time you do it."

"Bah, you do not!" TK laughs. "I slipped one in the Christmas card photo last year!"

His mother drops her hands and juts her hip out to the side, staring at TK. "I know. I couldn't send the damn things out, and I ordered a hundred. Now knock it off, and do it right," she says, that special quality added to her tone that means business. Wes smacks TK on the back of the head, and the three of them finally pose without any pranks.

After she takes a few pictures, she urges us all to gather for one together, then asks her boys to all gather with their dates for couple shots. She asks Wes and me to stand on our own last. She steps close to me, and her fingertips find the fringe at the bottom of my dress. She pulls it out a little before letting the fabric fall back in place.

"This is lovely," she smiles.

"Thank you," I say, my voice coming out a bit hoarse. I clear my throat, my hands gripping the sides of my dress, bunching it while I try to dry the sweat from my palms. "It's…it's new. I don't really do dresses."

"That's what I hear," she says quickly, smiling. She runs her palm down my arm and squeezes, then offers me her hand. "I'm Maggie. And Wes hasn't been able to shut up about you for the last two weeks. He…he doesn't talk about girls. Ever. So I figured you were pretty special."

I'm blushing—hard. I whisper, "Thank you," then tilt my head up to look at Wes at the feel of his hand squeezing mine. Maggie snaps a picture at that very moment.

"Do you think you could send me one? We didn't take any at my house," I ask.

"Sure. Here, just type in your number," she says, giving me her phone.

I look at the image she captured for a second before sending it to myself. When I give the phone back to her, she snaps a few more, but I know there won't be one I like any better than the image of me looking up at him and Wes staring down at me like I'm beautiful. For the first time ever, I feel that way.

"Okay, people. We're going to be late," Taryn says, motioning toward her car and Wes's truck. I laugh because Taryn is always late, and she shoots me a look. I shrug it off, following Wes to the truck. I climb in and slide close to him, making enough room for Levi and Bria to slide into the bench seat with us. Levi insists that Bria and I wear the lap belts, and he goes without.

The school isn't far from our home; we pull up to the outside of the gym, and the boys let us out, TK pulling Taryn's car into a spot down the hill. We wait at the curb, and when the boys leave the truck and car, they climb the hill back to us. It only takes a few seconds, but the scene feels like slow motion—like a glimpse into the future. The Stokes boys are lean and muscular, and I could watch them saunter toward us in the moonlight for hours and never get tired of looking.

After a second or two, though, Wes is all I see. His eyes never leave mine—not when he reaches me and threads my arm around his, not when he guides me through the balloon arch decorating the main doors to the gym, and not when he walks me through the rows of tables to the middle of the dance floor where everyone can see us—touching.

All. I. See.

"I still have my purse," I say against him, his arms heavy around me, cradling me as we sway off time to a song that I'm pretty sure is meant for fast dancing.

"I know, but one, that's not *really* a purse, and two—if I had let you sit down, it would have been hell trying to get you out here to dance with me," he says, his chin steady along my head. He won't break our hold because he knows if he does, I'll retreat to the safety of the tables. He's right.

"Good point," I say.

"You're a pretty good dancer, Jose," he says, the deep chuckle in his chest rumbling in my ear.

I kick him softly in the shin with the toe of my boot.

"Owwww," he says, faking to hop on one leg. I pull away, but only as a test. He tugs me back in close, his lips just above my ear. "You can kick and scream all you want. We're not leaving this dance floor until I've held you through three cheesy R&B songs."

"I know, right? What's up with today's R&B lyrics? They don't do it like they used to. Smokey, Marvin Gaye...that was good shit," I hum against his chest. He pulls back and looks at me, his hands still holding my waist tightly, though. "What?" I ask as he gazes down at me, one brow arched.

"You're like this perfect freakazoid girl," he laughs lightly with a shake of his head.

"Nice. *Freakazoid*. Real nice Wes," I roll my eyes.

"No, that's not what I mean. It's just...you can throw a ball harder than most of the guys on our team, and you can hit my best pitch—"

I interrupt him.

"Is that an admission? Did you just admit that I can hit your pitching?

Oh my god, did I…did I break the Wes Stokes ego code?" I tease.

"You broke it when you sent my best curve into the weeds at the elementary school weeks ago," he says, his lips an adorable half smirk with a deep dimple. I stand on my tiptoes to kiss it, then snuggle back into him to continue our sway while the song overhead raps loudly, the thump of the speakers vibrating near us.

"It was a changeup. Now, go on then, how am I a freak?" I ask.

"You throw out things like Marvin Gaye and Smokey Robinson, while most girls at our school would be singing along with the latest graduate of Disney's marketing machine or some winner from a pop-star reality show."

"Don't make fun of Kelly Clarkson. I love Kelly Clarkson—chick can belt," I say, my palm flat against his chest, my other finger pointing at him. He pauses our movement and looks at me, his lips slowly curling with his light laugh as he pulls my hand from his chest and kisses the knuckles.

"Got it, Kelly kicks ass. But you know what I mean," he says, his hands sliding to either cheek as his lips press a soft kiss on top of my head. I'm so very lost to this boy, it isn't even funny. I've given over my control, and as much as it scares the shit out of me, I'm more afraid of missing out on him—*anything* with him. I cede willingly, and I am racing to the next kiss, the next dance, the next touch of his hand. I've never felt my heart beat before like it does when I'm with Wes.

I melt into him again, and the music changes into an actual slow song meant for whatever it is we've been doing out here on the dance floor. I catch Taryn's eyes as she and TK move to a darker corner of the floor, spending more time kissing than actually dancing. I watch the lights shift around the floor, the reflections bouncing off overstuffed balloons and streamers and the rows of bleachers that have all been pushed in. It's the same gym it always is, only we've dressed it up to be something more. Kind of like me—a freakazoid dressed up like a western princess, dancing with the cute boy, while she slides around in her momma's boots.

I step back from Wes again and look him in the eyes, my hands finding a comfortable place around his neck. He looks at me like I matter.

"I'm just who I am," I say, his lips quirking up on one side with his raised brow. "Before...*freakazoid?* I know what you mean, that I'm different. But...I just...I never really fit into the right box. I like driving fast—not that I have a car to drive—but when I do drive, I drive fast. I like running through the street barefoot. You can't feel things through shoes, and I'm faster without them. I like winning. I hate losing. And when I lose, I front about it—I make up excuses and tell people I don't really care. But I do...care? I care so much when I lose that I find somewhere dark to cry. And then I lie about that too—about crying. I like the popular things too. I like movies where the guy gets the girl in the end, and songs that play on repeat ten times a day."

"And I also like the things you have to search for—the bands nobody knows and the movies with subtitles that are on late at night. I get pissed though, because I don't speak French or Spanish, and I wish I did. I like school, and I wish I was better at it. I think maybe if I tried all along, I would be. I'm mad at myself for giving up in the beginning. I'm also embarrassed that I don't know how to braid my own hair. That's why I don't put ribbons in it like the other girls on our team. I tried once, and I made a knot. Bows are stupid. But they're also pretty. And—"

Before I get out another word, Wes's lips are on mine, his mouth fitting against mine so perfectly, it's as if he's the exhale to my inhale, the end of my every breath. I freeze under the power of his kiss, my hands sliding to the back of his shirt, my fingers gripping to hold on as his come up to hold my cheeks and chin, his thumbs tracing a slow circle under each eye.

"You don't belong in a box. That's what makes you so amazing. You...you're a little bit of everything. And you're not ashamed to show any of it," he says.

"I don't know about that," I sigh. "I think I keep that shit in check," I laugh, but I quit trying to make a joke out of my insecurities when I meet his eyes again.

"I know about it, and I see it," he says, his thumb under my chin.

I breathe in deeply and let my head fall to the side.

"I always loved the way you looked at me," I say.

Wes's smile comes fast, and his strong arms swallow me whole. I embrace him so tightly I'm sure I'm ruining the hair work of art Taryn tacked to my head. I don't care, because when I'm with him, like this, no matter how I look, I feel pretty.

"I saw you cry once…" he breathes, his voice a low hum at my ear, his fingertips running circles over the bare skin along the top of my spine. His touch is hypnotic.

"When?" I whisper.

"When you were young. At school, the day of the first race I went to your house. I saw you cry. You didn't get picked for the solo in music class. Taryn did. You pretended you didn't care, and then you asked for a hall pass and hid around the corner from the bathroom to cry," he says.

He's right. I did. That memory has been buried under years of love for my friend. I never held it against her. And I don't now—not even in my memories. "I wanted Taryn to be happy. I felt selfish for being sad, so I hid," I say. Wes tugs my chin up with his fingertips, and I look at him, my cheek still resting on his chest.

"I know you did. That's what made it so amazing. You were this unbelievable friend. And I wanted a friend like you in the worst way," he says.

His eyes sink into mine, and I picture them on that sad boy I once knew.

"You remember all of that? I thought…you didn't remember me until you saw me?" I ask, still staring at his long lashes. His lip ticks up and his head tilts to the side.

"I had the memory, but the face was fuzzy. When I saw you again, you filled in so many blanks," he says.

I wonder how many blank spaces I filled, just how many memories of his I was starring in. I had millions of questions all battling to be the next one from my lips now that my big question—who he really was—had been answered. But they would have to wait. They'd wait because my other half, Kyle, was standing alone in the dark corner wearing a suit. And he looked sad.

"This is a really weird thing to ask my date, but can I dance with someone else? Just…just for a song?" I ask, my lips forming a tight line and my heart pounding in my stomach. I don't want him to get the wrong impression about Kyle, but I also can't let Kyle stand there, alone.

Wes follows the motion of my eyes to Kyle, then breathes in slowly, turning back into me, his hands sliding along my cheeks and his lips following to my mouth. "Like I said, you were always an unbelievable friend," he whispers against me before taking my bottom lip between both of his, holding it there for a few seconds then letting go.

Wes steps away and nods toward the table near the dance floor where Levi is sitting with his date. When he joins them, I turn to the right and walk slowly to my sweet friend. His suit is pressed, and I'm sure he's rented it—I've never seen one like this in his closet. The white shirt underneath is beaming, and I have a feeling that's new as well. He's painfully handsome, and in some other life, I would have been a fool not to fall for him. But this life had other plans for me, and somehow, Kyle has still decided to stay by my side—as my friend.

"Well don't you clean up nice, Kyle Marley," I say, stepping into the shadow with him. He chuckles and looks down, his thumbs hanging onto his pockets and his posture that of a boy ready to bolt.

"Thanks, Joss. You clean up pretty well yourself," he says, his head tilted just enough that his eyes meet mine. His smile only makes it across half his face, and his breath stops when he looks at me. His lips close tightly as he shakes his head, glancing down to his feet. "Nah, that's a lie. You don't clean up well. You're always beautiful. But tonight, you are breathtaking."

My chest collapses a little, and my eyes sting with his compliment.

"Thanks," I say, swinging my hand into his. Our pinkies link with my touch, and I let his hold on my hand linger for a few seconds before we both let go. "Where's your date?"

His eyes flash up to mine, and even though it's dark, I can tell he's blushing. He stretches his arms out before letting them fall to his sides. "I don't have one. I'm…I'm not staying long. I just wanted to see you. Taryn said Wes finally talked you into going, and I…I had to see Josselyn Winters in a dress," he smiles.

I squint at him, and he chuckles, shrugging with guilt.

"You shit! I rock this dress," I say, holding the skirt out a little on each side. His laughter fades when I do, and he brings one hand up to rub his chin.

"Yeah…you do," he says, his voice low as his eyes slide up to mine.

I suck in my bottom lip and look at his chest, not ready to take more praise from him so soon.

"Well since you're here…" I say, glancing up briefly.

"I'd love to have this dance," he says, pulling his hand from his pocket again and holding it out for me. I take it and let him lead me to the center of the dance floor, my eyes catching Wes's as Kyle pulls me in close, but not too close. Wes only smiles and continues talking with his brother. He understands, and I'm relieved he isn't jealous.

"I'm wearing my mom's boots," I say, stepping once to the side and twisting each foot on the heel so he can admire them. Kyle smiles.

"They fit you—in so many ways," he says.

I step into his embrace slowly, my own smile a timid one. "Thanks," I whisper. I both love and hate these boots. I hate that I love them. And I hate that I miss my mom tonight.

"She'd be sorry, Joss," Kyle says, his chin now resting on my head.

"Hmmm?" I question.

"Your mom; if she knew you now. She'd be sorry she missed so much of you. You're amazing, despite her. And she'd be sorry," he says. I squeeze him tightly, and his hands close around me and squeeze back.

I hold him like this for the rest of the song, and when it ends, he steps out of my arms and nods toward Wes. His eyes come back to me.

"I'm gonna go. There's a party at the river bottom. And I need to get this suit back in my dad's closet," he smirks. I laugh, also relieved that he didn't rent something special just for one dance.

"Thanks for the dance," I smile.

He shakes his head and shuts his eyes, opening them just as Wes reaches me and tugs my hand to his chest.

"It was my pleasure, Winters. Every single time," he says.

Wes shakes his hand, and without any words, Kyle leaves. Wes never asks what we talked about, and even though I know it wouldn't be any big deal to share, I keep it to myself. Kyle is still part of me, and I want to hold onto those small things that are just ours—even if they're transient and meaningless. And the fact that Wes lets me, makes my heart swell even more.

I never leave the dance floor. For an hour and a half, I let Wes sway me at the same tempo in a circle in a two-foot section of the gym floor. My purse remains slung around my body, and my friends only see me when they approach us. This stupid dance—it's the most amazing night of my life.

The clock says nine-thirty when Wes finally leads me out the door and to his truck. I don't ask where we're going, and I don't question the fact that we're abandoning Levi. I just follow him.

He pulls the passenger door open for me, then tucks my dress in safely before closing the door. The cab is dark when he climbs in, but the moonlight reflects off his eyes, and I lose myself in them as we pull away from campus. I let him drive me for several miles, until it dawns on me where he's taking me.

The flower fields.

Wes pulls over into the rough dirt on the side of the road, and climbs out of the truck, flipping the tailgate down before walking to my side and meeting me just as I'm about to step from my seat.

"Levi and his date are going to some party at the river. I…I didn't want to go. I hope that's okay with you?" His lips are crooked, and I'm struck by the fact that Wes wanted to get me alone, and he's slightly bashful about it.

"I love it here," I say, the only answer to give. The air is sweet. I've forgotten what it's like out here at night, and I'm sure that's why Wes brought me. The flowers are all sleeping, but their scent is almost like a potion for the soul. When I was a little girl, I was convinced that my hair would soak it up, and in the morning, I would sniff the strands in search of it. But it was always gone. The magic that happens out here—you can't bottle it. It doesn't come home with you. It stays with the petals and with the earth, ready and waiting for you to visit when you need to feel spellbound for a little while.

I need that right now.

Wes knew.

I climb into the bed of the truck where Wes has laid an open sleeping bag. I smile up at him, raising a brow, and his eyebrows shoot up.

"I swear to god, for stargazing. Cross my heart," he says, actually making the motion.

"I know," I roll my eyes. When I turn away, though, I think about how alone we are and how much I want his hands on my body. I pull my boots from my feet and set them along with my purse in the corner of the bed, then nestle into Wes's side, his fingers slowly curling around my arm. I love the tickle of his fingertips.

"You haven't checked your phone once tonight," Wes says, his head falling to the side until it rests against mine.

"I haven't," I realize. My father very well could have left after I did. But for some reason, I have this strange sense of faith that he stayed home. My instincts taunt me, preparing me for disappointment, but the faith remains.

"Your boss was okay with you taking the night off?" Wes asks.

"Sort of," I say. "He told me he'd save all of the gum from this weekend for next."

Wes turns his head to take me in fully and scrunches his face.

"That means *I'm* getting all the gum, doesn't it," he says.

"Pretty much," I say, ignoring his stare and snuggling back into his hold. He chuckles eventually, and I let my hand rest on his chest, feeling it shake with his laugh.

As we both grow quiet, the sound of the crickets in the fields takes over, and my eyes begin to wander around the sky. I haven't looked up in years. I notice the stars, but I don't really tend to them. I'm glad Wes made me do this.

"When I was little, after my mom left? I used to try to guess what star she was staring at, and it felt good to think that we were looking at the same one," I say. I feel his head shift, and I know he's looking at me. I swallow.

"You miss her," he says. It isn't a question. He's reading me. He's always read me.

"I do. It guts me sometimes," I say.

We lay in silence for a few more minutes before he asks for more. It's as if he knows I need to get used to shedding layers before I remove a new one.

"Tell me about her," he says.

My breath comes slow, and I let it fill me completely before I speak. I need this time to think of her, because I don't remember much. And that hurts most of all.

"She had blond hair—wavy, like mine. And she always wore ripped jeans and old T-shirts. She…she liked art. She had a potter's wheel in our spare bathroom. I used to put my Play-Doh on it when I was a kid. She never got mad," I say. It takes me a few quiet seconds to realize I'm smiling, and I start to correct it, to scowl, because that's what I've told myself to do when I think of her. But I stop, my head falling to look at Wes, and when his eyes catch mine, my mouth curves back into place. They are happy memories, and I'm allowed to have them.

"She sounds like she loved you," he says.

I consider his words for a moment, and I don't have a whole response. I only shrug, because I'm so unsure if she did. She left. She disappeared. And if she loved me, surely she would have stayed.

"When I was twelve, I thought about running away. I wanted to find her. Taryn was going to go with me. My dad found out about our plans, and that's when he started going to Jim's on Saturdays," I say, twisting back so my body is flush with the truck bed, my eyes locked on the stars

227

and the thin layer of clouds threatening to hide them.

"He was probably afraid of losing you," Wes says. I let go of a heavy breath, not wanting to give my father any excuse. "I'm not saying it was the right choice. But…I think he was just running scared. I also think he's done avoiding."

"We'll see," I whisper. "We'll see."

My mind lingers in hope for a while, and I let myself remember good times for just a little longer. It feels safe to remember out here in my flower fields, in Wes's arms. My thoughts never dive into worrying, and I never feel the urge to run. In fact, the longer Wes's fingers tickle up and down my arm, the more I want them to roam along more of me.

As long minutes turn into half an hour, my breathing shifts into a slow and quiet rhythm, and I become acutely aware of everywhere my body is touching Wes's. My right leg is against his, and my torso is turned just enough so my arm can reach over his chest, my fingers grabbing a fist full of his shirt to hold my hand in place. His body is just as still, and the more minutes that pass, the more I consider he may be inventorying the same touches.

"Wes?" I ask finally, my heart beating so hard it's drumming can be felt in my bones.

"Uh huh?" he says, his voice quiet as his face falls toward mine. His eyes are different—maybe a little hazed, definitely anxious.

"Now would be a killer time to kiss me," I say, pinning my lip in my teeth the second I do. My skin feels warm instantly, despite the cool air picking up with the late night breeze.

"Okay," he says, his voice cracking like a boy hitting puberty. I giggle at him, and he rolls his eyes closed. "Not cool, making fun of your boyfriend who is seriously panic-attack nervous about kissing you alone in the bed of his pickup truck."

"Boyfriend," I whisper, looking away from him and smiling. Wow, I hadn't thought about the word that goes along with him. I hadn't considered a label or any word for what we are. I just know I need him. God do I need him in my life. He's been missing.

I look back at him and smile so large my cheeks ache quickly.

"Yeah," he says, his voice deep, vibrating in his chest against my hand, which he reaches for and holds tightly. "Boyfriend."

I leave my eyes on his and let my lips tingle with expectation.

"You've kissed me before," I shrug slightly, the right side of my lip raising a little more, dimpling my cheek. He mimics me.

"Yeah, but not…not like this," he says, his smile sliding into a more serious look, his eyes moving from mine to my mouth. The tingling quickly becomes numbness under his scrutiny.

"I know," I breathe.

Inside my closed fist, the one wrapped in his hand, my palm is sweating. My heart is pounding, and my body is rushing with adrenaline. This is almost the same feeling I get when I step up into the box to swing against a really fast pitcher, only, I'm less sure of everything right now. My hookups and make-out sessions at parties and down at the river or the beach have been meaningless. But this—every *this* with Wes—it means everything.

I inhale deeply, lifting myself by pressing against his chest. He holds my weight and watches me carefully as I sit up next to him and slide one leg over his body, straddling his lap. We've been in this position before—the first time we kissed. Only this time, I feel different.

Wes's eyes study my every movement, and his breath stills. My hands slide down his chest, along the lines of buttons on his shirt, and I slowly pull each one through its hole. I push his shirt open and pull on the ends tucked in his pants, his stomach and chest now bare in front of me. My eyes widen at the contours of every muscle on his perfectly-formed body. Without pause, I lean forward and press my lips on his stomach, working my way up him until I kiss the center of his chest.

Wes takes a sharp breath as I blow coolness over the small area where my tongue tastes him, and I feel his hands begin to gather the skirt of my dress into his fists. I peer up at him as I lean forward and kiss him again, and I feel his muscles tighten. He's caught between being my savior and being my seducer, and right now, I don't need saving—I need his touch.

My hands find his, and I cover them, guiding them up my body with my dress until it's gathered around my waist and his fingers have found my bare skin underneath. His gaze bores into me, and I nod slowly, my movement continuing as his hands slide inches at a time under my dress until his palms have found my breasts.

I let my eyes fall closed as Wes sits up into me, his hands caressing every curve of my breasts until his thumbs finally stop along the lacy edge of the only nice bra I own. I wore it because Taryn bought it for me last year on my birthday. I wore it hoping Wes would see.

I wore it so he would take it off.

Impatient, I reach behind my own back and unclasp the hooks, and Wes's eyes flash with hunger. His head tilts slightly in question, for permission, and I lean my head back so I'm looking to the sky, all of me open to his touch.

The movement of his hands is gentle, his fingertips tracing my curves with a tickle, his thumbs gliding over the hard peaks as they move down my ribs to the bottom of my dress. Once there, Wes's confidence grows, and he pulls my dress higher until the only thing left is to remove it from me completely. He looks at me again here.

"I want you to. I trust you," I stare into him.

He lifts the layers of fabric over my head and his hands slide down my shoulders, pulling the straps of my bra along with them. My eyes can't quite make it to his as I sit before him, bare and wanting to be loved. The feel of his right hand on my cheek brings my gaze to him quickly, though.

"You're a beautiful girl, Josselyn," he says, using my full name. I sink into him, and close my eyes, my lips finding his quickly, not sure how to respond other than with this physical trust.

His mouth moves with mine until my lips are swollen and raw with our kiss, and slowly he kisses his way down my neck and shoulder until his mouth covers my right breast completely. My body grinds into him on instinct, his tongue on my nipple sending a wave of pulses down to my center. I push into him for relief, and his hands move from my ribs to my ass, pulling me against him as he groans.

He's careful with his touch, his fingertips flirting along the band where my panties hug my legs, but never breaching inside, though I'm desperate for him to. I lose myself in the feel of his teeth along my nipples though, and each time he sucks one into his mouth, I press into him below, until eventually the rhythm takes over control of my body in search of relief.

"Touch me, Wes. Please, just once. I need…" I beg, my center throbbing against the hardness underneath his pants. My hands move down his chest, wanting to feel him once, and just as I touch him, his hands slide under both sides of my panties, his fingers finding me wet and ready to explode.

"Wes…" I pant, unable to say anything more before his touch ignites a wave that rushes through me over and over again, my body moving with his touch and my hand moving against him. As I begin to come down, my core relaxing and my breath slowing, Wes pulls me against him tighter, his hand covering mine over his hard-on.

With his permission, I unzip his pants and release him, taking him completely in both hands and sliding my palms up and down, using the rise and fall of his chest as my guide. My head falls against his, and our lips barely touch, pausing between breaths as his teeth tug at my lower lip and drag across my sensitive skin. His hands grasp my ass firmly as he pulls me into him a few final times, and I feel him release under my touch, a deep groan escaping his throat.

I bury my head in his neck, my body flush against his, our skin hot. His hands loosen, but never let go totally, sliding up my back, tracing my spine, and folding around me so he can hug me close.

"I think we've pushed the limits of no traffic down the farm road. How about I help you get your dress back on?" he chuckles.

"I think that would be good," I say back, my voice coming out nervous, maybe a little embarrassed. Wes can tell, and as he pulls my dress to his side, he pauses, moving a hand to the side of my face, his eyes searching mine.

"Why are you looking at me?" I sigh, my face tingling from his attention.

"Don't do that," he shakes his head.

"What?" I say, looking down at my dress. I reach for it, but his hand catches mine.

"Feel ashamed. Don't do that," he says. I breathe in sharply once and flit my gaze back to him. "You're a beautiful girl, and you're allowed to *feel* things. And I wanted that…god, Joss, did I want that. If I pressured you…"

"You didn't," I look down, biting my lip. I look back up to him, my lip sliding loose with a smile. "You didn't. I wanted that too. And more."

"And more," he repeats after me. "God yes, and more."

I giggle and pull my dress up to my body, my arms and chest beginning to feel cold. He helps me pull it over my head, but leaves his hands on my cheeks after. "More can wait. I'm here with you…not because of *more*. I'm here because of *you*."

My body shivers, and I lean forward enough so my mouth dusts his with a kiss.

"I'm here because of you," I say, the meaning of that sentence deeper than Wes realizes.

CHAPTER 13

The pumpkins disappeared at midnight.

Wes brought me home, and my father was passed out in the middle of the hallway, halfway to his bedroom. He helped me carry him to bed, and I kicked myself for believing in change.

Wes told me it would take time, my dad was making progress, but it felt like more of the same. Only this time, he lifted my hopes before dropping them to the ground.

I assumed this morning was off. That's why I didn't set my alarm. But Wes called. He called six times, dialing over and over again until I answered. He and my father were at the field, and he wanted to make sure I was coming.

"Goddamned functioning alcoholic," I mutter to myself, my finger caught in the heel of my running shoe as I try to slip it on without untying it. I find my cleats in the garage and stuff them in the side pocket of my equipment bag, then sling it over my shoulder and pound my feet heavily in protest throughout my walk to the school fields.

I didn't want to go. I wanted to stand him up. But Wes asked me to. I'm coming for Wes. Not for him.

I clear the gate and my eyes zero in on my father crouching, and the boy I dreamt about all night throwing from the mound. The scene is exactly as it was the first time I saw them working together. It's like I'm on one side of the glass, and they're on the other. They're laughing, talking freely, but the closer I get, the less chatter I hear, until I'm upon them and their talk has stopped.

My bag slides from my shoulder, falling heavy on the ground, a cloud of dust kicking up with its impact. They both pause their throwing, my dad standing, wiggling his legs as he rights himself after catching.

"Well," I say, hands on my hips. "I'm here. I didn't want to come. Because you're a liar," I seethe, my hand motioning to my father. "But I think I'm good, and I think I can be great, and I decided sometime in the last week or two that I'm going to play Division I ball. And fuck if I don't need your help to do it, so…here I am."

My father's eyes are locked on me, his expression empty. It irritates me.

"Either get mad or say you're sorry or something. Don't just stand there like that," I say.

"Joss," Wes whispers, stepping up next to me. My eyes dart to his, and the anger extinguishes with one look from him. My eyes fall, and I bend down to grab the straps of my bag.

"Sorry," I whisper. "I'm just…disappointed."

I drag my bag to the dugout and pull my cleats out to switch my shoes.

"I know," Wes says, his hands hanging on the dugout roof, his body leaning in over the steps. My mind drifts to last night, to his touch, and it soothes me.

"Let's do this," I say, tossing my running shoes on the bench and pulling my favorite bat from my bag. I step up to the plate to swing from the left side, where my father has been frozen since I arrived. Wes moves out to the mound.

"Start with that bat, over there. The one on the fence," my dad says. I glare at him, then glance to the small bat propped up to the side.

"I think I'll stick with mine," I say, my lips bunching with my shrug.

"Yours is too heavy. You're going to be slow until you get used to it again. That one's three ounces lighter," he says.

"It's a fucking T-ball bat," I say, shaking my head. I tap the plate twice and spit into the dirt, covering it with a kick of my cleat.

I nod to Wes, and he motions for approval from my father, which irritates me. I dig in and wait as Wes holds a ball, winding up to throw it into the zone. I swing fast, but I'm late, so I dig in again.

"It's an awkward angle, because you're throwing overhand," I say. "Do it again."

"Do you want me to try to throw the softballs? I can go underhand, but I'm not as accurate," Wes says, holding the ball up, signaling he'll swap it out.

I open my mouth to answer him, but my father cuts me off.

"Horse shit. The angle's just fine. She's late because she's stubborn. Let her miss ten or twelve more and then maybe she'll listen to me," he says from behind me. Ah, the familiar tone is back.

"I'm not late," I say, kicking at the dirt and twisting my pivot foot, ready to load. My dad only chuckles.

Wes throws the ball again, and I miss. I can feel it, though, and I'm closer.

"Again," I say.

My dad tosses the ball back to him, and I hear him laughing. It fuels me.

Wes begins his windup, and I start my pre-swing early, my arms primed, and when the ball reaches the plate, my bat is there to send it hard and fast right down the line. I watch it roll all the way to the fence.

"Nice shot," Wes says, looking at it in the distance.

My father only laughs.

"What's funny? The fact that you were wrong?" I ask, leaning my weight on my bat like a cane.

My father looks down, pursing his lips, his glove bent with his hand against his hip. "What are you going to do?" he questions, kicking a rock out of the way before looking up at me. "Are you going to hope every pitcher throws you the same speed, the same pitch, exactly where you want it so you can start your swing early enough to hit it? Or are you going to pull your head out of your ass long enough to know that's not how this game works, and they are looking to strike you out, so you need to refine your weapons?"

He's making good points, but all I hear is *head out of my ass*, and I'm lit up.

"I can't do this," I say, shaking my head and tossing my bat end-over-end toward my things and the dugout. I pull the Velcro on my gloves away and look toward Wes, who's chewing at the inside of his cheek, disappointed in me.

"Don't you take his side. That…*that*…that isn't coaching. He doesn't even talk to you like that," I yell.

Wes chuckles once, and I glare at him.

"What?" he says, his arms out. "That's *exactly* how he talks to me. And it probably means I'm not listening when he does."

I pause and chew on his words before tugging my hands free of my gloves and glancing back at my father who is now standing with his arms folded, his face painted with the familiar disgust.

"Yeah, well, maybe it wouldn't be a big deal except that's how he talks to me about everything. And I'm his goddamned flesh and blood!" I yell, picking my bat up from the outside of the dugout and throwing it hard toward my bag, the metal ricocheting off the bench and sending a few balls rolling in stray directions. "Fuck!" I scream, throwing my gloves on top of the mess before sitting down to take my cleats off.

This was a mistake. A huge mistake. Believing was a mistake. Wanting something was a mistake. Striving was a mistake.

Goals are mistakes.

This was a pipedream.

I notice Wes walking over to my father while I pull my feet free and swap my cleats for my regular running shoes. I swear under my breath over the knot left in my laces, and I have to bring my shoe up to my mouth to tug the lace loose with my teeth, because my foot will no longer just slide in. The dirt hits my tongue, and I spit it out once I untangle the knot.

My bag packed, and my shoes finally on my feet, I tug the straps together and step out from the dugout, saluting Wes and giving my father the finger as I spin to walk away.

"Joss, don't leave. Just..." Wes says, and I feel bad, because I hear the pleading in his voice.

"Just, what, Wes? Just stay here and let him make me feel small and responsible for all of the bad shit in his life? Nah...I'm done doing that," I say, turning to leave again.

"Joss..." Wes calls. I pause, but only because he sounds desperate. "Eric...you have to tell her. She deserves to know."

What?

I turn to face them again only to see my dad's head slung forward, his hands on his hips, the glove on one hand and Wes leaning lower, trying to catch his gaze, to urge him to tell me...

My dad exhales a sigh that sounds as if it weighs a hundred pounds, then he flings the glove from his fingers onto the ground in front of him. He pinches the bridge of his nose with one hand and rubs the other on his neck. I study his small movements, until he finally lets go of his face and his eyes look at mine. The expression in them is the same one that was there the day I walked into the house and caught him fighting with my mom—the day she left and our relationship shifted into poison. His eyes are sad and regretful, but they're also angry and wild.

"What's going on?" I say, my feet moving back toward them without my control. "What is it? Is it...are you...are you sick? Is that what this is? Is this some elaborate set up so you can tell me you're sick? And that's...that's why I should feel sorry for you? That's what makes it okay for you to be an addict and for you to treat your only child like a worthless pile of crap? Because...what...you got sick?"

"Goddamn it, Josselyn! I'm not sick. It isn't me. I'm fine. It's...it's your mother," he says, his chest heaving with the extraction of those words. His face is ghost white, stripped of blood and life, and his eyes have cleared of every emotion but fear.

My mother.

I shake my head, and ignore the water forming at the corners of my eyes. We don't even know where she is. I haven't seen her in years. I barely remember her. I…"

"She's dead, Josselyn. She passed away two weeks ago," he says, and my legs can no longer hold me. I fall to the ground quickly, but Wes is there before impact, his arms under mine, his strength holding me up until I can make it to the first bleacher on the other side of the backstop. I sit down and he sits next to me, never letting go. I can't feel him.

I can't feel him!

"I don't understand," I say, my eyes lost in the dried blades of grass poking through the dirt in between my father and me. My dad steps closer, but doesn't walk to the other side of the backstop, instead leaving the fence barrier between us as his fingers cling to the metal and his foot steps up on the wood panels along the ground.

"Shit," he huffs.

My chest burns, and my mind is moving faster than I can handle. It's making my head hurt, and I bring my hands to my forehead, squeezing, wanting to make things stop, wanting to slow it all down for just a beat— one breath. I need one full breath.

"I thought you didn't know where she was? I thought she was dead to you? You hate her? Isn't that…how…how is she…"

I lean forward, dry heaving, nothing coming out but my stomach twisting and revolting against me. My instincts are begging me to fight, to flee, but I'm too weak. I don't understand, I don't understand, I don't understand, I don't…

"I haven't talked to her since she left. I…I got a call, two weeks ago Thursday. I didn't know the number, so I ignored it…it was during practice," he says, and I laugh once—a harsh laugh, because practice is precious. My mother was fucking dead, but can't interrupt practice with his boys.

"I got to my car and played the message. It was her mom, your other grandmother. She…she thought I'd want to know," he says, his voice breaking with the last word. He brings his hands back to the bridge of his nose and pinches tight, his eyes squeezing. He's trying to keep the pain at bay.

He shouldn't be allowed.

"How'd she die?" I ask, my eyes now centered on one blade of grass. It's a piece of rye, grown tall enough to blossom, five prongs of prickly grass poking out from the center like a skeletal flower. It's exactly how I feel. The wind is pounding it flat, but it's not breaking. It's stuck there, in the ground.

Stuck.

Feeling.

Hurting.

"How. Did. She. Die!" I seethe, my eyes darting from the place they were lost to my father's face in an attack.

He moves his lips, wetting them, as if he has to prime them to work, to speak, to say what is probably a terribly simple answer.

"Breast cancer," he says quietly, moving his hand back over his mouth and rubbing. I bet that's how the doctor delivered the diagnosis. Simple and quick. Two words. I shut my eyes.

"Joss…" My father says my name like he wants to comfort me.

"Don't," I say, standing and moving from Wes's hold. "You knew," I say, turning to Wes, walking backward toward my things. "You knew this whole time, didn't you? That's why you believed my father changed. That's why you told me to give him a chance. You knew!"

I start to cry, so I turn and grab my things quickly, picking up my pace. Wes rushes to my side and grabs at my bag. I jerk it away.

"You knew!" I scream. I yell loud enough for my father to hear several feet away, for him to look down in shame and retreat to the bleacher seats behind him.

"I knew," he says. He doesn't placate me, or fight me, or argue. He just agrees.

Good.

"I'm going home," I say, lifting my bag to a comfortable spot on my shoulder as I begin to walk the dirt path back to campus.

"I'll take you home," Wes starts, but he doesn't step toward me. I can tell by the fading of his voice that he's stayed where I left him behind me. He knows I don't want him to. I want to hide. I want to feel, without anyone seeing it.

My anger fuels the walk home, only when I reach my house, my feet keep going. By the time I push open the creaky door in Kyle's garage, my emotions have started to mix, and I'm so sick to my stomach that I pass directly by Kyle and the tangled web of cords for the video game console into the back bathroom. I slam the door closed behind me, but Kyle catches it with his hand, and when the contents of my stomach rip from my guts, Kyle quickly pulls my hair around my shoulder and places a hand on my back.

"I'm fine," I growl, standing back up, jerking away, and running my sleeve over my mouth.

Kyle stares at me, slowly crossing his arms. I flinch at him and squint my eyes—*game face*.

"My mouth tastes like shit," I brush past him, my steps picking up as I move to his dad's liquor cabinet, which is always unlocked. I pull the vodka out along with a glass and begin to pour. A hand grabs my wrist the second the glass touches my lips.

"Stop." I close my eyes and breathe through my nose. Wes doesn't yell. He doesn't pull or push. He gives me a quiet command, but even his hold on my wrist is just a touch.

"I can't…" I swallow hard in the middle of my words. "I can't handle this."

His hand moves along my wrist until it reaches the small glass, pulling it from my grasp and setting it on the table.

"You can," he whispers in my ear.

"She's gone…" I barely finish before the cry hits my chest with the force of a freight train. I double forward, my legs giving out again, and Wes's arms wrap around me from behind.

"I got you," he says, sliding one arm down to my legs, lifting me against him, and carrying me to the Marley sofa. I press into him, wanting to press so far, so hard, that I disappear. And I cry—an ugly cry that makes me choke.

Wes holds me. Kyle sits next to him and rubs my back. And my family—my friend, and my heart—let me be, holding me up when it starts to be too much, and pushing me through the barriers until I finally feel like my lungs can handle the sting of taking a breath.

An hour passes before I can speak again. I look at Wes, and let my head fall with the disappointment shadowed in my eyes.

"You knew," I say, the words heavy while quiet.

His eyes narrow on me, but his expression is soft—sincere. He nods slowly, and I let the weight of my head fall completely to the cushion next to me as he does the same. We stare into each other as I try to understand.

"You didn't tell me," I say.

"It wasn't mine to tell," he responds.

I feel the weight of the sofa shift behind me as Kyle stands. He moves around the couch, closing the liquor cabinet doors as he passes, then moves to a chair opposite Wes and me. He sits down, his hands folded and his elbows on his knees as he leans forward. His eyes are serious.

"You knew too," I say to him.

He offers the same quiet nod—the movement barely there, but just enough for me to understand.

"Your dad let it all out at practice. He…he had a pretty heavy breakdown the next day, and he begged us not to say anything," Kyle says.

I hear him. But I don't really *hear* him. I stare at him, until he grows so uncomfortable with the weight of being my center of focus that he has to stand and leave. My eyes move to the empty pillow that was behind his back instead, and I stare at the buttons and worn threads until my eyes burn from not blinking.

Eventually, the sickness of my life overcomes me, wrapping around me like a heavy blanket. Kyle's house is always my escape—it has been for years. But even it feels foreign now.

"I want to go home," I say, still staring.

"Okay," Wes says, his voice a quiet hum next to me. Neither of us move.

"Take me," I say.

"Okay," he says again.

After ten more minutes of nothing, I stand to my feet, and Wes rises with me. He pulls my hand in his, each finger weaving through mine, and he guides me out the door, raising my bag of equipment over his arm and tossing it into the back of his truck. He drives me home, and walks around to my door, lifting out my things from the back and holding the door open for me while I climb out.

"I need to be alone," I say, my focus on the ground, on the hundreds of steps before me that I have to trek to make it into this house, to pass my father, to lock myself in my room.

"I understand," he says. I don't let myself look him in the eye. If I do, I'll reach for him to hold me, and I won't be able to ask him to let go again.

He doesn't leave until I'm inside the house. Even then, I don't hear the truck pull away. I want him to go. But I also want him to stay there, ready—just in case.

My father is sitting in his chair. It's spun around toward the window, and he's leaning back with both of his hands behind his head. He's so still that if it were any other day, I would assume he'd passed out per his usual routine.

"I have questions," I say.

His hands move from his head, but he stays facing the window. I don't think he can look at me—he's not ready for the judgment. And I have judgment.

"Where was she? Was she…with family?" I swallow hard after I speak, adding my own mental addendum to my question—was she with *another* family?

"Kevin was there. They had…married," he says. I hear the heartbreak in his answer. I don't hear the usual blame that comes along with it.

Kevin. The man I only met once—when my father barely missed me trying to kill him with his car.

I hate Kevin.

"Was it…I don't know…fast?"

I don't know how to talk about cancer. I've never had a relative battle it. My grandparents, my dad's parents, both are alive and healthy. My dad's problems are all self-made, and none of my friends have dealt with something like this.

"She battled for a year," he says. His answer strikes something deep inside me, and a tear forms fast. I wipe it away and turn my head to look for my door.

"Did you go to her funeral?"

My dad is quiet for several long seconds, and I spend the time imagining her—what she must have looked like. Did she lose her hair? Did she have chemo or surgery? Was she thin and frail or strong, like I remember her? Was her hair still blond and her eyes hazel, like mine?

"No," my father finally answers. "It…"

His shoulders rise with expectation, and I hold my breath waiting for him to offer more. To say he didn't go because there wasn't a funeral. That he didn't go because my other grandmother told him not to, or out of respect for Kevin or a million reasons. He doesn't have one though.

"No," he says again, leaning back in his chair and pulling his hands behind his neck once more.

I stare at his knuckles. They're dry and cracked. His hair is thinning. His body has taken so much abuse. I stare at him and think about her. My mom is dead. I can't remember her. She didn't want me. And I'm left with this man.

I'm left with a shell.

"Are you going to get sober?" I ask, my belly thumping with adrenaline and nerves. My chest squeezes.

"I'm trying," he says.

I exhale quietly, running my hand under my eye to dry the last of the tears I'm allowing myself today. After a few minutes of silence, I nod to myself, and retreat to the quiet of my room. I drop my things on the floor by my door, kick my shoes from my feet and crawl on my hands and knees up my bed, folding half of my quilt over my body as I roll to the side.

My phone buzzes in my pocket, but I don't look right away. It's Wes, and I don't know what to say to him. After long enough, though, I realize I don't need to know. I just need him.

I'm still outside.

I read his text and my lips smile automatically.

I write back. *Thank you.*

Do you want to talk?

I think about his offer. I think about the millions of questions spawning millions more in my heart and head, and then I think about uttering them aloud. I can't. There won't be any answers to them. The questions are all for a woman who was supposed to love me more than the air she breathed. Now she's dead.

No. But…don't go. Maybe just text me about stupid things.

I picture him reading my text, propping his leg up against the door of his truck and tugging his hat lower, trying to think of something funny to write. My text box flashes dots for nearly a minute while he thinks and types. Eventually, his message comes.

Do you think there's going to be a lot of gum on the slide Friday?

I laugh out loud, and the gleeful noise surprises me. I cup my mouth, and cry with the mix of sweetness of his text and the sadness coming to rule me.

Your dad just left. I waved to him. He didn't look up at me.

My smile falls away and my hand rests against the bed with my phone clutched in it. My phone buzzes again, so I tilt my hand just enough to read his words.

Do you want me to come inside?

My body shivers from being alone. I reach my other hand to the side to type.

Yes.

In less than a minute, Wes pushes my door open, slips inside, and locks it behind him, climbing into my bed next to me and wrapping me in his arms. I exist there until the sun disappears and Wes kisses my head goodnight.

a boy like you.

I never once fall asleep.
My father doesn't come home.

CHAPTER 14

"Heyyyy," Taryn says, stretching the end of the word into a fade, as if somehow by saying the word slowly, hanging the *y*, makes me feel less like shit about my dead mom.

"Just drive to school," I say, pursing my lips and dipping my head to climb into her car. I stuff my backpack between my knees and pull my seatbelt on. I sense her still staring at me, so I huff and twist to the side to glare back at her. Her mouth makes the same straight line as mine, and we mirror each other for a breath before she finally turns back to her steering wheel, shifts her car, and pulls away from my curb.

Wes asked me if I wanted him to tell TK, Taryn, and Levi. In a moment of weakness while he sat with me in my room Sunday afternoon, I told him *yes*. I regret that now. I'm the girl with the fuck-up drunk, genius coach father, and dead mom. I'm ripe to get picked for a reality show; I can tell my story in a broken voice for the editors to play sappy music behind to get the audience to vote for me, to root me on. I bet I'd win with this story.

There is no audience in real life though. But there is someone rooting for me. He's the reason I came to school today. Maybe the only reason I keep going. He makes me believe there's a corner somewhere, that I'm going to turn it—and that I deserve more.

Taryn doesn't ask if I'm going to the library this time. She pulls into the spot near the gym and we both get out. The door is closed, and I hold my breath when we step up on the curb, listening for some sign of life inside. I hear the faint clanking of weights falling back in place, but that's all. No voices.

My father's in there. I see his car. He couldn't bother to make it home this weekend, but he managed to show up for his precious baseball team.

"You ready?" Taryn asks, her hand on the door handle, her eyes full of sympathy.

"Nope," I respond. I nod for her to go ahead and open the door anyhow, because I'm not ready for a lot of things that happen to me, yet somehow, I survive them.

My father is sitting at the desk near the front, his feet up on the desk as he works on lacing someone's glove. I look at him just long enough to see there's a smile on his face.

"Seriously," I mutter under my breath.

Kyle's spotting Wes, and I move over to the dumbbells, picking out the ones my father wrote on the paper for me. I watch Wes lift what looks to be about two hundred and seventy-five pounds from his chest easily, Kyle's fingers doing nothing more than tapping the bar lightly at the top to count each rep. When he finishes, he leans his head to the side, finding me. His smile is lopsided, or maybe it's just the way he's laying on the bench. If we were alone, I would lie down next to him and be content looking at him in silence.

With my small weights in my hands, I begin my workout, moving my arm slowly across my body first then punching back behind me. I notice Wes and Kyle move to another station behind me. They're both giving me space, but they're guarding me too.

"So, it's pretty weird that those two are getting along, huh?" Taryn says, folding her legs up as she sits on the stack of mats next to me. TK is busy working out with someone, so she's decided to follow me around this morning—or maybe it's her turn to watch over me. I look at her, waiting for her to bust into talk about my mom and questions if I'm all right, but she doesn't.

"Yeah, a little," I say, switching the weight from my right hand to my left to repeat the same set of ten.

"TK said it was weird that you went to Kyle's…" she trails off, looking down at her lap, her mouth too slow to stop the flow of thoughts from escaping. I let the barbell fall down to my side and tilt my head.

"What does that mean? I'm friends with Kyle," I say.

"Yeah, I know. That's what I told him, he just…" she stops, scrunching her face. I hate it when she gets like this—it's borderline gossipy. Only this time it's about me.

"He just what, Taryn?" I speak a little louder, and I notice it catches Wes's attention. I smile at him with tight lips, but I'm a horrible bluffer. His eyes narrow and his mouth pulls in on one side. I look back to Taryn. "He just what?" I say quieter.

She leans her head to the side and breathes out, almost frustrated with me.

"Wes mentioned it. To TK. That's all. When he told him about what you were going through, the last thing he said was 'when she found out, she went to Kyle—*not me*.'"

I hold her stare.

I did go to Kyle—out of habit, more than anything. I also went there in search of destruction, and an escape—also out of habit. I didn't go there because I thought Kyle could save me. I went there because he would enable me, like he usually does. Only this time, I kind of think he would have stopped me if Wes hadn't come. Because Kyle is really, honestly, a true friend. But he isn't my heart. That's someone else.

"I'm not going to make it to my morning classes," I say to Taryn, turning away before she can ask me any questions. I put the weights back on the rack near the wall and catch Wes's gaze in the reflection in the mirror. I tilt my head to the side, urging him to walk out into the hallway by the door. He says something to Kyle and steps over the bench, tossing the small towel from his neck to the floor.

My father's eyes catch me as I walk along the far side of the room toward the door, purposely taking this long route so I don't have to come near him. He watches as I step into the hallway. I know this from my sideways glances. I refuse to fully engage him.

I'm alone in the small alcove for a few seconds before Wes joins me in the darkened hallway.

"What's up?" he asks, his hands in his pockets, his body guarded. I'm a fragile thing right now in his mind, and I don't like that either.

"Do you have your wallet and keys?" I ask.

"They're in my bag, in the locker room," he says, brow lowered and suspicion painting his expression.

"Go get your things. Meet me at your truck," I say.

He stares into me for a few seconds, his face still, and his eyes studying mine with question.

"Okay," he blinks.

I slip through the door and walk to his truck, leaning on the passenger side, my teeth gripping at my thumbnail while I wait anxiously for Wes to finally appear through the opposite door of the boy's locker room. He walks toward me, but his eyes keep falling to the pavement in front of him, then they scan the parking lot around us. He never looks directly at me, not even when he unlocks the door on my side and holds it open for me to climb in.

He moves to the driver's side after tossing his backpack in the rear of the truck and turns the engine on to let the heat fill the cab. It's only chilly here in the mornings. He holds his hands in front of the vent for a few seconds, then looks toward my own hands that are fidgeting in my lap.

"What's up?" he asks.

I swallow, because I'm afraid of the dozens of tiny next-steps lying before me. I know the moment I take this first one, there won't really be any turning back—the row of dominoes will fall. But I'm ready to push them.

"I need you to take me home," I say.

His eyes come up at that, locking on mine for few seconds while he catches the tip of his tongue between his teeth.

"You forget something?" he asks, his hand moving to the gearshift, but not moving it yet. I watch his arm, the twitch of his muscles, the indecision and reservations he has. Those are about me.

"There's something I need to do. And I need you there." My eyes find his as I speak, and he holds me hostage again as seconds stretch into the feeling of long minutes. He nods slowly and turns his attention to the wheel, shifting and pulling us out of the parking lot.

"My dad's going to be pissed that I ditched class. TK got his ass handed to him when Taryn talked him into it the other day," Wes says. I laugh lightly, thinking back to the good boy who sat on Kyle's sofa nursing sips of a beer at the first party he came to. He is so good—all that is good. I will test him; this—what he's about to see—will test him.

I need him.

"Just tell him I made you do it," I smirk at him, my stomach sinking the closer we get to my house.

"Oh, I will. I plan on totally selling you out," he chuckles. I smile, knowing he wouldn't even if his own life depended on it. This is why he's the one I need. I feel selfish for it, but I think maybe it's my only chance.

We pull into my driveway, and I slip out of the passenger side before he has an opportunity to move to my side to open it for me. I leave my bag in his truck, so he does the same. I lift the garage door and open the small toolbox with the spare key inside, unlocking the back door to let us inside.

"That seems terribly unsafe," Wes says.

I look over my shoulder as we walk through the kitchen and down the hallway toward my room. "What could anyone possibly want from this house?" I laugh out.

Wes pauses at the entrance to my room while I walk inside, leaning on the side of the door. "You," he says. I stop and turn to look him in the eyes. "Someone could want you."

I suck in my bottom lip and nod. This is why I need him here today, for this.

"Come inside," I say, patting the top of my mattress. I crouch down and slide out a plastic bin where I keep my secrets, and I take my place next to Wes on the bed, pulling the lid free and tossing it to the side.

The first thing I pull out are the few letters I have paper-clipped together. I unfold the one on top because it's the most recently written. I penned this one when I was fourteen. I hand it to Wes and watch his eyes while he reads over the pathetic, desperate words of a naïve young girl.

"You wrote this," he says.

I nod.

"To your mom," he continues.

I nod again.

All of the letters are the same. I only wrote maybe five or six of them over the years, always late at night, always when I was at my lowest, when I wanted answers. I poured my anger and hurt into each one, asking her why she left, why she didn't love me, where she went, and if she had a family she liked better. I never signed the letters, because I never really intended on sending them. I'd write them until I slipped into slumber, or worse—until I was high.

I pull the small wooden box out from the bin next, twisting the tiny lock with the three-number combination. I stole the box from Taryn's sister—she used to hide her weed in it. I used it to hide pills.

I hand the box to Wes, the lid now open, and he pulls a few bottles out with names that aren't mine. There's a bag with a few blue pills inside too—oxy or some other prescription pill strong enough to make me sleep heavily and float in numbness for hours. The Ritalin bottles are almost empty. Those were my favorite. He shakes the few tiny pills left and twists the bottle in his hand so the label faces me. He doesn't ask, but he looks at me.

That look—it's heartbreaking.

"That's what I was at the elementary school for that day—the day I met you and your brothers. I was hoping this guy would show up who sells. He's always at the school," I say, taking the bottle from his hand and running my thumb over the rough edge of the lid. "I know you saw some of these—that one night, in our bathroom cabinet. There were more, I...I did more than just take a few pills to sleep. I took *lots* of pills. I hid them.

And I was almost out, so I went to find more."

His silence burns in my chest, but I keep speaking. I want him to know all of me—even the ugly parts.

"I wrote my last letter that night. It was the most honest letter I'd written, so I burned it when I was done. I hate my mother for leaving us. And now she's dead."

His movement is slow and careful. Wes lays out the rest of the things in the small box—a photo of my father and me, the stack of letters and the pen I'd used to write, the ink now dry. Then he dumps the few remaining pills out on the mattress, gliding his hand over them as if he's spreading out ingredients. I've done this too—so many times—spread out my options to leave the pain. I've come so close to pushing the limits.

"I haven't taken anything in months. But I could never get myself to throw it away. I wanted the safety net of the escape," I say, my eyes coming up to meet his, my raw and most embarrassing secrets spread out between us. "But now I have you. I come to *you*, Wes. I went to Kyle because I thought he would let me fall into this…my old comfort, for just a while. But then I saw you—you showed up at his house. And you were all I wanted and needed."

"Kyle wouldn't have let you," Wes says, his head falling to the side. "He…" Wes swallows hard. "He loves you too much."

I suck in a breath hearing him say something I already know. My eyes stay on his.

"He told me," Wes says, his attention looking back to the bedspread, to my addictions.

"I'm sorry," I say, guilt that I've broken Kyle's heart hitting me like a bullet in the gut. "I'm not sure why he told you that."

"Because he asked me if I loved you just as much. He wanted to make sure I was for real, that I was in this for real," Wes says, his hand gathering my things and stuffing them back inside the small box. He closes the lid and holds the box tightly in both palms.

"What…what did you say?" My body is pounding nervously, my heartbeat felt in my fingers, toes, and head—the rhythm wild.

Wes sets my past to the side and moves closer to me, his hand sweeping my hair behind my ear and his head coming to rest against mine.

"I told him the truth. You had me the first time I saw you, and I'll be in love with Josselyn Grace Winters until I die."

I draw in a long, deep breath, and the pain that I've felt in the middle of my chest since the moment my father told me about my mom subsides just a little—relief comes for this moment, and I consume it. My eyes close as Wes traces his thumb over my cheek in a slow pattern.

"You said you memorized my name. In class, when we were young. My *full* name. Why? Why were you waiting to hear my name? What was it about me?"

I feel Wes breathe in, the weight of his body balanced where our heads touch. His head rolls slightly back and forth.

"You sat at my table the first day I started at that school. Do you remember?" His voice is low. I shake my head because I don't. I remember slices of time with him—small interactions and things I wish I could take back—and then I remember how he took care of me when I needed someone most. That's when Wesley Christopher became the ruler of my heart. I regret it hadn't happened sooner.

He chuckles softly.

"I get it," he says. "I was a freak. I know. Weird kid who didn't talk. I wore the same clothes every day. My life then…it was pretty awful."

"I'm so sorry," I say, but his thumb finds my mouth, the pad running over my bottom lip as he quiets me.

"No, it's…don't be," he says, lifting his head up from mine, his hands cupping my face as he looks over me, adoringly. His mouth shifts into a soft smile. "That first lunch, when you sat next to me, I wanted to talk to you so badly. Introduce myself, or something. I don't know. I didn't know how, though. I was wearing these clothes that didn't fit, stuff the Woodmansees gave me that didn't fit their real kids any more. The shirt had a stain on it, and I was embarrassed. So I sat there quietly."

"You hummed," I smirk. His eyes widen, and I feel bad instantly. "It was cute. Don't be embarrassed."

He rubs his hand over his face.

"It was weird, but you're sweet to call it cute," he says. He lays back and twists to his side, propping his head up on his elbow. I do the same.

"The next day at school, I had to wear the same clothes. I didn't have a choice. I wore whatever the Woodmansees put out for me. And they pulled my clothes from the dirty pile and flattened them on the floor next to my sleeping bag, said they'd be fine to wear one more day," he says, his eyes blinking as he looks down to my bedspread, his hand sliding the distance between us along the cloth. His lip ticks up on one side as his eyes meet mine again. "Kids are mean. I showed up in the same clothes, and some of the boys picked up on it right away. I had to walk to school because there wasn't enough room in the car for us all. And when I started walking through the bike-rack area, a few of the boys pushed me over the rack, tripping me and pulling on my clothes."

"They ripped your shirt," I say, my own voice surprising me.

I remember. When he tells the story, the vision in my head fills in the rest. For me, it was just a regular morning—only a few boys were starting to pick on some kid, knocking my bike over in their quest to be mean. I screamed at them, and kicked the main boy in the knee, telling him he broke my bike. He didn't, but the fact that he knocked it over pissed me off. My bike was new—my dad had just bought it for me. When they knocked it over, the paint chipped. The boys started laughing at me, and Christopher shoved one of them, telling them to stop. That's when they started hurting him for real. That's when they ripped his shirt. And that's when I got sent home early from school for fighting because I leapt on the main assaulter, my fists pounding at his head and back until he got off Christopher and left him alone.

When it began, it was about my bike. But then it became about the boy being hurt and my need to save him.

"You fought for me," he says, the faint smile drawing me close. I move toward him, my head nestling into his chest, his arms circling me. "This scrappy, scratchy, tough-as-hell girl was fighting *for me!* Nobody had ever done that."

"I should have fought more," I say, thinking of how Taryn and I made fun of him sometimes, how we dared each other to sit near him for a full minute. All he wanted was my attention, and I toyed with him. "I'm sorry if I ever…"

"You let me stay in the race. When nobody wanted me around, you made sure I could stay," he says, sweeping my hair back again. "I know what peer pressure is like. I don't hold it against you."

"Still, if I could go back…"

He interrupts me with a soft kiss.

"There are dozens of things everyone would do differently if they could just go back. How about instead, you move forward," he says, reaching down and taking the box in his hands. I sit up and take it from him, then stand and carry it to my bathroom. I dump the few remaining pills into the toilet and flush them away, watching the water swirl as they disappear. Except for this weekend, I haven't craved them for months—but now that they're gone, I feel weak.

"How are you so strong?" I ask Wes, my eyes still on the water. I need to know, because I feel so helpless right now, but I also still have so many questions about him.

"I'm not," he says.

My eyes close as a breathy laugh escapes me. I nod slowly, but then begin shaking my head, moving to the bathtub edge where I sit down, my hands gripping either side while I look at him.

"You are. You know what I mean," I say, my head sideways. He holds my stare for nearly a minute before pulling his hands from his pockets and looking at them, stretching the fingers out slowly, his face void of any expression at first, until his brow pinches and he grows pensive.

"I was helping TK change the oil on the truck last night," he begins. My chest tightens, because I feel like he's avoiding my question. I'm frustrated, and my eyes flutter while my mind races, wanting to beg him to stop avoiding my question. But something about the way he keeps telling the story halts me. I listen. "We were using the jack, the one for tire changing?" His eyes come up to meet mine, and he holds his breath for several seconds before looking back into his palms. "I was under the truck when the jack slipped."

He steps forward, open palms facing me.

"I grabbed the axle and exhaust," he says, his eyes on the same hands I'm looking at—the ones that are soft, no calluses or scars. His hands are virgin of any trauma at all. "I told TK I rolled out just in time. But I didn't. It should have burnt the shit out of my hands."

My gaze flicks up to him, but his eyes are still on his palms, his face wearing a hint of shock. I run my fingers lightly over his skin until my hands are flat against his. I let their weight fall into his hold and his fingers slowly curl around mine.

"I don't know what's wrong with me, Joss. I don't know why I don't get hurt, or how I can anticipate things before they happen. The first time I did it was with you, when we were kids," he says, his eyes squarely on mine now. He doesn't blink, and his gaze burns through me. He looks scared.

"Maybe you're just special," I smile, standing up to be closer to him. I can feel his body shake slightly.

"Joss," he whispers, looking back down at our hands, weaving them together more tightly, pulling them into his chest. "I'm not special. But I'm strong…I guess. Or maybe I'm fast. I don't know. I can stop a lot of bad things from happening. But I can't stop that…" he says, his gaze moving to the empty box on the edge of the tub, then to the toilet where I just flushed my pills.

"I can't save you from that," he says, his eyes drifting to our feet. "That's my limit. I cannot keep you safe from *you*. You have to do that for me. And I'm so afraid you won't."

His confession slams into me. That's why I brought him here, why I needed him to hold my hand through this, through getting rid of the poison I used to seek to take me away. I knew it would be hard. And I know I am inherently weak when it comes to feeling. I have wounds from my mother's leaving and my father's drinking that have been bleeding for years. The Band-Aids have only put off coping with the actual source of the pain. But I don't know if I'm strong enough to keep walking away…not without him holding my hand.

"I'll fight so hard, Wes. I promise," I say, my eyes swimming in his. He doesn't respond, but the way he pulls me tight tells me he believes me. He knows I'm a fighter. That's what he loves about me—the way I fight.

He loves me.

He said so.

And I love him back so very much.

CHAPTER 15

"Your dad is pissssssssed off!" Kyle says as I round the gym toward my locker room. He grabs my arm and walks me backward, until we're hidden behind the maintenance shed and giant dumpsters.

It stinks here.

"Nothing really new there, and can we not have this conversation by the lunch leftovers? It fucking smells," I say, folding my arm over my face. Kyle pulls me against the wall next to him.

"No, your dad is on the other side of the building—so no, we can't. I just wanted to warn you," he says, craning his neck and looking around the wall. He steps out a little and lets out a puff of air, his shoulders relaxing. "I think he went back inside."

I smack him in the chest hard to get his attention.

"Owwww, damn!" he says, brow knitted as he looks at me, offended.

"What's up with the kidnapping?" I ask, my arms out.

He purses his lips and shakes his head. "You went AWOL all day, and for once, your dad was looking for you. He tried to pull you out of third period," Kyle says.

"What? Doesn't he have some PE class or something during that time? And whatever. I went home, Wes was with me. I had shit to deal with. I kinda have a lot on my mind, and that's kinda his fault..." I say, stopping when I see the expression fall over Kyle.

Wes was with me.

"I'm sorry," I say, taking a deep breath. I let my gaze fall down to the ground and I kick my foot forward, swinging it. I look back up to find him sucking in his top lip.

"It's okay," he shakes his head.

"No, it's not. It's awkward, you hearing about me being with Wes, and I'm sorry I just blurted it out like that," I say.

His eyes come up to meet mine, and his smile is crooked.

"Yeah, it's…awkward. But still…don't hide it. You shouldn't have to hide it. And I'm good with Wes," he says.

I hold my tongue and keep my gaze on his just long enough to know he's telling me the truth. I'll probably still try to shield him from Wes and me, but it's good to know that he doesn't resent me, or Wes, for our feelings. There was no stopping them.

"Speaking of the shit you're dealing with. Are you…are you *dealing*?" Kyle lets the question linger, and it means so many things. He knows I like talking about my mom almost as much as he likes talking about his since his parents divorced a few years ago. Kyle and I turn to destruction to cope when life gets hard—and we've always turned to one another as allies for distraction. But it's starting to feel like we can lean on each other differently now, without risk.

"I'm dealing. I haven't done anything stupid either, if that's what you mean," I say, resting back against the large recycling bin hiding us from view.

"Well that's a relief. I know how you like stupid things," Kyle says, his familiar grin punctuating his response.

"I like you, don't I?" I say, punching his arm lightly. He laughs, but it fades quickly.

"Yeah, well…I'm a pretty stupid thing," he says.

The awkward quiet starts to creep in, but before it becomes too much, I return us to the reason Kyle dragged me back here.

"So why's my dad looking for me? What's wrong? Any other estranged relatives pass away? Or is he just looking for a designated driver?" I don't bother to laugh through my sarcasm; it rings too true.

"Your dad quit the team this morning, Joss," Kyle says, his lip pulled into his teeth while he looks at me as if this is something I should already know. My mind is still trying to understand the words Kyle just said. The thought of my dad giving up the team feels like a goodbye, it makes me worry—*for him.*

"What?" I ask, my wide eyes a direct reflection of the shock I'm going through.

"You didn't know? Shit, I thought he at least told you that much. This morning, he told us all…damn…after you and Wes left," Kyle says, piecing it together. "He said it was time, that he had to refocus on his life, and that the assistant coaches were ready, blah blah. I don't know, the timing was all just really weird."

"No," I say, stepping away from him. I look around the corner, spotting my father's car—it's still in the lot. "It's not weird timing at all. He's shutting down. He was gone so much last week, Kyle."

I scan the campus, but everyone has gone. I notice a few players starting to straggle from the boy's locker room, and I know Wes will be coming out soon too, expecting my father to be there waiting for him, to mentor him.

I'm sorry, Wes. Eric Winters has just quit on you too.

"I'm sorry, Joss," Kyle says, stepping up behind me, his hand on my shoulder.

"Thanks," I whisper. "Hey, you should go get ready. I have practice too."

Kyle slides around me, and takes a few steps backward, his eyes searching mine to make sure I'm really okay. I'm not. He knows I'm not. But I've also been worse. I shake his worry off, and he eventually turns to jog to the locker room and I cut around the back of the gym to go into mine.

The girls are all mostly ready, except Taryn, who's manically trying to pull on her sliding pants over her cleats as she dresses in the wrong order. Even with her mad dash to get ready, the locker room is eerily quiet. My teammates are all sitting, waiting, with their gloves and bags in their hands, and there are a few whispers while I line my things up and get ready at my own pace. The way I see it, Coach is lucky I'm showing up to practice today.

I straddle the bench to put on my cleats, and my eyes lock with Bria's across the room. She smiles at me quickly, the kind of smile filled with condolences. *Shit. They all know about my mom.*

I drop my gaze back to my hands and feet, tying my laces and shoving my regular clothes into my locker, dumping my equipment bag on the ground. The clanging sound when my bat bounces on the floor makes a few girls near me flinch.

"Sorry," I say, to no one in particular. I pick my bag up and sling it over my shoulder, clicking the lock on my door with my right hand and walking with purposeful steps until I'm outside and away from the stares and uninvited sympathy.

I get all the way out to the field and begin my jogging, stretching, and warm-ups on my own. Several minutes pass before Taryn begins to make the long walk through the outfield. I notice Wes has already made it to the baseball field, and the boys are all circled with the assistant coaches— no doubt trying to figure out how they could possibly move forward without the genius that is Coach Winters.

The rest of the girls finally make it to the field, and Taryn and I begin throwing along the baseline. The quiet is still there. It doesn't belong, but I don't know how to end it.

"I wish people would understand that I'm fine," I say to my friend. She holds the ball, tucking it in her glove and resting it at her hip. "What? I am. I am fine."

Taryn looks down the line of girls throwing next to us and shakes her head, jogging over to me. I sigh as she gets closer.

"Stop it," she says.

I flinch.

"I'm...sorry?" I begin to laugh, but I'm not that amused.

"Stop pretending you're fine. Your mom died, Joss. And your dad just quit the baseball team. So clearly *he's* not fine," she says.

"I hardly knew her," I say quickly. The power of that statement hits my chest, stripping my breath away a little. My eyes sting, so I look down and sniff. I won't cry over her any more.

"But she was your mom. And the fact that you hardly knew her has sort of been a big deal in your life for a long time," Taryn says. I keep my eyes at the ground, because I can feel the others start to look our direction. The throwing sounds have stopped.

I do not want a group hug.

"Fine, all right? Whatever. I'm messed up about it. But I also don't want to deal with it, and now that my dad quit the one thing he loved, I've probably got bigger problems on my—"

Taryn stops me mid-sentence, her hand wrapping around my arm. I look up into her confused face, her eyes over my shoulder.

"Hey, Joss? I think maybe…you…maybe *do* have bigger problems…" Taryn's voice trails off, and I turn slowly, my face into the sun, to see my father standing next to Coach Adams. He's dressed for practice.

"Motherfuck—" I breathe.

Taryn laughs once, the sound like a rim shot to the punch line of my joke of a life.

Coach Adams blows his whistle, but I don't hear it. I only see him pull the small piece to his lips and watch as everyone else reacts, jogging over, whispering, nervous. These girls should be nervous. I am only sick.

I'm the last to join the circle around them, and everyone sits down, but me. I'll stand in the back, ready to leave. I want to leave. This can't happen. This field is *mine*. He can't have it.

"Joss, mind taking a seat?" Coach Adams asks.

"I do," I say, clearing my throat. "If it's all right with you…I'll just stand."

"Joss, sit your ass down," my father says.

This is why this won't work. I straighten my posture and shift my glove against my body, narrowing my gaze on my father.

"Why are you here?" I ask.

His chest puffs slowly with the intake of breath, and his eyes shift to Coach Adams. His voice is low, but we all still hear him.

"I didn't get to talk to her today. She was…*out,*" he says. He says it like I was out doing some illegal activity, like I didn't have a good reason to leave the school, like I'm a disappointment.

"Sorry, finding out your estranged mother died sort of makes you act up. Guess it's the same when it's your estranged wife," I bite.

"Josselyn!" My father's nostrils flair, and I blink rapidly from his tone. This scolding is different. It's full of authority. I crossed a line. I keep my stare on him, my eyes slits, because I'm still so angry I could punch him, but he's right—that was a low blow. I don't regret saying any of it, but I regret saying it in front of the team. I shake my head and kneel down under the scrutiny of everyone's stare.

Coach Adams coughs a few times, moving the clipboard in his hands to rest against his chest as he straddles his legs out wider to stand in front of us. "Ladies, I'm sure some of you know Coach Winters," he says, his eyes scanning over us, stopping on mine. I feel trapped by it, so I look away.

"Coach Winters is joining us for the rest of the season. I've had some things come up, personally. Nothing bad. Good things, actually. My wife and I are expecting twins, but the pregnancy is a risky one, so she's on bed rest. I just want to be there, in case she needs something," he says, and I can't stop the laugh that escapes my lips, amused by the irony that one dad is stepping away to be there for his family while the other— mine—is doing anything he can to hide from his. I cup my mouth and hold up a hand in apology.

"Thank you for the introduction, Dave," my father says, his lips pursed, and smile tight. He talks to our *real* coach as if they have some special respect or connection, as if my father hasn't torn apart every single coaching decision Coach Adams ever made.

"Ladies, I see a lot of potential out here," my father starts, and I tune him out, my eyes wandering over to the baseball field where the boys are now running. I catch a glance from Wes, and I shrug, not sure if he can see my small movement. His eyes stay on me for the first few steps when he turns to run the other way.

"Joss!"

My neck snaps. I'm sitting here alone. Seriously, Taryn? Couldn't, like, nudge me or something. I stand and brush the dead grass clippings from my legs and socks and begin to run to join the rest of the team.

"You're with me," my father says. I halt and roll my eyes before turning to face him.

"Is this funny to you?" I fold my arms.

He stares at me, his eyes unwavering, his expression unchanged.

"Why are you doing this? I mean you're taking things pretty far just to prove a point, that you can teach me how to hit lefty. You didn't need to go and quit the baseball team just to prove you're right. Could have saved us both some torture."

He continues to stare. I hold his gaze, trying to outmatch him, but eventually I break and look to the ground, kicking my cleat into the dried grass.

"Fine, whatever. I'll get a bat," I say, stepping toward the dugout.

"No," my father says.

I sigh and spin around with my arms out to the side, tossing my glove onto the ground. My head tilted up to the sky, I laugh in exasperation.

"No, he says," I chuckle. "What is this, some test? What are we doing? Why are you here? What's the point of this?"

My head falls forward, my eyes expecting to take in the same hard man looking at me seconds ago, but my father's face has softened. It catches me by surprise.

"We're going to talk," my dad says.

I blink at him. Talking is not one of our strong points. Yelling—we yell. That's what the tiny Winters family does. We don't share. We don't care. And we never talk.

"Fine. How was your day? Oh, wait…you quit the job you love just so you could ruin the only thing I love. Oh me? I'm fine. Or…I was fine. Now I'm not. You're right, Dad. This talking thing—it's awesome."

"I made you this way," he says, shaking his head.

My breath pauses while I think about his reaction. He's right. He did. He made me this way. He fucked me up. My mom fucked us both up. Wes saved me, but only what's left of me.

"Are you trying to go back? Is that what this is about for you, Dad? Making up for lost time? All those games you missed?" I ask, my voice lower. I'm not trying to be difficult with this line of questioning any more. I genuinely want to know. Because there's too much for him to make up for; there's no rewriting our history.

"I guess I was…yeah," my dad admits. My eyes grow wide with my surprise at his honesty.

"It doesn't work that way," I say, wrapping my arms tighter around my body. I look around us, scanning to make sure we're alone. I don't want anyone hearing us.

"I know," my father says. He glances over my shoulder and I turn to see the baseball team starting to throw, Wes and Kyle moving to the bullpen.

"They're the ones who really need you," I say.

His eyes stay on them for several seconds, but eventually slide over to meet mine.

"You need me more," he says.

It's such a simple truth, and as much as I want to reject it, my gut knows it. I don't answer him back. My throat feels dry and my body is beating with the thump of my nervous heart. As much as this is my nightmare, it's also my dream. I just don't want to jump into it, to live it, because I'm afraid it could change from one to the other at the blink of an eye. I'm not sure what I'm in right now—a fantasy or tragedy. Perhaps it's both. Maybe it's always been both. Maybe that's what life is—a beautiful mess.

"Can we hit while we talk?" I ask, tucking my cheek between my teeth. It feels so unnatural to have a candid conversation with my father. I'm not sure it will ever feel quite right.

"We can," he says, nodding toward the plate.

265

I walk to the dugout to put on my batting gloves while my father drags a large pop-up net around the backstop, placing it a few feet in front of the plate to give me a target. He spills the balls from the bucket, pushing them together with his feet before tipping the bucket upside down to sit on. When I step closer, he nods to the other batter's box, urging me to step in.

I steady my feet, digging my back one into the dirt, ready for my swing, but my father spins the ball loosely in his hand instead of tossing it up.

"Your swing is fine. You've been late. I want you to force yourself to hold on, as long as you think you can, before the ball drops out of your zone. Then hit it," he says.

I don't react. He grimaces, and I know he thinks I'm going to ignore him like last time, but I'm not. He was right then. He's right now. And he can make me better.

I want this.

I do as he says, and top the ball with my first swing, bouncing it into the net.

"Good," he says, leaning to the side as he spits a cluster of seed shells into the dirt. He pulls another handful from his pocket and pokes some seeds in his mouth. He grabs another ball from the ground, spinning it in his hand, then speaks from the side of his mouth. "Again."

I dig in and hold my breath, my lips pushed tight with my need to grunt with my swing, and I wait—just long enough. This time I hit the ball squarely, right up the middle into the net.

"Good," he says. It's the same good as last time. No false praise. No sugarcoated response or muted approval. I followed his directions and got the right result.

Good.

"Again," he says, picking up another ball and doing the same. My hands tucked inside, I hit the ball squarely again, only with more power.

"Good."

Our work continues, our conversation single words, small actions and tiny adjustments, until I've cleared every ball and the rest of the team is starting to move toward us for a water break.

"Let's hit some live," my father says, standing up and tipping the bucket over in his hand. I start to pick up the balls from the net, but he stops me, his hand squeezing the net closed.

"I got this," he says, his eyes clear for the first time since I can remember. He looks at me, then toward the dugout. "Go join your team."

I nod, and whisper *thanks* as I turn to jog away.

For the next hour, I hit balls from the left side, poking holes in our defense while my dad works to tighten them up. I hit where he tells me to, and I never let up—often showing our weaknesses. That's what he wants. It's what he's good at. And after one day under my father's guidance, we've turned a small percentage of our failures into strengths.

Coach Adams and my father put the heavy equipment back into the gated area near the backstop, and I pack up my gear. Bria stops at the end of the bench between Taryn and me.

"I'm sorry about your mom, Joss," she says. Nobody else hears her, which I'm relieved about. But her small condolence also feels nice. I can tell she was nervous to say those words to me, so I suck in my bottom lip and nod.

"Thank you," I say softly. "Nice job at practice today."

She grins, and her eyes shift over to Taryn then down to her feet.

"Thanks," she says, tugging her bag up her shoulder and walking up the path to the locker room.

"That was nice of you," Taryn says.

"Shut up," I joke. I glance at her and roll my eyes and return my attention to my shoes. I slip my feet from my cleats and pull out my slide sandals as Taryn wheels her equipment bag behind me, and I know she's trying to leave before me, to force me to be alone with my father. At first, I hurry with my laces, wanting to catch up with her, but I realize quickly I won't be able to.

Maybe, I shouldn't.

Talk. He wants to talk.

The baseball team is still practicing, but I know they'll be done soon, so I stay in my seat, twisting my body to face my father as he steps into the other side, taking a seat on the opposite end of the bench.

"Great work today, Joss," Coach Adams says as he passes.

"I know," I smirk, making my father chuckle. Coach Adams is already well on his way to his car, to his home, to be with his wife and unborn children. He couldn't have cared less about my response.

"You know, arrogance isn't a great team-building trait," my father says, pulling the bag of sunflower seeds from his pocket and raising it in an offer to me. I nod and he tosses it to me.

"Yeah, well, we're cocky sons of bitches, us Winters," I say just before dumping a handful of seeds in my mouth. I push them to the side and break them apart letting the salt coat my tongue. My father chuckles.

"Yeah, we are," he says, snapping for me to throw back the seeds.

"Wow, what are you, an addict or something?" He frowns at my joke. He probably should. It wasn't really a joke. I was being snarky.

"Chewing on something keeps me from having cravings," he says, pouring another handful into his mouth. I spit out a few of my shells and work the remaining ones open in my mouth. He's right—chewing on something works. I've gone through sixteen packs of gum since I've quit smoking.

"You planning on sticking around the house tonight then?" I ask, one eye squinting as I look up at him, the sunset reflecting off the metal fencing.

"Gonna try to. It's been hard though," he says. I laugh once quickly, and it catches his attention, his eyes landing on me. I chew harder on my remaining seeds, then bend to the side to spit them out.

"Yeah, it's hard to stay sober when you keep slipping up and sneaking out to the bar at night. But I gotta hand it to you, you haven't called me from Jim's in days," I say, squeezing the bench sides in my hands, leaning forward and waiting for my dad's excuse to come back to me.

"I haven't been at Jim's," he says.

I laugh again, but he doesn't protest. The longer I look down at the graffiti marks on the bench, the more curious I grow, until I peer up at him. He's fidgeting with his watch, twisting the metal band around his arm, clasping and unclasping. It's a nervous habit he's done since I was a kid. I remember he threw a surprise party for my mom once, and all I remember was him standing in front of the kitchen window doing just this.

"Where have you been then? Gotta new place?" I ask, blinking as I look at him, my eyes moving from his wrist.

"I've been visiting a friend," he says.

My gaze narrows. My father sighs, moving his hands behind him and leaning back on the bench.

"She's an older woman. Her name is Meredith. She…" he pauses, smirking at the face I'm making. My father is dating an older woman. I'm a little freaked out. "Ha…no. Not like that. She runs a group. You know, for recovering alcoholics?"

Oh.

"So you're in, like, the twelve-step or whatever?" I ask. My stomach is fluttering with my heartbeat. That's hope I'm feeling. I hate it.

My father chuckles.

"I guess, sort of. Though, it's not really anything formal. I tried formal, Joss," he says, his eyes meeting mine. His self-disappointment worn like a mask. "I'm not good at groups and sharing in front of others. It's too much for me to overcome on top of my problems."

I look down, twisting my hands together as I nod. I understand.

"But I failed enough that the last time I went to a meeting, Meredith gave me her number. She told me when I wanted to really try, to call her. She just sort of *listens.* Sometimes, ha…" he breaks into a small laugh, looking off to the side. "Honestly, sometimes I just call her up and go over there to fix things around her house. It's old, and her husband passed away years ago. I think she knows it keeps me busy, so I swear she breaks things just to make sure I have something to fix.

"Sometimes we talk too. She's been here—*rock bottom?* She lost her daughter in a terrible car crash when her little girl was only four or five. Meredith was hurt pretty bad, and she got addicted to the pain pills. Her husband threatened to leave many times, and one day, he had a heart attack. She went in for treatment after that. I guess she was strong enough to know she couldn't function at all on her own…not like this."

I take in my father's words, and I picture Meredith in my mind. I hope she's strong, because Eric Winters has sunk below bottom. He's one foot in the grave.

"Did Grandma Grace tell you where she was? Where she's been?" I keep my eyes low for this question. Rock bottom is tricky territory, and I hesitate asking questions while my father's dwelling there for fear it might push him deeper. But…I want to know things.

I spare a glance up and my father tilts his head up at the exact same time, his mouth curling in a smirk when our eyes meet. He looks out to the baseball field and his eyes grow distant.

"Tucson. I guess. At least, that's where the funeral was," he says, kicking his foot into the grass below our bench, digging a small divot with his toe. "I couldn't go. It didn't feel right. My goodbye, it's…complicated and different."

Mine too.

I look down at my fingers and think about how I would have felt— walking into a room full of strangers, knowing I have the right to be there to send my mother off to heaven or hell, but also knowing everyone's eyes would be on me, pitying me, or wondering about my real story and how my mom exited it.

"I don't blame you for not going," I whisper.

We sit in silence for a few minutes, the only sound my father pulling the bag of seeds open and dipping his hand inside one more time. The crack of the bat a hundred yards away gets both of our attention, and we look to where Wes is standing on the mound and Levi is rounding first base, pumping a fist over the fact that he's gotten a hit off his brother.

"You would have liked Grace—your grandmother?" my father says, his eyes staying on the team he left—the team he left…*for me.* "You have her name, but you've got so much more of her…ya know? I wish…" he sighs. "I wish you would have gotten to know her, at least. I should have kept that relationship there—for you."

His eyes dart to me. I don't respond, but I look at him long enough to ease some of that guilt away. I always wished I knew her better too. My dad's parents—they're like him. Short with words, cold on love. I wonder if Grace is warm?

"Well," my dad stands, kicking one leg over the bench as he gets to his feet. He tugs his pants up. His belly is thin—too thin. It's because he rarely eats, and his body has been his source of abuse for years. "Looks like practice is over. I'm gonna go make nice with the boys a little. Maybe you can take care of Wes for me?"

He winks, and I smile because that small gesture is one that I've yearned to see him make for so long. He rounds the gate through the dugout and starts to step over the dirt berm that separates the two fields when I stop him.

"Hey Coach?" I say. He turns on his heels, but keeps making small steps backward. "Welcome to the team."

His feet stumble, just enough that I notice. He pulls on the brim of his hat with a slight nod and his lips begin a smile that never fully manifests. When he turns, he puts his hands in his pockets and his shoulders slump a little. This change is killing him. But it isn't selfish or greedy.

This was for me. I see that now.

Wes and my father pass one another and have a short conversation, but soon Wes is walking toward me. I pick up my things and step out of the dugout, meeting him halfway.

"Looks like you've got a new coach?" He tilts his head to the side, lifting his hat a little to scratch at his hairline, his lips cocked in a half smile.

"Seems so," I say, sucking in my bottom lip.

"Big game tomorrow, I hear. You all are traveling north to play Los Banos. Chico State folks coming out to your game to see what you can do," he says. My stomach flutters with the anticipation, and the brief fantasy that I could do this—play college ball one day—flashes through my mind.

271

"That's the rumor," I say, stepping closer to him. His hand reaches for mine and the entire thing feels like habit. I notice it—the way our fingers fold together, naturally, as if this is how they were meant to exist. I've never been comfortable with someone like this. I've never trusted, or cared how someone felt. But when I'm not with Wes, my hand is cold. It's always looking for its other half.

"You nervous?" he asks as we get closer to his truck. I drop my bag into the back and turn into him, shrugging. "Liar," he laughs.

"Yeah, okay. I'm a little nervous," I say. He pulls the door open to let me inside, but before he closes the door, he steps in between my legs, his hands rushing through my hair, loosening the tie from the back and letting my strands fall free. His thumbs run along my cheeks as he cups my face and urges my chin up so he can kiss me lightly.

"Don't be nervous. You're going to be amazing. And your dad knows so too," he says. My focus swings from one of his eyes to the other, and I notice the orange hue cast in their blue pools, reflections of the sunset behind me.

"You make me less nervous," I say. He smiles softly, stepping in close enough to cradle my head against his chest, his hands running slowly, soothingly up and down my back.

"I want this, Wes. My dad. This game. This…life. I want it so bad," I say, my voice barely above a whisper.

Wes's lips fall down on top of my head and he holds his kiss to me briefly before rolling his to the side so his cheek rests on my hair.

"I know you do, Joss. I want it for you," he breathes. His chest fills slowly, and his exhale follows even slower. The tempo soothes me. "I'm gonna make sure you get it."

CHAPTER 16

I'm nervous.

The more I come to realize I'm nervous, the worse it gets. My first two years of high school softball were spent playing a game. There wasn't anything on the line—I didn't even really care if we won or not. I skipped practice, going when I felt like it. I rarely felt like it. The games were a chance for me to stretch my muscles, to remind my arms of what they could do and my legs of just how strong they were. It was a chance to show off—to be the *hot shot*. And if I blew it—I never gave a fuck.

I give a fuck now.

I kind of think there was this dormant part of me that always did. She's awake. And she's hungry.

The rain has been constant. It started sometime late last night, and the drops have pounded the school's roof most of the day. The boy's games were cancelled. The fields flooded. But apparently two hours to the north, California was dry. We were playing Los Banos today. A conference matchup that my father told me this morning had a small paragraph mentioning it in the paper.

This morning.

That was strange too. My father waited for me before leaving the house, insisted I ride with him—just to try it once.

It was nice. I may do it again someday, maybe even someday soon.

My father cut the article out and posted it to the fridge with tape because we lack magnets. There weren't many years of hanging my art and report cards up. But he hung this small clipping from the paper up with pride:

PITCHING PROWESS OF LOS BANOS FACES HEAVY BAT OF BAKERSFIELD SOUTH'S WINTERS

The article went on to mention my record number of RBIs and the speed with which Caitlyn Moore throws the ball. And then, there was the prediction that she and I—both juniors—would probably face off in a state title next year.

I wonder if Chico is coming to see Caitlyn or me?

The two-hour bus trip meant skipping photography today. It was my day to present my flower images for critique, and for once, I was prepared for something. Instead, Wes is going. He's not presenting the photos he showed me. Those were just for my eyes and my eyes only, he said. Instead, he took some shots of his brothers and father, but only of their legs—the way they line up, ankles crossed all the same, on the sofa while watching sports. He showed me the shots—and they felt special too.

With the baseball games cancelled, Wes, TK, Kyle, and Levi all planned to drive up to Los Banos for our game. I wanted to sneak Wes on the bus with me, to calm my nerves, but Taryn would have to do.

My father sits up front next to Coach Adams. It was odd to see both of their heads on either side of the bus, flanking the front seats as the rest of the team climbed in.

The bus feels cavernous, and I stop before I get too many rows toward the back, sliding into a seat near the middle. Taryn takes the seat across from me, and we both sit lengthwise, our feet almost touching in the aisle. Our team only has thirteen players, so most of the seats remain empty. It feels wasteful to take an entire bus, but the same bus is used for everything at South High. While North has extra vans painted with the team's colors, we're happy to have working windows and tires.

My father sits up on one knee, and my eyes catch his across the rows of seats. The bus rumbles to a start, and while everyone else turns around to settle in, he keeps his stare on me as I poke my earbuds into my ears. No lecturing. No reminders. He looks at me to make sure I'm taking this seriously, and I look at him like I used to when I was seven and he'd send me up to bat against a boy.

With fire in my eyes.

My thumb runs along my iPod, and I hit play, letting Wes's playlist stream into my ears and warm my chest. He put songs on here purposely, some of them with hidden messages, about the quiet boy loving the firecracker girl. I know he did it for me, to tell me how he felt before he really had the courage to say it aloud. We haven't discussed it, other than when he asked me if I liked the songs. I simply told him *yes.*

I'm calm for the ride to the school, and I remain calm until Taryn decides she needs to talk to me as the bus exits the highway to ride up the main road through town. She kicks my foot from the seat, and I startle as I sit up, pulling the music that was distracting me away from my ears. All so she could ask me if she thought coach would let her ride home with TK and the guys.

"No," I say, my eyes blinking in disbelief. What I didn't add to the conversation was that if she even as much as asked my father not to ride with the team, he'd probably make her push the bus for the first mile. That's not an exaggeration. It's rumored he made one of his ballplayers do something very similar a few years ago. I remember a suspension. I also remember that suspension getting lifted the moment the baseball team dropped two games to region rivals.

Taryn grimaces at my answer, but eventually shrugs and moves to sit up in her seat. I pull my gear bag up to my lap and fold my arms over it, resting my head to the side to stare out the window.

Los Banos is a lot like Bakersfield, only smaller. Poor neighborhoods, and less-poor neighborhoods—it's a city where people have to work hard. I always wanted out of Bakersfield, but now looking at this small town, the mother holding her son's hand as they walk along the side of the road, groceries in a bag wrapped around her other wrist—I kind of like the spirit of places like this and Bakersfield.

The other team is already warming up when our bus ambles up the dirt driveway behind the field. The air outside is cooler than normal, and it hits me like a slap. It's the wind. I pull my jacket from my bag, zipping it closed in the front before slinging my bag over my shoulder, my hands pink with chill in my pockets.

"Remember, this weather is worse on her," my father says softly as he strides up next to me. He's pulling a large wagon with the buckets of balls, our nets, and the water cooler. I smile when I glance over him, and he cocks an eyebrow. "What? You don't believe me? She won't throw nearly as hard if her hands are cold. And that rain—it's coming."

"No, no...I believe you. I totally knew what you meant, I was just sort of..." I stop my words and shake my head, looking down to my feet. "I don't know, caught up in seeing you pull that wagon."

My father chuckles.

"I miss the Little League wagon," he says, wiggling the handle of the rusted metal one he's pulling now. "Our old wagon was a lot nicer than this piece of crap. Maybe I'll see if I can get some of that baseball money over here."

"Now you're talking," I smirk, splitting away from him while he pulls the wagon to one of the dugouts and I hang my bag on the other.

"I'm cold. The boys got cancelled. We should have been cancelled too," Taryn says, following it up with a sniffle as she tosses her bag into the corner next to mine. I chuckle to myself, because while the wind is chilly, the temperature is still in the seventies, I'm sure. Taryn's a bigger baby than I am. "Come on. Run with me. I need to move," she says, tugging lightly on my sleeve.

"All right, hang on," I say, switching out my shoes. Taryn rolls her neck and watches me change to my cleats. She never switches her shoes, which is why she's worn the spikes down to nearly nothing. I brought it up once and she only stared at me, wide-eyed, then pointed out that she doesn't need to be fast hanging out in right field and doing nothing all day.

It was a good point.

My shoes on, I step from the dugout and begin a slow run toward the main road and back again. I feel Taryn next to me for most of the trip, but when I reach the roadway and turn to run back, I realize that the rest of the girls are all close by too. Not ahead, though. No. They're following.

More accurately, I'm leading.

The red jackets stepping from the car near our bus catch my eyes first, and I jog over to the bucket of balls, my gaze on the team of coaches from Chico State. I don't know what they're looking for, and I've thought most of the day that the reason they're really here is to see if Caitlyn Moore can strike me out. I know she's their target. But if she doesn't…

My teammates are watching the red jackets too.

"We're gonna make you look good today," Bria says, patting my back with her flat palm as she picks up a ball from the bucket and jogs to the opposite end to begin throwing with her partner.

My eyes flit to Taryn, and she grins with half her mouth, blowing a bubble with her gum out the other side.

"Bows and all, these are your girls," she says.

I toss the ball in my hand a few times as she walks backward to her spot, and then I glance at the row of girls next to me. Their faces are serious, and they're hardly talking. They're nervous—nervous for me.

"Hey, Bria!" I shout, holding the ball up for Taryn to see and acknowledge before I throw it at her. She catches my throw and returns it. My eyes stay on her, while Bria answers.

"What's up?" she says.

"We should have a party. Like…a real team party. Maybe at the beach. Bonfire. Just the girls," I say.

I don't look at her, but I can tell she's smiling. A few seconds pass, but she answers.

"That'd be cool," she says.

"Only girls?" Taryn whines. I whip the ball back at her a little faster.

"Yeah, you can make it one night," I say.

She holds the ball in her glove for a beat, resting it on her hip as she pushes some loose hairs under her visor.

"Yeah, but can you?" she teases.

I narrow my gaze and lean my head to the side, pushing my tongue into the corner of my mouth.

"Yes, I can handle a girls night. Especially with *these fine ladies,*" I say, exaggerating my words and speaking loud enough that the rest of the girls pick up on our conversation.

"Woot! Party Friday night!" Shannon, one of the more quiet girls near the end says. I laugh lightly to myself and glance at her. She's smiling as she throws, and her expression infects my mouth too, my lips unable to stop their curve into my cheeks.

"All right," I say, catching the ball from Taryn then waving her to take a few steps back. The rest of the girls follow. I lead—they follow. "Friday it is," I say. "But it has to be late. I've got work."

And I can't miss out on gum scraping with Wesley Stokes. Not even for the girls.

The quiet starts to fade, and soon there's a mixture of laughter and camaraderie along with the sounds of the balls smacking into the leather of our mitts. It's the sound of friends. I haven't heard it since I was little.

Maybe, I haven't been listening.

After warm-ups, we line the dugout, and there's a moment I notice that nobody else does. Coach Adams hands the blue lineup card to my father, and for a brief moment, both of their hands are holding it, their fingers pinching it in place. My father takes it completely, his lip twitching in a small acknowledgement to his counterpart. Taking the lineup card to the umpire is something the head coach does. This was the passing of trust.

We'll bat first, because we're visiting, so I pull my bat from my gear bag and step around the dugout to take a few practice swings. My father joins me a minute later, nodding over his shoulder for me to join him behind the brick side of the dugout. He's hung a small net against the fence and brought a few balls with him.

"Take a few swings for real, from the left," he says, kneeling down to steady himself in place to toss the balls for me to hit.

I glance behind me at the sound of Caitlyn's pitch hitting the catcher's glove with a commanding *pop*. She's throwing hard.

"You sure I should hit left today? She's throwing hard. I'm not sure I'm ready," I say, loading my bat over my shoulder.

"You're ready. You were ready before practice. You just needed to remember what you were capable of," my father says.

I smile, briefly, and take a quick but deep breath through my nose. I focus my attention on the ball in his hand as he spins it around, his fingers finding the seams.

"Ready?" he asks.

I nod.

He tosses, and I swing through the ball, hitting it hard into the net, the sound it makes when it pushes far enough through to hit the brick where the chain of the fence connects making an equally confident sound. I tuck my chin into my shoulder, but my eyes glance over at Caitlyn. She's watching.

"She see that?" my father says, the cocky smile spreading quickly on his face.

A few drops of rain pelt my eyelids.

"Yeah, she saw that," I say, swinging my bat around and laying it back on my shoulder. "Go again."

I swing a few more times while Caitlyn takes her warm-ups, each of us battling to be more impressive. She throws harder—I *hit* harder. Finally, after about ten swings, I help my father pick up the few balls, and we walk around the dugout to step back under the eave. The rain is picking up.

"They're going to have to cancel," I say, sighing.

We both cling to the fence and look out at the storm rolling our direction. The clouds are a dark gray, heavy with rain. One of those clouds is bound to open up, and it's going to completely flood this field.

"Maybe you'll get your bat in first," my dad says, zipping his jacket up and tugging his hat down over his thinning hair.

"That's some serious rain, Coach," a familiar voice says behind us. My father and I both turn at the same time to see the boys—TK, Levi, Kyle, and Wes.

"Gentlemen," my father says, his voice serious. He'll never really stop being their coach. "I see you made it here in record time. Not sure I want to know how you did that."

"Kyle drove," Wes says, selling my friend out. Kyle shoots a glance his way, his eyes wide. Wes just shrugs. "Dude, your driving scares the crap out of me. I'm not going to pretend it's better than it is. It's fast though."

"Ah yes, the Marley lead foot," my father says, his gaze coming back to Kyle. "I hope your father's truck made it here in one piece?"

"It's my truck now, sir. I'm paying it off. And yeah, it's in one piece," he says, rolling his eyes at Wes before looking at me. I offer him a half smile.

"You do drive fast," I say.

"Yeah, nobody was complaining when they wanted to get here on time," he says.

Wes chews at the inside of his cheek before leaning his elbow into Kyle. "You're right, man. Thanks for driving—like a fucking maniac," he says.

Kyle stares at him again for a few seconds then nods. "You're welcome," he says, holding his knuckles against the chain link between him and me. I meet his knuckles with my own for a quick pound and he steps over to the bleachers to sit next to Levi and TK.

"Thanks for coming," I say, stepping toward the far end of the dugout while our lead-off batter steps out to the plate. I hit in the fourth spot, so I have a batter or two to get myself ready for this.

"Wouldn't have missed it," Wes says, his head leaning forward against the fence. I slide my fingers over his where they grip the metal links.

"How was photography?" I ask.

"Good. I think he gave me a *B*. He said I was supposed to use an object," he shrugs.

"Your brothers' legs aren't objects?" I say, one eyebrow up.

"That's what I asked," he laughs. "He sighed and wrote *B* on my paper, so I think maybe he just split the difference. Whatever, I'm good with a *B*," he says. His eyes come up to meet mine, and we lock our gaze for a few seconds while the noise of everything else fades away. His lip ticks up on one side before he looks back down at our feet, letting his right foot kick into the bottom of the fence.

"The Chico guys are here," I say, glancing over to the home plate where Bria is now facing two strikes.

"Yeah, I saw them," he says.

"Strike three!" the ump calls. Bria jogs back to the dugout, her expression dejected as she runs by me. I pat her helmet as she moves to the corner.

"You'll get her next time," I say.

"She's too fast," Bria says, stuffing her helmet into the pocket on the bottom of her bag. She pulls her gloves off and grabs her gear to get ready to take the field. My attention comes back to Wes.

I breathe in slowly, our eyes locked again. No smiles. Just nerves from me. I look down at my gloves and adjust the Velcro tighter.

"You're faster," he says. I chuckle once. "I'm serious. I'm not feeding you bullshit. You're faster, and you know it."

I sigh and turn around to grab my bat from the place I hooked it through the fence. "They're here to see her. I'm kidding myself thinking that anyone gives a shit about me," I say.

"Stop it," Wes interrupts. I pause, one leg propped up on the bench as I lean my weight into the fence. His hand reaches in between the links to find mine and I let go of my bat to feel him. My eyes flit up to his to find his stare challenging me. "Make them notice you. She throws hard. You hit hard. They're going to want you both on their roster. Make them. Then fuck 'em, and go play for Stanford."

A sharp breath of a laugh escapes me, and my mouth smiles.

Shannon walks to first, so I move to step out of the dugout, Wes walking along the other side until I get to the gate.

"Fuck 'em, huh?" I say quietly, swinging my bat over my shoulder.

His cheek dimples with his lopsided smile as he pulls his hat from his head once to smooth out his hair. He wiggles it back into place with both hands and lifts his chin at me slightly.

"Yeah, fuck 'em," he says.

I bite my lip, nodding, and step out to the damp grass alongside the field to begin taking a few warm-up swings. As if the sky is announcing my arrival, the air crackles with a long rolling thunder, the sound no longer far in the distance, but only a mile or two away.

The raindrops start to come down harder, each drop bigger, carrying more weight. The small drumming along the ground and nearby rooftops picks up speed, and within seconds it's a steady drumroll, with powerful winds coming in behind the fall of water, blowing the rain so hard it stings my face to look at it.

"To the bus ladies," Coach Adams yells, waving his arms. I run into the dugout for my things, and my father grabs them from me, ordering me to get to the bus while he loads the small wagon with everything he can fit from our dugout. The boys help him, and we all climb inside while the team from Los Banos runs toward the brick building near the outfield fence.

We all climb on the bus, and I look out the back window to see Wes along with the other boys stuffed into the three seats of the cab of Kyle's truck. The rain is hammering their windshield so much I can barely make out their faces.

My father pushes the gear in through the back of the bus, and Taryn and I climb to the rear to haul bags and bats inside. I drag my bag to my seat and reach into the bottom pocket, pulling out my phone. I try to send a text to Wes, but it only sits in the queue, spinning. No signal.

"That came fast," my father says, brushing the water from the arms of his jacket as he stands at the main door of the bus. He starts to pull the door closed, but the coach from the other team runs over to talk to him. He climbs up the few steps and we all watch as he talks with my dad.

After a minute, my dad shakes his hand and pulls the door closed behind the other coach, who runs across the field with his jacket drawn tight around his body, the neck yanked over his head to shield him from the heavy rain.

"Cancelled?" I ask, my eyes wincing.

"Yeah, this storm's pretty deep. The fields are going to be covered in water for days when this is done. We'll reschedule," he says, taking the seat in front of me. I like that he sits here, in the middle of the bus. I'm disappointed, and I want him close.

I lean back against the window and slide my feet down, letting them dangle into the aisle. My father does the same, turning his head to the side to face me.

"We'll face her again. You'll get your shot," he says.

"I guess I get more practice now first," I say, holding the right side of my mouth up. My father's hand rises to pat the top of mine where I'm holding on to the back of his seat.

"That's the spirit," he says. He pats two more times, and before his touch disappears, I reach for him, my fingers catching his before they disappear into his pockets or lap. I squeeze his hand, keeping my eyes on it. He squeezes back. When he lets go, I feel more ready than I did before—ready to face Caitlyn Moore, ready to take the first step with my father.

The bus rumbles to life, and I look out the side window as Kyle pulls his truck next to us before we drive out onto the road. It's hard to see him, but his hand presses flush against the window as a signal they're leaving along with us.

We pull out behind them onto the main road, and the rain only grows stronger as we drive slowly through the central part of town, the tires of our bus forming waves that send the water rushing along the sidewalks. The people that were walking outside on our way into town, have now all gone inside. The streets are dark and empty, and the flashes of lightening and roll of thunder is continuous.

I stare at Taryn, both of us with our phones in our laps. She holds hers up and shrugs.

"I can't get a signal either," I say.

It takes us nearly twice as long to reach the highway, and the bus vibrates, idling for several minutes while we wait through the line of cars all trying to merge onto the highway. The traffic isn't thick, but it's slow.

Eventually, we turn onto the highway and I rest my head against my seatback and the window, closing my eyes and focusing on nothing but the long drag of the windshield wipers along the front window glass and the drumming rain on our metal roof.

I was going to be great.

I let myself have that thought. I've fended it off, not wanting to be too confident. My usual comfort on the field wasn't enough today. I wanted to have that edge, to keep myself ready. I wanted to surprise myself, to do more than I thought I could. I knew I could hit her, but I didn't just want to get on base hitting from the left side. I wanted to hit that ball over the fence.

I was going to make them all notice me.

Me.

I wanted this. I still want it. I'll wait. It will come.

My eyes flash open when even my dreams begin to feel off balance. The bus is dark, the wheels are skidding, and nobody onboard is making a sound. We're all alert as slow motion begins to take over. The river and washes zigzagging under our roadway have all been overcome with rain— the water is rushing fast.

The roadway is gone.

Gone.

It crumples underneath the weight of us, and our driver is leaning hard to one side, trying to keep the wheels right enough to keep us from falling. But she can't. It doesn't matter how strong she is. It wouldn't matter if Wes were driving right now.

This is nature—and it's violent and aggressive. It goes where it wants, takes what it wants.

It's taking us.

The bus creaks as the tires give way and our precious balance loses its battle, the giant vehicle slowly collapsing to the side. I see my father. He sees me. Our eyes lock as our bodies both press against the wall, our arms moving as quickly as we can will them to in order to brace us from the impact.

Cracked pieces of roadway smash into our glass windows, shattering everything, crumpling the wall of the bus. The wheels are visible through a gaping hole suddenly opening up in the floor. The bus is rolling. The bridge is collapsing. The water is rushing.

The screaming begins.

"Hold on!" my father yells, his hands pressed flat on the roof. I reach too slowly, and as the bus rolls completely, I tumble around the seats, my head slamming into the bench seat opposite me, my body colliding with Taryn's.

I blink and my body is on the opposite side from where it was a second before, my leg now pinned between the broken window casing and some piece from the underbelly of the bus. The tires are spinning, and the roar of the rain and water makes it hard to hear anything other than the shrill screams of my teammates.

For the briefest moment—long enough for a single inhale—everything stops. The bus is no longer sliding, the bridge is balanced on its own pieces, and the water is rushing around us, the rest of the roadway high above us. But we're still. The world is holding on to us.

When I look up, my eyes find Wes's waiting for me. He's too far for me to reach him, but our eyes lock. My mouth opens to begin its call for help. The world begins to move again. There's a very specific sound metal makes when it bends to forces far stronger—that moaning sound, of the aluminum and steel giving way, echoes like a siren right now.

Gravity.

Water.

Weight.

It all pushes at once. My eyes meet my father's quickly with the snap of my head, and the sureness that was there during our game is gone. It's fear. It's familiar terror. It's far worse than any I've ever seen painted across his eyes before.

"Daddy!" I scream, the bus sliding with my call, the rotation slow at first, then happening all at once. The bus tumbles end-over-end into the water, pieces breaking away and water rising around us.

Floods happen quickly. The water explodes in the sky and fills the hungry earth, the dirt too dry to accept everything. It washes everything away, and we go along with it.

My father holds fast to a giant yellow slab of metal, and I work to free my leg, my mind swiveling between panic over the pain and worry for the world I'm at risk of losing. Then, without any effort at all, my leg is free and my body is being lifted from the bus, pulled through the tangled scraps left of the window. My heart thumps wildly, but stops the moment Wes's arms wrap around me.

I'm home.

I'm safe.

I'm cold.

I see things in small snapshots, as if it's all unfolding in frames from a comic book: Wes carrying me through the shallow but rising water, up jagged rocks toward the highway, the bridge behind him in half, metal cords dangling—support systems that gave way, failed when we needed them. It's all broken.

Taryn is pulling herself through the water next to us. My teammates are climbing from the wreckage. Others have already made it to safer grounds.

The rain is coming down in sharp, slanted lines. It's almost a constant stream of water, as if someone is dumping it on us rather than rain falling from the sky.

The bus begins to jerk loose from the jagged rocks it's settled on. Wes sets me on the asphalt of the highway, dozens of feet above others still trapped—holding on in the rush of the waters, to what's left of our bus. The metal beast tears free from the rocks and the water pushes it into the small strip of metal my father and Bria are clinging to for safety.

I blink and they disappear.

"Daddy! Daddy!" I scream so loudly my voice cracks and grows hoarse. My eyes burn, and my throat aches. My heart yearns. It's breaking.

"I got him," Wes says, rushing down the edge of the ravine, rocks giving way under each step he takes until his body is caught in a massive slide of mud and debris that crashes into the water. The mud is thick, but I see Wes's arms pound at the water. I see his body fight.

I begin to scream for him now too.

I try to stand, but the pain is sharp—it sears through my entire body, and I collapse on the ground in tears.

"You're really hurt, Joss. You're bleeding. Oh my god, so bad!" Taryn is next to me; she's holding my leg then covering her mouth. I don't look down. Whatever she sees makes her sick.

"He'll get him. It's okay, Joss," Kyle says, moving to my other side. He pulls his wet jacket from his body and wraps it tightly around my leg, moving his face in front of my view.

I'm shivering. I can't see my leg. I can't see the water below. I can't see my father or Wes. I only see Kyle. His eyes are drilling into mine. He's nodding slowly.

"You're okay. They'll be okay," he says, every now and then glancing over me until I feel the hands of others on me and see the blue uniforms of paramedics and firefighters take control of everything that surrounds me.

Kyle stays though. I strain my neck to see—to see anything. But he doesn't let me look.

"Wes will get him. Don't worry. Let them help you now, Joss," he says, his mouth a hard line. His jaw flexes with the grinding of his teeth. He doesn't want to have to lie to me.

He's afraid he's lying to me.

The pain is overwhelming. Everything is so cold. My body can't feel anything. The world is yellow.

Bright.

And so very quiet.

CHAPTER 17

"She's going to hate all of that crap hooked up to her," Kyle whispers.

I don't know why they're all whispering. I can hear them. They don't think I can. They think I'm heavily drugged. I am. But I'm also awake…and so very aware.

Painfully aware.

My body is numbed. The pain was too much. It made me black out. And when the doctors tried to repair me, I fought them.

I'm a fighter.

So they subdued me.

I think maybe everyone was hoping that my memory would disappear with the pain meds too. That it would wash away with the waters that destroyed me.

But I remember.

That's why I lay here with my eyes closed. That's why I don't show how awake I am. I'll rest. I'll hide. And I'll keep hiding until they find him.

I know my father made it. I've heard bits and pieces. I've heard his voice. He somehow found enough to grab in the rush of waters to cling for life until a rescuer could reach him. He had no idea Wes was searching.

I don't hear Wes's voice.

But he's alive. I know he's alive.

I feel it.

He's too strong. Water is nothing to Wesley Christopher Stokes.

"Mr. Winters? It really should just be family in here, sir," the nurse reminds my father. He has the same answer every time.

"It's just me. And Kyle is like a brother," he says. It's the fifth time he's said this, second time to this nurse. I recognize her voice.

"Okay, but he'll need to leave when visiting hours are over," she says. That's the same response from her as well.

"Right," my father says, his gravelly voice a fraction of himself. "Right," he says, the sound even fainter.

I'm not sure how long it's been. When I first heard the voices, I thought it had only been a few hours. But I've come to realize that it's really been days. Two...I think? Maybe three.

I can't feel my body. The drugs numb me. They don't numb my mind, though. That races, replaying everything that happened, hyper-focusing on the details. The bridge collapsed in the rush of floodwaters. This stupid state and their goddamned budget problems skipped a few inspections here and there. They bet on certain areas never getting rain. And then the rain came.

My father has had the news on in my room. I've heard it—the bridge collapse on one-eighty-five. They talk about our bus. They have footage of the wreckage. They've tried to talk to my father about me. They've ambushed my friends. I was the one injured, the only one injured—other than the bus driver who had a concussion and my father who had a broken arm.

Nobody talks about Wes. Even my father whispers when Kyle asks if he's heard anything. I heard a small blip, once, that there was a search for one of the students who was caught in the floodwaters. But then nothing.

"It's late, Kyle," my father says. I hear a chair shift and Kyle's heavy feet hit the floor.

"It's okay. I don't have to work today. I...he said I could take time off," Kyle says. His voice is sleepy. He's losing it. He used to lose his voice when he'd stay awake all night with me at his house. *Go home, Kyle. You're tired.*

"Nothing's going to change, Ky," my father says. My eyes twitch under their lids hearing him speak to my friend with the familiar name he used to give him—shortened Ky. They have each other. "Go on, get home. You can come back tomorrow. I don't give a shit what the nurses say about you visiting."

Good. I don't give a shit either.

It's quiet for a few minutes, but eventually the chair slides again, and I hear it move all the way to the opposite side of the room. I feel Kyle step closer. I should open my eyes. But I don't want to—not yet. I'm going to stay in this dream for a little longer; avoid the nightmare.

"Hey, JJ," he says. I feel his hand grab mine, and I fight my instinct to squeeze it back. "I'll see ya tomorrow."

His hand slips away, and a few seconds later, I hear the door close. My father's sigh is long, but he's not leaving. His own chair moves, and I feel the bed shift slightly as he rests a leg up on the end. He's getting comfortable for the night. He won't leave. I heard the nurse say he hasn't left since they set his arm.

"Are they still looking for him?" I ask. My lips are so dry, the words crack them open when I speak. My voice is a whisper, and it cuts my throat.

My father's foot remains still. He's quiet. But I hear him breathe slowly, a long inhale and exhale. I'm pretty sure he knew I was awake, but he's also relieved. I don't look at him, but I can hear him tremble when he speaks.

"They're still looking," he says.

I don't say anything more. He doesn't ask any questions. I feel the threat of my first tear form in one eye, and I let it fall to the cool sheet under my head. After a few minutes, I feel my father's hand close around mine, and his head falls against my shoulder. The weight of it shakes with small tremors. He's crying. I squeeze his hand back, and he stops. He leaves his head on my arm, and I hear the sniffles as he tries to be strong.

He's not ready to tell me the rest. I'm not ready to hear it. But I know my leg is gone.

The pretending could only go on for so long. The next morning, it was time to start the long climb through reality.

Infection. Nerve damage. The bone snapped completely. Everyone who spoke to me gave me the same details and timeline—they had to make decisions fast. They worked to repair what they could right after the accident, but the infection was spreading quickly. It was making me sick, risking more of my leg—risking my life. I had been here for four days, almost five. At the beginning of day two, the decision was made to cut off my right leg below the knee. Mid-calf, I'm told. I wouldn't know. I won't look at it. I refuse.

As much as I can't feel anything…somehow, I still feel my missing lower leg. That's the first thing I felt when I started to wake—pain. A sensation that wasn't there because my leg—it wasn't there. Then that ache shifted to my heart.

"Joss, I'm going to change the dressing. We're going to set a hard cast over everything later today, which means you'll get to go home," the doctor says. He seems really impressed with his work. I hate the way he admires it.

"Okay," I say. I've also learned I have to respond. If I don't, the adults begin to whisper. They start to talk to me in that fragile voice, the one used on infants and people who are at risk of losing it.

I've lost everything, so what does it matter?

"Okay," I say to her next question.

I never smile. I don't make eye contact. For the last twenty hours, I've done nothing but stare out the University Hospital window, my eyes searching for something. I'm searching for him.

Several minutes pass. I move for the nurse and her assistant. I do what I need to do so they'll leave, so I can go home—even though I know I'll hate it there even more. At least at home I can hide in the familiar.

"I called the Jungle Gym. Kyle said he talked to your boss too. You can take as long as you need. He said he'd hold the job for you," my father says. Like I'm what? Getting over a fucking cold?

"Call him back and tell him I quit," I say, my eyes wide on the window. The cars far below weave in a pattern I've memorized. It's the timing of the lights. Six get to turn, twenty get to pass, and then it starts all over again.

"Joss, don't give up on something. You might want to go back; you loved that job. The psychologist said familiar is good…" my father says. He sounds like a brochure.

"Have they found him yet?" I say, ignoring his plea to keep my shitty job because it's good for me mentally. The only thing I liked about that job was the boy who gave me a ride home at night. Find him and I'll go back.

What if they never find him?

"They're still searching," my father answers. His response is several seconds late. He doesn't think they will. He doesn't know Wes.

"It looks like you get to come home tonight…if they get you through the cast part early enough. Kyle is at the house. So is Conner. They helped move some things around, so you can…"

He doesn't finish. They moved furniture so I could get to my room in a wheelchair. I logged that part of our conversation with the doctor too. I said crutches were fine, but my father heard it might make it harder for me to learn my center of balance when I get a prosthetic.

"I'm not going to play ever again, you know?" I say, my back still to him. I think it's more comfortable for him this way too. He never answers me. Maybe he needs to believe that he can make me better—be part of my miracle. I let him.

The sound of the television clicking *on* drowns out everything else, and I let the white noise of some college basketball game take over for our conversation. Hours pass, and my father and I don't say another word to each other. He trails behind as I'm wheeled to another room where my cast is set. They want to protect the skin, let it heal without me risking any setbacks or damage to the wound.

I never want to move. I'm not sure how I could do any damage to anything other than my soul, and that's already gone. Or at least…it's missing.

When we get back to my room, my things are all packed. There's a bag on the bed—my duffel from home. My phone is sitting on top of the zipped part. I haven't looked at it other than once, briefly, to see if any of the hundreds of texts and messages were from Wes. They weren't.

"I'm leaving now?" I say, my eyes zeroing in on how small my bag is. My things fit in such a small space, and I'm going to another small space, to live a small life.

"Heyyyyy…." Taryn's voice hums from behind me. My eyes flutter to a close. That's her awkward *hey*—the one she spoke when my mom died. She used it the first time I needed stitches, and she was staring at the cut on my chin. She used it the first time I tried cutting a chunk out of my hair in the back because my dad wouldn't take me to shave it. She's using it now.

"Hey," I say back. I almost amuse myself. Almost.

"I packed your things. I told your dad I'd help you get settled in," she says, shifting to sit in front of me. She perches on the edge of my bed, ready to sprint. I don't like how everyone feels like they have to catch me. I just want to be left alone.

My mouth is in a straight line, and I don't have anything to say. The discomfort of the silence grows until she has to stand. She walks behind me, my bag in tow, and someone pushes me in the chair until we stop at my doctor—the one impressed with his cutting-and-sewing job.

"If things heal well, we're looking at fitting her in two, maybe three months. It's going to be important that she maintains her strength, and we want to try to keep her off crutches, as much as possible," the doctor says. He's not looking at me. He's speaking to my father.

"Why?" I butt in.

They both turn to me, then to each other. After a few seconds filled with glances that feel like I am only getting part of the story, the doctor sits on the arm of a chair, folding his clipboard to his chest, and begins a lengthy explanation about gait and my ability to return to normal activity more quickly if my center of balance doesn't get used to depending on my *sound* limb.

"What's...normal activity?" I ask. The doctor glances at my father, who chews at his lips and adjusts the way he's standing.

"Well," the doctor begins, looking at his hands clasped around his clipboard, his brow pulled forward. "Normal depends on the goals you set for yourself, Josselyn. If you push yourself, there's no reason you can't participate in sports again. Maybe in a year or two..."

I knew that's where this was going. In a year. A year! What good would that do? I can join some rec league in Bakersfield and fill my Tuesday and Thursday nights after class at the community college with some slow-pitch softball league? I'm never playing again. I'm never going to be the girl with the fire again. I'm never going to get a hit off Caitlyn Moore's fastball and prove myself to college scouts, and my grades are shit. My path ran right into a cliff, and I jumped off.

Now all I'm doing is falling. And Wes isn't even here to catch me.

"Let's go," I say, my eyes focusing on the long hallway before us.

After a few seconds, the doctor stands from the arm of the chair, stepping over to give my father a few more directions, as if he'll remember any of it. He's barely learning to take care of himself. Taryn walks alongside me as the nurse begins to push us down the hallway, and when we get to the curb outside the lobby, Taryn waits with me while my father goes to get his car. She doesn't ask any questions. My friend knows better than that.

The drive home is just as quiet, and I tune her and my father out while they arrange my things. The house looks ridiculous—all of the furniture pushed to the side, making wide paths for me. What's worse is I feel like I should be able to get up, to be able to stand whenever I want to. I catch myself more than a few times pushing my weight on my arms, lifting to try to reach for something, only to fall back into my seat. I'm trapped; my body is a prison.

After an hour, my father leaves us to go to the pharmacy to pick up my prescriptions. I stay by my window, wishing it were bigger—higher. I want to go to the river. I want to find him. They say they're searching, but how is anyone looking—everyone is here. They've all been here. And I've seen the news. The camera shots are of volunteers and guys in wet suits walking through the area where the bus collapsed upside down into the water. Nobody is looking for Wes. They won't find him this way.

"Why are they all lying to me?" I ask Taryn.

She's quiet. I keep my stare on the small, dried dots where the rain hit my window several days ago and left salt deposits behind.

"Tell me, T."

I hear her move toward my bed, and I finally turn to look at her. Her eyes flit to me, but move away when they meet mine. Maybe it's guilt. Maybe it's empathy. Whatever it is it has her tongue-tied and our friendship twisted.

"Tell me," I repeat, my eyes heavy on her, waiting for her to look up. She finally does, and the glassiness is the first sign I've seen of anything real and honest in a week.

"The police called off the search two days ago," she says, her head falling to the side. My heart is ripping open, the tear slow and painful, but not a shock. I think I've been ripping it open every day to get used to the pain.

"He's out there," I say. Her eyes close and her head falls forward completely.

"TK and Levi…they keep searching," she says. She brings an arm up to run along her nose and eyes.

"I want to go there," I say.

Her body shakes with one short laugh.

"Take me," I say. Her head shakes with a *no.*

"Why?" I ask.

Her eyes come up to meet mine, and her lips are tight before she finally speaks. "It won't do any good, Joss. And how am I going to get you there? How are you going to help look?"

My eyes narrow on her, and she stands, turning her back to me. My eyes fall to my lap, to my one good leg, and I know she's right. But he's out there somewhere. He has to be.

"Just…" I swallow hard. "Just drive me through the area. Just once. I need to see it. Please."

It's quiet—the only sound her moving a few of my things, hanging shirts that I never bothered to hang before the accident. My gear is still in the bag, piled in the corner, and I turn to see her lift it in her hand, but then she sets it back down.

"Put that away. In the garage," I say.

She doesn't look up, but stills, her fingers flexing a few times before she nods and bends to pick up the bag. She leaves my room with it, and I hear the sound that signals the garage door opening and closing, the bats clanking on the floor, my old life being packed away.

When she comes back, she has a harder time looking at me. At first, I almost challenge her, dipping my head with her movement around my room, trying to catch her sightline. After a few minutes, though, I give up and let my eyes go back to the comfortable bliss of searching out my window, staring into the endless sky.

"I have to go," she says softly. I nod. "I'll be back tomorrow, and I'll bring your school things. They approved you for home study until you can go back."

Back. I'm never going back.

I nod again, and after several long, quiet seconds, I hear my door close. I'm alone.

CHAPTER 18

Three and a half months later

"Joss. It's time," my dad says.

It's the same routine every morning. My father knocks lightly on my door before pushing it open enough to poke his face inside. He tells me it's time. I ignore him. And we battle it out between both of our obstinacies until I give in and go to rehab, only to fail and have to come back home to homework I don't understand and a tutor who makes me want to punch him.

His name is Todd. He's a teacher's aide. One of those men in their thirties who decided the corporate world was too corrupt, so he wanted to give back, in a meaningful way, by teaching. He would get eaten alive in a classroom. He can barely handle me, and that's one-on-one, and I can't run away.

My only solace is that I'm in my final week of school. I will have one science credit to take over the summer—to make up for a failing grade— but that won't require Todd's visits or help. I failed because I quit trying mid-semester. One bad test sent my grade below fifty percent. Honestly, it made more sense just to let it ride and retake it over the summer. My dad agreed. Or maybe he has to pick his battles. Either way, I won that round.

I won't win this one though. I'm too tired to argue this morning. I pull my body up and work my prosthetic on. The process may get faster one day, but I'm still too new at it. I've only had the temporary leg for a few weeks. I spend a lot of time with the sock and finding my balance. My walking is still not good. My dad says it's because I don't try. I quit arguing with him about that too. It doesn't do any good.

I make my way slowly down the hall, and he's already waiting with the door held open, half a peanut-butter sandwich in his mouth and another half wrapped in a paper towel for me to eat in the car.

It's five in the morning. We go to the rehab center early, so my father can make it to work after. I suppose the hours and my constant needs have had one positive effect—he hasn't fallen off the wagon. At least, not that I know of. I met Meredith last week. She showed up for dinner and stayed late, talking out in the living room with him until almost midnight. At first, I listened in on their conversation, expecting him to confess cravings or slips he's had. But there weren't any confessions. They talked about family, about me when I was younger, and about my progress. I guess he just needed someone other than a bottle to listen.

It takes me a few tries to get into the car. I'm still not great at maneuvering myself. My dad looks away when I move awkwardly. I'm hard to look at.

The rehab center is in the downtown, so my dad and I nibble slowly at our sandwiches, taking up half of the ride there, avoiding conversation. My father moves right into his daily recap of what we did the morning before, and my new goals. I let him talk, but I never react. I just listen, my eyes looking out at the empty streets of downtown Bakersfield as we drive to the clinic.

My eyes are still searching for Wes. But I'm starting to believe I'll never find him. His family is starting to believe it too.

I made Taryn take me to visit them last week. I've seen them one-on-one, when Levi came to visit me with Kyle or when TK was with Taryn, but it was different seeing them in their home. It was so incredibly evident that a piece of them was missing. The home wasn't the same.

Bruce was warm as always, hugging me, and begging me to stay for dinner. But I couldn't. One look in his wife's eyes was all I needed. She was as broken as I was, missing her son. There couldn't be two of us at that dinner table.

Before I left, Bruce mentioned that they were probably going to go through some of Wes's things this week. Not to get rid of, but just to put away, so Maggie didn't have to look at them with any false expectations that Wes would one day return to claim them—that he wouldn't step through the door and slide out of his shoes and into his favorite sweatshirt. He invited me to come back to take anything I'd like. I couldn't tell him no, but I didn't tell him yes.

There's a part of me that doesn't want the false hope either. Then, there's another part that wants to keep that hope alive and where it belongs—in Wes's home, in his room, with his brothers. It feels like we're picking apart the pieces, like vultures.

"Joss? Ready?" My father's question startles me from my thoughts.

I nod.

He holds the door of his car open while I find my balance and step out. There's an older man walking in front of us with his wife. He's been here at the same time as me for the last week, and I notice he's making better progress. Then again, he's trying.

I notice my dad's eyes on him, and when his gaze moves to me as he holds the door to the center open, I see the judgment. He masks it quickly, but not before a hint of it slips through. I'm not trying hard enough. But I guess I don't see the point in rushing. What am I rushing to?

We're past needing to fill out paperwork and formally check in. The therapists all know me. My dad made sure of that too. I wished he hadn't told them I was an athlete. I'm not. Not anymore. And all he's done is put high expectations in place that I will never reach.

"Are we ready for the bolster work, Joss?" asks Stephanie, my main therapist. My dad requested her, thinking I'd work better with a woman. Stephanie is peppy, and her lips are always pink with glitter. My dad has no idea who I am at all.

"Sure," I say, ambling toward the table. I lift myself up and push my hips higher with my hands, lifting my legs while Stephanie slides the round bolster in place for me to complete a series of hip flexers and leg raises. The goal is to strengthen my muscles in other places to improve my gait and let me walk with my prosthesis for longer periods of time. Right now, my legs hurt after a couple hours, especially the stump.

My dad is usually right next to me, coaching me through the exercises. But this morning he steps to the other side of the therapy room. The peace is welcome, and without his watchful eye, I coast through my sets. I'm operating at maybe thirty percent of my normal output, but Stephanie is still clapping and praising every exercise I complete. She's walking confetti.

I finish my bolster work and push myself to sit while Stephanie puts it away. My eyes catch my father's across the room. His arms are folded, and he's talking out of the side of his mouth to a woman next to him. She's in a black sweat suit, one made for runners. Her hair is dark, long and pulled back tight. Her face is hard, and she doesn't smile. She stares at me for several seconds, and I look back, daring her to look away. She never does, but she raises her hand, cupping her mouth, whispering something to my dad.

They're talking about me.

Stephanie helps me to my feet, and I answer a few questions about the fit of my new leg, any trouble I've been having with it, any adjustments I might need.

"I don't really think there's anything you can do to make it much better than it is now. It sort of is what it is, ya know?" I say, looking at the top of Stephanie's head while she bends down in front of me and tugs on the socket, feeling around my stump.

"There are plenty of things that can be done," a woman's voice says. Her tone isn't nice, and it causes me to jerk up and meet her hard eyes quickly. "You're failing yourself, you know."

I'm a little stunned, as is Stephanie, who stands up quickly and places her small, sparkly body between me and the woman in the dark track suit.

It's like watching a bad guy in a Superman comic have a showdown with a pixie.

"I'm sorry, but our sessions are private, unless the patient approves of you being here," Stephanie says. I smirk slightly, impressed at her ballsy response. The woman looks to my dad as he steps up, his hand rubbing on the side of his face.

"Actually, it's okay. This is Becca Fontain. She's here to work with Joss. Not…not to replace what you do, but just to…supplement it some," my dad says, barely navigating through hurting my therapist's feelings.

"I'm sorry?" I say, leaning to the side from behind Stephanie's big hair. She turns to me, blinking away tears. Apparently, my dad didn't navigate delicately enough.

"I'll be right back," she says, squeezing my shoulder and moving to the back room where I know she's going to wipe away the evidence of her emotions.

"Great, you made my pixie mad," I say, rolling my eyes. My legs are tired from the morning, so I rest one hand on the table behind me.

"You're tired from standing. How do you expect to ever get on the field again, to compete, if you can't stand and have a conversation?" Becca says, her eyes shifting from my hand on the table, which I quickly remove, to my face.

"I'm sorry, how do I…what?" I'm too stunned to respond to her. I look at my dad to fill in the blanks—and there are dozens of blanks. Maybe even hundreds.

"Becca, give me a second," he says. The woman nods and steps back to the other side of the room, pulling a cellphone from her pocket and flipping through apps on how to be evil to pixies and new amputees.

My dad clears his throat, looking over his shoulder to the table I'd just let go of. He urges me to sit, but I refuse. Becca might see me resting, and fuck if I need another dose of her today. My father leans against the table, crossing his arms. He looks down for a few seconds before he begins to speak.

"I thought you'd get more out of sessions if you had someone like

Becca to work with. She's a para-athlete. She was one of the first women in the Iron Man competition…"

"What's wrong with her?" I ask, my eyes raking over her hard body, wondering what her tracksuit is hiding.

"She lost her right leg, below the knee. Just like you," he says. My eyes shoot to his, and my lips push together hard. She didn't lose anything just like me. Nobody lost anything like me. I lost everything.

"And she's here because you think…" I don't finish, my jaw working back and forth as I fail to complete that sentence. I let my dad fill it in.

"She's here because you're an athlete, Joss. Because she can get you back on that field, and if you work hard enough—in time for you to play your senior year," he says.

I laugh hard once and stare at him.

His chest rises slowly as he draws in a long breath, his demanding eyes full of expectation. The coddling period is gone. He's returned to being the coach. But what if I just need a father? What if I just need someone to hold me and tell me it's okay that I'm only going to be what I am now? What if I need a daddy to tell me another boy will love me one day, just like the one who disappeared?

Just like the one who died.

That thought flashes through me unwanted, and my eyes burn instantly. I run my arm over my face and turn away.

"I'm done playing. You need to get over it. I have. I'm done for today too," I say, walking as quickly as I can to the main door. Stephanie rushes out to help me, but I hold a hand up, telling her I'll see her tomorrow. She looks hurt, and I feel bad. I know she's only trying to help me. That's what all of her positivity is about—about making me feel good about the tiny strides I made. But that's all they are. Tiny. And those small things exhaust me; they feel impossible to the point where I will myself to believe I'll never achieve them. It's easier than being disappointed at the end.

I get to the car and stand at it, my arms draped over the roof, my fingers tapping urgently while I wait for my dad to come out behind me. It takes him nearly ten minutes to leave the clinic, and I see him take a card and program a few things into his phone with Becca before they shake hands and he strides my way. She pushes her sunglasses on her face and keeps her body pointed my direction, watching me. This time, I break the hold and look down.

"That was rude," my dad says, unlocking the car and getting inside.

I laugh and open my door, climbing in after him.

I shake my head and buckle my belt, every move of my arm an angry jerking motion. I fold my arms over my body and let my good leg bounce nervously, my teeth clenched. I hold back everything I want to say, but I rehearse it in my head in an effort to rid my system of it. It has the opposite effect, and by the time we pull into our driveway, I'm so mad I want to kick a hole through the car door and take off running, never looking back.

But I can't. I barely walk.

My father leaves the car and doesn't look my way, and his dismissal of what just happened fires me up. I step from the car and slam the door.

"Fuck!" I yell.

He freezes, spinning in his spot before taking several steps toward me. He points his finger, his head cocked to one side, and his jaw clenched.

"You DO NOT talk to me like that!" he yells.

"Like what? Like your broken, disabled, disappointment of a daughter? Fuck! Fuck, fuck, fu…"

My father's hands rise up and I flinch, almost falling backward. But he doesn't hit me. I don't know why I thought he would. He has never put a hand on me in violence. Instead, his hands grip my shoulders, and his hold is hard and rigid, forcing me to face him.

"I can't," I say, my eyes wide and trying to focus on anything but him. I begin to blink, the tears coming. "I can't."

"Yes, you can!" he yells, shaking me lightly, willing me to listen. My head falls forward and the sobs come.

"I'm never going to be what I was…I can't. I just…" The cry takes over everything, and my dad pulls me into him, his hands clutching my back at first and soon his palms work along my spine and shoulder blades, attempting to soothe me.

I mourn. And in our driveway, the sun barely up, the summer heat threatening to begin already, my dad holds me. He holds me without saying a word. He doesn't bring up his opinion, what he thinks I can do, or what his plan is with Becca with the laser eyes and the sharp tongue. He just holds me.

When I needed him, for once…he's there.

I cry in his embrace for several minutes, until we both know that Todd, my tutor, will arrive soon. We walk inside, my dad's hand on my back until I move down the hallway toward my room. He pulls out my books and leaves them for me on the table, and after freshening up in the bathroom, I begin my studies silently, preparing myself for my last test of the year while my dad leaves for his job.

Todd comes, and I let him proctor my exam without my usual snarky remarks. He waits for them, and his eyebrows narrow more than once when I don't deliver. I catch him about to speak a few times, his mouth making the movement of drawing in a breath, but each time he halts himself. When I open the door to let him out, my test tucked away in his polished-leather briefcase, I laugh quietly to myself. I think Todd was worried about me, but didn't want to ruin the easy day—his last with me.

His hands are washed of me, just like everyone else.

I move to my room and lay on my bed, removing the socket and pulling my leg across my body to stretch. I wonder if this will ever feel like routine. I wonder if I'll quit waiting to wake up.

I pull out my phone and run through the few texts from Kyle and Taryn, both complaining about the other being a pain in the ass. They fight over who gets to help me and bring work home for me from school, and their kindergarten-like banter amuses me for a few minutes. I write them back, calling them babies, then move to the messages I have saved from Wes. There aren't many. Mostly short notes that he's outside my work, or that he'll wait for me after practice. It's the last one that gets me the most—he wrote it in the parking lot, while the rain was pounding the bus and his truck. It probably sat in his queue waiting to be sent for several minutes, finally clearing and coming to me just before he jumped into the water to save my dad.

You would have been great today. Nature just wasn't ready for you to show that girl up yet.

I laugh lightly and let the tear fall down my cheek. I feel him every time I read those words. Wes believed in me more than anyone. He believed in me differently than my dad, different from Kyle or Taryn. He knew my weaknesses, and loved them, and he loved my doubts too. He told me they were what made me strong, but lately, they're too heavy to bear. They're swallowing me, and I'm not sure there's any of that girl left inside.

The coolness of the sheets against my face lulls me eventually, and I let my phone fall from my hands onto the bed next to me, my eyelids heavy as the sound of wind whistles through my window. I sleep hard, and I dream of Wes.

In my dream, he's at his family's house. I drive up in my father's car, on my own, without any help, and I step from the car and run to him. My leg is still gone, but I'm able to run. Wes sees me, and he holds his arms wide, catching me when I leap to him. I feel his arms around me, and the warmth seeps into my bones. It's all so real, which only makes the pain more intense when I wake up an hour later to the sound of my front door opening.

"Joss, it's me," my dad's voice echoes down the hallway.

"I'm in here. I took a short nap," I say, my voice groggy and my eyes puffy. I'm pretty sure I cried in my sleep.

My dad knocks lightly, but pulls his hand into a fist quickly when the door falls open. "Sorry, I know you don't like the knocking thing," he says.

I smile lopsided and push myself up to sit, stretching my arms over my head before shrugging.

"It's okay. I would probably find a problem with anything you did to wake me up," I admit.

He chuckles.

"Oh, hey. I stopped to pick up the mail. There are some magazines in here, and a few of those catalogues you used to like," he says, tossing the pile of mail on the bed next to me. I glance down to see the one on top for an online store where a girl can order almost anything and have her name put on it.

"I have always wanted a Joss spoon-and-fork set," I say, lifting it and holding it in front of me on display, my finger tapping at the picture.

"You'll have to ask Santa for that," my dad says with a wink. That was always his comeback, for everything I asked for. Santa never followed through on most of it. "I have your last homework assignments. Taryn said she was going to the Stokes' house right after school and Kyle had a meeting. I said I'd deliver."

My dad throws the homework pile on my desk just inside my door. It's thin enough to fit into the file folder, which is a relief.

"What kind of meeting did Kyle have?" I ask, thumbing through the name catalogue in my lap.

My dad doesn't answer right away, so I glance up at him. When I do, my stomach knots. I know before he says it.

"Cal State's looking at him. They have to meet at the school, with his dad, since he's still a junior," he says, his lips pursed as his eyes drift down and to the side.

"That's great," I swallow. I mean it, even though it sounds pathetic and half-hearted. I want Kyle to get noticed. I just wasn't prepared for the disappointment I would feel lamenting my own dream.

"Anyway…I'm gonna see if I can get something going on the grill later. I'm going to run to the store. Any special requests?" he asks, diverting the topic.

"I'm good with whatever," I say. His face starts to fall so I smile and nod. "Really. I'm good. And I like anything from the grill. Maybe burgers, if you want."

"Burgers it is," my dad smiles. He pushes his hand into his pocket for his keys, but leaves it there, his posture half of what it once was. "I won't be long."

I watch him leave and wait for the sound of the door closing before I let out the breath I've been holding. My lips flap and the sound makes me laugh. I pull the catalogue back up to my face and read the name in the sample: *Florenza.* I chuckle to myself. Nobody has that name. And if they do, they aren't buying vanity bottle openers.

Rolling my eyes, I toss the catalogue back down on my bed, and it slides sideways along the stack of mail, a small, cream envelope sticking out. I glide it forward with my thumb and pick it up between my thumb and forefinger. It's addressed to me, with no return address on the front or back. The envelope is the kind that's sent along with greeting cards, but my birthday isn't for another two months. It's been years since my dad's mom has sent me money for no reason, and I'm not sure my mom's mom, Grace, would just send me something out of the blue.

I turn the envelope on its side and push my finger through the one space that isn't glued down, pulling the flap away and tearing along the seam. There's a regular piece of notebook paper inside, folded in thirds, but I can tell from the backside that there isn't any writing on it.

I pull it from the envelope and unfold it in my lap as the small ticket slides loose, landing on the bare skin of my leg. My breath hitches.

"Oh my god," I whisper.

My heart begins to drum loudly in my chest, the sound filling my ears. I lift the tiny ticket in my fingers and hold it up to examine it:

ADMIT ONE TO TARYN AND JOSS'S RACE

The words are faint, and the finger smudge is permanent. The edges are soft, worn from being kept in a pocket or hidden in a box—wherever Wes kept his secrets. I'm the only other place he's shared them. And somehow, he's sent me this for safekeeping.

Somehow, meaning he's…alive.

I don't call anyone. I don't ask for help. I just begin pulling on my leg, starting with the sock then the socket, fitting everything in place, my hands fumbling as I try to work quickly on something I'm far from comfortable with yet.

Once it's on, I stand, finding my balance, and stuffing my keys and phone into my back pocket. I leave a note on the counter for my dad, telling him I'm trying a short walk. He'll be pleased. Maybe less so, if he knew how far I was really going. Or maybe that would please him more, to know I'm pushing myself.

I leave through the garage, avoiding the few small steps on our concrete porch. I'm not good at climbing and navigating obstacles yet, but the driveway is clear, as is the garage. My dad makes sure of it.

The slant gives me a little speed, and I work hard to keep the pace up as I make it to the end of our block. The pressure hurts, and I pause at the brick fence on the corner, sitting on the short wall and rubbing my hands down my thighs, working my circulation. The pain is setting in, but I can't stop.

After a few minutes, I stand and begin to walk again, slower this time, but I force myself to keep putting one foot in front of the other. I walk beyond Kyle's street until I find the familiar corner to the Stokes' home, taking one more small break, holding onto the stop-sign pole, before I cover the final distance to Wes's home.

There's an older-looking van out front, a ramp on the side for a chair lift, and the garage is open, some boxes stacked near the opening.

"You want me to put these in too then?" TK says, his back to me as he steps through the door of their home.

"That would be great," I hear his dad from inside.

He turns and jumps, swearing lightly under his breath when he sees me, but shaking it off and reaching for a hug quickly.

"Damn, I'm sorry. You…you snuck up on me," he says.

I hold onto his arms, my fingers wrapping around them, searching for ways they feel like Wes's. They don't, but they're welcome anyhow.

"I'm so sorry. I…I was just trying to walk a little, and I found myself here," I lie. My eyes inspect everything around him while he talks, looking for a sign. Why would Wes be hiding here?

"That's great," he says, glancing down, but moving his eyes up to mine. He's trying not to offend me by looking at my leg.

"It's okay. You can check it out," I say. "Actually…I could use a break for a minute?"

"Oh...yeah. Here, I'll put these in the van later. Come into the house. Dad would love to see you anyhow. Mom's home too," he says.

He sets down the boxes that were in his hands on the small stack by the driveway. I notice a few of them are labeled with things like JERSEYS and BASEBALL CARDS. I think they're some of Wes's things.

I don't ask TK, but instead follow him into the house, moving as quickly as I can to the table and chair, my legs ready to rest as I collapse into it.

"Thanks," I say, stretching my limb out and rubbing the thigh again with my hands.

"Does it hurt?" TK asks. Levi walks up behind him and smacks the back of his head.

"Hey...owwwww! I was just curious," he says. Levi narrows his eyes on his brother.

"It's okay," I say through a soft laugh. "Really. I'd rather people ask questions than try to ignore it. And yeah, right now? It hurts like a bitch."

Both of them look down as I roll up part of my sweatpants, showing where the socket fits to my leg. The skin is red and irritated, which I know I will pay for tomorrow. Hell, I'm paying for it now.

"You're still bad-ass, though," TK says, his eyes on the metal rod that connects to a very simple-looking foot and shoe.

I laugh once. "I'm *always* going to be more bad-ass than you," I say.

Levi belts out an over-exaggerated laugh and points to his brother, backing out of the kitchen and sliding past his father. This feeling—the interaction—I've missed it more than I thought I had. It soothes.

"Joss," Bruce says my name with the reverence of a long-lost relative. He's next to me quickly, his big arm around my shoulders, pulling me into him for a hug. "So glad you stopped by."

"Thanks," I say, looking up into his face.

The sadness is there, but he clears his throat, pushing it away for long enough so we can have a conversation. We both feel it though—it's the hole from Wes. Only...the ticket. I want to show him. But I also somehow know I can't, or shouldn't.

"I'm sorry we haven't stopped by. We talked to your dad at the school, and meant to come to the house. It's just been a little hectic," he says, running his hand through the thinning strands of hair.

"It's okay; I understand," I say.

Taryn has kept me up-to-date on the major details. I know that the boys kept looking for Wes long after the official search was called off. The media trucks left their block after the first week, moving on to the next disaster or tragedy. Meanwhile, Bruce, Maggie and their boys were trying to find ways to pick up the pieces, to move on.

"Josselyn," Maggie says, filing in behind her husband. Her smile lands on me with the weight of a gentle feather.

"Hi," I say, smiling back. As much as I wanted to tell Bruce about the ticket, I want to tell Maggie more. She needs hope. But I don't know what it means. And as much as she needs hope, she also doesn't need a false promise.

"How's your dad doing?" she asks, her eyes never once dipping below my chin. It's different than when other's try not to look at my prosthetic. I can tell. She's not avoiding my leg because she's uncomfortable with my injury; she's avoiding looking at it because of its connection to her son.

"He's good. He's…he's picking up dinner actually. I should head back. I was just trying to get a good walk in," I say, repeating the same fib from before.

It takes Maggie a few seconds to react, her thoughts lost and her face drifting into the distance. "Oh, well…please. Come see us again soon? Maybe…dinner or something," she says.

She squeezes her husband's arm and heads back down the hallway she came from. Bruce's eyes follow her until she disappears, his gaze remaining on the empty space she just left.

"She's struggling," he says, taking a deep breath. "We all are."

"Me, too," I say, the words slipping out. I pull my lips tight and look down at my hands; in this house, it doesn't feel right to admit to any strife bigger than the one this family is feeling now. They wear the grief like heavy coats, their bodies trudging along and trying to remember how to be normal, but the spirit is dark and blue.

It takes me longer to get to my feet this time, the fatigue setting in and the pain from the long walk there reminding me of the hill I have yet to climb. I follow TK and Levi out through the garage, Bruce a few steps behind me, and the hope that carried me here feels thinner now. I know that ticket—I know it was Wes's and I know he sent it to me. It's not something he would share with anyone else. But maybe somehow, it got hung-up in the postal system, lodged in our box, or delivered to the wrong address first. Maybe the timing of it was nothing more than a fluke.

"So these are it?" A heavy voice bellows just out of sight through the garage door. I step forward a little more quickly to see a large man— maybe five or ten years older than Bruce, but so similar to him—sitting in a wheelchair and bending forward to lift one of the boxes onto his lap.

As he bends back up, his eyes stop, catching a glimpse of my leg, and he freezes.

"Ah glad you're still here. Shawn, I want you to meet someone," Bruce says, stepping around me. My mind filters through fragments of memories and things Wes told me, rummaging through facts, not sure if I remember them correctly, but my instincts telling me...

"Shawn, this is Josselyn. She was one of Wes's friends. Still is. Her dad coached all the boys," Bruce says, stumbling through the introduction, careful to make sure it's acknowledged that I'm still very much a part of their family and lives. His words are sweet, but I don't dwell in them long. My ears lock in on the name. Shawn. *Shawn.* "Joss, Shawn's my brother. He was Wes's first caseworker, at the state."

Yes. I knew it. I knew it the minute I heard the familiar timber of his voice that he was related to Bruce, and my heart told me who he was. This man—this man is Wes's savior, in every possible way. And he was supposed to be dead.

"Shawn, it's nice to meet you," I say, taking small steps forward and reaching for his hand. He takes my palm in his and covers the top with his other hand, his eyes crinkled with the cautious smile that splays out under his glasses.

"Nice to meet you too, Joss," he says, looking at me more directly than anyone has in months.

He keeps my hand in his for a few seconds, his eyes studying me, his smirk faint, but there. It's like a tango, each of us glancing at the other, trying to decide who to trust and what the other knows.

"Shawn is holding onto a few of Wes's things, just to store. We're not erasing him or anything. It's only…"

"I understand. It's hard to see sometimes," I say, my eyes lingering on Shawn's before coming to Bruce as I let go of his brother's hand. "It must be hard on Maggie."

He inhales slowly, and holds his mouth in a tight line, nodding as his chin tucks into his chest. "It is," he concedes.

I look back up to see Shawn now moving down the driveway, TK walking with him carrying the rest of the boxes. I trail behind with Bruce and watch as they load the last items in and help Shawn position his chair on the lift that's now flattened in the street. With a push of a button, it raises him to the car-floor level and he moves to the open area where he lifts himself from his chair to the swiveling driver's seat.

TK steps forward to slam the sliding door closed, but Shawn holds up a hand to stop him, then his finger points at me.

"When my doctor said I had to go on disability, and stick to a wheelchair, he told me it meant no more driving," Shawn says, his finger suddenly pointing down to his seat. "I said bullshit. Don't let circumstances dictate what you're capable of. We're all special in our own way. Wes taught me that."

I look at him silently and smile with a nod, but my eyes hold his a little longer than the rest of them realize. We are all special. And Wes—he's special too. You know it. I know it. And he's alive.

"I'll remember that," I say. TK closes the door, but Shawn and I look into each other for another breath before he turns to face the wheel.

"You need a ride home Joss?" Bruce asks. I open my mouth to utter *yes*, but instead close it, gritting my teeth because I know it's going to hurt to turn this down—physically *hurt*. But I do. Because bullshit. Because I can walk home. And I am special too.

"I'm okay. It's good for me—to set a goal," I say, one eyebrow lifted at him.

"All right," he says, the smooth chuckle of his laugh almost stripping the sadness from his eyes for a second. "Well, if you change your mind—call."

I hold up my phone, waving it once, and I give him a nod. I turn away and begin my much slower trip home, glancing once or twice to see the Stokes family still standing at the end of their driveway, watching over me as long as they can, to make sure I'm okay.

When I turn the block, I pull my phone out and thumb through my texts, settling again on my favorite one from Wes. I start to type several times, quitting each, thinking I'm being far-fetched and ridiculous. Eventually, I figure I have nothing to lose, so I type and send a note to my hero.

Thank you.

I stare at it for a long while, and for the first block I walk, my body tingles with anticipation that I will get some message back. After a while, I tuck my phone in my pocket, pulling it out every minute or two to check again. Each time, my words are the last line typed.

By the time I get to the house, my father is pacing in the driveway. He starts to walk toward me, but when he sees the look of determination on my face, he stops, his hands folded behind his neck as his chest lifts and lowers with heavy breaths.

"I'm sorry. I should have called or texted," I say when I reach him. He looks down at my leg, his eyes still heavy—he's worried. "It's sore. But I wanted...I wanted to know my limits."

He nods, his brow pinched as his hand comes up to cover his chin. He fidgets in place, exchanging one hand for the other, trying to cover his emotion. But I see it. It's there. I'm fighting, for the first time in months. It's all he's wanted for me.

"Your limits," he whispers through loose fingers, his breath catching with a cry.

I suck in my bottom lip, nodding, reaching my hand for him to grab my arm, to help me steady myself.

"Turns out, I don't have any."

His body shakes with his laugh, a short burst that carries his release.

"Well then. How about I make us something to eat," he says, arm around my back, my weight relying on him more than I've ever let it. My father carries me.

I let him.

"Joss, it's time."

My father knocks. The same knock, the same quiet wake-up call. The same pattern we've lived morning after morning. Today, though—I'm up. I'm ready.

"Let's go," I say, pushing the door the rest of the way. My father lets me pass him in our darkened hallway. The sun is just rising. I've been awake for hours. Not from pain. I've just been waiting for the day to arrive. I'm ready for it.

I pick up the wrapped half of a sandwich from the counter and glance at my father, standing with his folders and messy briefcase behind me. His smile is subtle. He hides it. It's part of his technique, not that a parent should have a *technique* with their child, but he's been a coach more than he's been a father, the lines blur. When my father coaches me, and I do something well, he grins, but only on the right side, and only for a blink. It always disappears, sometimes before I catch it, but other times I get a glimpse just before it's gone.

I saw it just now.

We leave the house, the door slamming heavy behind us, my father's keys jangling in the lock. He pulls the garage shut and locks it in place while I wait at the passenger door in the driveway. He clicks his key fob, and I get in.

We both devour our sandwiches in the car, but we don't rush to talk. I'm glad he doesn't have questions. I don't have the thoughts formed yet. My mind hasn't put my priorities in order. But I know what I want. I know what I'm *capable* of. And it's a lot.

My father knew too. That's why he's been pushing. In his way.

My eyes still scan the landscape. If anything, I think I'll be doing that more now, now that I know. Wes is somewhere. I'm not sure why he's hiding, but I trust there's a good reason. More importantly, my heart trusts that I will see him again. I'll keep his secret safe—whatever that secret is.

We pull up to the rehabilitation clinic, but before we leave the car, I unbuckle my belt and lean to the side, looking at my father. He takes a deep breath and lets his hands fall from the steering wheel.

"I want it all," I say.

He doesn't look at me, but that smile ticks up the right cheek again, sticking around a little longer than before.

"What can Becca do for me?"

I looked Becca Fontaine up late last night. She's impressive—even for an able-bodied competitor. She's also incredibly open about dealing with depression and how important it is to have a place to channel your emotions. She channels hers into training others, in between training for her own goals—which she's achieved in the form of several gold medals. She's based in Los Angeles, and I also saw that her training rates are by request only. That means she's expensive.

"She can get you back on the field, at a high level that will make people notice," my father says, his head falling to the side as his eyes land on me.

"The cost…"

"Is taken care of," my father stops me before I fully ask. He steps from the car, ending the conversation, but I open the door and pull myself out as quickly as I can.

"Dad, that's not true, and you know it. We can't afford this, so how can I help?" I ask. He pauses at the front of the car for a few seconds before leaning back to rest his palm on the hood, his head falling forward.

"Josselyn, I have made mistakes," he says, a breath of silence before a sad laugh escapes him, his shoulders rising as his head shakes. "Monumental mistakes…that I will probably spend a lifetime trying to correct. And when I die…" he says, turning to face me, his eyes glossy, "I will still come up short with you no matter how hard I work to get back to even. I have failed you. I left you when you needed a father most. I fell into a selfish, dark, demon-kinda hole, and it claws at me still—probably always will. But damn it to hell if I'm going to abandon you again. Not now. No baby girl. Not now."

I hold his gaze with my own, my lips tingle, my heart affected by his words. I pull my mouth together tightly and breathe in through my nose.

"Is this some twelve-step box you have to check, because I'm pretty sure we still can't afford this," I say, making light of the heaviness of our conversation, but also only half kidding.

My father chuckles and steps closer to me.

"No...and yes," my father says. "I talked this over with Meredith. About how I need to really step up now, and how hard that's going to be. But we'll make the money work. There's more insurance that needs to pay out, and I'm not about to be quiet until you get what you deserve."

"No, I guess quiet isn't your thing," I say through a pointed laugh.

He reaches a hand for mine, and I stretch to him, threading my fingers through his older, callused ones—a touch I haven't felt since I held his hands when I learned to skate in our driveway as a child.

"Come on; let's head inside. Becca's waiting," he says. My head twitches at his words and my mouth twists in curiosity. He laughs harder, unhooking our hands and sliding his arm around me as we walk slowly to the front door. "I took a gamble that you'd change your mind. I asked her to come back again yesterday."

"What if I refused to come today?" I ask as he holds the door open for me.

He shrugs.

"Then I'd have her come back the next day until I wore your ass down," he says. I narrow my eyes on him with a smirk. "Truthfully, I knew you would eventually. You're a lion."

"Lioness," I correct.

"Right...see? Quick to correct me. Always right. Always for the win," he says, taking in a deep breath as his eyes fall down to my feet and back up to my face again, as if he's inventorying all of my assets and weaknesses. "Heaven help the soul who gets into a battle with you."

I roll my eyes and smile, but my expression turns more serious when my father walks on ahead of me, thoughts of Wes weighing heavy inside my heart. I inhale and hold the air in my lungs, spreading his spirit throughout my body. The simple act makes me feel stronger. I can't wait to tell him what I've done—when I've made it.

When I'm on top.

Because I will be.

And he'll be waiting.

CHAPTER 19

Summer's End

My body is the sheer, physical form of exhaustion. It has been for months, and it is tonight. I've been working with Becca for the summer—every day, for three hours a day, sometimes more. She broke me down—beyond my injury and leg—to the core of everything I knew about being an athlete. She fine-tuned me—turning me into something more.

I wouldn't have seen the text until morning had it not been for the pain. It comes and goes, and I'm learning to tolerate it more—my muscles in other places all working to support things that I can no longer count on physically. But tonight…tonight my body hurt.

That pain is nothing now. It's barely a memory. It evaporated with the small buzz of my phone in the darkness of my room.

I rolled to my side, reaching for it on the night table, expecting to get some note from Taryn or Kyle about school's start next week, end-of-the-summer parties, or something like that. But instead, it was the familiar flashing dots indicating that someone was writing—Wes was writing, or at least someone with Wes's phone.

My last message to him was sent two months ago. Two words: Thank you. I sent it the day I opened the envelope and found the ticket, and I've carried that small piece of paper with me for every grueling workout, the failures and missteps during my rehabilitation. I've clutched it in my hands through every late-night cry, and I've squeezed it in my palm when I learned to run again. That tiny ticket gives me strength when I need it most.

I'm holding it now.

No words were sent this time, at least not yet. The buzz was for a photo. More accurately, a photo of a photo—my photo…of the peony barely blooming at the start of spring. The image that was just sent to me from Wes's phone is of that picture positioned against the dried and spent bushes of my favorite field. This image is recent—my heart says it was taken hours ago.

Wes is the only one who could have taken it from the classroom—from my display for my presentations. He's the only one who would know where it belongs, the setting—the exact spot along the road.

I need to go.

Kyle was awake when I called. He's been working my shifts along with his at the Gym in an effort to pay the rest of his truck off this summer. I'm going to work there again during the school year, but in the afternoon, and at the front counter. Climbing through the slides is too tricky.

I could hear the question in his voice when I asked him to come to my house, to be quiet when he pulled up, but to leave the motor running. He didn't ask though—he only said to give him five minutes. It's been four, and I see his lights at the end of the street.

I've walked a few houses away from my own, and Kyle's brow is wrinkled with his famous worry lines as he slows to the curb. I rush around to the passenger side and get in, closing the door gently.

"I didn't want to wake my dad up. He'll ask questions…or worry," I say, holding a finger up and circling it in the air. "You're going to need to turn around and leave from that end."

"Yeah…imagine that…asking questions," Kyle jokes, pulling on the wheel and flipping a U-turn in the middle of my street. He glances my way when he rights the truck again, twisting his hat backward on his head. I laugh at it because of what it symbolizes. My father is a baseball traditionalist—you don't wear your hat any way but forward with the brim bent. Kyle's is always flat, and half the time he flips it around. He started doing it as a way to show his solidarity with me, but over the years, it's just become habit and our thing. Whenever we're up to no good, that hat spins around.

Good timing.

"So...do I get to ask any? You know...questions?" he says, his eyes moving from me to the road. He stops at the corner, and I direct him out to the highway.

"Maybe," I say at first. He raises one brow, glancing at me before turning his eyes back to the roadway. "Okay, probably. And I'll fill you in later because I'm going to need you for something big...before school starts. But right now, I just need you to drive down Cotton Lane until it turns into the State Route.

Kyle pulls up to the final stoplight before we turn left, out of the glare of the municipal lights, into the darkness. It's one in the morning, and there isn't another car to be seen, so when the light goes green, he remains still. His arms stretch out as he pushes his back into the seat and his chest fills with a long breath.

"Okay," he says, finally.

I smile, and my grin grows larger as he punches the gas, driving us deep into the night. He doesn't ask any more questions. He won't have to. I'll tell him everything. Kyle is me, and I'm him—he can handle my secrets. He'll respect them.

I twist in my seat and press my hands on his window, dropping one lower to the armrest, feeling around until I find the button to roll it down. I lean my head out, my other hand gripping my hair at the base of my neck, and I shut my eyes for a few seconds, breathing in the scent of the flower fields. Their season is ending, and the fall flowers aren't as sweet. But if I search hard enough—inhale deeply enough—I can still sense the trace left from the spring and summer blossoms.

"Here," I say, leaning back inside the cab.

I roll the window up while Kyle pulls to the side of the road. He shifts the truck into park, but leaves it running, the lights on for our benefit as we both step out into the field. I move close to the small ravine of the canal, and Kyle quickly grips my arm, helping me find my balance so I can jump across. I've learned to let people help me sometimes.

We both trudge through the dead bushes, many of them ground up from a recent tractor pull. The dirt is still wet on top, and the lines dug between the rows of plants are still fresh—this happened tonight, after the picture was taken.

I panic at the thought that the photo—my clue—could be gone, ground up in the blades of a John Deere or pushed into the earth to make compost for the next season. My eyes dart wildly as I kneel down for a better view.

"What are you looking for, JJ?" Kyle says, his feet stopping just behind me.

"Something…a sign. I…I don't know. I'll know it when I see it," I say. I hear him sigh heavily through his nose, and I know he's worried and confused. But I can't explain it until I know for sure—I need to see it.

I lean forward, my palms against the dirt, and slowly lower myself to the ground.

"Here," Kyle says, pulling his shirt from his body, handing it to me. "You'll get dirty."

I take it from him, laying it down beneath my ribs, my left arm folded under my head and my cheek pressed flat against it. I smile at the memory of the last time I laid like this.

"Turn your lights off. Just for a minute," I say. After a second or two, Kyle walks back to the truck, flipping the switch until the fields are bathed in nothing but moonlight again.

It takes my eyes a few minutes to adjust, but when they do, I can see the silhouette of the ground in every direction. I begin at the top and slowly scan down, disappointment growing the farther along the field my eyes roam. And then, there it is—the corner of the photo jutting up like a late bloom from the peony plant.

I rush to stand, dusting off my body and tossing Kyle his shirt. My legs move quickly a few rows in, and I bend at the waist, my fingers pausing briefly before grasping the photo.

My pulse quickens as I pull the photo into view. It's mine—the one I took. The small glue dots dried on every corner; I feel them with my fingers.

"What is it?" Kyle says, leaning over my shoulder to look.

He can't see the smile on my face, or the tears forming in the corners of my eyes, but they are there. It's going to be hard to get them to go away now.

"It's a message," I say quietly, my own words filling me with thought as I turn the photo over in my hands.

You can do anything. I'll be watching.

He wrote it in a permanent marker. He left it here for me to find. But he's still hiding. Something has him afraid; there's something more to Wesley Christopher Stokes' story, and I intend to find out.

"Can you take this week off from work? Before school starts?" I ask Kyle, turning to him quickly. He spins his hat forward, then gives up and just pulls it from his head completely, his other hand scratching through his hair.

"Uh, I don't know. I...I guess I can ask? Why?" he asks, his face a combination of expressions—those full of questions, and those that know me enough to trust anything. "Where are we going?"

"To Tucson first. I want to see where they buried my mom, and I want to meet my grandmother," I say, nodding toward his truck, taking his hand again to step over the canal. He feels the photo in my hand and takes it from me when we get to my passenger door. I wait while his eyes read over the words on the back. They flit to me, and I can tell all I need to do is say it out loud. My eyes hold his. I breathe once, and then I tell him what's next.

"And then, we're going to find Wes, and convince him to come home."

THE END

COMING SUMMER 2017

The journey continues.
Book 2

A Girl Like Me

ACKNOWLEDGEMENTS

Thank you for taking this leap with me. I know this book is different, but I also believe it's special. And I know I left you there…in that place, with questions…and hope. I can promise you this: *I've got you. I won't let you fall.* Book two will be just as magical, and perhaps even more special…because Joss Winters says so.

I don't think I have ever loved a heroine I've written more than this feisty blonde tomboy. I'd like to think I wove a little of me into Joss's fabric. Certainly, the drive to win, the touch of stubborn feminism and, if I may be so bold, the ability to line-drive a ball at someone's knees. Yeah, that part's all me. But as I read her again and again in edits and proofs, I came to realize that a lot of the parts I wove may instead be characteristics I wish I had. No, not the penchant for danger and self-destruction. But the ability to face adversity with such grit and to admit failures and weaknesses, even if only to herself. While Wes may be the one who's physically strong, Joss is the one who's unbreakable. I've learned from Joss.

I've learned from this story.

I have so much more I want to say, but I can't. I can't because there are threads I still need to unravel for you. Book 2, A Girl Like Me, will fill in the gaps. And the ride is going to be sweet. I don't want to ruin it.

With that, however, there are several people I need to thank for getting me to the point where I was ready for this story…for something still *very* me, but also…*different*. I dedicated this to my dad. And no…not because he has a lot in common with Eric Winters in this story. But the good parts of Joss's father? Yeah…he's there. My dad taught me to throw a ball. Even when he thought it might be hopeless, he'd stand in the back yard with me for hours, begging me to just try not throwing underhand once. I can remember vividly when it all finally clicked. It wasn't much unlike that scene in Forrest Gump when he's running and the braces just fly off of his legs. One minute, I was arching the ball into bushes, and then the next…I zinged it so hard into his mitt that it bruised his hand. Many more bruises would follow. Fence slats were broken when I learned to hit. Balls were lost over the fence at the elementary school. My dad's shins were nailed by my low liners, and I giggled as he packed up to go home, mad but proud as hell. While the magical touches, angst and love story are vital to this story, I think just as important is that relationship between Joss and her dad. It shaped her.

It shaped me.

So, thanks, Dad, for being my Ted Williams on the field and off.

I also need to give special thanks to fellow author BT Urruela. BT is a combat wounded amputee and purple heart recipient, but he also happens to swing a decent bat and…oh…have this killer smile that's graced the cover of several romance novels. I met him when the idea for this book was a kernel in my mind that was keeping me awake at night. I knew the storyline, and I knew what would happen to Joss in this story. But what terrified me was getting it right. I'm moved by fighters—seeing people punch adversity in the face, bend it to their will and turn it into a strength. I wanted Joss to embody this, but I knew it couldn't be a switch she simply flipped. It had to be authentic, and pay homage to the struggle that comes with the kind of climb she took and will continue to make. BT, I called you…and I was perhaps a little nervous. You answered, and you shared. You laid the ground for my research, pointed me in the right direction for more, and made that fear that I couldn't pull this off take a seat. Thank you for all you do, but selfishly, thank you for chatting with me on the phone most.

I also have to give special thanks to Mike Booi, assistant athletic trainer for the Arizona Coyotes, for his guidance on training techniques and rehabilitation for competitive athletes. And enormous thanks to the Advanced Prosthetics Center for your detailed research materials.

When it comes to the words, there's a group of women I could not get through this book business without. As always, thank you Jen, Ashley, Bianca and Shelley for taking my chapters as I fed them to you. I know waiting through this one was a wee bit torturous. I hope I treated you right. I could never thank you enough.

And BilliJoy Carson and Tina Scott—my editing queens. Let me just say that you are my heroes. Capes for you both.

None of this would be possible without the support of my boys. Tim and Carter, you are my world. When I say "I can't," you turn me around and just tell me to "go do." When I waver, you remind me you're proud. When I chew my nails to nubs on release night, you tell me this story is your favorite (I don't even care that you say it every time). I love you, my boys. You're it for me. And every book is really for you.

And to my readers—to the bloggers, posters, Goodreaders, reviewers, late-night Facebook message senders, emailers, teens, moms, grandmas, dads, brothers, students, and oh-but-never-least Ninjas—thank you. Each one of you cracked open a cover (swiped is probably more accurate for e-readers). Thank you for taking that first chance, for thinking one of my little stories was worth your time. I swear I'll never take it for granted. In fact, I'm going to get to work right now, because you have questions you need answered, and a cute missing boy you need to know about, and a girl on a mission you need to follow.

And I made you all a promise.

I've got you.

ABOUT THE AUTHOR

Ginger Scott is an Amazon-bestselling and Goodreads Choice Award-nominated author of several young and new adult romances, including Waiting on the Sidelines, Going Long, Blindness, How We Deal With Gravity, This Is Falling, You and Everything After, The Girl I Was Before, In Your Dreams, Wild Reckless, Wicked Restless, The Hard Count, Hold My Breath and A Boy Like You.

A sucker for a good romance, Ginger's other passion is sports, and she often blends the two in her stories. Ginger has been writing and editing for newspapers, magazines and blogs for…well…ever. She has told the stories of Olympians, politicians, actors, scientists, cowboys, criminals and towns. For more on her and her work, visit her website at http://www.littlemisswrite.com.

When she's not writing, the odds are high that she's somewhere near a baseball diamond, either watching her son field pop flies like Bryce Harper or cheering on her favorite baseball team, the Arizona Diamondbacks. Ginger lives in Arizona and is married to her college sweetheart whom she met at ASU (fork 'em, Devils).

Ginger Online

@TheGingerScott
www.facebook.com/GingerScottAuthor
www.littlemisswrite.com

BOOKS BY GINGER SCOTT

The Like You Duet
A Boy Like You
A Girl Like Me (Summer 2017)

Read The Complete Falling Series
This Is Falling
You And Everything After
The Girl I Was Before
In Your Dreams (spin-off standalone)

The Waiting Series
Waiting on the Sidelines
Going Long

The Harper Boys
Wild Reckless
Wicked Restless

Standalones
Blindness
How We Deal With Gravity
The Hard Count
Hold My Breath

www.ingramcontent.com/pod-product-compliance
Lightning Source LLC
Chambersburg PA
CBHW072126250626
47159CB00007B/2579